"I thought you'd like to see this," he said.

Suzie stepped out of Tucker's truck and stared at the huge trees that he'd parked beneath. Cottonwoods.

"I've never seen this many of them together!" It was a beautiful sight when the cotton tufts were floating from the branches on their slow free fall to earth. It looked like it was snowing in the middle of May!

"I've always liked this spot this time of year," Tucker said, coming to stand beside her. Smiling down at her, he plucked a bit of cotton from her hair. "It looks good on you," he said.

She wasn't thinking about the cotton any longer. "Which way will we go?" she asked, butterflies sifting inside her chest.

"Which way do you want to go?"

She stared at him, her insides completely aflutter. His deep blue eyes were steady and unwavering as they seemed to see every emotional hiding place within her.

"I don't know." Were they talking about which way to go to check fences…or something more?

D1400620

A sixth generation Texan, award-winning author **Debra Clopton** and her husband, Chuck, live on a ranch in Texas. She loves to travel and spend time with her family and watch NASCAR whenever time allows. She is surrounded by cows, dogs and even renegade donkey herds that keep her writing authentic and often find their way into her stories. She loves helping people smile with her fun, fast-paced stories.

Belle Calhoune grew up in a small town in Massachusetts. Married to her college sweetheart, she is raising two lovely daughters in Connecticut. A dog lover, she has one mini poodle and a chocolate Lab. Writing for the Love Inspired line is a dream come true. Working at home in her pajamas is one of the best perks of the job. Belle enjoys summers in Cape Cod, traveling and reading.

Her Unlikely Cowboy

Debra Clopton

&

Her Alaskan Cowboy

Belle Calhoune

LOVE INSPIRED
INSPIRATIONAL ROMANCE

LOVE INSPIRED®

INSPIRATIONAL ROMANCE

ISBN-13: 978-1-335-20196-6

Her Unlikely Cowboy & Her Alaskan Cowboy

Copyright © 2020 by Harlequin Books S.A.

Her Unlikely Cowboy
First published in 2014. This edition published in 2020.
Copyright © 2014 by Debra Clopton

Her Alaskan Cowboy
First published in 2018. This edition published in 2020.
Copyright © 2018 by Sandra Calhoune

Recycling programs for this product may not exist in your area.

This edition published by arrangement with Harlequin Books S.A.

For questions and comments about the quality of this book, please contact us at CustomerService@Harlequin.com.

Love Inspired
22 Adelaide St. West, 40th Floor
Toronto, Ontario M5H 4E3, Canada
www.Harlequin.com

Printed in U.S.A.

CONTENTS

HER UNLIKELY COWBOY

Debra Clopton

This book is dedicated,
with much gratitude and sorrow, to the family
of *and* to US Marine Sergeant Wade Wilson.
Your sacrifice and selfless act of heroism
for our freedom will not be forgotten. 1989–2012

Greater love hath no man than this,
that a man lay down his life for his friends.
—*John* 15:13

Chapter One

More dread than hope filled Suzie Kent's heart as she drove around a wide curve toward Dew Drop, Texas. Suddenly, the flash of police lights startled her just as a mass of short, fat donkeys standing in her path yanked her out of her depressed state. Suzie gasped, "Oh!"

"Mom! Stop!" Abe yelled.

A tall man in a cowboy hat, jeans and the tan uniform of a Texas sheriff stood in the middle of the donkeys, waving his arms for her to halt. One minute he was standing, and the next—

"He went down!" Abe yelled again as the sheriff buckled and fell over.

Suzie stomped on the brakes of the monstrosity of a moving truck. The heavy vehicle groaned and rebelled, but fortunately the brakes grabbed and the bulky box on wheels lunged—once, twice, three times before stopping hard. She and Abe strained forward against their seat belts with the force.

Even intent on halting, she was shaken by what they'd witnessed. One of the cute donkeys had just taken down an officer with a well-placed kick.

Abe had his seat belt off and was out the door before Suzie even had time to tell him to be careful. At fifteen he wasn't listening to her anymore, and this was no different. Hurrying to get out of the truck, she pushed the flashers on then locked her gaze back on her son. He approached the donkeys, yelling and waving his arms wildly. She was thankful when the creatures parted down the road's yellow center stripe, scurrying like mice out of his way. This gave her a clear view of the downed officer. Sirens sounded in the distance and she hoped their shrill cry signaled help was on the way.

Abe skidded to a halt beside the black-haired man holding his hip and struggling to get up. His back was to them but it was easy to tell he was well built as he struggled to one knee, holding his injured leg straight.

"Mom, he's hurt!" Abe yelled over his shoulder, bending down and blocking her view of the officer. "I can help you stand up. If you can," he said. "That donkey blasted you."

"Thanks," the officer grunted. "That'd be much appreciated. Donkeys might be innocent-looking, but they can sure make an impact."

Though she hadn't yet glimpsed his face, Suzie quickened her pace. The officer looped his arm over Abe's shoulders just as she reached them.

"Here let me help, too." She scooted beneath his other arm, placing her hand on his stomach—his very firm stomach. The officer was in shape. Looking up she met his deep marine-blue gaze and froze.

Tucker McDermott!

"Thanks, Suzie. It's good to see you." Tucker McDermott's eyes bored into her, but concern stamped his expression, as if he knew the dismay shooting through her.

Her breath had flown from her lungs and she had no words as she looked into the face of the man she held responsible for her husband's death.

The man she was also counting on to help her save her son.... Suzie's world tilted as she realized whose clean, tangy aftershave was teasing her senses and whose unbelievably intense gaze had her insides suddenly rioting. His hair was jet-black and his skin deeply tanned, making his midnight-blue eyes startling in their intensity.

"Tucker," she managed, hoping her voice didn't wobble.

Moving to Dew Drop, Texas, to Tucker's family's Sunrise Ranch, and asking for his help had taken everything she had left emotionally—and that hadn't been much since her husband had given his life in the line of duty for fellow marine Tucker, two years earlier.

And now, as circumstances would have it, she was forced to rely on his help.

Tucker grimaced, trying to keep most of his weight off of Suzie and Abe, but his hip clearly hurt.

"Thanks for the rescue. I'm glad y'all saw the pack and stopped in time. I had just arrived and it wouldn't have been good if you'd wrecked because of these hairy pests."

Suzie realized the donkey must have kicked him in his bad hip.

Shot.

The word ricocheted through her. He'd been shot in the hip and gone down in a firefight—a firefight after being ambushed.

The firefight in which her husband, Gordon, had stepped in front of him and drawn fire.

Acid rolled in the pit of her stomach thinking about it.

"Thank y'all for helping me up," he said, his gaze snagging on hers again and holding. "I've got it from here, though." He pulled one arm from around her and the other from around Abe.

"Are you sure?" she asked, even though she wanted to step away from him in the worst way. Wanted to break the disturbing connection radiating between them. "Do we need to help you to your vehicle?"

"Yeah," Abe added, looking just as uncertain as she did.

Tucker limped a few painful steps away from them. "I'm okay," he said, gruffly. "It'll just take a few minutes for the throbbing to go away." He glanced ruefully at the donkeys. "What a mess."

"There's a bunch of them," Abe said excitedly, accepting Tucker at his word and moving back to focus on the herd of innocent-looking donkeys.

Suzie's heart caught. Abe's reaction—from the first moment they'd spotted the donkeys—was the first time in weeks, even months, that she'd heard any kind of positive excitement in his voice. Now he was actually grinning at the short, squat animals.

"They act like they own the road," he added, looking as if he wanted to pet one of them.

Tucker frowned. "And that's the problem. They could easily have caused a serious wreck."

"They sure took you out." Abe chuckled.

Suzie suddenly felt as though she was in a time warp, glimpsing the son she'd had before his father died. A lump lodged in her throat and her eyes welled with tears. She fought both down.

Tucker's lip hitched upward in a quick lopsided grin.

"It's my own fault. A donkey's God-given instinct is to kick and they have a range of motion that would surprise a prize fighter. That's why they're used to protect herds from predators."

"Seriously?" Abe gaped at Tucker then at the docile, unassuming animals.

"Seriously," Tucker said. "They may not look like much, but those are some kickboxing masters right there."

"Cool," Abe said, swinging around as, siren blaring, a Dew Drop Sheriff's Department car rolled to a halt beside Tucker's SUV. "Looks like backup has arrived."

A young officer emerged from his patrol car, and strode their way. "Hey, Tucker, got here as soon as I could." A cocky grin widened across his suntanned skin. "Couldn't handle the misfit delinquents yourself?"

Delinquent. The word hit Suzie in the heart and wiped the smile off Abe's face instantly. He'd become too acquainted with the term of late, and the mention was all it took for shadows of mistrust to cloud his blue eyes. She almost cried out as she saw the veil of anger fall, the veil that he'd disappeared behind months ago. Her gaze shot to Tucker and she realized that he'd witnessed Abe's reaction.

"Yeah, the donkeys are troublemakers, all right," he clarified smoothly. "Help me get them off the road, Cody," he instructed the deputy, then focused on Abe. "By the way, I'm Tucker McDermott. I was a friend of your dad's and I owe him my life. He was an amazing man." Tucker cleared his throat. "I'm glad you've come to Dew Drop. And the boys of Sunrise Ranch are looking forward to meeting you."

Abe's expression flashed bright with anger as he

stared at Tucker, then, glaring daggers at the deputy, he stalked back toward their moving truck. "This is ridiculous, Mom. Why'd we have to come here?"

Her mild-looking, blue-eyed, blond-haired son was a time bomb. Feeling sick, she glanced back at Tucker. He hadn't moved and was still favoring his hip. She wasn't sure he could move. "Tell me this is going to work out."

The weight of the world—her world—settled heavily on her and she felt suddenly weary and far, far older than her thirty-two years.

Tucker's fierce gaze engulfed her. "You have my word, Suzie. This is going to work out. I promise."

Tears sprang to her eyes, and all she could do was nod. She was so tired of handling everything on her own. So very tired. Tucker was offering her a strong support system and strong words that she needed to believe in.

"Hey, Abe," he called. "Could you help us herd these donkeys off the road before someone gets hurt?"

Abe spun back, his stance still belligerent but his expression interested. "Sure."

Tearing her gaze from her son, she looked back at Tucker, amazed.

"I hate to ask," Tucker said, as if nothing out of the ordinary had just happened—but surely he knew it had. "Could you help, too? I'm not moving as fast as I need to and we need them off this road. The trailer will be here soon but…"

"Um, yes, just tell me what to do."

"Move slow and wave your arms if one starts to come at you. Contrary to what you witnessed, they aren't aggressive. They're pretty tame. Until you sneak up on them like I did. Or try to ride them. I hear they don't like that at all."

"Okay." She glanced at Abe, who was already urging a group of three to move toward the edge of the road. "Abe, be careful," she called.

"Mom, I've got this," he huffed, impatient with her mothering.

"I'll get this end," the other officer called from where he'd moved to the far side of the group.

That left the middle of the herd for her and Tucker. Feeling that she wasn't doing it right, she waved her arms somewhat weakly, moving toward the donkey closest to her.

Not intimidated in the least, fuzzy whiskers lifted her way and deep brown eyes studied her. Clearly distracted from nuzzling the yellow line, the animal blinked dark eyelashes, pawed the pavement twice—then *charged*.

Suzie gasped, her arms dropped like lead as she spun and ran—straight into Tucker McDermott's arms.

"Hold on," Tucker said, pulling her protectively against his body and shifting so the crazy donkey aimed at him instead of her. "Yah!" he yelled at the miserable beast and waved his arm in a not-so-weak manner.

The donkey skidded to a halt instantly.

Tucker held her tightly with one arm and shooed the silly animal away. It turned and trotted off, as if it hadn't just tried to mow her down.

"They just get excited sometimes. No harm meant," Tucker assured her. His soft chuckle washed over her. "It's okay."

Suzie was mortified that she'd run to him. That she was now in his arms. And her crazy heart was pounding, even as his low rumbling chuckle resonated through her. What was wrong with her? She was reacting to Tucker's touch as if…as if she were attracted to him. Even the thought made her ill, made her feel like a traitor.

True, she hadn't been held like this in almost three years because when Gordon died it'd been months since she'd seen him. But still, *Tucker McDermott*.

This was disturbing and wrong on so many levels that she couldn't stand it. Yet, even as she worried, Tucker's aftershave, manly and teasing, filled her senses as he soothingly rubbed her back.

This was the man she held responsible for her husband's death.

"You're trembling."

"Yes," she forced, pulling away. "I'm not used to charging animals. And I'm embarrassed. I don't make a habit of running into strange men's arms."

He looked confused. "You don't have anything to be embarrassed about. You didn't know. If an animal does that again, yell loud and make an aggressive move of your own. It will run for the hills. Usually."

Like she hadn't tried that. "Fine," she snapped. "Thanks, um, for the lesson. I believe I'll wait in the truck." She stumbled over her words, turned and strode toward the van, daring even one of the measly animals to come her way! It was all she could do not to run as humiliation and indignation collided.

Yanking the door of the moving truck open, she climbed inside, glancing out at Abe as she tried to compose herself. He appeared sullen but, surprisingly, continued helping move the varmints off the road. Her gaze shifted back to Tucker. His expression was grim as he stared after her, probably wondering why she was acting so strange.

After a moment he turned away, and she watched him take a step, stiff at first, then better after a couple of steps. Still, though his expression didn't show it, she sensed he was in real pain.

Good.

The mean-spirited thought jumped into her mind instantaneously. Shame engulfed her. She'd been outspoken in the past, when needed, but never mean-spirited.

Death changed a person. Hardened up the heart like a cement block—she hated it.

She hated everything about this process of loss and its life-altering aftermath.

The truth was, she had no choice but to be here and hope with all her heart that Tucker McDermott and the Sunrise Ranch could help her son. Abe was the only reason she was here.

Her fifteen-year-old was hurting so bad on the inside that the only way he could cope was to lash out in ways that scared her for him. Her son, who needed more than she'd been able to give him.

Over the phone when she'd spoken with Tucker, before coming here, he'd given her his word that all would be well. She was praying that Tucker's word meant as much as Gordon believed it meant...

Gordon had been a few years younger than Tucker when he'd come to live at Tucker's family's ranch. A working cattle ranch that was also a foster home for boys who'd been abandoned and were alone in the world. Gordon had looked up to Tucker and he'd told her he'd become a marine because Tucker was a marine.

Gordon would have walked through fire for Tucker

and had told her if anything ever happened to him she should turn to him for help.

As it turned out, her husband had given his life for Tucker...

And left her to raise their son alone.

Tucker McDermott was the last person she wanted to turn to for help, but her son was in trouble and Suzie would do whatever it took to save him.

An hour after he'd been kicked, Tucker watched the trailer loaded with donkeys drive away. His hip throbbed like the pounding of a heavy-metal band... and since he had a metal plate in his thigh, it stood to reason. It was feeling better, he thought as he eased into the seat and closed the door. Totally conscious that he was being watched from the rented moving truck twenty yards away, he turned off his lights, backed up, then headed toward the ranch with Suzie following.

He'd been shaken to look down at the flaxen-haired woman helping him and discover Suzie Kent's remarkable blue-green eyes.

So much had crashed through his mind at that moment. Guilt for being alive when her husband was dead. Sorrow for what the war had cost her and her son—and Gordon. But there was the other emotion that swept through him strong and swift and deep...attraction.

Gordon had shown him her picture over and over when they were stationed in the Middle East. No one in the unit had missed seeing Suzie's photo. He'd been so proud and so in love with her. And Tucker could completely understand why—not just because of how beautiful she was, but because of the person his comments set her up to be. She'd sounded like a kind and caring woman, and her actions proved it. She didn't just send letters to her husband, but also care packages filled with his favorite things. And she always sent along plenty for the other marines in his unit—a thoughtful gesture appreciated by all.

Suzie Kent was the real deal and Gordon had been a lucky man.

Tucker hadn't been so lucky in love, before his stint in the marines or since. He'd been too in love with his career—this had been pointed out to him several times and it had been true. Driven to make a difference in the world was what he'd called it.

He wasn't marriage material back then, still wasn't. But he knew finding what Gordon and Suzie had found together wasn't easy.

He'd been happy for Gordon, though, and drawn to look at Suzie's pictures as often as Gordon wanted to show them. Everything was raw and harsh and brutal where they'd been, and looking into Suzie Kent's sparkling eyes had made him feel that there was hope in this world.

That he was fighting for goodness to prevail.

Moments ago, Tucker had looked down and Suzie hadn't been a photo any longer. She'd been real, and staring into her eyes, brutal reality had struck him like a bolt of lightning. Suzie Kent had once been full of life, fun and vivacious. Now she was sad and struggling to hide it.

Worry was etched into her expression and imprinted in the depths of her eyes. She seemed skittish, too, and uncertain.

And it was because of him.

If he'd died and Gordon had lived, she wouldn't be having the trouble she was having with her son or her life.

And, as much as he wanted to help Abe, Tucker wanted just as much to bring back the girl in those photos.

He knew deep in his soul that Gordon would have wanted that.

And as he began the drive toward the ranch with Suzie following, Tucker vowed once more that he would not let his fallen friend down.

Chapter Two

Turmoil rolled in Suzie's stomach like bad chicken salad as she followed Tucker down the country road. Pastures spread out on either side of the road, and yellow flowers were everywhere, carpeting the hillside in sunny yellow—goatweed, she knew, but pretty nonetheless.

When a majestic, wooden entrance came into view she knew this was Sunrise Ranch before she saw the name and before Tucker slowed and turned into the drive. Gordon had described everything perfectly.

In the distance, she could see the tops of the ranch buildings. She didn't look at Abe, but she felt him straighten in his seat and bend forward slightly, as if to get a better view. Her heart squeezed tight with hope.

They topped the hill, and the ranch spread out before them.

"This is where your dad came to live about the age you are now," she said, even though he already knew this. "He loved it here. I can see why."

Abe had stopped talking much about Gordon over the past year. It was as if he were angry with him for not being around. She understood. She had her own anger issues to deal with.

"Your dad had described it just like this," she said, loving the look of the place as she pulled to a halt beside Tucker at the rear of the large ranch house—a welcoming two-story house with an expansive back porch, inviting one to sit a spell overlooking the ranch compound. Out to the side of the house, an office and then a chow hall sat connected by porches and plank sidewalks. Small wooden signs swinging from the covered porches confirmed this, but she knew it from Gordon's descriptions.

Directly across the white rock parking lot was an older, but extremely well-maintained red stable that he'd said was at least a hundred years old. Gordon had loved the stable—she could still hear the awe in his tone when he talked of the baby horses being born there.

Beside the stable was a massive silver barn with an arena and corral attached. And out in the distance sat another building with playground equipment behind it—this was the schoolhouse.

There were boys everywhere, it seemed. Some were in the arena with a few cattle, others were on horses, riding toward them across the pasture. No sooner had Suzie parked than it seemed their truck was surrounded.

Suzie could easily tell that the bright-eyed boys were all ages, the youngest seemed to be eight or nine but there were all heights and ages.

Surely one of these boys would be a good friend to Abe.

She was about to open her door, but a dark-headed kid who looked amazingly like a young Elvis pulled it open for her.

"Hi, ma'am. Welcome to Sunrise Ranch. I'm Tony."

She could not help but smile. Not only from the fact that he did, indeed, sound like Elvis, but also because just the simple act of courtesy gave her another swift surge of hope. His eyes twinkled with goodwill and happiness—as her Abe's once had. *Please, God, let this be the answer.*

She heard Abe's door squeak open and glanced over her shoulder to see him getting out. Tucker was exiting his truck at the same time and said something to him as Abe closed his door. She turned back and smiled at Tony and the other boys, all talking at the same time.

"You done brung us another boy," said a small, plump boy, who looked to be the youngest. He looked from her to Abe on the other side of the truck.

"You want us to show you how to rope?" one called to Abe.

"Are you going to live here?"

"Can you ride a horse?"

Questions bombarded them from all directions.

She laughed, not knowing who to answer first.

"Whoa, boys," Tucker said, rounding the end of the truck with Abe. "Take it slow. This here is Abe. Yes, he's going to be going to school with y'all. And yes, he'll also need some help learning to ride and rope and work cows."

Suzie watched as everyone started introducing themselves. It was going to take her forever to learn all of their names. She *would* remember Tony. He seemed to be close to Abe's age.

Over the tops of their heads, her gaze met Tucker's and her pulse kicked into a gallop. His deep blue eyes seemed to reach for her and she felt suddenly breathless. What was wrong with her? These were emotions of attraction.

And they had no place between her and Tucker McDermott.

No place at all.

Abruptly the office door opened, and a tall, straight-backed woman with a gray ponytail and a wide grin came striding outside—Ruby Ann McDermott. She was followed by Randolph McDermott. Both had come to Gordon's funeral and stood beside her as if they were his family. They'd loved Gordon and he'd loved them, having considered them the family he'd never had since his parents abandoned him early in life. At the service, they'd given their condolences and offered to help her in any way they could. She'd refused their help at the time.

Randolph, a handsome man in his mid-fifties had threads of white at the temples of his charcoal hair. He'd marked his sons with the same dark hair and George Strait good looks.

Crossing to her now, she was struck again by his kind eyes as he took her hand in his.

"We are so glad you've come," he said. "We loved Gordon and are honored to get the opportunity to know you and Abe through Sunrise Ranch. This was Gordon's home and he loved it here."

"Thank you. He did love it."

Ruby Ann, or Nana as Gordon said he and all the boys affectionately called her, wrapped her arms around Suzie, just as she'd done at the funeral two years earlier. "Welcome to Sunrise Ranch, precious girl," she said. "I'm so glad you've come. We all are."

Randolph's eyes held hers. "We are forever in Gordon's debt for the sacrifice he made, and the sacrifice you and Abe made. His home is your home."

She fought back tears, her emotions were on edge today. She'd heard so many similar declarations over the past two years. But none of them changed what had happened.

And yet people were sincere, and that meant so much to her.

"Thank you. And I'm very grateful for what you're doing for us. For Abe," she said softly, not wanting him to hear, though he was now encircled by the other boys and she doubted he could hear anything she might say. Her heart swelled with gratefulness, despite the turmoil raging inside of her at having to turn to Tucker. Without the hope they were giving her with this opportunity for Abe she didn't know what she would have done.

Nana smiled warmly. "You think nothing of it. That boy needs this place. I can feel it in my soul. There's healing here at Sunrise Ranch. You needn't worry. Time and God's goodness will heal his broken heart."

Glancing back at Abe she caught Tucker's gaze again. A shiver raced down her spine when she thought she glimpsed pain in his eyes. She looked away and was glad when Randolph and Nana moved in to meet Abe.

She pushed aside the thought that Tucker might be hurting, too—and not just in his wounded hip. For two years she'd blamed him, never once thinking about what he'd been through, and now, upon meeting him, she had started thinking about his feelings.

It made her nervous and she wasn't sure why. She hadn't had long to think about it when one of the littler boys tugged on her arm.

"We're gonna show you and your boy how to rodeo,"

he said. "Oh, and I'm Sammy." A wide, enthusiastic smile spread big and bright across his thin face, and he puffed his chest way out. "I'm gettin' good and I've only been here a little over a year. Just think how good I'm going to be next month."

She laughed. He was so adorable and it was obvious he was thriving here.

To her surprise, the boys had planned a mini rodeo for them and, within minutes, in the midst of a flurry of action, she and Abe found themselves over by the arena watching the boys riding their horses and roping and chasing calves. Abe looked sullen, but at least he wasn't storming off to be alone.

"So, we're all excited you bought Joyce and Lester's flower shop," Nana said, coming to stand beside her at the arena fence.

"I am, too." Finding the flower shop for sale had been a bonus incentive for coming to Dew Drop. It wasn't as if she could just pick up and move to the town without a job to support them. That had been a worry. But she'd worked at a florist's for years, and when she'd started looking at possible jobs she'd come across the for-sale ad for the Dew Drop Petal. The price had been unbelievably reasonable, and she'd known exactly what to use part of her life insurance settlement on.

The flower shop had been a great blessing. And after feeling as though God had turned his back on them since Gordon's death, it had been very welcoming to her bruised faith.

"Dew Drop's not that big, but you should do well. And if there is anything I can do, I'd be happy to help. And our Tucker there, he'll assist you any way he can. That man has a huge cloud of guilt hanging over his head where Gordon is concerned. He loved Gordon as a brother. He'll want to help you in any way he can."

Suzie didn't want to think about his guilty feelings. "I came here for him to help with Abe. That's all I'll need from him."

Nana studied her with deep blue eyes that unsettled her. After a moment, she patted Suzie's arm. "God's got a plan, Suzie. I think maybe you don't believe that. But He does. He always does."

Suzie yanked her gaze away and, without meaning to, found herself looking at the broad-shouldered form of Tucker leaning on the fence beside Abe, pointing at the boys, explaining to her son what was going on in the arena.

She was clinging to the hope of a plan, but it didn't have anything to do with spending unnecessary time with Tucker McDermott.

As a matter of fact, the less time she spent around him, the better.

"Hey, you want me to show you how to rope?"

Tucker took a swig of his iced tea. The cold, sweet liquid did nothing to cool the burning tension in the pit of his stomach as Abe gave Caleb an angry glare. Caleb was trying to pull Abe out of his shell, but the boy wasn't interested. Fortunately, the boys of Sunrise Ranch were used to this kind of behavior and had probably been on the giving end when they'd first arrived at the ranch, alone, lost and feeling as if their world had come to an end.

The emotions that warred behind Abe's chilly blue gaze were not uncommon.

Tucker's dad always halted chores and school and

held some small welcome event for each boy upon his arrival, to showcase the fun that was in store for him. This helped ease their transition and break them into life on the ranch by snagging their interest.

During the mini rodeo for Abe and Suzie, Tucker spent time explaining what each event was to Abe. Though the kid hadn't joined in on the conversation, the fact that he'd listened was a plus, and Tucker believed he was interested.

When the rodeo was over, Nana called everyone to the chow hall, where they'd decided to have their first meal with Suzie and Abe. Sometimes Nana would have the guests and all the boys over at the house, but it was a rowdy event and they'd decided it would be better to eat in the chow hall. It would be good for Suzie to see where Abe would be having his meals during school hours. Abe would eat supper at the ranch house with Suzie and Nana, since the boys ate their evening meal with their house parents at the two foster homes on the ranch.

Tucker had given Suzie some space not long after the mini rodeo started, staying out of her way for a couple of hours. She was clearly not comfortable around him, and so he'd let his dad and his grandmother and his other family members try to put her at ease. His brother Morgan was there with his wife, Jolie, who was the teacher of the school. And his youngest brother, Rowdy, was there also, though his fiancée, Lucy, was at an art show in New York and couldn't make it. Everyone had tried hard to make Suzie and Abe feel welcome and she'd seemed to respond well with them. Even seemed to relax and he'd thought some of the tension had eased from her eyes.

But dinner was over now. Pans of homemade lasagna and Nana's handmade rolls had been devoured and only the crumbs remained. The huge bowls of her cream-cheese banana pudding slathered in whipped cream were practically licked clean. And the boys were walking around smacking their lips in satisfaction.

His nana knew how to make boys happy. She gave them plenty of love and nurturing, and filled them with the best food in Texas, and plenty of it.

As the sun started to dip under the horizon, he knew it was time to talk; he'd put it off as long as possible.

Suzie and Nana were on the porch, and as he walked over he forced the nerves rattling around in his gut like barbed wire to go away. He'd faced more than his share of danger, and yet facing Suzie made him feel like a coward.

"I hate to interrupt, but, Suzie, could we take a walk? I think it would be a good idea for us to discuss a few things."

She minded. It was written clearly in her eyes.

"No, not at all. If you'll excuse me, Nana, Tucker is right. We need to talk."

Nana squeezed Suzie's arm. "You go along, dear. When you get back I'll show you upstairs to your room and you can get you and Abe settled into the ranch house."

"Thanks. Thanks for everything."

Nana waved off the gratitude. "You are family, just like Gordon was. My house is your house. Helping is what families do. Now go, it will do the two of you good to talk."

There were kids all around the yard and the barn, and despite Abe's reluctance to join in, Tony and Caleb, along with Jake, one of the newest teens, had gotten him to go to the stable to see the horses. Horses were always good for the boys.

"We can walk out to the school, if you'd like. I'm sure you'd like to see where Abe will be tomorrow."

Placing her hand on her stomach, as if to calm her nerves, she nodded and fell into step with him.

In her running shoes, she came to just below his chin. So when she looked at him she was looking up slightly and it made her seem even more vulnerable than he knew she was.

"How's Abe doing since we talked?" They'd had a couple of conversations on the phone prior to her move. She'd explained that she needed help, that Abe was hanging with a crowd of older boys who were constantly in trouble and that she was afraid for him. He'd heard the fear and distress in her voice over the long-distance line.

Two of the boys Abe had been hanging out with had just been sent to juvenile jail. Abe had been sneaking out at night, several times that she knew of, and he refused to tell her what he'd been doing. She'd called Tucker out of desperation and he knew it—because she blamed him for Gordon being dead. She'd made that clear when he'd gone to see her after being released from the hospital. She'd refused his help and refused to have anything to do with him.

Until now.

Her eyes flashed and he could have punched himself.

"You saw him," she said tightly. "He's like a bomb waiting to explode. He's been that way since he lost his father. It's just getting worse." The accusation vibrated in her words and the vein in her throat beat so hard it was obvious that her blood pressure had skyrocketed. He hated that he'd done this. His own blood was pounding in his ears. He hadn't been trained for this.

Silence stretched between them, the only sound the soft crunch of gravel as they followed the path across the pasture toward the school.

He started over. "What I meant to say was—how long after losing his father was it before he started hanging around this group of kids?"

Her shoulders slumped as she pushed her silky hair behind her ear. "It was about a year ago. We'd had a tough first year. Lots of tears and angry outbursts and sullenness. We saw a counselor, but Abe wouldn't open up and eventually he refused to return. I should have found him another counselor—one he would talk to. I should have continued until I found the right one. But he refused and said if I took him to another one, he would run away. And I believed him."

There was anguish in her voice and it tore at Tucker. He said a silent prayer that God would lead him in helping Suzie. His faith had been the strength that had sustained him through all of this. His faith that God would not let this family down.

"I understand. And after that?"

She took a deep breath. "After that, things went downhill. He started skipping school and sneaking out at night, even though he was barely thirteen. He was in detention much of the time. The school tried. They felt for him. He met one of these boys in detention. The other was a dropout."

"You can't blame yourself."

She looked up at him. "I don't."

Her eyes were hard where he'd seen softness and love

in the photos of her smiling at her husband. Tucker's gut clenched and he felt like throwing up.

"At least I try not to. I blame the war. I blame you. Even though I know it's unreasonable. I do. But still, I feel guilty because I couldn't hold it together without Gordon. He was made of stauncher stuff. He believed in me. And in the end, I've let him down." Tears were in her eyes. "He believed in you, too. And so I've come. Maybe his trust in you is worth more than his trust in me."

Her throat worked as she tried not to cry. It was clear in her expression that she was fighting breaking down.

"No, it isn't," he offered bluntly, feeling awkward. How was he supposed to answer something like that? "I'm sure you're probably exhausted from the move, too," he said, when she looked away as if embarrassed that she was crying. It took everything Tucker had not to wipe away the tears trailing down her cheeks. He vowed he would fix this as best it could be fixed without Gordon rising from the dead.

She wiped away the tears herself and took a shuddering breath. He watched her stiffen her shoulders.

He cleared his own throat. "Your husband loved you more than life itself. It was evident to all who came within ten feet of him. Your picture was shown around more than a pinup, and he talked about how strong and good you were. He would never believe you let him down. You should know that."

She looked away. "If we don't find a way to save Abe from this destructive path he's on, nothing else matters. Sunrise Ranch and you are my last hope."

"We'll all get through. This is a place of healing. My mother had a dream to see scared and scarred boys find a place to belong and mend. She knew…" He paused and looked across the pastures at the setting sun and the beauty surrounding them. When he looked back at Suzie she had followed his gaze and was staring toward the sunset, too.

"You've seen the boys who are here. They are happy, regular boys now. Yes, they have deep hurts and issues that they deal with, but we are their support group. Their family. Just as Gordon was part of our family. You saw some of that tonight with Nana. Even if no one else makes any headway with Abe, Nana and her food and love will smooth a path for others to reach him. It happens all the time."

They started walking again. "She is wonderful." There was wistful hope in her voice.

That breathless sound eased a knot slightly that had formed beneath his rib cage. They'd reached the school and stopped beside the porch. "She is," he agreed. "So rest assured. And I promise it will work out. It may not be easy but Abe will be all right." He'd never made promises he meant more than the ones he was making to Suzie.

Tucker prayed God's plan and his plan were the same.

"Let me show you the school," he said, opening the door. "It's a simple three-room structure with restrooms." They walked into the large, open room full of desks and bookshelves and exploding with color. "As you know, Jolie is the teacher. And she loves bright colors."

She paused in the doorway, and her breath caught. "I love it! It radiates with happiness. Just like she does."

Glad for something positive to latch on to, he smiled looking at some of the bulletin boards. "That's true,

Jolie is a very happy person and it shows. Jolie loves color and light. She had Rowdy's fiancée, Lucy, paint the mural of the outdoor scene around the chalkboard."

"I love that. It brings the outside in."

He was feeling hopeful now, hearing the excitement in Suzie's voice. "She loves the outdoors, and holds class outside a lot. At her request we added more picnic tables out back under the trees. She's great."

"She and Morgan were really nice at dinner. I heard the boys saying she was a champion kayaker."

"Yes. World-class. But her heart is here now. The boys are enthralled with her."

"I can see why. It's rather intimidating to think about."

"Tell me about it. I certainly don't know how kayakers do what they do, and I don't want to. But the boys like the idea that their teacher has an adventurous spirit. It helps her to be able to talk to them. Plus, she was raised here. Her parents were house parents, and she went to school here with me, Morgan and Rowdy, when the school first started. She has witnessed the power of Sunrise Ranch. She'll be good for Abe."

Suzie nodded. "I like that. This is certainly going to be different than the school he was attending."

"We found having a smaller group setting was a better option for the boys here at the ranch. It will be good for Abe." He prayed it was so.

He showed her the rest of the school, then took her out back to the picnic tables and swings that sat beneath the oak trees. A breeze rustled through the leaves, and the sunset had turned into a pink glow, making a beautiful horizon.

Suzie turned to him. "Thank you for agreeing to do this."

He could tell that was costing her. What must she feel about him behind those beautiful, sad eyes?

Tucker yanked his thoughts back. He had a good head on his shoulders. He knew how to handle tough situations and make clear decisions under stressful ones. The emotions assaulting him as he stared into Suzie's eyes were dangerous. Having a crush on the wife of the man whose death you felt responsible for just was not acceptable.

And if she even got a hint of what he was feeling, she would surely leave this ranch and never come back.

And he wouldn't blame her at all.

Chapter Three

"Abe, can I come in?" Suzie asked, tapping softly on the door of his room. There was a muffled "Whatever" from the other side of the door, so she opened it. Abe was stretched out on the bed staring at the ceiling. The fluffy green bedspread made him seem small, even though she knew he was growing like a weed.

She walked across the room and sat down on the edge of the bed. He kept his gaze firmly locked on the ceiling, and didn't even glance at her. Her fingers itched to push the lock of hair out of his eyes.

"I just wanted to tell you good-night." She touched his arm gently, but he pulled away. The boy she'd glimpsed earlier on the road with the donkeys seemed like a dream gone away. As if she'd imagined him for a moment. "The boys seem nice. Tony and Caleb must be about your age, too."

His jaw tightened. "They're okay," he said at last. "Now can I go to sleep?"

"Abe, I won't have you being disrespectful," she said, shaken by his coldness. His eyes suddenly glistened with unshed tears. Her heart broke one more time....

How could a heart break over and over again? How…?
Dear God, help me. Help my son.

After a moment she stood, knowing that hugging him was asking too much.

"Abe, what happened to us—losing your father—that wasn't fair. But life isn't fair always. Your dad would want you to be happy. This ranch, these people. They made him happy. I just want you to give it all a chance."

His gaze met hers finally, but only for a desolate moment, then he rolled over and turned his back to her.

"I love you, son." It felt like she was saying the words to a brick wall. Her heart ached.

Abe's going to be all right. I promise. Tucker's words echoed through her thoughts and gave her strength.

Still, it took everything in her to stand up, walk out and close the door.

Tomorrow a new day would begin.

And Suzie was going to trust that it would be their new start. She was going to think positive and give it everything she had. For Abe.

The next morning, Suzie's sense of hope continued to prevail as she drove into town. Abe had eaten a huge breakfast with the other boys—Nana relayed the info, because Suzie had forced herself not to hover. Not to go peek through the windows, either—though it was exactly what she wanted to do.

Sometimes a mother's job was hard—stepping back was one of the harder things.

But when she'd walked across the hall to his room she'd been surprised to find him already up and dressed and she'd taken that as a great sign. He'd startled her more by revealing that he'd decided to help feed the horses.

Evidently he'd been invited to do so, and after a night of thinking about it, he'd decided to help. It was a positive start and Suzie, not knowing what to expect when she'd awakened that morning, was thrilled.

Now, heading into town, she found herself relaxing in the seat of her small car, which Tucker had unhitched from the moving truck the previous night. She had the truck for another day, so she was going to have to find a place to rent, though the McDermotts had assured her that she and Abe were welcome to stay as long as needed. And she was wondering if prolonging their stay for a little while might be a good thing, if spending mornings, days and nights there would put him more in the action for a little while.

There was an apartment on the second story of the building that housed the florist's shop, but she'd been told it was in some disrepair. She wasn't sure she wanted to live above the store, anyway—how good would that be for Abe? But it was an option.

For now, she'd use it to store her things until she decided what she wanted to do.

The town was darling. The four-story, redbrick Dew Drop Inn reigned supreme across from a quaint town park that was surrounded by four rows of small businesses. On the far corner across the street from the Dew Drop Inn was the Spotted Cow Café with a sunny yellow door and red geraniums. Like a welcome sign, it begged a person to come visit.

On the bench outside the newspaper office just down the street sat two older gentlemen who waved as she passed. They were whittling and added to the feeling that Mayberry had come to life. Suzie instantly imagined Sheriff Andy Taylor walking the streets—but then, Tucker McDermott's image replaced the fictional sheriff's image and Dew Drop seemed suddenly a little more exciting than Mayberry. *Stop with that, already!*

Pulling into the empty parking spot three doors down from the weathered church pew where the gentlemen were sitting, a wave of nerves suddenly attacked her like stinging bees.

The ugly chipped door of her new business was directly in front of her, kind of a toss-up between mud-brown and murky gray.

"First order of business," she muttered. "Paint that door."

To say it was bad was the understatement of the year. And hopefully not a foreshadowing of things to come once she opened it and stepped inside.

The two older men came hurrying down the sidewalk, their boots scuffing as they came.

"We've been expecting you this morning," the taller one said, grinning wide. He looked as though he smiled often because of the crinkles around his pale green eyes. "We made sure and got here early, just so we could welcome you. Right, Drewbaker?"

"Right, Chili," the other man agreed. "We usually show up in the afternoon after we get our cows fed, but we snuck away this morning." He winked, making her chuckle at the pure teasing in his manner.

"Thank you so much for coming. I'm Suzie Kent."

"Oh, we know who you are. But I'm Chili Crump and that's Drewbaker Mackintosh."

Mr. Mackintosh nodded. "We heard all about you buying the place from Joyce and Lester. Those two were so excited to hook a buyer, they told the world it had sold before the papers were signed."

"Ain't that the truth," Mr. Crump said, scratching his jaw. "Why, they packed up their motor home and left town almost before we could wave goodbye. You'd think they couldn't wait to get rid of us."

Mr. Mackintosh's entire face fell with his frown. "Yeah, kind of felt like we weren't wanted anymore," he said, then winked again. "They really wanted to get out of town before you changed your mind."

"That bad?" she asked, enjoying herself, despite the ominous teasing.

Both men grinned and followed her to the door, watching as she stuck in the key. Opening the door felt as if she was opening the best gift at Christmas, even as the musty scent of age wafted out in greeting.

"Well, gentlemen, let's see what I've got, shall we?" She couldn't help but feel happy walking in. Comical expressions of doom and gloom lit her new friends' faces—half teasing, she knew, and yet the place had certainly seen better times.

Entering, she had to step lively to get out of their way as they crowded in behind her.

Someone flicked the lights on—not really a good thing, since it illuminated the lost and forlorn look of the empty flower shop. Glass cases that had to be some of the first ever made lined one wall. A single forgotten vase of flowers sat wilted behind the glass. The floors were old planks, rough and worn so that they had a shine to them like pebbles under a constant stream of water. Their footsteps rang out in the cavernous room.

The back room wasn't any better. The tables all looked as though they were made from leftover wood, with plywood tops that had no charm at all. Turning back to the front room she studied the small front counter, more of a podium, with barely enough room for a purchase tablet much less a computer—even a small laptop. That would have to be remedied. Bad, to say the least, and yet…light streamed in from the large, old plate-glass window and made a sunny spot in the center of the room. It was to that sunny spot that Suzie walked and stood as she readjusted her eyes.

"It ain't much to look at."

"Mr. Mackintosh, you're right, it has its bad points."

"Call me Drewbaker. Ever'body does."

"And the same here. Call me Chili, little lady."

She smiled. "Drewbaker and Chili, then. It does have its bad points. But, for the money I paid, I got a steal of a deal. That's a huge plus. And look up. Isn't that tin ceiling amazing? What charm."

Both of them cranked their necks back and frowned.

"You've got better eyes than me," Drewbaker said. "Ain't no charm in here."

Chili agreed with his silence and the skeptical expression on his craggy face.

"Now, it's not that bad," Tucker said from the doorway. "Good morning, Suzie. Fellas."

Suzie's pulse bucked into rodeo mode upon seeing him—it was very disturbing.

"Good morning," she said. Then, not waiting for any more encouraging declarations, she walked over to the glass cases and tried the sliding doors. "These work great. That's a plus. They would be the most expensive pieces for me to purchase, so as long as they keep the flowers cool, everything else is workable. You'll be amazed what a little paint will do."

"That's right," Tucker said, coming over to test the doors himself. "You have a great attitude."

"Well, I have two choices. See only the bad or start thinking positive. I want to think positive. Paint will work wonders. And scrubbing and rearranging.

"And flowers," she added. "Flowers everywhere will change the whole atmosphere."

And scent. What was that odor?

Candles. Candles and flowers would change the scent.

Yes, she had a plan.

She dropped her fists to her hips and did a full turn, taking in the room, trying not to think about Tucker watching her.

She came to a halt at the comical expressions of dismay on Chili's and Drewbaker's faces.

"This place is a dump. To tell you the truth, we haven't been in here in years." Drewbaker scratched his head. "My wife always said I'd pick a neighbor's rose and give it to her before I'd pay for one, and I reckon she was right."

Suzie chuckled. "Sadly, you aren't alone."

"I bought a few in my day," Chili said, with a sheepish grin. "But it's been a while. I might have to buy some once you get this joint up and going. Matter of fact, you put me down as your first customer. You just let me know when you start making deliveries."

Tucker shot him a glance.

"You're serious?" Drewbaker asked.

"I am. A man's got to make a move sometime."

Drewbaker's laugh nearly busted out the windows. "Well, I'll be getting me some entertainment from this. What do you think, Tucker?"

"Might be interesting," Tucker agreed, his eyes dancing with laughter.

Suzie couldn't help but be curious, but she'd learned not to ask personal questions about flowers unless it was absolutely necessary. Privacy was part of her business. So she'd wait. "I'll certainly let you know the date," she said.

"Okay, Romeo," Drewbaker grunted. "You and me both have hungry cows waitin' on us. We bes' get a move on."

The two said their goodbyes and were gone, leaving Suzie and Tucker alone. The room seemed suddenly much smaller than it had before.

"How long have you been a florist?" he asked. "You seem to really enjoy it."

"I do. I started working in a shop for a friend not long after Abe was born. Opening my own place is a dream I've had for a long time."

He smiled and the room grew even smaller. "You'll make people smile with each arrangement."

It startled her realizing how easy she found talking to Tucker. She'd just opened up to him about her dreams.... "I need to check out the upstairs," she said, heading out the door and onto the street, needing to break the moment.

Tucker followed her, of course, opting not to stand alone inside her shop while she came out onto the sidewalk. The man was like a bright, shiny penny, with his badge and buckle both glinting in the sun. And those eyes—and that warm smile spreading across his ruggedly good-looking face had Suzie's insides fluttering to life with renewed awareness.

Instantly ruining a great morning.

* * *

Tucker hadn't slept much after leaving the ranch last night. He'd gone home to his place, which was on a small piece of land just on the outskirts of Dew Drop. After moving back, he'd decided to move in closer to town. When he'd become sheriff, he found he was often barraged by calls at all times of the day and night—it was better to be closer to his office. Getting to the office quickly in an emergency situation was important to him. He'd live on the land he loved again, one day, but for now, while he'd taken the oath to serve and protect, he'd live close by. Plus, he'd felt the need to be alone at times. Especially in the beginning when nightmares kept him awake—he pushed the thought away and focused on Suzie. Helping her was the only thing that could give him some redemption from the past.

She seemed different this morning. She was upbeat and striving. He liked that. Liked it a lot that she was fighting, and that would be good for her. The woman he'd seen in the pictures didn't seem so far away right now.

"I'm sure that old shop will look like a different place when you're done. I'm pretty sure the apartment isn't livable, though. It'll be a good place to store your things until you find what you want."

"I guess we'll just go up and look," she said, starting up the steps.

Tucker followed her. The steps creaked beneath their feet but seemed sturdy. Suzie rested her hand on the banister as she went.

"Did Lester and Joyce live up here?"

"No. They had a little house over near the lake. They didn't really use this, I don't think. That's one reason I thought I might come up with you. I'm not sure if they ever came up here or if they even did anything with the stuff that had been here before they left."

She paused on the steps. "Everyone is saying they left town quickly. It sounds like they were really ready to not be tied to a business any longer."

She was a step ahead of him, and that made her almost exactly his height. He could look her straight in the eyes.

She rested her hip against the railing. "Do you think there was some other reason they left so quickly?"

"I don't know. They'd had the place up for sale for a couple of years, and I think they had almost decided just to leave anyway. Your offer came while they were packing up, so I think they didn't pause to look back."

Just as the last words were out of his mouth an ominous crack sounded and the banister Suzie was leaning against broke.

Suzie felt the board she was barely resting against give under her hip. She tried to catch her balance, arms flailing, but as the board broke there was nothing stopping her from tipping backward into open space. She was twelve feet above the ground with nothing but gravel and dirt below her.

Suddenly, a strong arm snaked around her waist and she was yanked from thin air and pulled hard against Tucker's firm chest.

"I've got you," he assured her as he swung around, throwing their momentum in the opposite direction. One moment she'd been free-falling and the next she found herself held snuggled in his arms against the brick wall of the building.

Both of them were breathing hard as she stared into his eyes. Her feet dangled beneath her and she was nose to nose, eye to eye with Tucker. Her gaze dropped to the mere inch between their lips.

"Thank you," she managed as her pulse thundered. Her mouth went dry when she met his gaze and realized he'd watched her studying his beautiful mouth.

What am I thinking! I almost plunged twelve feet to the ground and now I'm thinking about kissing Tucker. What is wrong with me? This is so wrong.

"No thanks required," Tucker said, taking a deep breath as if he, too, had just remembered to breathe.

She pulled away and they moved in sync, him moving down a step, her shifting up away from him. Even separated from him, her skin tingled with sensation.

"That will have to be fixed," she said, as if he didn't realize that. Silly, but it was the first thing that popped out of her numbed brain.

Spinning away from him and keeping close to the building, she stared at the steps. She moved up one step at a time to the small landing outside the door. Key. She needed a key.

Digging in her jeans pocket she produced it and, with trembling fingers, inserted it into the lock and twisted.

Tucker had followed close behind her, not saying anything, but she knew he was as shaken as she was. She'd read it in his eyes. The tension radiated between them as she pushed open the door and stepped into the murky room.

Her thoughts were just as murky as suddenly the lights came on, and she saw Tucker had flipped the switch.

Relief washed over her, seeing that the room wasn't

as full of leftover stuff as she'd feared. She moved farther inside, putting space between them.

In her mind she wanted to be grateful that he'd caught her.

But she was too shaken by the experience.

"What do you think?" Tucker's baritone radiated through the room.

Think? *That I've lost my mind.* "It, ah, isn't as bad as it could be."

"It might take a little while to get it cleaned up if you're thinking about living up here. But we could help or, if you want some walls moved around and would rather hire it done, I know a great contractor."

Suzie grabbed hold of this new topic of conversation, glad to focus on something other than how being around Tucker was affecting her. "I think we'll just store my stuff up here for now. I might decide to find a rental property instead. You know, something with a yard, so Abe could have a dog. After I get the business going, though. Maybe I can think clearer about what would be best then. Tackling the store downstairs should be my priority."

"That sounds like a plan. And you know, the ranch is your home as long as you want it. There is plenty of room. And Nana will love having you in the house with her." He was studying her, as if he were trying to read the thoughts flickering through her mind.

"But," she added quickly, "I need to have that banister repaired."

"Count it already done. I'm heading over to the lumber company right now, and I'll have that fixed before lunch."

She wanted to say she'd get someone else, but she

needed it done as soon as possible, before they began traipsing up and down with her things. Anyone could fall and she would blame herself. "Thank you again," she said. "I seem to be indebted to you over and over."

Tucker frowned. "No debt. That's all mine." With that said, he went to inspect the next room.

Suzie followed, slowly, startled that for an instant she'd forgotten what Tucker had cost her and her child. That if it wasn't for him Gordon would be alive and they wouldn't be here.

No thanks required.

That's what he'd said and it was true.

Chapter Four

Tucker called in Cody, his deputy, so he could take the morning off to get the banister rebuilt. And he needed the physical exertion—needed something to occupy his mind, but it wasn't working. He'd been thinking of nothing except holding Suzie in his arms all morning.

What a jerk he'd been. He'd rescued her, and then instantly his pulse had ramped up and he'd been looking at her as if she was his long-lost love. And she'd seen it, too.

He slammed the hammer to the nail with enough force to test the foundation poles holding the stairs in the air. He needed the exertion that working with his hands would provide. Riding his horse across the ranch would have been his number one choice to exert his pent-up frustrations—as far away from Suzie Kent as he could get. But she needed the banister and despite knowing that she was just inside the building, it was where he needed to be.

His reaction to her had stunned him. She was the wife of the man he owed his life to. *Widow.* His brain corrected. *And free to find a new love.*

That his thoughts had even hinted at going there angered him. He owed Gordon his life, and he owed Gordon's widow and child his support to help them maneuver through the wreckage he'd caused in their lives. But to think about her in terms of a love interest—nope, she was way out of bounds to him.

And yet there was no denying that he was attracted to her. *Or that she's the kind of woman I've been looking for all of my life.*

But there was no chance for there to ever be anything between them—and he had no right even thinking about it. Feeling cornered, he placed another nail in the base of the banister railing and then moved up the steps to hammer in the next one. Six more to go, and not near enough to get rid of the anger fighting inside of him.

He was a man who took action. He'd had to watch his mother die of cancer when he was fourteen and there had been nothing he could do about it. He'd sworn then that he'd make a difference in the lives of others and the marines had drawn him. He'd wanted to make a difference in the world. Time after time he'd pulled his men back from death, or as many as he possibly could. He'd been able to make a difference in their lives and those of their families. Unlike his own. Cancer was a war that many were able to defeat, but his mom had not been one of them.

He'd never thought about what watching helplessly as one of his men gave his life for him would cost—not only the soldier's family, but him.

He didn't like it. He couldn't control it. But he was going to fix it. And being attracted to Gordon's widow was the ultimate betrayal of his friend. Tucker had been sixteen when that first group of boys had started filtering in, and Gordon had been two years younger when he'd come to Sunrise Ranch the year it opened. Tucker and Gordon had hit it off instantly.

It had been a surprise when Gordon had ended up in his marine unit. They'd celebrated, not realizing that it would come down to one of them living and the other dying.

Tucker closed his eyes, thinking about it. Kenny Chesney's "Who You'd Be Today" played through his mind, as it did so many times when he thought about Gordon and the others who didn't come home.

"Woo-hoo, Tucker!"

At the excited singsong holler he opened his eyes, to see Mabel Tilsby, owner of the Dew Drop Inn, weaving her way across the street toward him. A tall, stout woman, she had the heart of a missionary, and that was a good thing because Tucker was pretty sure an angry Mabel could take care of herself.

"You are doing one great job," she said, drawing to a halt at the bottom of the stairs. "These old stairs have been here since the beginning of time, and they did need repairing." Hands on hips, she grinned up at him. "I was out front this morning when I saw them break. Thank goodness you were there to save our new resident!"

He glanced across the street and saw that she had a straight shot of the stairs from her front door. He groaned inwardly knowing exactly what Mabel saw—him holding Suzie in his arms longer than necessary.

"Yeah, I should have checked these out a long time ago when I was making my rounds at night." It was known by everyone that he still walked the square on foot each evening to make sure everything was secure. An odd thing, some might say, since Dew Drop was such a small place and the crime rate was low, but even small towns had problems. And it was his job to make sure his tiny hometown stayed safe.

"You can't fix everything, even though you think you're our superhero sheriff," she said jovially.

Tucker had always liked Mabel. She was a tower of a woman, and with her big-boned frame could almost have been a linebacker if she'd been born a male. His mother used to say that a tall person needed bigger feet to balance out their height, and that Mabel needed her larger size to balance out her large and loving personality. He believed it, too. Mabel would just as soon pick you up and hug you in half as shake your hand.

"Nope, but I can try." He grinned back at her.

She waved him off. "You got it honestly from both sides of your family. I'm going to go inside and introduce myself. Have to tell that girl how much I loved Gordon. I always smile thinking about that boy. Ta-ta for now."

And she was gone, disappearing inside the shop. Suzie would hear a lot of good stories about Gordon from Mabel since he'd worked for her as a bellboy whenever she needed help.

Tucker went back to hammering.

And his mind went straight back to thinking about how Suzie Kent had felt in his arms.

Though the previous owners had left the shop in decent shape, such as it was, there were spiderwebs and dust in the nooks and crannies. She had busied herself cleaning, getting it ready to paint. Paint worked wonders, and she was counting on it for the store.

The thump of the hammer outside was a continual

reminder that she'd made a fool of herself by looking up into Tucker McDermott's eyes like a love-starved widow. How humiliating that cliché was. The more she thought about it, the worse it got.

In addition came the guilt that she'd done so with Tucker. It would have been bad with anyone—but Tucker? It was awful. Guilt engulfed her. And even if Tucker hadn't been the man she blamed for Gordon's death, he was in law enforcement. She could never again risk falling for a man who worked in the line of fire. And yet, she couldn't deny that the man affected her in startling ways.

When a large woman came barreling through the open door, Suzie was more than ready for company.

"Hello, hello. I'm Mabel Tilsby, owner of the Dew Drop Inn—hope you don't mind me dropping in on you." She grinned, taking Suzie's hands in hers for an extended moment.

"Not at all. I'm glad to meet you."

"I have to tell you that I loved your husband. That Gordon was a good young man. He'd had a rough life, but he came right to this town and brightened it with his smile and good humor. Do you know he rescued me that first summer?"

Suzie couldn't speak at first, startled by Mabel's declaration. Of course there would be stories of Gordon. This was his home. She was touched and then remembered him mentioning the owner of the hotel. "He mentioned you," she said, smiling. "I remember he said you were a wonderful lady."

That made Mabel blush, her eyes misted. "That boy always was a sweetheart. And just look at you. So beautiful and young. I know he must have loved you very much."

It was Suzie's turn to get misty-eyed. She nodded. "He did."

"Well." Mabel heaved a deep breath in then expelled it. "He'd be happy you've come home and brought his boy. You've got a lot of life ahead of you. He'd want you to move forward—or in his case he'd want you to plow forward like he always did."

Suzie laughed at that. "Yes, he did move at a fast pace."

Mabel nodded and then studied the shop.

"This old place needed new blood in it. So, what do you think?"

Suzie had been destroying a large web in the upper corner of the ceiling when Mabel burst into the building. She smiled. "Minus all the spiders, let's just say I'm counting on paint to make a whole new world in here. Paint and flowers."

"It is ancient."

"Yes, but serviceable, and that's what counts. As long as I get some orders for flowers when I open the doors."

"You'll get them. And you have such a handsome handyman outside. That has to be a plus."

"He's not my handyman. He's just—" *What? Fixing your banister. Being your handyman.* "It broke while we were going up to look upstairs. Mr. McDermott and Rowdy are going to come in a little while and help Tucker unload my moving truck and store my things up there for now. I think some of the boys are coming, too, and we didn't want anyone getting hurt."

"I understand. Falling from those stairs wouldn't be good. I saw you almost tumble off this morning.

Thank goodness our fabulous sheriff was there. I almost screamed from the steps of the Inn when I realized what was happening. But then, just like that, you were in his arms and safe." Mabel sighed as she finished and her eyes got dreamy—it was enough to make Suzie worry.

And she felt the heat of a blush race over her as though she'd just been doused in warm cherry juice. "So, come over here and see what you think about the colors I'm going to paint the shop," she said, changing the subject.

She popped the top of the can of paint in a soft buttery-yellow that she'd picked up at the lumber store.

"Oh, I like that," Mabel gushed enthusiastically.

Suzie was learning that everything Mabel did was with enthusiasm. It was kind of contagious.

"I think it's a happy color. It'll make a perky background for the flowers."

"I most certainly agree, hon. I'll go tell the girls and we'll have a full-scale painting party. How does that sound? All you have to do is tell us where you want it, and we can slap it up there in no time. Matter of fact, have you had lunch?"

Suzie looked at her watch and was startled to see that it was past noon. "No, but—"

"Nope, no buts allowed. You're coming with me. Seal up that can and let's go. When were you planning on painting?"

She found herself swept out of the shop and managed to squeeze in "I'll be back" to Tucker—not that it was any of his business, but he was working on her stairs and he would be lugging her furniture up them before too much later. He nodded that he heard and went back to hammering. They headed down the street with Mabel talking nonstop.

"That man sure looks good swinging a hammer," Mabel sighed, elbowing her in the ribs before continuing to talk about paint. Before they made it to the café she'd learned that mission trips and fixing things up for folks in need were high priorities for Mabel. It hit Suzie that she'd just been added to the top of Mabel's folks-in-need list.

She'd become a mission project.

Suzie wasn't sure how to take that. She took care of herself, or had been trying to. But as they took their seats in the diner and were joined by Ms. Jo, the owner, who was Mabel's buddy and also Nana's, Suzie had the oddest sensation that she'd been embraced. Embraced by a town. Being helped just came with the deal.

Gordon would be happy. The knowledge echoed through her heart and she had to fight off a sudden wave of emotion.

Her being happy again would have been what he'd wanted. It felt good knowing that, here in Dew Drop, it was a possibility.

Despite Tucker and her conflicting emotions.

Later that afternoon, after an already full day, Tucker watched his dad back the moving truck up to the newly renovated stairs. Just as Randolph and Morgan climbed from the truck, Rowdy pulled in beside them with a truck full of the older boys, including Abe.

"Hey, guys," he said. "Thanks for coming to help."

"Sure thing," Jake said. He was new at the ranch, having taken one of the vacant spots left when Joseph and Wes, two of the older boys, headed off to college.

Jake didn't speak much about what he'd been through before he came to them, but he'd had it rough, even lived on the streets for a while. The kid had taken to the ranch as if he'd been born a cowboy, always ready to mount up and herd cattle or pitch in where needed.

Tucker noticed Abe stood back from the group and didn't look pleased to be here.

"So, did you check out the apartment up there?" Randolph asked, striding over to stand beside him.

Morgan nodded toward Tucker's handyman project. "Hopefully, it's more stable now."

"Yeah," Rowdy said, grabbing the banister and tugging to test its sturdiness. "Did they teach you to be a carpenter in the marines? Because I don't remember you ever building anything before now. You sure this thing will hold us?"

"Oh, it'll hold," Tucker assured them, heading toward the moving van instead of thinking about that banister breaking and him pulling Suzie into his arms.

As if on cue, Suzie stepped out of the office right at that moment, and she smiled—not at him but at everyone else.

"Thank you all for coming," she said, warmly. She'd been painting already, and there was a splotch of yellow paint on her jaw. He busied himself opening the cargo doors as the boys gathered around.

"Abe, how was school today?" she asked.

"All right, I guess," Abe answered, his voice flat.

"Well, good. I'm glad it was all right," she said and Tucker liked that she was trying to be positive.

"He's gonna ride a horse when we get back to the ranch. Isn't that right?" Jake prompted.

Though he remained silent, Abe's scowl was a definite "no."

"Come on," Tony encouraged. "You said you would."

"Yeah, I heard you," Caleb challenged.

"Fine, whatever. I'll ride," Abe agreed, but he continued to frown.

Jake grinned. "That's what I'm talking about!"

"Abe, that's wonderful," Suzie said. "I might try riding sometime, too."

Tucker knew she was putting on a front but was probably worried about the obvious mood Abe was in.

"We've got extremely gentle horses for beginners," Randolph told her. "So anytime you want to ride, you tell us or Walter Pepper, our horse foreman, and we'll get you on one and make sure you have a good time."

Tucker opened the doors wide and noted that it wasn't crammed full. "Suzie, if you'll tell us how you want this done we'll get it finished in no time. Won't we, boys?"

Within minutes it was settled and the unloading began. Tucker and Rowdy took control of getting the couch up the stairs, which proved tricky. The task of getting it through the door and across the small landing was precarious.

"Don't fall over the banister," Suzie warned.

Tucker's position on the end tested his handyman skills to the limit as he had to bend backward over the banister while holding the couch, and then push it through the door. He hiked a brow at Suzie from his dangerous position.

"Just testing my double-reinforced banister for you, ma'am," he drawled, bringing a smile to her worried expression as he moved past her through the doorway.

"So that was what all the hammering was about." She

laughed. "I have never in all my life heard that much hammering at one time."

"Yup, it'll hold," he grunted, pushing through and into the building as Rowdy pulled on the other end of the couch. He didn't tell her that there were enough nails in that banister to reinforce Texas, if need be. And still, he hadn't gotten rid of the frustrations that holding her in his arms had generated.

They managed to test the banister a few more times bringing up a chest of drawers and her kitchen table. He figured if there had been a kitchen sink to haul up, that that might have done it in. But, fortunately, there wasn't one. The boys were over in a corner trying on old hats they found in a box of Joyce and Lester's left-over stuff. Everyone was watching them. Even Abe put on an old derby hat and almost smiled. Almost—it was a Kodak moment. If they'd had a camera, which they didn't. Of course she did have her cell phone camera, but Abe would have been mortified if she'd asked to take his picture.

"Hey up there, I brought y'all some pie."

Ms. Jo's holler from downstairs had them all reacting. No one turned down her pie. The boys sounded like a cattle stampede tromping down the stairs.

Tucker held back, watching the rush from the top of the landing. Tiny Ms. Jo, with her cap of dark gray hair, had set a tray on the empty floor of the moving van and smiled happily as she began dishing out the pie onto paper plates. From his vantage point, he could see the wonder on Suzie's face as she watched Ms. Jo's hospitality.

He would have to give Ms. Jo a hug later for knowing the perfect way to end the day. Like his nana, she had a knack for making folks smile.

The fact that it was Suzie's smile he was seeing, as she savored the taste of Ms. Jo's Triple Chocolate Wonder pie, made watching all the sweeter to him.

Chapter Five

It had been an eventful day, from beginning till evening, but Suzie's spirits were humming with energy as she arrived back at the ranch. Maybe it was a sugar high from Ms. Jo's amazing chocolate pie but Suzie knew that was just part of it. It had just been an amazing day—despite the shaky moment of being in Tucker's arms, the rest had been wonderful.

"Suzie, come up and join us."

She hadn't even realized Nana was on the porch and she wasn't alone. "Sure," she called, heading that way. Jolie was there and so was another woman, a stunning blonde.

It turned out to be Lucy, Rowdy's fiancée, the talented artist. Suzie suddenly felt like a plain, ordinary female in the presence of these two accomplished women. After her mother had grown ill, Suzie had been unable to finish high school, much less move on to any kind of greatness. Her biggest claim to fame was Abe, and she'd managed to mess that up, too, by not holding it together after losing Gordon.

"Sit down and let me pour you a glass of tea," Nana said, after introducing Lucy.

"Thank you," Suzie said, feeling exhausted all of a sudden. She sank onto a brown wicker chair with red cushions and met the smiles of Jolie and Lucy with a forced one of her own. "It's been a long day," she explained. "How did Abe do at school?"

"Fair," Jolie said, honestly. "He was quiet, frowned a lot, but not disrespectful. He's taking it all in right now, figuring out what he thinks about everything."

"Thank you for working with him."

Jolie's Julia Roberts smile was wide and encouraging. "I love it. Working with these boys is a joy. Lucy teaches them art for me, and they love her, too."

"Yes, that's what I hear. I saw some of the artwork yesterday when Tucker showed the school to me."

Lucy's eyes twinkled. "I had no idea when I moved here that I was going to fall in love and get to work with these boys."

"I can see how it would be rewarding. And I loved the mural with the young cowboys."

"Me, too! I've always been partial to roads and landscapes but then I came here and now, all I want to paint are paintings that showcase the boys and Rowdy branding calves. She hiked a brow above her gorgeous eyes—everything about the pint-size artist was beautiful. "It's been a wonderful blessing coming here, in more ways than one."

"I can't wait to see more of your work. It sounds amazing."

Nana paused before sipping her tea. "We have a weekly art class at her place on Tuesday nights. You should come—although, that evening we're working on decorations for Lucy and Rowdy's wedding in two weeks."

"Um, I've never painted anything other than walls of a room. But I would love to help with the decorations."

"Sure, that would be great. We could use your help on the silk flowers. And no worries about the painting," Jolie said, pointing at Lucy. "That woman there can make you feel like an artist even if you paint stick art. She has a gift."

"I'm so excited you'll come help," Lucy said. "But you have to promise that when I get back from our honeymoon you'll come to art night. It's our ladies' night out. We're a wild bunch." They all laughed at that, and Suzie couldn't help but look forward to being around them more.

"I'll come," she said. "It sounds like too much fun to pass up."

"Wonderful." Lucy nodded toward Rowdy in the arena with a horse and one of the boys. "I love watching that man work with a horse."

"He looks like a good instructor," Suzie said, seeing his patience.

"He loves it." Lucy smiled as she watched her fiancé.

"All of them do," Nana added. "My grandsons had as much love bestowed on them by my daughter-in-law as any kids could ever have. In the short time that Lydia got to be here with her boys, she lavished them with an abundance of love and nurturing. Never saw a woman with as big a heart as she had. So my grandsons know what these other boys are missing in their lives. Most of them were abandoned, either physically or emotionally, and never understood what a real family was like." Nana smiled gently at her. "Unlike your son. Abe has obviously been very loved. Like my grandsons, his parent died, forcing his parent to leave. But the parents of the boys who come to the ranch—their parents willingly gave them up."

Suzie's heart clutched in her chest as if someone had stomped hard on the brakes. She could only nod. A revelation spiked across her thoughts.

"What I'm trying to say is that there is no better place for Abe to recover than here, with the leadership of these strong men Lydia's sons have become."

"And we came together specifically this afternoon to let you know that we want to be here as a support group for you," Jolie added. "None of us have walked in your shoes, but we are here for you. In any way you need us."

"That's right," Nana agreed. "Mabel called to tell us about the painting party tomorrow at your shop. How does that sound?"

Shocked, Suzie took a shaky breath and looked about the group. "Thank you. That means a lot to me." She teared up, looking at their smiling faces she could barely speak. "All of it does."

"That's what friends are for," Nana said. "You just relax and this is all going to work out."

"That's right. Abe will get through this," Jolie continued. "All of these boys have lost both of their parents, whether through the courts or through death. When they come to us they are boys who will never be sent back to their birth parents, the majority anyway, and because of that, they need nurturing men and women involved in their lives. If you ever feel led to volunteer or just want to help out, we would love it. Just so you know."

The idea appealed to her, even though she had a business to get up and running. "After I get situated I'd love to get involved."

"You'll be blessed by it, I can promise," Lucy said, her eyes twinkling.

"I'm sure I will." Suzie nodded, following Lucy's gaze as it went back to Rowdy and the little boy.

"There's a lot to learn from these boys," Jolie added. "Their circumstances could have made them victims but they're survivors. They didn't have a choice about the lot they were given, but they do have a choice how they react to it."

Suzie agreed with her, but Nana's words echoed through her mind. *Like my grandsons, his parent died, forcing his parent to leave. But the parents of the boys who come to the ranch—their parents willingly gave them up.*

Suddenly fighting back more tears, it hit Suzie and she knew Nana had been wrong. Abe's dad had dived in front of Tucker McDermott of his own free will. He'd chosen to let Tucker live and his son grow up without a dad. That was the lot Abe had been given, and he wasn't handling it well.

Abe's father had, in a way, willingly abandoned him, just as these other boys' parents had done.

And she believed that knowledge was at the root of Abe's problems.

It was certainly at the root of hers. Because Gordon had abandoned her, too…and she hadn't handled it well.

Had she allowed herself to be a victim?

Stunned, Suzie hid her emotions and took a sip of her drink, pretending everything was fine.

But the revelation was hard to take.

* * *

Tucker had peeked in the flower shop window every night for a week as he made his rounds and the inside had begun to look like a different place.

He had been proud of the way Mabel, Ms. Jo, Nana, Jolie and Lucy had jumped in to help Suzie. The second day she'd shown up to open the shop they'd all come running—all but Jolie, who'd had to work. She'd joined them as soon as school was out and they'd had the shop painted in no time.

He'd thought of every excuse in the book to come see the progress in the daytime and had to force himself not to do it. Suzie needed time to adjust without him trailing her about.

But he'd been keeping up. At a distance.

He needed to talk to her today, though. The door was open and he walked into the freshly painted room. The soft buttery tone was a far sight from the drab place he'd looked at the first of the week.

"Suzie, are you here?" He could hear humming and headed that way. "Suzie," he said again as he stepped through the archway into the back room. Suzie stood at the back wall, her back to him as she sang softly while she painted one of the cabinets deep red.

"Suzie," he said, louder, hoping not to startle her— failing when she screamed and spun around. Disaster happened quickly as her elbow caught the can of paint and sent it flying.

Tucker tried to grab it but succeeded only in stepping into the line of fire. The can hit his outstretched hands and launched the contents straight at him. It got his tan uniform with a direct hit. He had red paint dripping from his badge to his boots.

"Oh, my stars!" Suzie squealed. Only seconds had passed since he'd startled her. "What have I done?"

Feeling bad for her and berating himself for walking in and scaring her, he shrugged. "You didn't do anything. I know not to walk up on someone like that."

She thought about that for a blink of an eye. "True. You do. But look at you." Hurrying to a roll of paper towels she came over and started blotting him down, going for his radio and phone first. The rest was hopeless.

"It's water-based paint, but still, your uniform is ruined."

"I have more," Tucker assured her. He couldn't have cared less about the uniform as he stared at Suzie, flashing back to the day on the stairs.

Her hair had fallen loose from behind her ear and swung free as she tried unsuccessfully to dab the paint from him. A few strands of pale blond hair now had red paint on them, too.

Instinctively he reached for those strands and rubbed the paint off with his fingers. Her brows dipped and suddenly her concerned eyes flared.

She stepped away from him.

"Water. You should go put water on this now. I have a hose hooked up outside by the back door for cleaning paint rollers and pans."

"I'll do that. Then I'll help clean up the floor."

Suzie's look of horror at what she'd done turned more alarmed. "You will not clean up the floor. I'm the one who doused you. I'll take care of this. Hurry, you might be able to save your uniform if you wet it down before it dries."

Striding across the room and out the door before he

made a complete idiot out of himself, Tucker took his radio and cell phone off and set them on a small table by the back door.

Finding the hose, he twisted the knob and drenched himself with the water. He needed something to snap him out of the continual lapses of bad judgment on his part where Suzie was concerned.

Red paint, even water-based, was not the easiest thing to wash away. It looked as though he'd cut an artery or something as the paint ran off him and pooled in the scraggly grass and dirt.

After a few minutes Suzie came out the back door carrying a towel covered in the crimson paint.

"How's it looking in there?" he asked, feeling like a drowned rat. Soaking himself down might not have been the best solution to this situation.

She bit her lip and he could tell she was fighting back a smile. "Better than it looks like it's going out here."

He cocked his head. "That's a plus. I'd hate for you to continually have to tell people what the big red stain on the floor is."

She smiled. "That would get old after a while. Folks might start thinking I'd committed some terrible crime, Sheriff."

"Good thing most of it got on me."

She bit her lip, holding back a smile, and held the towel out. "You look terrible."

"Thanks." He laughed. "All I can say is you have great reflexes and on-target instincts. If someone tried to sneak up on you they'd be in for a surprise, even if you weren't wielding a can of paint."

Her eyes twinkled as she shook her head. "I'm glad

I have something going for me. Could you point that water this way and let me rinse this out?"

"Why, I'd be happy to do that," he teased, and swung the hose toward her. It hit the towel, and the force of the water splattered red paint all over her, instantly making her look as though she had the measles.

She gasped.

Tucker did, too, shocked at what he'd done.

They stared at each other, pink and red spots everywhere—and burst into laughter.

"I promise you I did not do that in retaliation," he said, between chuckles.

"I wouldn't blame you if you did."

She was so beautiful. Without thinking he gently wiped a spot from her cheek.

Her laughter died. She swayed toward him and then suddenly backed away. "I… I'm here for Abe," she snapped, shaking her head, looking confused.

"I'm just here to help. That's all."

She didn't look as if she believed him and that was his own fault. How many times had he grabbed her or touched her? Too many.

"You have nothing to fear from me," he said. Moving to the faucet he turned the water off, stopping the flood around them. "I'd better head home and change."

He picked up his phone and radio, and started toward the side of the building, his boots sloshing and his jeans dragging. He climbed into his SUV, not even caring that he was dripping murky pink water all over everything.

He'd almost kissed Suzie again—no wonder she was leery of him. They'd been laughing and relaxed, a good thing in the dynamics of their working together to help Abe.

But no, he'd lost his head.

He was a man who never lost his head. He was cool under fire and clear thinking through the worst of times. And yet, around Suzie he didn't think.

His phone rang before he backed out of the parking lot. Glancing at the name, he punched the talk button. "Hey, Dad," he said, his voice calm, giving away none of the turmoil eating at him.

"Tucker, we have a situation out here."

Chapter Six

She should have just stayed inside earlier. But no, she'd had to go check on Tucker. Had to go outside after him and just look what had happened. Suzie's face was hot as she stormed back into the shop, snatched a towel up and swiped the last puddle of paint off the wooden floor.

She'd behaved like a fool.

Part of it had been due to the fact that she'd decided she was being a simpering victim when it came to dealing with being a widow.

She'd been so angry for the past two years. Angry at God. Angry at the military. At Gordon. And especially at Tucker. And then this situation with Abe had started, and she'd gotten angrier.

She was a mess and she knew it. She had things to work through, things to change about herself. And the one thing she didn't need complicating matters was this attraction—there, she'd said it. There was an attraction between her and Tucker that had no place there. Hopefully he understood that.

Hopefully she'd made that perfectly clear just now.

The door to the shop opened and Tucker poked his

head inside. "Suzie, we have a problem at the school. It's going to be all right, but I need you to come with me."

Her heart dropped to her knees. "What's happened?" she asked, rushing across the room, tossing the rag to the floor as she went.

"Abe and Jake got into a fight."

"Are they hurt?"

"They're fine. Lock up. I'll drive."

Nodding, full of questions and turmoil, she hurried to grab her purse, locking both the back door and the front door. Still dripping wet, Tucker held the door of the SUV open for her then trudged around to his side. He was so wet he looked uncomfortable as they buckled up and he drove toward the ranch.

"A fight?" she said. "With Jake. I thought they had been becoming friends."

"Boys fight sometimes, Suzie. This could be nothing."

The miles to the ranch seemed endless when, in reality, it took twenty minutes to travel the country roads. In the city it could have taken hours in traffic, and she kept reminding herself of this as she watched the pastures flow by.

Tucker pulled up to the ranch office and they got out. She waited for him to lead the way, aware that they were being watched from the arena by young eyes. His boots squished as he strode across the wooden porch and held the door open for her.

Though he wasn't dripping now, he looked terrible, his tan uniform shirt had turned a marbled crimson and pink, and his jeans were not much different. "I'm so sorry," she said, everything that had happened forgotten other than he was dealing with her problems looking like this and it was her fault.

"It'll be fine," he said. "We're here to find out what's going on between Abe and Jake, and to help them resolve the issue."

"Thank you" was all she could say as she followed him inside and through the door to one of the offices.

Jake and Abe sat in the rich brown leather chairs in front of the large desk, each one of them had a cut lip and an ice pack. Dirt and sprigs of grass clung to their clothing and their rumpled hair.

Randolph sat behind the desk looking serious, but not overly upset. Unlike Suzie, whose insides were curled up in a ball. Her hands were shaking, she was so upset. How many other times had she been called to the school office over the past year for Abe's problems? She had hoped that it would change here.

But there he sat looking as if he didn't care about anything.

Randolph stood. "Suzie, why don't you come sit here, in my chair?" He gave her a reassuring smile and she did as he asked because her knees were too wobbly to hold her.

"Thank you," she said, walking around the desk and taking the seat. "What happened?"

Neither of the boys would look at her.

"We don't know for sure, since they aren't talking," Randolph answered. "Jolie found them taking swings at each other behind the school when she was leaving—about thirty minutes after school had been dismissed for the day."

"You fellas want to tell us what's going on?" Tucker asked, drawing sullen looks from both.

"What happened to you?" Jake asked, taking in Tucker's appearance.

"It's a long story, but it's your story I'm interested in right now. Not mine."

Jake looked almost embarrassed as his gaze shifted away and he firmly clamped his lips together.

"Abe," Tucker said. "How about you? Want to tell us what's going on between the two of you?"

Suzie studied her son. "Abe, answer Sheriff Tucker."

He shot her a sullen look.

Tucker gave her a hint of a smile. "I do have on my uniform—or what remains of my uniform," he said, his smile lifting to his eyes. "But, so you boys will know, I'm not here as the sheriff. I'm here as a member of this family. Dad called me because we have a family situation and we need to work together to get it resolved."

"That's right," Randolph added, patting Suzie on the shoulder. "Both of you boys are new here, and this is how we do things. We mess up as a family and we resolve issues as a family. I don't know what's going on between the two of you and if you're not going to tell me, I'm not going to force you. Sometimes a man has a reason for keeping silent. But if either of you need to speak in private there is always that option."

Tucker had leaned a shoulder against the wall and looked very relaxed now, watching the boys. Suzie realized that he might appear completely at ease, but he was taking in everything. "We're all here to talk about anything bothering either one of you," he said.

Suzie liked how they emphasized family. Nana had done that same thing.

"So, if you have nothing to say, then head on back outside," Randolph said. Both boys stood up as if they'd been shot from a cannon. Jake looked relieved and Abe looked a little disbelieving. After all, at his previous school he would have received detention. Here he was being set free with no penalties. Suzie was about to say something about that. She was worried about Abe but he had to know there were consequences for his actions. Even among family. They were almost to the door when Randolph halted them.

"There is one more thing, fellas." They turned toward him, both only a step from exiting. "I don't like fighting. A man has to do what a man has to do sometimes. But for the most part a fight is avoidable. There are other ways to resolve your differences. Talking about it is usually the best way. So, to give you the opportunity to resolve this issue on your own, you're both assigned two weeks of mucking out the horse stables every evening together."

There was no hiding their dismay. "Yes, sir," Jake said, but Abe only shrugged.

"You can go now. I'll let Pepper know there won't be a rotation for a couple of weeks." After they had gone and Tucker pulled the door closed, Randolph patted her shoulder again.

"It happens. Boys fight, so don't get too upset. Working together will either push whatever's bugging them to the surface and it'll come out or they'll resolve the issue and move forward."

Tucker grinned. "It's amazing how much life-changing bonding can go on when you're cleaning out stalls on a regular basis."

Suzie wouldn't know, having never done it, but it sounded like something she wouldn't enjoy at all. "I'll take your word for it."

Randolph looked from Tucker to Suzie and she was suddenly reminded that though not as bad as Tucker's, her clothing wasn't much better off. "Now, mind explaining what happened to y'all?"

Tucker chuckled. "I'll just offer this piece of advice, Dad. Never surprise a woman standing near a can of paint."

Randolph laughed. "Sounds like a great piece of advice. Thanks."

Tucker winked at her and despite all that had happened, she laughed.

After they left the office Tucker closed the door of his SUV and looked across at Suzie. "I'd like to drive over to the school before I take you back to town, if that's okay with you."

"Of course, do whatever you need to do. What are you looking for?"

"Something started that altercation between Abe and Jake and I don't like that they aren't talking. I want to look around where the fight happened."

"Sure, that sounds like a good idea. I know you have to be miserable in those clothes. I am so sorry."

"It's fine. They're drying. A few more minutes won't matter anyway."

He drove across the pasture and pulled around behind the school where Jolie had found them fighting. He would talk to her himself when he saw her. "I know I said I wasn't here as the sheriff and I meant that. But still, we need to get to the bottom of this even if the boys choose not to tell us what was going on."

"I agree."

Tucker walked over and surveyed the area. It was

clear where the fight had ended, because the grass and dirt were disturbed. Tucker stood beside the area and surveyed the school and the grounds. Noticing something in the bushes he walked over and moved a limb out of the way as he reached for the fluorescent orange can.

"What is it?" Suzie came to stand beside him.

Looking up at her he frowned. "A can of spray paint."

Instantly, her face fell. "No."

"What do you think?" he asked, having his own suspicions but wanting her thoughts first.

"Abe got in trouble vandalizing property with spray paint."

He nodded. "So did Jake."

Her brows crinkled and her expression grew stormy. "I just don't know, Tucker. I don't get it. Abe can be mad, he can be furious and hurt about what happened to his dad, but I don't understand destroying people's property. I just don't understand it. As soon as I get back to the ranch I'm going to have a long talk with my son. This is ridiculous."

"As his parent, that's your prerogative. But my opinion is to hold off for a little while. See if the boys come clean about what they were doing. And of course there is the possibility this doesn't belong to them."

"You don't really believe that, do you?"

He shook his head. "No. But in my line of duty, a man is innocent until proven guilty or he confesses. And Dad is trying to let them work through this together."

"Okay. He doesn't listen to me right now anyway, so I'll go along with you and Randolph and we'll see if they step up."

"Good. I'm disappointed in both of them, but the

opportunity to fess up gives them the opportunity to redeem themselves. Which is Dad's hope."

"Then we'll go with that. Thank you, Tucker."

He tugged his hat snugger on his head. "No thanks needed." He started back toward the vehicle. "Okay, now it's time for me to find some dry clothes."

"Yes, better hurry before some new disaster arises."

"Agreed. Let's roll."

"Are you all right?" Rowdy asked the morning after the paint fiasco. "You're not looking so good."

The donkeys had escaped again and the men were loading them into a trailer bound for Sunrise Ranch, where they would remain until their escape route was discovered.

"See, there you go hurting your big brother's feelings," Tucker said, teasing his way out of this conversation. "Just because you got the real looks of the family, you don't have to always rub it in."

Rowdy stared at him, knowing full well what he was doing. "Hey, I can't help it if I got the looks. At least you got the height."

"True, there is that." Tucker chuckled as the last of the donkeys stepped up into the trailer with the enthusiasm of a kid going to the dentist. At six-two he was just a hair taller than his brother.

"There you go, Tucker. Our work here is done." Tony grinned and pushed the ever-present lock of thick black hair out of his left eye. Tony would be taking his driving test in a week and they were giving him every opportunity to practice. "Thanks, Tony, couldn't have done it without you."

"I know." He grinned. "Hey, did you hear Wes is riding bulls?"

Wes had just turned eighteen, as had Joseph. Both had been raised on the ranch and were now in their first semester at Sam Houston. "He always did want to do that," Tucker said, not surprised.

Rowdy closed the trailer gate. "He's good. Got on the team as a walk-on, but hasn't told anyone till now."

Bull riding was the one rodeo sport their dad, Randolph, didn't allow at Sunrise Ranch. Tucker and Rowdy both knew you didn't just walk on to a college team without prior experience. No one had talked about it much last year, but they'd all suspected that Wes had been riding on weekends and not saying anything about it. This was proof. Randolph didn't allow bull riding *on* the ranch, but he'd never specifically forbidden it away from the ranch. It was that gray area Wes had operated under. Just as Tucker and his brothers had growing up, the older boys had use of trucks and the rights to spend time off the ranch with their friends.

Tucker knew there had been something inside of Wes that drew him to bull riding. Though good-natured, he had been pulled to anything that had an edge to it. Tucker had been a lot like that as a kid. But instead of bulls, he'd been fascinated by the marines. Gordon had been the same way. When a man truly wanted to do something, there was no stopping him. Tucker recognized that in Wes and hadn't butted in when he'd suspected he was riding.

"He'll be all right," he said. "If he rides a bull half as well as he rides a horse, then he'll be at the National Finals Rodeo before you know it. I better get to town— if y'all can haul them to the ranch that'd be great. We'll get the boys and go over to Chili's this weekend to ride his fence line. We've got to find out how these misfits are getting out before someone gets hurt."

"Will do," Rowdy said. He watched Tony head toward the driver's seat of the truck. "That boy can't get enough of driving," he added. "If Chili spent a little more time ranching instead of sitting in town whittling, these donkeys wouldn't be such troublemakers."

"That's the truth." Tucker started toward his SUV, remembering the painful walk to it the last time they'd dealt with the donkeys. He was thankful an ice pack had fixed him up. He'd made certain to stay out of their way this time.

"You sure you're all right?"

Tucker knew what Rowdy was asking. Rowdy knew the weight of his guilt. Anyone who knew him, and understood the code that drove him, knew that he'd taken full responsibility for their friend—their *brother's*—death.

"I'm making it," he offered. "I can't let them down, Rowdy."

Rowdy's eyes narrowed. "You won't, bro. You've never let anyone down. Gordon was a marine, same as you. If you hadn't been shot, you would have been the one to draw fire—you'd done it before. Gordon was no different and you know that. You have to accept it."

"Yeah, well, that doesn't make it any easier. I have to do right by his son. By his wife."

Rowdy clamped him on the shoulder. "You will."

"Thanks for the confidence. Tony didn't happen to say anything about the fight between Abe and Jake this morning, did he?"

"Nope. If any of them know what happened between those two, they aren't saying."

"Yeah, that's what I figured. Talk to you later. Duty calls."

He was almost to his truck when Rowdy's words stopped him. "You like her, don't you?"

Tucker hadn't expected Rowdy's question. He scowled. "You better go. Your driver will leave you."

"Yup. Just what I thought."

"Now, Rowdy, don't get any ideas. Yeah, I like her. But nothing could ever come of that. Nothing."

"And why not?"

"That's a crazy question. You know why. She would never be able to look at me and not think of Gordon. And as much as I like to look at her, he is always on my mind, too."

"That's some tough stuff," Rowdy said. "I don't like it, but I get it. And if that's how you really feel then I would be extra careful. Don't get in too deep."

"Hey, you don't need to be worrying about me. You have a wedding in two weeks."

Rowdy grinned. "Don't worry, Tuck. Thinking about that beautiful lady walking down the aisle wins every time."

Tucker slapped his brother on the back as he turned to head toward his truck.

Don't get in too deep. Tucker thought about that advice for the rest of the day. He hoped it was that easy, but he had a bad feeling he'd already dug a hole he was going to have a hard time crawling out of.

Chapter Seven

Breakfast in the chow hall was just getting finished when Suzie saw the trailer filled with renegade donkeys wheel into the yard. Tony was driving and waved as he and Rowdy passed by.

Suzie walked to her car, watching as he backed the trailer up to the unloading pen at the far end of the arena. The beasts were staying here, it seemed.

Seconds later, the boys came flooding out of the chow hall to see what was going on. Obviously they'd known Tony had gone to help Rowdy load the animals, since he wasn't at breakfast. She had helped in the kitchen today, reluctant about leaving Abe. He'd remained closemouthed about the fight and had hardly spoken at all last night.

Whoops went up as the boys gathered around the trailer, watching Tony herd the donkeys into the pen. Abe jumped onto the fence, his excitement evident from the way he scrambled to the top to lean out and watch the animals. Rowdy had emerged from the passenger's side of the truck and looked as if he was joking around with the guys.

She wondered where Tucker was. She assumed he'd been involved. Not that it was her business where he was, she reminded herself. Taking one more glance at Abe, she forced herself to get into her car and drive to the shop. If he got into another fight she was confident that Randolph would handle it wisely. She hadn't slept much, thinking about the spray can and what it meant.

It had been nearly nine-thirty when Abe had come into the house, and though he left his boots on the porch, he still smelled like a barn. Mucking that many stalls with only one other person to help was a huge job. Tired, stinky and quiet, he'd disappeared into the hall bathroom. She'd been in her room ordering business supplies for the shop when she'd heard him exit the shower and pad down the hall to his room.

Still feeling conflicted about what to say, she'd given him a few minutes and then knocked lightly on his door. When there was no answer, she'd opened the door. He was already asleep in the dark room. At first, she'd thought he might be pretending in order to avoid talking to her, but there was no faking the soft snores.

Which was a good thing, she'd decided, heading back to her room. Maybe he'd be too tired to get into any more trouble.

Maybe that was another motive behind Randolph's plan.

Too bad some of that sleep hadn't rubbed off on her, she'd thought later as she lay in bed staring up at the ceiling fan. Despite the fact that it had been a long, hectic two days, it seemed she was doomed to let the events roll around in her head with no peace. She'd come here to get help resolving Abe's issues. She hadn't realized when she'd come to Sunrise Ranch that she would also be coming to terms with issues of her own.

Issues she had no idea how to react to.

When she'd finally drifted off to a restless sleep, it was with Tucker's laughing, paint-dotted face squarely in the center of her thoughts.

Tucker gathered the boys up late the evening after picking up the donkeys and ferried them to Chili's ranch to check fence lines. He'd had another crazy day. Though it hadn't involved paint, it had had its own un-usual set of odd circumstances—lots of them. A semi driver had fallen asleep and flipped his rig out on the interstate. He'd been carried off to the hospital with minor injuries. Tucker was left to clean up the mess—clean up the chickens, to be exact.

Thousands of squawking chickens! Running, hop-ping, crazy chickens scattered everywhere—it was bad. He'd had to call all his deputies in to help deal with the traffic and the poultry. The only good thing he had to say about it was that he was wearing a clean, dry uni-form.

By the time he and the boys arrived at Chili's place, they were practically rolling on the floorboards laugh-ing at his tale of woe.

They agreed that looking for the donkey escape route was a breeze compared to chasing chickens. Even Abe, though quiet, hadn't been able to hold back a few chuck-les. Of course, the kid had been mucking out stalls for two days with twelve more to go. Compared to that, chicken chasing might appeal.

Same with Jake, who seemed fine but stayed clear of Abe. Tucker had brought only the older fellas along, wanting time to observe the two and see if anything came out into the open.

"Welcome, boys," Chili greeted them when they arrived. "Thanks for coming out to look for holes in my fence." He'd driven his truck and trailer out behind Tucker and the boys to the area that ran along the road.

"If we can't find the break, then tomorrow after we work cows, we'll bring the whole crew. The younger boys are wearing their lips on the ground, they were so disappointed that I didn't let them come. I promised them Saturday was their day to ride roughshod on your place if nothing showed up this afternoon."

Chili chuckled. "Them boys are a hoot and a half. Bring 'em on over here. They ain't gonna tear up nothin'."

They got the horses unloaded and everyone saddled up. Though Abe wasn't great on a horse, he was fair. Time in the saddle would improve that naturally.

Chili grunted as he climbed up into the saddle. "I don't saddle up as easy as I used to, with these old creaky bones of mine. But let's ride, boys. If we see something worth looking at it'll be nice to watch all you young 'uns check it out for me.

"I don't recognize you, son," Chili continued, his gaze stalling on Abe. "You must be Suzie's boy. We met her the other day at the shop."

Tucker saw a flash of something volatile in his eyes.

"She's my mom."

"Nice lady. What's your name?"

"Abe." It was more of a grunt.

Tucker didn't like his attitude. "Abe, you're going to ride with me. The others will go with Chili. That way we can split up. That okay with you, Chili?"

"You're the boss," Chili said, shooting Tucker a sharp-eyed look that told him that the older man hadn't missed the bad attitude.

The others had mounted up and within moments they were riding across Chili's pasture. The boys loved this. They smiled and leaned forward in their saddles. Tucker knew that, if they could, they'd be galloping across the pastures. Instead, he held them back, talking to them about what he wanted them to do when they got there. When they arrived at the fence that ran beside the road, they split up into west or east groups.

"Watch for tracks or anything that alerts you to many donkeys tramping around," he said, as they started out in silence. Abe looked sullen and uninterested.

The sun was out and bright in their eyes. Tucker squinted from beneath his hat at Abe. "So how's it going?" he finally asked.

Abe hiked a shoulder. "It's going."

"You like the boys?"

"Sure. Most of them are okay."

Obviously, Abe was fond of the word *okay.* "You seemed bothered a minute ago. Want to share what that was about?"

He studied the fence intently. "He called me *son.* I didn't like it."

"I thought that might have bothered you."

Abe frowned. "I'm no man's son anymore."

"You will always be Gordon's son."

He shrugged. After a moment he asked, "Did he talk about me much?"

The question shocked Tucker. "He talked about you all the time, Abe. He was proud of you and loved you so much. You and your mother. He showed us pictures all the time. And he said y'all were the best things that ever happened to him."

Abe's Adam's apple bobbed and his nostrils flared, but no tears came. When he looked at Tucker, his eyes were eerily dry. "Do you feel weird being alive and my dad being dead?"

Leave it to kids to cut to the point. "Yes, I do. And I'll never get over feeling like it should have been me and not your dad." Tucker prayed for words that could help this boy. He felt powerless, even more so than he had felt with Suzie. "This may sound stupid and might not be something you want to hear, but God does have a plan. He can make good from bad. Even something this bad."

"Nothing is gonna bring him back. And now I'm riding a fence with you and not my dad."

The blow hit Tucker in the chest. "I'm not going to lie to you. I can apologize till I'm blue in the face and it won't change a thing. But you have a wonderful mom who loves you and a whole support group at the ranch who care for you, me included. And I can promise you that I'll honor your dad by being here for you and your mom till the day I die. I promise you that, even if it doesn't mean much to you now."

Abe stared at him for a long time as the horses moved slowly forward beneath them. This was what riding the range was good for—Tucker and his dad had ridden many a fence line together after his mother's death.

Abe just nodded and went back to studying the fence.

"I'm hoping you'll let go of this anger you're holding in, Abe. It's only going to hurt you," Tucker added.

With the fighting incident, it was time to do something. He needed Abe to be comfortable with him, so he could build a bridge of trust.

"So?"

Tucker hated his sullenness. Sometimes hurt seemed all there was. "Well, I'm here if you need me. And I'm here to keep you out of trouble, too, standing in for your dad, so remember that."

His shoulders stiff, Abe rode ahead, leaving Tucker a few yards behind. It was going to be another long afternoon. But this was a complicated puzzle of the heart—a child's heart—and Tucker planned to tread very carefully.

Two weeks after she'd arrived in town, Suzie opened her shop. It was both nerve-racking and exciting at the same time. To her surprise, everyone came to wish her well, creating a grand opening that she would never forget.

She had planned on getting opened and then, after settling in and getting some orders under her belt, she would have an open house or something, but on the Saturday morning she was actually going to start business, in walked Mabel, Ms. Jo and Nana with trays of refreshments and decorations.

"Good morning!" Mabel exclaimed, first in the door. "We are here to party! And help out any way we can."

"Oh, what? Why?" Suzie stumbled over her words as they marched through the door and took over.

"You just go about your business," Ms. Jo said. "We've got this under control."

"That's right," Nana said. "By eleven, this place will be a regular Grand Central station."

Flustered and touched, Suzie hugged each of them

and went back to arranging her very first preordered flower arrangement. Chili had looked a little green around the collar when she'd asked him if he still wanted it, and she'd thought he was going to back out. Then Drewbaker had grinned as if knowing he'd planned to back out all along, and Chili had staunchly reiterated that he did, indeed, want the order.

So here she was working on a bouquet of sunflowers. She had to admit she was curious about who they were for. When she'd asked Chili what he wanted in the bouquet he'd been specific: sunflowers and magenta zinnias. As she was putting the arrangement together, she couldn't help but wonder if Chili had any idea what the meaning of these flowers were.

Surely not. He was an old rancher who barely set foot in a florist's and had admitted such. True, the colors complemented each other, but then, any deep rose-colored flower could have done the same.

Sunflowers and magenta zinnias: adoration and lasting affection.

Who, Suzie wanted to know, did Chili adore with lasting affection?

"That is beautiful," Nana said, coming to stand beside her. "I adore sunflowers, don't you?"

"Very much so." Suzie's radar went up—could it be? "Nana, can I ask about your husband?"

Nana got a gentle look in her eye. "I'm seventy-two and he's been gone nearly thirty years now, but not a day goes by that I don't think of Harrison Randolph Mc-Dermott. When you've been loved by and loved a man like my Harry, you never forget. Oops, I left the plates in the truck. I better run and get them."

Suzie watched her go. She didn't know what had

happened to Nana's Harry, but Nana had been somewhere near fifty when he'd died. And she was strong, independent, and had done amazing things with this ranch and these boys.

She inspired Suzie to require more of herself than she had, so far. A person had to move past grief. Past anger.

A person had to move forward.

Taking in her shop with the colorful gift items and the silk arrangements and colorful vases, she felt a flicker of joy ignite inside of her.

She smiled.

If she could feel this, surely Abe would feel it someday soon.

There was movement outside the window as cars and trucks began pulling into the parking spaces. Within moments, the grand opening was in full swing.

Tucker came in, right behind Chili and Drewbaker. And by that time, there was hardly room to move around in the small front space. "Congratulations," he said, over the laughter and hum of conversation. "It looks great in here, and I assume there isn't any evidence in the back room of any heinous crimes being committed."

She laughed. "No, there isn't. All the evidence of the terrible crime I committed has been destroyed. How is your shirt?"

"I'm afraid it didn't survive."

"I was afraid of that." She sighed. "But I'd be glad to replace it."

"Thanks, but no need for that. I have a closetful. Those are pretty," he said, nodding toward the arrangement.

"Yes. My first order."

"Are those the ones from Chili?"

"Yes, and I have to say the man knows his flowers. I'm very curious."

Tucker's smile spread wide and his eyes crinkled around the edges.

"You know who they're for, don't you? No, don't tell me. I'll wait until he tells me." Was her suspicion right? Were they for Nana?

"I wasn't going to say anything. But yes, I'm fairly certain I know who they're for. It should be interesting."

"That's what Drewbaker said the day Chili ordered them."

He laughed. "Only because it's true," he said, just as she saw Drewbaker spot the flowers from across the room.

She knew he had, because he elbowed Chili in the ribs and pointed straight at them.

Chili turned, and his head ducked momentarily, as if looking for a table to crawl under.

"Those must be your flowers, Chili," Drewbaker roared.

Chili gulped, his Adam's apple bobbing low. "Maybe so," he said, glancing around.

Beside Suzie, Tucker chuckled softly. "Like I said, interesting."

Edwina, Ms. Jo's waitress, had popped in for the party and her gritty voice rose over the crowd. "Well, Chili, you old Romeo, those are beautiful—not that I've ever gotten flowers. My four ex-husbands' idea of giving me flowers was to buy me a roll of flower-printed paper towels. Don't laugh," she said, dryly. "I kid you not."

From across the room, Suzie saw Nana spin, her thick gray ponytail swinging out like a horse's mane.

Her gaze hit Chili and the little man turned redder than Tucker's shirt had been during the paint fiasco.

And in that instant, Suzie knew she'd been right. She glanced at Tucker.

"Yup. Head over heels for her for years. Poor fella."

"I had no idea until moments ago. Would never have dreamed it. They, well, they just don't fit."

"The heart doesn't always listen to reality," Tucker said, holding her gaze for a beat too long. Suzie's knees melted momentarily as her heart bucked. "You're in the flower business. I'd think you'd know that."

While they'd been speaking, Chili pushed his chest forward and marched across the room to her. "You did a fine job on those. May I take them?"

"S-sure," she said, hurrying around the counter and handing the flowers over. "Do you want a card?"

There was startling determination in his eyes. "Nope. No card needed. Ruby Ann McDermott knows everything there is about a flower. She'll read the message in the flowers themselves."

Suzie's heart skipped a beat. His message: I adore you with lasting affection.

He crossed the room straight to Nana. "Ruby Ann, if anyone deserves flowers, it'd be you."

Shocked though she was, Nana took the beautiful green vase in her arms and studied the flowers. "They're lovely. And I thank you," she said. Beside her, Ms. Jo and Mabel were actually speechless.

Chili thrust his chest out a little more, and beamed. "You're welcome." That said, he strode—no, he strutted to the door.

"Now, don't go getting ideas," Nana called after

him, and Suzie thought she saw alarm in Nana's usually calm eyes.

Was Chili listening? No. He just grinned and continued out the door. It really was a great exit.

"I have to give him credit. He cowboy'd up on that one," Tucker said. "Nana needed that."

"Really?"

He looked at her. "Every woman needs flowers. Even if she thinks she doesn't. I've got to go to work."

Her pulse skipped at his low declaration. He turned to go.

"Tucker, wait. How did Abe act when you took them to ride fence at Chili's?" She'd meant to ask him earlier.

"It was all right. He's wound up tight, like you said. I talked to him a little. He asked about Gordon. The good thing was, he did talk some. And he asked a few questions. I take that as a good thing. But he's expressing his feelings with action. So keep an eye out, and call me anytime, day or night, if you're worried about anything. You might try to set him up with a counselor. Whether he wants it or not. I think he might need it."

"Thanks," she said.

His radio crackled to life. "Duty calls," he said, and tipped his hat.

This had been a great day, but she would give it all up to have Abe happy again.

This girl didn't want flowers, she just wanted her son happy. And she didn't want to have to call for help— she'd much rather not need it.

Chapter Eight

She didn't have to call Tucker; he called her later that day, right after lunch. He asked what time she was closing, and when she told him two o'clock, he asked her if she wanted to go with him and all the boys to check fences at Chili's.

She said no, at first, until he reminded her it would be good to spend time doing something with Abe. Of course she agreed to that.

Now she was riding shotgun beside Tucker in his truck full of boys as he led the other trucks across the pastures toward a stand of trees.

It looked as if it was snowing in the middle of May.

"I thought you'd like to see this," he said, pulling to a halt.

Suzie stepped out of Tucker's truck and stared at the huge trees that he'd parked beneath. Cottonwoods.

"I've never seen this many of them together!" It was a beautiful sight when the cotton tufts floated from the branches in a slow free fall to earth.

She'd seen one or two in yards, but there had to be fifteen in this shady cluster. "These trees are amazing!

And huge," she said, opening her arms and turning in the midst of the falling cotton.

"What is this stuff?" B.J., the youngest boy, asked. He immediately began jumping and diving, trying to catch handfuls of the downy fluff. "It looks like snow."

All the younger boys joined him in running after the floaters. The older boys, Abe included, were helping unload the trailers of horses.

"I've always liked this spot, this time of year," Tucker said, coming to stand beside her. Smiling down at her, he plucked a bit of cotton from her hair. "It looks good on you," he said, holding the small piece of fuzz up for her to see.

She wasn't thinking about the cotton any longer. "Which way will we go?" she asked, butterflies shifting in her chest.

"Which way do you want to go?"

She stared at him, her insides completely aflutter. "I…" She looked to the left, then to the right and back at him. "I don't know." Were they talking about which way to go to check fences? His deep blue eyes were steady and unwavering as they seemed to see every emotional hiding place within her.

Which way did she want to go?

Looking at Tucker she was suddenly filled with the longing to be free to feel again.

She wished, at least for a little while, to be free from the bitterness and the grief that bound her.

Tucker couldn't tear his gaze away from Suzie in the soft white rain from the huge old cottonwood trees. She was beautiful. He'd enjoyed talking and laughing with her at the grand opening that morning…. Now he wanted to pull her into his arms and kiss her beneath the cottonwoods.

Wanted to be more to her than the man she held responsible for making her a widow.

He wanted to kiss her and wipe all of her fears and worries and sadness away.

"I better get the horses so we can ride the fence." Spinning away, he strode toward the older boys. Abe and Jake were leading horses out of the trailer, and Caleb and Tony were busy unloading the other horses from the trailer Tony had driven over. He'd gotten his license the day before and was one proud kid.

Tucker waved the four over. "Y'all know what to do. I'm sending you east along the line and I'll take the younger ones in the opposite direction. Tony, you have the cell. Call me if y'all find anything. I know you'll do a great job. Abe, I'd like you to come with us—"

"I'd like to go with the guys," he said, his expression tight.

Tucker studied him, then Jake. "You two going to get along? No fighting—and I mean none."

Jake nodded. "Fine by me."

"Me, too." Abe rubbed the back of his neck and let out a hard breath.

"Do I have your word?"

Both teens nodded.

"Fine, I'm going to trust that you'll do this job, and I'm going to hope that you have a good time. I still don't know what's going on between the two of you, but here's another chance to prove you're mending your differences. You both did good work with the stalls."

"Yes, sir," Jake said readily, making Tucker more

and more certain that whatever had happened between the two had more to do with Abe than Jake.

"Yes, sir," Abe said a moment later.

"Good. See you in three hours."

Seconds later they rode off. He'd watched many men head out under his command, and it felt good to know these boys weren't riding out into a war zone.

"I thought I was supposed to be spending time with Abe," Suzie said, coming up beside him.

"Yeah, about that. Abe wanted to ride with the older guys."

"He and Jake okay?"

"I think so. They promised they wouldn't fight."

She smiled. "Then that's a very good thing."

"Even if you're stuck with me and the rowdy bunch?"

She winced. "I'll manage." She chuckled, looking toward the boys playing in the summer snowstorm. "We better head out, or they'll be trying to ski soon."

"True. Thanks for coming," he said, then called the boys to mount up. They shot up from wrestling in the cotton. It was stuck to them like chicken feathers as they raced each other to their horses.

"This will be fun," Suzie said, taking him by surprise. "Thank you for inviting me. I haven't ridden that much in my life." She stared critically at the horse he'd untied for her.

"This is our trusty Cupcake. She'll do right by you."

"I learned on ol' Cupcake and she's a good ol' horse," Sammy called. "She won't toss you."

"She sure won't," B.J. agreed. "I learned on her, too."

The other boys all joined in encouraging her as they nudged closer on their horses to encircle them.

Suzie laughed. "Thanks, boys, I need your support."

Grabbing the saddle horn, she stuck her foot into the stirrup and hauled herself up, then threw her leg over. Cupcake stood docile as a kitten, making Tucker proud of the old horse.

"There you go," he said, moving to stand at her knee and handing her the reins. "You'll be fine." He snagged his own horse's reins and stepped up and into the saddle. "Okay, let's head out. You boys can lead the way. Here we go." Tucker went ahead of Suzie and knew that Cupcake would follow. It wouldn't take a lot of experience or work on Suzie's part today. "Just give her a nudge when she slows down too much, or a little pressure with your knees, and that should do it."

He held his horse at a slow walk while she got adjusted to Cupcake. "See, you're doing good."

"Thanks," she said. "And thanks for helping with Abe."

"We'll just keep letting him be more and more a part of the family."

"So, how did the party go after I left?" he asked, enjoying her riding beside him more than he should.

"You saw the highlight. The rest was just friendly chitchat. Much of it was about Nana's flowers. I'll confess, the shop makes me a little nervous."

"Really, what part?"

She hesitated. "Not the actual designing. But the actual running of the business." She took a deep breath and expelled it slowly. "I never finished school. I dropped out right before my senior year."

"Really? What happened that caused you to drop out of school? That doesn't fit." He was shocked she'd done such a thing and knew there had to be a reason.

"It was just my mom and me. And Mom got really

ill. She was in and out of the hospital and we needed the money, so I went to work full time as a waitress."

"I'm sorry." Her doing that fit with the kind of person he'd come to know her as. "How's your mom?"

"She passed away at the end of that year. I met Gordon not long after she died and we got married. I could have gone back to school, but I got pregnant."

"So you didn't go back."

"No."

"That happens a lot. So, now, trying to open your own business makes you nervous."

"It does. But I'll make it. I just feel like I'm faking it or something. Does that sound odd?"

He studied the fence and glanced at the boys ahead to make sure they weren't getting too wild. "Have you ever thought about going back to school? Maybe get your GED and then some college courses. It would eliminate that fake sense that you have, and it would also be a positive move for you with Abe. It's always good for kids to see their parents work for a goal and accomplish it."

She grew quiet and stared ahead, deep in thought. "I honestly have toyed with that idea, especially since Gordon's death."

"You know," he added, "Jolie is a good person to ask about that, I'm sure."

"I'm sure she would be a help." Suzie smiled. "I think I'll talk to her. And find a place to take the course." Reaching across the distance between them she touched his arm. "Thank you."

Her touch was warm, and Tucker wanted to place his hand over hers and hold tight. "No thanks necessary," he said, his voice tight with wanting things he could never have.

"Suzie," he said, gently. "Gordon would be proud of what you're doing. You should know that. Everything you're doing is for Abe's welfare."

She raked her fingers through her hair. "I hope so. I was so very proud of him."

"We found it!"

The whoop and excited yells came from the boys.

"I better go see what they've found." Tucker urged his horse into a trot and headed toward the boys, though his thoughts were not on finding the donkey escape route anymore. He was thinking how his skin still radiated with the touch of Suzie's hand. And wondering what it would be like for Suzie to be proud of him.

To have that soft edge to her eyes when she thought of him, the way she did when she thought of Gordon.

It was wrong to even think about wanting that.

But he did.

He was in so much trouble.

The remodeled barn that housed Lucy's paint studio was full of silk flowers, lace and ribbons. They'd been having a great Girls' Night, as they were calling it, while they worked on decorations for Lucy's upcoming wedding. Suzie had enjoyed the first Monday of business at her flower shop. There'd been a lot of traffic. She'd sold several gift and home decor items, and filled a few orders for flowers. It had been a very encouraging day.

And now she was enjoying helping with Lucy's decorations. Lucy had tried to pay her for her services but she'd refused. They'd finally come to an agreement that she would do the flowers for the wedding party and her bouquet for a price. Lucy had been adamant about that and so Suzie had agreed. After all, as Lucy had pointed out, she was running a business and had to show a profit. Suzie knew she was right.

Still, looking at the room, satisfaction and joy filled her to be pitching in as a friend on this part of the decorating. It was her way of paying back some of the goodness they'd shown her and Abe.

And it was beautiful. Greenery wrapped around wreaths with small daisies scattered throughout them were garnished with ribbons in silky cream and soft fern colors. To add sparkle and romance, the women were also decorating twig balls with tiny lights and ribbons. These would hang suspended throughout the reception hall.

Suzie and Jolie were working together to attach tiny strings of lights to large twig balls.

Suzie decided now was a good time to ask for help. Being a private person, opening up about her past was hard, especially to someone as accomplished as Jolie. But she trusted her new friend.

"Jolie, I never finished high school and I've been thinking I'd like to get my GED. Can you help me with that?"

Jolie's eyes lit up like fireflies. "I would love to help you! It's wonderful you've decided to do this. So many people never finish for a wide array of reasons. Trying again will be a good example for Abe."

"That's the major determining factor. Tucker, actually, is the one who pushed me to do it. We were talking, and I told him I hadn't finished school. And that I felt a little intimidated, opening my own business. He suggested I might feel better if I had that certificate. And I might go on to do some community college courses."

"I think that's a great idea. I'll check into it first thing tomorrow. What grade level were you at?"

Suzie said she just lacked twelfth grade when she'd had to quit. "I don't regret what I did. I'm glad I was able to help out with my mom being so ill. I don't know what would have happened if I hadn't." With no other family, it struck her again how important it was to have Abe here, at the ranch.

"Raising a child on my own is no easy task and there is that fear that if something happened to me, if I were to get ill, like my mother did, what would happen to Abe? I'm glad he has you and everyone here at the ranch to count as family."

Jolie leaned across the table and grabbed her hand. "We're so glad y'all are here."

They worked and talked about what getting the GED would consist of. After a while Jolie asked, "Do you ever think of remarrying?"

The question took Suzie by surprise. "I haven't." Tucker flashed before her and her insides tilted uneasily. "I'm not sure I can risk it, for one. It's scary thinking about falling in love and running the risk of losing him again."

If she ever did feel she was ready to take that risk, it would be with someone who had a desk job.

Not a military man. Not a lawman.

"You know, from what I've heard about Gordon, he would want you to be happy."

Suzie tugged the ribbon a little harder than needed at the top of the ball she was working on. "I'm doing all right."

"Sure you are. You're doing great. But Gordon sounds like a guy who would want you to move on, to find someone else to be a part of your life, yours and Abe's."

"You're right, that's what he would have wanted. But this is about what I want now." Suzie studied the finished ball, lost in memories for a moment. "I met Gordon right after my mother died. He was stationed in San Antonio working in the recruitment office. I fell for him instantly. And you're right, he was a giving guy. We only dated two months before we got married."

"Really, that sounds like Lucy and Rowdy."

Suzie smiled at that. "Some people think that's crazy. But it isn't."

She'd never been instantly attracted to anyone the way she'd been attracted to Gordon. Never.

That's a lie, and you know it. The words whispered through her mind and caused her heart to ache. *You felt similar attraction that first day when Tucker wrapped his arm around your shoulders and you looked into his eyes.*

She pushed the thoughts from her head. Things were so tangled. *This is the man you hold responsible for Gordon's death.*

Didn't she? He'd been so good to them. He held himself responsible. But even if she no longer held Tucker responsible for Gordon's death, he would never be someone she could consider marrying. Those emotions were still too tangled up. Besides, he might be a sheriff in a small town, but he still put his life on the line every day. Death was still a possibility every time he strapped on his gun and pinned on his badge.

Why was she even entertaining these thoughts about Tucker?

They were on a tenuous tightrope toward friendship,

and for the sake of their common goal—Abe's health and happiness—friendship made sense.

Anything else did not.

That she felt irresistibly drawn to him in moments when her guard was down didn't matter. That was understandable.

Admitting that those emotions were there eased the tight knot of tension in her chest just a little. It was… explainable.

She'd been young and vulnerable when she'd met and fallen for Gordon. She was not so young anymore, but she was vulnerable again. Gordon had helped her during the loss of her mother. Tucker was helping her with Abe, with coping with the aftermath of Gordon's death. Completely explainable.

She had no one else to turn to and Tucker, along with his family, was filling that void.

Yes, having her shop open and finishing her education would help fix that. Knowledge equaled strength and stability for her.

Exactly what she needed.

Chapter Nine

Tucker was running late as he turned his SUV onto the blacktop road and headed toward the ranch. Everyone would understand, though; his job had a timetable all its own. This time he'd been called out to aid in a domestic violence case in a neighboring small town. No matter how many times he did it, he would never get used to responding to a case and finding a female with a bruised and bloody face. But there had been a twist to the scenario: the male, after having beaten his wife, had been the one to call 911 when she'd retaliated with a baseball bat.

Tucker had arrived on the scene first to find the man had actually climbed a tree to get away from his fed up, abused wife.

Tucker took one look at her face and the man had been ordered from the tree, handcuffed and escorted to jail. Tucker hoped she would press charges. But he had learned that most times people didn't. Still, today, he had hope. Thinking about the lowlife cowering in the tree had him chuckling as he drove toward the ranch.

It had taken a long time after losing Gordon for

Tucker to smile again. He'd been different when he'd finally come home after spending time in the hospital. Making the stop to see Suzie and offer his condolences, and his aid and support, hadn't helped him. She'd been so angry—so grief-stricken and full of blame toward him that it had cut him to the bone. Helping Gordon's family had been his only means of redemption and when Suzie refused him, it crushed that option.

He'd been in a very dark hole.

It had taken his family a long time to talk him into running for sheriff. But in the end, God had led him to accept the post. Most days, small-town sheriff duties were about as redneck as could be, what with chasing chickens and herding escaped donkeys. But then, times like today, when he got to see the human spirit fight back against wrong, and he got the opportunity to be a part of that—he knew he was making a difference. And that was his redemption.

Now that Abe and Suzie were here, he'd come full circle. God was giving him the opportunity to make a difference in the life of Gordon's family.

If he just didn't mess it up.

And that meant he had to stop thinking about Suzie standing in the sunlight, cotton in her hair, and eyes as sparkling and changing as the ocean.

Eyes he continually found himself getting lost in.

No, he needed to focus on the life he'd been dealt, the good he was able to do and the wrongs his job enabled him to right.

With Suzie, he had been careful. And he would be, not because of his own feelings, but because his getting in too deep would harm the friendship and trust that he needed to build with Suzie.

Anything more, any romantic notions that continually knocked the wind out of him when he looked into her eyes, were absolutely off-limits.

Rolling to a halt in front of the horse barn, he rammed the shifter into Park with more power than needed, just to ram home the thoughts in his head.

He was here to see Wes and Joseph. They were arriving home from college today to attend Rowdy and Lucy's wedding in two days. Tucker had to be at the ranch to welcome them home.

"Hey, Dad. Pepper," he said, walking over to the stable, where his dad stood with Walter Pepper, their horse foreman. "Have you heard from them? Are they running on time?"

Nana had had someone string a welcome-home banner across the front of the chow hall and folks were arriving for the welcome party they were throwing Wes and Joseph.

Pepper's sky-blue eyes crinkled at the edges, standing out against his pure white hair. "I'd say those two might not make it till tomorrow, but then they haven't had Nana's cooking in three months, so I'm sure they have the pedal to the metal and will be here by two o'clock, just like they said."

Randolph hiked a black brow, reminding Tucker of George Strait with his black hair, lean face and easygoing smile. "I agree with Pepper. Haven't heard from them, but I'm sure they'll be here on time. If not, their nana will probably jump in her truck and go looking for them. Or expect you to turn on the missing-persons alert sirens."

"True." Tucker looked at his watch. "Well, they have ten minutes." Suzie was standing beside Nana. She wore a soft turquoise blouse with her jeans and was as fresh as a flower. He couldn't look away—and just like that, she caught him staring. The small, tight smile she sent him was enough to cause his pulse to break the speed limit. He smiled in reaction then forced himself to turn back to the conversation.

"There they come!" A shout went up from the boys in the arena as a black truck sped over the hill, dust flying out behind it. Sixteen boys scrambled from every corner of the yard, arena and horse barn. They came running with whoops and yells and laughter.

His dad crossed his arms and smiled in satisfaction. "Tucker, your mother would be proud. That right there…" He nodded toward the gathering of excited boys as Wes and Joseph came to a halt. Wes had his cowboy hat hanging out the window and was waving and yelling, while Joseph drove and waved and grinned. "That right there is family. Just like Lydia wanted it to be."

Tucker's throat tightened. His mother had had a dream. And it had come true over and over again across the years at Sunrise Ranch. And it gave him purpose and meaning, knowing that he'd had a part in it and would continue to have a part in it as long as he was breathing.

Looking across the way at Abe, and then at Suzie, he knew they were witnessing how it had been for Gordon. And he hoped Abe's heart was more and more at peace being here.

Suzie watched, amazed at the excitement of the boys as their friends jumped from the truck. One was a stout, happy-faced young man with blond curls and eyes full of mischief. The other was tall and lanky with a long, thin face and the kindest brown eyes she'd ever seen.

The happy-faced one grinned, opened his arms wide and yelled, "Hey, hey, little brothers. What's up?"

The younger boys literally tackled him, yelling, "Wes, Wes!"

The pure tenderness of the show of affection between them was beautiful.

"Glad y'all are home, Joseph," Tony said, hugging the kind-eyed young man.

He laughed. "It's good to be here. Wes always steals the show, though," he teased.

"Hey, we can jump on you, too, but we're a little big for that," Jake offered, and hugged him followed by Caleb. Joseph didn't have to wait long before the younger ones finished mugging Wes and came after him with just as much excitement. They'd been gone and now they were home.

It hit her in that moment that these weren't friends. These truly were brothers in all the best senses of the word. There was a camaraderie they shared that was touching. And she marveled more at what the McDermotts had accomplished.

Gordon had told her that they'd changed his life. The day the social worker pulled his file and decided that he, a teenager who'd been abandoned by his parents as a toddler then bounced from one foster home to the next, was a perfect fit for the new boys ranch that had just opened up. He'd told her that, but until this moment it hadn't hit her how deeply he'd meant what he'd said.

"Okay, okay," Nana called, moving into the fray. "Now it's my turn. Come give your nana some lovin' hugs, boys."

Instantly Wes broke free and grabbed Nana in a bear hug. Then Joseph did the same. Nana laughed and teared up—so did Suzie as she watched.

After Nana had her hugs, the McDermott men moved in and there was a bunch of manly handshaking and more bear hugs. It was clear that Tucker and his dad and brothers had true love and affection for Wes and Joseph.

"Hubba-hubba," Wes said, when Jolie stepped up and gave him a hug. Looking over Jolie's shoulder, he winked at Morgan. "I'm still in love."

Jolie chuckled, grabbed his beat-up hat off his head and scrubbed his curls. "It's good to have you home, funny man. Joseph, give me a hug." Reaching over, she engulfed him. "It's good to have you both home."

Then it was Lucy's turn, and it was the same warm welcome.

Abe stood to the side and took it all in.

"Hey, dude," Wes said, moving his way. "You're new. What's your name?"

"Abe."

Wes's brows lifted and his eyes twinkled like Christmas lights. "Well, Abe, my man, you're going to have to hang with me and Joseph some before we head back to school. Got to get to know our new brother."

Abe shrugged. "Sure."

Wes reaching out to Abe had Suzie's eyes misting up again, even though Abe wasn't as receptive as she'd hoped he would be. These boys had learned to be inclusive living here on the ranch. It came naturally to them. Suzie stepped out of the way toward the chow hall, not wanting to mar the moment with tears. This was how Gordon had grown up. She could only imagine the welcome he would have had if he'd have come home from war.

"Are you all right?" Tucker asked, coming up behind her. She hadn't even realized he was near.

She hadn't seen him since she'd checked fences with him and the boys almost a week ago. It seemed longer than that. "I'm fine. Just overwhelmed by the reunion. Gordon truly did have a home here, didn't he?"

"Yes. And Gordon was, in many ways, like Wes there. He was a warm kid with a willingness to take care of others, and he did it by teasing the dickens out of them most of the time. Little kids loved Gordon."

"That sounds like him. I'm sure he was like that with the guys in his unit, too."

Tucker held her eyes, steady and sure. "Yes, he was. He led by example."

Led by example.

The phrase drove deep into her heart. That was what heroes did, and he'd led by example right to his death. She pushed the thoughts away. Gordon was a hero in every sense of the word. It was just hard to accept that it had cost them all so much.

"I guess Rowdy is as excited about the wedding as Lucy is."

"He was ready the day he asked her five months ago."

"It will be a lovely wedding."

Tucker smiled. She knew he knew that she was diverting the conversation away from Gordon.

"I'm excited for them," he said. "It's been great watching how the Lord has worked in both Morgan's and Rowdy's lives. I've always wanted the best for my brothers and they're getting that in Jolie and Lucy."

That suddenly had Suzie wondering about him.

"Have you ever been in love, Tucker?" Why was she asking him this? *Because you need to know.*

Was that sadness or anger she saw flash in the depths of his deep, deep blue eyes?

"Not me," he said. "I've never been marriage material. Hey, I need to get back. Do you want to walk over and let me introduce you while I give 'em a hug before I head back to work?"

"Sure," she said, following him as he'd started walking without waiting for her answer. Wes and Joseph hugged him, grinning so wide their faces had to hurt. They were well loved.

"This is Suzie, Abe's mother. Abe's dad, Gordon, was part of our family here, too, when he was younger." Tucker introduced her as soon as the hugging stopped. Then she was swept into conversation with the young men, and Nana joined in on the conversation, too. Tucker took his leave and headed to his truck.

Suzie's gaze followed him as he climbed into his SUV, which stirred up dust as he left. She wondered if it would be another week before she saw him again, and then remembered absently that he would be at the wedding in two days.

Funny, how that suddenly seemed a long time away.

It wasn't until a few minutes later, when she was helping serve the feast that Nana had made, that Suzie realized Abe hadn't come to load up a plate of food like the other teens. Looking around, she spotted him riding a horse alone at the far end of the large arena.

She watched him for a few minutes. *Please, Lord,* she found herself praying… *Please.*

She didn't even put words to the pleading prayer. God knew what she was asking. God knew what Abe needed.

As if God knew what *she* needed, Nana came up beside her and watched Abe ride, too. "He'll come around, you know. I've seen boys work out their grief, their abandonment, any number of issues of the heart and soul."

Suzie sighed. "It would be wonderful if he was just a regular kid out there riding for the love of riding."

"One day he will be. You just keep thinking about that. Every day is one day closer to that day."

Suzie had hired Camy, a high school student, to work a few hours in the afternoons, and today was her first day. It had worked out well, giving Suzie the time to help with the welcome-home party for Wes and Joseph. It was after five, and Suzie was feeling restless as she headed back to town to make sure Camy had locked up good. She also wanted to begin Lucy's wedding bouquet while it was quiet and no one was popping in and out. She'd been touched when Lucy had decided to forgo simple silk arrangements and hired Suzie to do the wedding party flowers.

When Suzie told Abe she was going to be in town for the evening, he'd surprised her by wanting to go, too.

Any hope she'd had that he might be a happy companion was immediately dashed when he got into the car, slammed the door and sulked in the passenger seat.

Anger flashed through Suzie, her patience wearing thin. "Abe, what is wrong with you? It was a nice afternoon. Didn't you like Wes and Joseph?"

"Yeah, sure, Mom. It was one big happy family out

there. It always is. Only I don't want that family. I want my dad."

"Of course you do."

He was at an age when he really needed his dad.

"I want to go home. Back to San Antonio."

"Our home is here now, Abe. All you did there was get into trouble. It's better here. You'll fit in better every day."

Even though she was watching the road intently, her hands gripping the steering wheel as if it were her last great hope, she could feel his angry glare.

"They're too happy, Mom!"

"Too happy?" She shot him a glance, disbelieving that he was serious. He was, though, his dark expression made that clear.

"It's like they all just got to the ranch and suddenly everything was wonderful."

She pulled into her parking space in front of the shop. "I don't understand, Abe. I don't."

His voice had been rising with each declaration. "Their lives were crummy before they got here. Lousy. Their dads were deadbeats, drunks and losers. Their home lives were the pits. Jake's was so bad he was on the street! And he was trying to tell me everything was going to be A-okay. I told him he was only saying that because he didn't know any better. I knew better. My dad was great, Mom. You were great."

His voice dropped low. "We were happy. I *know* what I lost. Don't you get it?"

Suzie did. Looking at him she finally understood what he was feeling, what he was struggling with. Tears blinded her as she reached out to touch him.

He yanked away. "I want to go home," he snapped. He jerked on the door handle then thrust open the door. Before Suzie could find her voice he had flung himself from the car and charged across the street. He disappeared within seconds.

Chapter Ten

"This way." Tucker directed the dangerously inebriated man through the side door of the jailhouse. Handcuffed as he was, the man was in danger of stumbling and sprawling onto the concrete floor with no way to break his fall. Tucker had a firm grip on the foul-smelling, somewhat subdued man, not wanting to have to spend the rest of what had turned out to be a miserable day in the emergency room because of this yahoo.

"Whoa," Cody said, swinging his boots off the desk where he'd had them crossed while reclining in his seat. "I can smell him from here."

Tucker frowned. "Well, it's about to get worse. He's all yours. Watch out for his right hook."

The drunk ran off a string of slurred words that Tucker didn't even try to decipher. He was just glad he'd pulled him over when he did, or someone might have been hurt or killed.

"Thanks for the heads-up. Okay, that is just wrong," Cody said, leaning back as he got a whiff up close.

Tucker headed straight for the sink by the coffeepot in the corner and washed his hands.

The door of the office opened, and he turned to see Suzie, pale and teary-eyed, rush inside.

"Suzie, what's going on?"

"It's Abe. He's run off."

"At the ranch?"

She shook her head, swiping her eyes with her fingertips. "Just now."

He grabbed a tissue from the box on the sidebar and handed it to her. "Here? Tell me what's happened."

"Just a few minutes ago. He ran off. He wanted to ride into town with me and was upset. Tucker, part of what happened between him and Jake was he said some terrible things to Jake about how bad his life had been, and that Jake didn't understand how good Abe's had been. He doesn't want to fit in here. He wants his old life back—his life with me and Gordon in San Antonio."

Poor kid. And Suzie, Tucker had to fight not to pull her close and wipe her tears away. "Let's go find him," he said. He took a second to stick his head through the door to the back of the jail and tell Cory he was going out. "He can't have gone far," he said, reassuring Suzie as he took her arm and led her onto the deserted street. Dew Drop wasn't the busiest place after stores closed down at five. People were in and out of the Spotted Cow Café, but the stores on the square were pretty much shut down.

Suzie had stopped crying now; he was glad. He wasn't real comfortable with tears. Growing up with all guys and then joining the marines didn't give him a lot of experience with tears. And Suzie's tears cut straight to his heart.

"Thanks for helping me. He ran across the street,

toward the inn, but I didn't see which street he went down."

Tucker's office was on a side street just off the square. "We'd better take the SUV. We can make better time than on foot." He led her around the corner of the building to where his vehicle was parked. Within moments they were driving across town.

"Let's go down the alley beside the Dew Drop Inn first and then we'll start the backstreets. He'll turn up." He gave her a reassuring smile. "Our streets are about as safe as you can get. So that's a positive."

"That's what I keep telling myself. I know he's safe. He's just so upset."

Tucker was scanning the backs of the buildings as he drove down the road that cut behind the buildings on that side of town. Suzie was doing the same.

"Tucker, I have to find a way to help Abe be stronger. I don't want this to make him grow up feeling sorry for himself. Which is what I think is happening. Does that make sense? Or does that sound terrible on my part? It's been two years. And I'm afraid I may have contributed to this without realizing it."

"It makes sense. You want him to be a survivor and take control, not let the loss of his dad be something that ruins his life. I'm not sure what you mean about your contributing to it, though."

She looked at him. "He knows how I've held this grudge against you. He's seen the anger in me. The problem I've had blaming you for Gordon's death. I'm sorry about that, Tucker. I've realized I was wrong."

He'd stopped at a stop sign and stared straight ahead as he took in her words. "You don't have anything to be sorry about."

She reached across the space between them, placing her hand on his forearm. "No—I do. Gordon was a U.S. marine. A *marine*. You know more than anyone what that means. You know what that commitment is. Gordon was a hero. He made choices that were true to the man he was. I accept that. I should have done that before now. I let my anger and…some self-pitying attitude overpower my thoughts."

What did he say to that? She didn't give him a chance to figure it out as she continued.

"You were the one that pointed out that Gordon led by example. And you're right. He did." She smiled. "I've spent two years stealing that from him. His son should have been taught to be proud of what his dad did. But no, I overshadowed his bravery and his sacrifice by putting blame on you. I've led by example, and it was a bad example."

Tucker's heart was thundering in his chest from the touch of her hands and the sincerity in her eyes. Her words didn't take away the guilt he felt toward himself for being alive while Gordon was dead. But it made him proud of Suzie. "That means a great deal to me. Gordon deserves that respect. It's going to be all right. Abe's stronger than he thinks."

"Yes, he is."

Tucker drove across the street and began scanning the area again. The elementary school was on this side of town. On a hunch Tucker hung a left and drove toward the back of the school. And there was Abe. He had climbed to the top of the nine-foot slide and was sitting with his feet on the ladder. He looked about as alone as a kid could be.

"There he is." He pointed, drawing Suzie's gaze from where she'd been scanning the houses across the road.

"Praise the Lord," she said, softly.

Tucker pulled into the empty parking space on the street and they walked across the playground. Abe watched them. The sun was starting to lower in the sky. Purple and blue streaks glowed behind Abe on the slide.

Tucker started praying as they walked. Suzie was right. Abe was going to have to get stronger. Something bad had happened in his life. He'd lost a parent and it was a wrong and terrible thing to happen to a kid. Tucker knew from experience. But he and his brothers had each gone through their own mourning period and then they'd moved on. They'd grown from it and used it to become the adults they knew would have pleased their mother. But they'd each had a rough go of it.

Abe would have to find that within himself, and the truth was that only Abe could do it. Abe would have to make the choice of how he would let, not only his father's death, but his life and sacrifice, affect him. Just as Tucker and Suzie were having to do.

Life went on. No matter what, the wheels of life stopped for no one. Tucker prayed for strength for Abe. And peace.

He prayed for the same for Suzie.

But for himself—until Suzie and Abe were okay, there would be no peace.

Abe looked sullen and Suzie could tell by the redness around his eyes that he'd been crying. Her mind was whirling—what did she need to say to him?

Instead of glaring at her he stared down at her with zero emotion. His face was lax and his eyes dull as if he'd been so furious moments ago that he'd exhausted everything he had.

"Abe, are you okay?" No, it was clear to see that he wasn't okay, and yet a mother had to ask.

"What do you think?" he said, dully.

I know what I lost. His earlier words echoed through her heart. "I think we have to find a way to deal with this," she said, holding her voice steady. Falling apart wouldn't help anyone. Her child needed her to lead.

"I want to go back home."

She knew he was talking about San Antonio. "Abe, that isn't an option. Our life is here now. Our…our life…" She fought the hard lump of emotions. She glanced at Tucker. He didn't say anything, but the edges of his eyes softened and he gave a slight nod of encouragement. She drew strength from his support. Momentarily she wished…what? "Our life will never be the same as it was. But it can be good again. God— Oh, Abe, God *does* have a plan—"

"Yeah, whatever." Abe stood up abruptly on the top rung of the ladder, cutting off her words. He stomped down the rungs. "Let's just go back. No one understands."

"Give it some time. Give the guys a chance. They're a great bunch and they like you."

"Fine, I guess I'm like them, after all." He looked so lost it hurt. "Dad loved the marines more than me, anyway. I'll meet you at the shop."

"Abe, that's not true."

"Your dad loved you very much, Abe," Tucker spoke up as Abe stalked past him.

"Whatever," Abe said again and kept walking. "It is what it is."

Suzie felt weak watching him go. "How has this happened?" she asked Tucker. "He seemed better, and suddenly he's angrier than ever."

"Grief comes in waves, Suzie, you know that. You've experienced it, I'm sure. But he's really angry at Gordon. And now the boys."

"I know...." She rubbed her forehead, a pain throbbing there. "This seems so raw. So new."

"Has he been angry at Gordon all this time?"

They started walking toward the SUV as Abe disappeared around the edge of the school, heading up the sidewalk. At the rate he was walking, it would take him thirty minutes to make the two blocks to the shop.

"Subconsciously, yes. Me, too. I think— Do you think this could be his hurt coming to the surface finally?" She stopped and turned toward Tucker, raking a hand through her hair in frustration. "The boys of Sunrise Ranch have been abandoned by their families. And I've felt deep down that Abe has felt abandoned by Gordon—though he might not have voiced it in any way but through anger." She paused, the realization coming full force. "I believe being here among them has made him feel like one of them. And he doesn't want to feel like one of them."

"He's fighting it even though he feels that in his heart," Tucker finished for her.

"Does that make sense?" She started walking again, knowing they were on to something. Feeling it deep down.

"Yes, it does." They'd reached the vehicle and he opened the door for her. "How about you, do you feel that way? Do you feel like Gordon abandoned you? Because he didn't. He loved you too much."

And there it was. "I did. But not now. The emotions are so convoluted. In a situation like this, I guess they all rise to the top."

"I think so. I can give you a counselor's name. She's good and a Christian. This may be something deeper than we can help him with."

"I'll try to talk him into it."

"Y'all will get through this."

"We have to, Tucker. There is no other option."

And there wasn't. Nothing else except Abe getting better was acceptable.

Tucker sat on his porch that night, thinking about Suzie and what she was going through. He'd wanted to take her in his arms and just hold her, she'd looked so alone. As alone as Abe had looked sitting at the top of that slide.

But, as much as he'd wanted to wrap his arms around her, he knew he couldn't. The best thing he could do to offer comfort to Suzie was to help Abe. He'd been surprised at the revelation that the kid was angry with Gordon. Suzie's anger had been at him, not Gordon, and that was what he'd expected from Abe. The abandonment issue had taken him completely by surprise. And that was directly linked to the choice Gordon had made when he took the bullets meant for him.

He felt nauseated thinking about that. Sick in his heart, too.

And all the more certain that he had to fix this.

He'd never backed away from a challenge in his life or a man in need of his help. And he didn't plan on doing it now.

Grief was hard. His mother's death lived with him

and always would, but time had helped ease the loss, though he hadn't believed it would as a child. He hadn't bottled it up like Abe. Hadn't had the same issues.

He'd kept silent at the slide that afternoon, letting Suzie take point. But when the time was right he would talk to Abe. He would wait for God to present the right opportunity.

Tucker just needed to be prayed up and ready when that time came. As for Suzie…she'd turned a corner in their relationship by not holding him responsible for Gordon's death. But he needed to remember that there was no room for a relationship between them. He was here to offer help and support where Abe was concerned. Holding her, comforting her, was off-limits. Something between them would only complicate matters and they were already complicated enough.

Still, it was just getting harder and harder to maintain and believe when every fiber in his body wanted something different.

Chapter Eleven

❧

"Stick with the plan."

Suzie said the words out loud as she left for work on Friday morning. She'd come to Dew Drop to start a new life for her and Abe and that was what she planned to do. Being at Sunrise Ranch made more sense to her now than ever.

She needed everyone's support.

"Abe needs it, too," she told herself firmly, her hands tightening on the steering wheel as she gave herself a pep talk. "Staying at the ranch or at least in Dew Drop is for his own good."

Before leaving for work, she'd gone to the classroom to see Jolie, while the boys finished breakfast. Suzie explained what had happened the day before so Jolie would be aware of what was going on with Abe. Strong and encouraging, Jolie had assured Suzie she would watch out for him and call immediately if something went wrong. And then she'd asked Suzie if they could pray together.

Suzie had needed that connection so much and agreed wholeheartedly. Jolie reaching out to her with prayer lifted Suzie's spirits and was affirmation from God that He was listening. And that she was right where she needed to be, surrounded by an amazing support group.

With her spirits renewed, she walked into her shop and went straight to the phone and called the counselor Tucker had suggested to her. She made herself an appointment. Before she made Abe an appointment, she wanted the doctor's advice.

That done, she got busy.

Today was a full day, with work and then the wedding rehearsal that night. Though she wasn't in the wedding party, Lucy had asked her to be in charge of the wedding book and involved her with the decorating, and so Lucy had insisted she come to the rehearsal dinner.

When she finished work, Suzie would see how Abe's day had gone and decide if she could make the dinner or not.

She felt energized as she worked on the wedding flowers. They had to be extra special for Rowdy and Lucy, and it was a blessing to be busy. As she worked, her thoughts kept going to Abe.

And to Tucker.

He amazed her. That he would continue to stand by her in the face of all the anger she'd harbored toward him spoke of the man he was.

He was strong of character. A man she could lean on, and there had been moments when she'd longed to lean her head against his chest.

Those thoughts she didn't dwell on.... In fact, she moved past them forcibly.

Her life was complicated enough, as it was. She was staying in Dew Drop but Abe was her only concern right now.

Tucker wasn't himself as he headed toward the ranch. He'd missed the wedding rehearsal but knew everyone was eating at the ranch and decorating the barn for the reception.

His day had been a full one. He'd had to go before the monthly grand jury meeting and present several cases. Since the cases were pretty cut-and-dried he felt as though the grand jury would make the indictments so trial dates could be set. One of the cases he'd presented was the wife-abusing tree climber, and Tucker was very proud of the wife for following through with the charges. Sure enough, the jury had indicted the husband.

He'd been on his way back to Dew Drop from the county seat when one of the officers from a nearby community radioed in for backup. Tucker had been close and responded. A situation had evolved into a car chase down a country road with bullets being fired. It'd been dicey there, for a while, but no one was injured.

They could have been, though.

Tucker hadn't had that much action since the marines. He hadn't been prepared for the aftermath…for the flashbacks that had hit him during the gunfire.

Pulling up in front of the barn, he pushed the memories from his mind and exited the truck. Laughter and music filled the air as he approached. In the dusk the glow from the lit-up interior was welcoming. Though he'd really wanted to go home and be alone, he'd known that he needed to show up for Rowdy and Lucy.

Boys were everywhere. Joseph and Wes had a trailer loaded with square hay bales backed to the rear of the building, and they were tossing bales down to the boys, who were stacking them around the barn. Nana was directing them where and how to stack them for seating arrangements and decorations.

At a table in the center of the room stood a group of ladies: Mabel, Ms. Jo, Jolie and Suzie.

With turmoil roiling inside of him, he walked over to say hello and see what he could do to help.

The barn was spotless. It had been cleaned to the point that there was no sign livestock had ever been inside. There was only the fresh scent of the new hay bales being brought in.

"Hey'ya, Tucker," Wes called from his position on the top of the load of hay as he tossed the bales down.

"Hey, yourself, Wes. Looks like the good ol' days of you and Joseph hauling hay all summer."

Joseph grinned affably beside Wes. "Those were some fun times."

"Yup, sure were," Wes agreed, grabbing a square bale as if it was a tin can. "Tony, Jake, Caleb and my boy Abe over there held their own loading this stuff up today."

Joseph gave a thumbs-up. "That's right."

"You two relax. You've got great backup taking up the slack, and we're really proud of them. Couldn't run the place without your dedication or theirs."

"That's what I'm talkin' about," Wes said. "My dudes are making me proud."

Tucker gave them a tip of his hat, not missing that

Abe didn't look at him. At least he'd pitched in and was helping. Hanging out with the guys was the best thing for him.

Morgan came in and set a box down.

"Missed you at the rehearsal. Must have been bad."

Tucker had called Morgan to let him know he wasn't going to make it to the church on time. "Yeah, it was. I'll fill you in later. You'll make sure I know what I'm doing tomorrow, right?"

Morgan grinned. "I don't know, it's pretty hard to walk out there and stand beside your brother. Then watch a string of pretty ladies and a beautiful bride come strolling down the aisle."

Tucker had to chuckle at that. "Yeah, I was afraid things might have changed in the months since your wedding."

"Nope, still the same. You'll be fine. Come help unload the boxes of decorations from my truck. I've never seen so much stuff. The gals must have been warehousing this stuff over at Lucy's studio."

"Be right there. Let me say hello to the women."

"Sure, just don't let them snare you into helping till we finish unloading the truck." He laughed and headed back out the rear door.

Tucker didn't stay long saying hi to the ladies. They were chattering like a bunch of magpies anyway, laughing and having a great time. Suzie was gathering a bunch of greenery wrapped with lights and she stepped away from the table as he walked toward her. She looked beautiful, and though she appeared to be smiling and in good spirits, he thought he could detect worry creasing the edges of her eyes.

He wanted to talk to her, ask her how her day went

and how Abe had done. He wanted to hold her in his arms—he broke that thought off. "Are you about to hang that somewhere?" he asked, spotting the tall ladder in the center of the room.

"She's about to climb that thing," Ms. Jo called. "You showed up just in time, Tucker. Climb that ladder and hang that garland for her, please."

"Oh, that is a perfect thing for you to do," Mabel added, smiling like an opossum. "And you stay over there and make sure he gets it done right, Suzie. You know these men don't know the first thing about decorating with flowers and such."

Tucker wasn't unhappy at all about the opportunity to spend time with Suzie. "I'd be glad to do that. You ladies just tell me what to do."

The tension coiled inside of him eased as he and Suzie walked toward the ladder. She glanced at him, studying him for a minute. "You've had a hard day."

It wasn't a question and he shrugged it off; suddenly, looking at her, everything seemed better. "It had its tough spots. But it all turned out good." And it had. It hadn't turned out like the day Gordon died, despite the flashbacks that had hit him as the bullets flew past.

"Maybe, after we decorate, you can tell me about it if you need to talk. You've tried so hard to help me, it would be nice to repay the kindness."

They just looked at each other for a moment. "How's Abe today?" he asked, after a beat or two. "I see he's helping with the hay."

"Jolie said he was silent during class. That he didn't participate, but he wasn't rude. I'm worried about him, but he was helping Wes and Joseph with the hay when I got here and I thought that was a good sign."

"It can't hurt. So, what do you want me to do with this stuff?" he asked, reaching to take it from her hands. Their fingers touched.

"We're wrapping it around those beams, so it's going to take a little time. Are you sure you have time to do this? I'm not afraid of a ladder."

"I'm here to help. But you will have to direct me or there is no telling what it will look like."

She chuckled, and the sound sent his pulse racing. "I'll stay close. Don't worry."

He nodded and climbed the ladder as fast as he could. He liked the thought of her staying close far too much to linger beside her listening to her laughter.

The evening had passed by quickly and Suzie stared at how lovely the barn looked. The garland was hung from the rafters, thanks to Tucker and Morgan, who'd been roped into joining in as soon as he'd looked as though he had nothing to do. It had been a fun experience listening to him and Tucker complain to each other, teasing the women with their moaning and groaning.

As soon as the boys had finished unloading the hay, they'd gone off and she'd lost track of Abe, though she'd relaxed a little during the evening seeing him interact with the boys. She just had to give it time. She couldn't panic, and she couldn't pull up stakes and move just because he wanted her to.

She was standing by the stables after waving goodnight to everyone. The younger boys had been gathered up earlier by their house parents and taken to their homes on the ranch. The older boys had a later curfew on Friday night and were hanging out at the end of the arena under the lights, riding and cutting up. She could spot Abe and prayed that today had been good for him. She planned to talk to him before he went to bed.

She was standing in the shadows watching the boys, and remained there for a few minutes, not ready to go in just yet. She told herself she wasn't lingering to talk to Tucker before he headed home, but she wasn't convinced that was the truth. He'd gone into the stables with his dad and Pepper earlier and she wondered how long they would be. She got her answer soon when they emerged, all smiles. They greeted her, then Pepper waved and headed to his truck.

"Rowdy brought in a few new horses today," Randolph said. "They're beauties. You should get Tucker to show them to you. I'm heading to bed. Got to get my beauty sleep, you know." He gave her a quick hug before leaving. His home was elsewhere on the ranch, as Morgan's and Rowdy's were.

Suddenly she found herself alone with Tucker. He looked so handsome in the moonlight. She'd known just by looking at him earlier that something had happened at work. Something stressful. She knew it had been important if he missed the rehearsal because of it.

But now, he seemed more relaxed. Still she'd been curious about what had happened. Had it been dangerous?

"Do you want to see the colts?"

"Sure, I'd love that."

He smiled. "Then follow me."

Single bulbs down the center of the alleyway lit the stable, and they glowed bright as they entered. Soft nickers came from the stalls as they walked toward the tack room on the right, down a few stalls to where a beautiful tan horse stood watching them. It was the color of caramel with a vanilla mane and huge chocolate eyes.

"How gorgeous," Suzie said, loving the color.

"This is Bow. He's going to be as good a cutting horse as he is beautiful once Rowdy finishes training him. And this next big fella is Cisco, and we have high hopes for him, too."

Cisco was coffee-brown with black eyes and he jerked his head up and down, as if nodding agreement. Suzie laughed at the sight. "Hey, boy," she said to him. "You're a confident fella. I like that."

He nickered and pawed his foot on the ground. Tucker chuckled beside her, and she was suddenly very aware of how close they were standing. Her pulse skipped.

"I think he's going to be competitive," she said, running her hand down the side of his neck, which had Bow sticking his head over his stall gate and nudging her shoulder for some loving. "Okay, didn't mean to leave you out, handsome. You're both going to be competitive and confident."

Tucker was watching her with a thoughtful smile. "They like you. They haven't been this friendly to anyone. Rowdy may have you out here helping him if you're not careful."

"I think I'll stick to flower arranging. No offense, boys," she added, giving each horse one last rub on the nose. "This barn is really old, isn't it? I mean, I think I heard your nana talking about it to someone."

"Yeah, it is. My great-great-grandfather built it back in the early 1900s. We've diligently taken care of it over the years. Those harnesses hanging on the back wall over there are antiques, too.

"Come here and I'll show you the saddles." He opened the door to the tack room and flipped on a light.

Suzie entered first. It was a long room with saddle racks along both sides of the room. On a ranch with this many boys, one expected there to be a lot of saddles and there were. "Wow!" she gasped. "That is amazing. How many of them are there?"

Tucker moved into the narrow room with her, and when she looked up at him, butterflies immediately erupted in her chest.

"There's about thirty in this room," Tucker said, holding her gaze before looking back at the saddle. "One for each boy and then everyone else's. We have a separate place for the hands to store theirs. But these aren't what I was going to show you. It's those at the back."

"Oh." Suzie was flustered by the way she was reacting and moved quickly toward the back wall, putting space between them.

On the back wall were six saddles, three on the bottom row and three sitting on wall-mounted racks above the bottom three. It was clear these weren't regular saddles. The tooling on them was too fancy and there were also things written on them.

"These were my grandfather's, my great-grandfather's and my great-great-grandfather's and grandmother's saddles."

"Oh, wow, they are amazing."

"Yeah, it shows how, given a little tender loving care, things last. The initials TRM on this one here stand for Tucker Randolph McDermott, who was my great-great-granddad. This saddle is actually mine now. I just can't bring myself to take it out of the place it's always set, so I leave it here to remind the boys of the roots this place has."

"I wouldn't be able to take it from here, either." She ran her fingertips over the smooth leather. "Abe hanging out with the guys today was a good sign," she said, glancing at him, "I think he's going to get over this abandonment issue, just like I have." She couldn't look away from him.

Tucker touched her then; he lifted his hand and cupped her jaw gently. "I think so. Whatever you need, I'm here. I'm glad we're talking now, like this."

She nodded, fighting the urge to close her eyes and enjoy the warmth of his touch. A noise outside the open door broke the moment and she smiled, stepping away. "Thank you. I think it's going to be much better for Abe. I guess I'd better go in now."

"Right," he agreed, tucking the hand that had been cupping her jaw into the front pocket of his jeans. "I'll go check on the boys. It's time for even the older fellas to turn in. I'll send Abe your way."

"Great. I'd appreciate that." She was moving fast now—needing space between them. She was not comfortable with the way his touch melted her mind and made her respond.

"Talk to you tomorrow," she said, and left him there. It took resolve on her part not to jog across the lot to the porch.

Not being angry and blaming Tucker for Gordon's death created a new problem. It allowed the attraction she'd been fighting to gain footing.

What was she going to do about that?

Chapter Twelve

Tucker wasn't in the best of moods when he woke the next morning. He was in trouble and he knew it. He was falling for Suzie, and he wasn't at all sure how to handle that.

Gordon weighed heavy on his mind all night. The guilt weighed heaviest—despite accepting that his friend was a marine, just as he was, and accepted the risk and responsibility that came with taking that oath.

He was in his SUV heading to the office when his cell phone rang. "Good morning, Pepper," he said, having seen the caller ID.

"Tucker, you need to get back out here," Pepper demanded, not bothering to greet him. "We've got problems here in the horse barn."

He could hear the seriousness in his friend's voice. "What's going on?"

"You just need to get out here and don't tell anyone why until you meet me at the barn. I need to show you something in the tack room." Tucker started to say he'd just been there last night but Pepper wasn't one to make demanding, ominous remarks so Tucker didn't waste time, instead he made a quick U-turn and pressed the gas.

He walked into the barn a few minutes later, managing to avoid being stopped by anyone as he arrived. Pepper was waiting.

"What's up, Pepper?"

He shook his head. "You're not gonna like it." He led the way to the tack room and unlocked it. He never locked the tack room. That room had been unlocked for all of Tucker's life.

"I got here at sunup and saw the door open. The boys know the rules."

The rule being that no matter what—the door to the tack room was *always* closed to protect the saddles and the other gear. Tucker replayed the night before, knowing he'd shut the door securely when he and Suzie had left. It had been nearly eleven o'clock by that time.

Pepper looked over his shoulder. "This is what I found." He pushed open the door and let Tucker inside. Pepper slipped in and closed the door behind them.

Tucker's heart jerked, his trained eye instantly going to the back wall. His saddle, the one that had belonged to his great-great-granddad, had been destroyed. It was spray-painted red and black, and the discarded spray cans had been thrown on the ground beside it.

From where Tucker stood at the far end of the room, it didn't look as though anything could repair the ruined handcrafted leather. His great-great-grandfather had hand-tooled the designs himself, the hours and hours of labor and artistry now destroyed. Unless something could remove the paint it was ruined, but even then it would never be the same.

Tucker's mouth went dry; the heat of anger swept through him like a grassfire. Swift and charring.

"I'm sorry, Tucker."

Tucker had to clear the lump out of his throat. "Not your fault, Pepper." He forced himself to walk the endless length of the room to the saddle. Close up, it was as bad as he'd thought. Vandalism at its highest. The letters TRM were filled with paint so thick that even the groove where Great-great-granddad Tucker had dug his tool into the leather was almost invisible.

Unless the culprit had worn gloves, the cans at his feet would make identifying the responsible party easy—if his fingerprints were on record. Tucker seriously doubted gloves had been worn. But he knew it didn't matter. He knew who had done this.

This was the work of an angry teen. And Tucker hated it, hated thinking what he was thinking, and knowing with certainty in his heart who the prints would reveal.

Abe wasn't getting better, as Suzie hoped.

"Who else has seen this, Pepper?"

"No one, I don't think. I locked it up right after I found it and called you." Pepper had worked at the ranch since being hired on as a teen by Tucker's granddad in the early years when he'd first started the ranch. He knew the sentimental value that saddle held for Tucker. "There is a lot of hurt in this."

"Yeah. I know I don't have to tell you, but we need to keep this to ourselves for right now."

"I figured as much, for more reasons than one. I'm thinking Rowdy and Lucy's wedding doesn't need to be marred by this, if possible."

"Exactly. And the other is, I need to get the prints."

"Not that you need the prints if my, and I'm sure your, suspicion is correct?"

Pepper knew the boys, and had seen every kid who'd come through Sunrise Ranch since its inception. He was a keen observer of behavior—both of human and horse. Not much got by him and that was why the wise older cowboy was such a valuable asset to the ranch. Tucker laid a hand on his shoulder. "I need some time. I'll do an official investigation and gather evidence, then we can clean this up and no one will be the wiser. Till then, the door stays locked. No one is going to need a saddle out of here till after the wedding, anyway."

"You got it," Pepper said, as they slipped out and he locked up behind them.

Tucker left; he needed to think. He'd learned what was valuable in life and it wasn't things acquired, whether they were sentimental or valuable. He'd live, even though he hated what had been done to the antique. The question was—what was the best thing to be done for Abe? And though a man was considered innocent till proven guilty, Tucker had good instincts honed from years of experience and this had Abe written all over it.

The church looked absolutely beautiful, but it didn't even compare to Lucy as she stood in the doorway beside her father as the wedding music began. Suzie had come to love the beautiful blonde in the short time they'd known each other.

"She looks like a princess doll," B.J. said, the moment he spotted Lucy standing in the door of the church.

"Wow," Sammy echoed beside him.

Wes leaned forward. "Shhh, hold it down, little

dudes. You're going to make Rowdy jealous." He chuckled, and Suzie and everyone else did, too.

Rowdy was so handsome in his black suit. His white shirt set off his jet-black hair and that dazzling smile was as large as it could get. His eyes twinkled watching Lucy. She practically floated down the aisle toward him.

She did look like a fairy princess meeting her prince. The music came to a halt as she and her father reached the front of the church. Beside Rowdy, Tucker and Morgan looked just as handsome.

Jolie was Lucy's bridesmaid, and her best friend from school had flown in to be her maid of honor. Kimberly had gleaming blond hair and her emerald eyes kept roaming to Tucker. Since she and Lucy had gone to dinner last night with Lucy's parents, and since Tucker had missed the rehearsal, they hadn't met until just before the wedding.

Suzie took Kimberly's immediate infatuation with Tucker as a sure sign she'd been right. Tucker affected all women the way he affected her. It made her feel better.

Somewhat. Thoughts of standing beside him in the tack room had her confused.

Pushing those thoughts away, she concentrated on the ceremony. Lucy's father had given her away and now Rowdy had taken her hand and led her to stand before the preacher.

Watching the sweet ceremony, Suzie's heart swelled and she prayed they would live a long and happy life together. She prayed for a happy ever after for them.

"Are they married yet?" B.J. hissed, looking over his shoulder at Wes. "Can I whoop?"

The preacher chuckled, since there was no use pretending that everyone hadn't heard his loud whisper. "Not yet, son, hold your horses."

That got laughter everywhere.

"Hey, I'm just as anxious as he is." Rowdy grinned at B.J., then winked at Lucy.

The pastor went on to tell how God had created marriage and what a sacred union it was between a man and a woman. And then he pronounced them man and wife.

Rowdy almost kissed Lucy before the preacher told him to. Suzie misted up with tenderness, she was so happy for them.

Feeling a gentle prick of awareness, her gaze shifted, and there was Tucker watching her. As her eyes met his he gave a slight lift to his lips and then the music started and he moved to offer his arm to Kimberly. The boys were clapping and whooping and hooting as Rowdy and Lucy headed toward the doors. Then came Tucker and Kimberly—who was smiling up at him as if he'd just slayed dragons for her.

Jolie and Morgan came striding by next, looking like the perfect couple. From the front row, Nana had turned to watch everyone leave.

Did Suzie's expression convey some of the internal turmoil being around Tucker threw her into? She'd never been able to hide her feelings well, but in this instance it was purely about crazy, mixed-up emotions that even she didn't understand.

Or didn't want to understand.

The words echoed in the back of her thoughts, disturbing yet…completely true.

Tucker stood to the side of the barn, watching the festivities. Rowdy and Lucy were dancing their first dance to Clint Black's duet with his wife, Lisa Hartman Black, "When I Said I Do." They looked so happy. It was as if no one else was in the room.

He was glad for them, though as the evening wore down, his mood was growing darker and darker. Suzie looked beautiful, and she was avoiding him. Not to mention that Lucy's friend was a really nice woman, but it had taken him half the night to politely extract himself from her company.

As Tucker visited with relatives and friends his gaze kept finding Suzie in the crowd. She was having a good evening and he was glad he'd chosen to keep the vandalism hidden until after the wedding. Everyone deserved to loosen up a little and that went double for Suzie. She'd know soon enough what Abe had done, but she wouldn't know it until he had absolute proof.

Raking his hands through his hair, he wondered if his life could get any more complicated.

Suzie kept her distance from him and had been busy helping with the reception, so that made it easy. But when he saw her slip out the side door, he was immediately torn, wanting to follow her and make sure she was okay.

The tension he'd been feeling all day wound tighter inside of him. After a moment, he made the decision and slipped out the side door, too.

The cool night enveloped him—one of those perfect summer nights two people could get lost in. The moon washed everything in a silvery glow that elongated shadows and promised romance.

He fought that thought. His frustration twisting tighter, he scanned the landscape, searching for Suzie. It almost seemed that you could see a mile in the moon's glow.

Behind him in the barn, Clint and Lisa's song finished and the live band took over with another slow romantic ballad. Spotting Suzie's silhouette over at the rear of the horse barn beside the round pens, his gut twisted as he headed that way. He just needed to check on her and make sure she was all right, he told himself.

"Suzie," he called softly, with twenty feet to go before reaching her, not wanting to startle her.

"Hi," she said, glancing over her shoulder. She remained where she was, with her elbows resting on the railing, watching the colts playing in the moonlight in the center of the arena.

He moved to stand beside her. "Everything okay?"

She took a deep breath and didn't look at him. He placed his elbows on the railing, too.

"It was a beautiful wedding."

"Yes, it was. Like I said, my brothers are lucky men."

"I think so, too. Jolie and Lucy are wonderful."

"I consider Gordon my brother, too. He was a lucky man, also."

She slanted her head toward him. "I'm glad he had this amazing place to grow up in. He never really talked about his family life before the ranch, but I know it wasn't good. He preferred to talk about the ranch and all of you."

"Most of the boys don't talk about their past. When the pain of rejection eases after they arrive, and the joy of living seeps into them, they choose not to talk about it."

She took that in silently. "And yet they still hurt some, don't they?"

"Sure they do. Our past never leaves us. You and I know that. It stays with us forever. But we learn to live with the scars. To share space with them. The good and the bad." He let his words sink in. "Wes and Joseph have moved on and are seeking their own lives. They've come to peace with their lives. I sometimes believe that Wes is still slaying memories that haunt him. He has a rage that hides inside him despite the joy you see.... A little like Abe."

"But Wes is so happy," she said, before he could move on. "I wouldn't think he was still fighting his past."

"Sometimes what you see on the outside isn't what is truly going on inside. Wes, he's always been a great cheerleader for the boys and will make you laugh at the drop of a hat, but he's fighting something. He chooses to fight it alone. Something I'm hoping Abe will choose not to do."

Suzie turned her back to the arena and leaned against the bars, studying him across one shoulder. He moved toward her, the soft, sweet scent of her drawing him. She wore a sleeveless pale apricot dress that shimmered against her skin in the soft light. She was radiant in the moonlight. And his thinking got fuzzy when he looked into her eyes.

"And Joseph, what a sweet guy."

Tucker had to focus. "Joseph is. They don't get any better than that kid." Tucker didn't want to talk about the boys. His gaze dropped to her lips and he fought the strong need to kiss her. Her skin looked so silky in the golden light.

"You're a nice guy, too, Tucker." The words were soft, and the she probably wished she hadn't said them the moment they crossed her pretty lips. But they meant the world to him.

She would never know how deep they went. "I try. Strong and dependable are what I strive for."

"I..." She started to say something but the words trailed off.

They were both caught in an invisible force that seemed unshakable. He touched her shoulder ever so lightly, traced the curve, and held her gaze. Fighting every instinct inside of him to maintain his distance, it all went out the window when she shifted slightly toward him, as if drawn to him. Leaning forward, he hesitated for a second, holding her gaze, then touched his lips to hers.

Time stalled.

His hand came up under her chin, lifting it slightly as she stepped into the shadow of his body.

The kiss was gentle, a prelude to what could be between them, and bittersweet at the same moment because of what couldn't be. But for a brief moment he felt freedom and peace...and promise.

Reality slammed into him full force.

He pulled away, knowing that even if Suzie gave in to this right now, in this moment, beneath the romance of the sky and the soft music from the wedding reception, she would feel as though it was a mistake.

Grabbing the arena rails, he turned to stare at the colts once more.

Every nerve in his body hummed with the need to pull her close, to wrap her fully in his embrace and kiss her soundly...and freely. But that would never happen.

She had turned back to the horses, too. "I don't know what this is. There is too much past."

Tucker closed his eyes, her words sank in deeper. "Gordon was a marine and a good one. The burden of his death is hard on me, but I only take it to a point. After that point, though, it was his choice. Taking that away wrongs him, Suzie. You said it yourself the other day at the playground. It steals some of the pride he had for his country and the sacrifice he was willing to make for it. For you and Abe. It's unjust." He ground the last words out with stern assurance and knew the truth at last. Knew he could no longer steal that from his brother-in-arms. It wasn't his to steal. "Gordon would have done what he did for any of his unit. It wasn't about me, Suzie." The truth hit him in that moment. It was raw and powerful, and it was freeing.

He turned to stare into Suzie's eyes. "It wasn't about me." He almost laughed, he felt so free in that moment. "Gordon was my brother and I hated what happened. But I'm letting go, Suzie, because he didn't give his life for me. He gave it for his fellow marine—his marine brother. He would have done it for anyone in that unit."

She stared at him, and he realized that he'd taken her by the arms sometime in the past minute. He gently tugged her toward him again, hugging her with relief. "You felt what I felt when I kissed you."

"Tucker, this is all too soon."

"This is not just a fleeting infatuation and you know it."

"Tucker, I've just stopped resenting you. This…" She waved her hand between them, having backed out of his arms. "This is too soon. I'm not ready."

"Not ready or scared?"

Her brows dipped. "Both. Yes, I feel this, this electricity that hums between us, just as well as you do."

He smiled at that admission. "Do you, now?"

Her eyes flashed. "Don't tease me. This is important."

"Oh, it's important. Believe me, I know that. I've felt this bond with you from day one and denied it. But after that kiss, whether it should have happened or not, there is no more denying. Suzie, that kiss gave me clarity to see through the fog of guilt. I see the truth. So you know how important that was for me? Life changing."

She backed a step away from him. "I came here for Abe. I can't get involved with you or anyone right now. Abe couldn't handle it."

The saddle vandalism. How had he forgotten about that? He'd been too caught up in the emotions of the moment.

"I can only think about Abe right now," she said, her eyes full of turmoil. Spinning away, she hurried back toward the barn and the festivities.

Tucker started to go after her, every instinct wanted to. Instead he watched her leave. He needed time to think.

He'd been an idiot kissing her.

What had he thought it would accomplish?

That was the problem... He hadn't thought at all.

He'd brought his fingerprint kit and now was the perfect time to put his mind where it belonged and take fingerprints and evidence from the tack room. Was it what he wanted to be doing? No. He wanted to be kissing Suzie.

Not finding out if her son had destroyed a family memory.

Chapter Thirteen

Two days after the wedding, Suzie had orders for a funeral flooding in and it kept her busy. She needed to be busy. Though she hated that the poor man had passed away, that was the nature of her business. She just had to do it to the best of her ability so that her flowers gave joy or comfort in someone's time of need. It was the aspect of the business that she loved.

Abe had continued to be distant and aloof, though he was spending every minute he wasn't in school with Wes and Joseph. She kept thinking about what Tucker had said about Wes and prayed that Wes might have a good influence on Abe. The door opened and Chili stuck his head in. "Place is looking good."

"Thanks, Chili. Have you come for another flower arrangement?"

He got a hound-dog expression. "Ha! Ruby won't hardly talk to me these days."

Drewbaker stepped in beside him. "She sure won't. I told him to send her another arrangement, but he's chicken."

"I'm not falling for that again."

"Well, Nana's a nice lady. I'm sure time will heal this situation."

She thought about her own situation with Tucker. Things had gotten so complicated.

Drewbaker got a twinkle in his eyes. "True love always finds a way is what I told him."

Suzie chuckled. "You two are a mess. I meant to tell you that I enjoyed your fiddle and banjo playing with the band."

They beamed and the conversation switched to their music. Suzie had learned to just keep on working when they came by or she might not get any work done. Today she enjoyed the distraction they gave her from thinking about Tucker.

However, as soon as they walked out the door, five minutes didn't pass before Tucker came walking in.

She hadn't forgotten their kiss. She didn't think she would ever forget it.

"Suzie, we need to talk," he said, before he had the door closed. His tone alerted her instantly.

"What's wrong?"

He placed a manila envelope on the counter. She glanced from it to him.

"What's this?"

His expression grim, he pushed the envelope toward her. "It's about Abe."

She felt the color drain from her face and her stomach turn over. Tucker wouldn't look so disturbed if this wasn't something bad. She knew him well and while she had no control over her expressions, he was the opposite.

"What's in that?" She wanted to recoil. Foreboding hung like the stench of bad eggs in the air.

"You need to look at this." His gaze shifted, turning amazingly tender.

She inhaled a shaky breath, disturbed even more.

"It's going to be all right, Suzie. But you need to see these pictures and then we'll come up with a plan. Together."

She needed to sit down, but refused to give in to the weakness. She picked the envelope up and lifted the flap.

"What?" The word came out weakly as she pulled them out. There were five photos. Fingers shaking, she spread them on the counter.

They were of what had once been a beautiful saddle. It had been ruined with red and black spray paint, every inch a motley mixture of offensive coating. She swallowed the lump in her throat; it refused to go away. She didn't want to look at Tucker. Didn't want to see what she knew she was going to see in his eyes. The truth— but she had to. His eyes were full of compassion when she finally lifted hers to meet his.

"Please tell me this wasn't Abe."

His lips flattened together, momentarily locked, as if he didn't want to tell her. "I took fingerprints before I could talk to you. I'm sorry, but they belong to Abe."

She grasped the edge of the counter for support. "When? When did he do this?"

"The night that I showed the saddles to you. Pepper found it like this when he came to work that morning."

She closed her eyes, not wanting to believe it. "Wait. You *knew* this the night of the wedding?"

"I knew, but I didn't know who. I had my suspicions, but no proof."

"And you didn't tell me? You kissed me! Instead of telling me something this important—"

"I know you're angry at me for that. That wasn't meant to happen. But this isn't about me kissing you, Suzie." He waved at the photos. "This is separate. This is about Abe."

"And you think I'm not aware of that." She fought the urge to snatch the vase and throw it against the wall. She never threw things.

"His fingerprints are all over everything." Tucker inhaled heavily. "There is a lot of anger here. Suzie, this was directed at me. You can't tell it in this picture but that is the saddle with TRM engraved on it."

"No," she gasped, her hand going to her heart as the sentimental value of this heirloom dawned. "I'm so sorry. It was priceless."

"It was. But it's not the saddle itself that matters, it's why he chose this saddle, my saddle, out of those sitting there. I don't believe that was a random act."

She shook her head. "No. I don't believe it was. Remember that noise we heard? Do you think he overheard us talking? Maybe looked in and saw us?"

"Those are my same suspicions. I think he heard me talking about the initials and knew that was my saddle. No one but Pepper knows about this. He discovered it and called me, keeping it locked up until I could gather the evidence."

At the word *evidence* Suzie couldn't stop the tears. Couldn't stop the dam that broke. This was San Antonio all over again.

Tucker watched her tears flow, wanting to pull Suzie into his arms but knowing she didn't want him to. He'd really messed up kissing her before they'd made it through the trouble facing them. And now he couldn't even console her.

Couldn't console the woman he loved.

The truth settled over him with the ease of rightness. Rightness for him, but not for Suzie.

"Look at me, Suzie," he said, gently. "This is going to be all right. There was anger and vandalism here, but not real violence. He just expressed his frustration. If I believed differently I'd suggest radical steps. But I've seen a lot in my life and this isn't the end of the world. I know it feels like it to you. And I knew that when I had to come and tell you, and that was why I dreaded it. Still, it's not the end of the world. It's time for action."

"I've called the therapist." She dried her tears. Took a deep breath and nodded. "I was going to talk to her myself first. But I'll call her and tell her what has happened and see what she thinks I should do. If she says bring him in before she sees me first, then that's what I'll do."

"I'll talk to the counselor with you if you need me."

"Thank you. But I can do it."

He put the photos back in the envelope and closed it. "Okay, but let me know if I can help. I'm not pursuing this officially."

"Thank you." She crossed her arms, hugging herself. As if giving herself comfort that he longed to give her. "I'm fine. I better call her now."

Feeling lousy, he gave a short nod and left.

He had to find a way to fix this, but he was feeling out of control. And he had never done out of control well.

As he was climbing into his SUV he caught sight of Drewbaker and Chili sitting on the church pew. Both of them were grinning like hyenas and giving him a thumbs-up.

Crazy old fellas—if they only knew.

Chapter Fourteen

Suzie dried her tears after Tucker left and called the counselor. She was done crying. And she was done letting her son get away with something so wrong. That saddle was irreplaceable. After talking with the counselor she hung up, locked the door and went to the ranch.

She couldn't get over how understanding Tucker had been. It was amazing, really.

When she pulled into the yard and got out, she scanned the area looking for Abe.

B.J. spotted her and came hurrying toward her. "Hi, Suzie. You lookin' for your boy?"

Sweet kid. "Yes, I am. Have you seen him?" She gave him a hug and he returned it fiercely. He smelled of sweaty little boy and she was reminded of Abe at the age of eight. Oh, how life was simpler then. But that was then and this was now, and she had to stop wishing for the way things had been.

And so did Abe.

"He's mucking out stalls."

"Thanks, little man." She winked at him and headed that way.

"You're a nice momma."

She turned back at B.J.'s words. "Oh, thank you. You're a nice boy."

He giggled. "Thanks. I got to run. I got trash duty today."

She watched him race toward the chow hall. Then she headed toward the stables just as Abe was coming out.

"Hi, Abe, I need you to come with me," she said, firmly.

"Where?"

"I'll tell you on the way. Come on."

"I don't want to go."

She looked at him. "Abe, I didn't ask you." He stared at her and she held her gaze steady. There was a time to be firm and this was it. Making decisions alone had been hard. And she had to admit that there had been times when it was easier not to push issues. But that time had passed.

"Get in the car, Abe. Now."

His eyes flashed, but he did as she asked. Stomping to the other side of the car, he yanked open the door and slouched in the car seat.

"Buckle up," she said, as she got in. "We have a long drive."

He sat up then. "Are we going back home?"

She started the car and backed out. "No, Abe, this is our home now. And it's time you got used to that. Now buckle up."

He yanked the seat belt over and buckled it.

"I'm not sure if you thought destroying Tucker's saddle was going to make me give in and take you back to San Antonio. I'm not sure what you were thinking when you did such a horrible thing. But I can tell you that some things are going to change, Abe Kent. And the first thing is that you're going to see a counselor."

"I don't want to see a shrink!"

She turned onto the blacktop and kept her eyes on the road. She knew his expression wouldn't be good. "She's nice, Abe. She'll listen to anything you have to say. Anything you need to talk about that is bothering you. But you have to open up. You have to let go of what is eating at you."

"I'm not talking."

She glanced at him. "I'll take you anyway. You can sit in her office, silent for every appointment, but you'll be there anyway. This has to stop. And you will not manipulate me into giving you what you want through bad behavior."

Was she doing this the right way? She didn't know, but one thing she did know was that giving in and being soft hadn't worked. She'd been so thankful when Dr. Livingston had said she did evening appointments and she'd had a cancellation. It had clearly been a gift from God, and she'd grabbed the opportunity immediately.

Still, the miles ticked by slowly after that. He didn't speak and she felt it best to not push any more. This was for his own good. She decided the time would be better spent in prayer.

For both of them.

Moonlight cast Tucker's front yard in a silvery glow. Alone, in shadow of his porch, he was still reeling from the afternoon in Suzie's shop. He was free. Despite every doubt and every feeling of guilt and remorse he'd carried over the past two years, he was finally free of it. Free because he'd realized finally that Gordon had done what he had to do—that it hadn't been about giving his life for Tucker but instead about honoring the oath he'd taken when he'd become a marine.

The pain was still there, the wish that he could turn back time and change what had happened. But the burden that he'd carried was no longer there.

But where did that leave him with Suzie?

Did that mean he was free to want Suzie?

Because he did.

He wanted her in his life and he wanted her to want him...to want a life with him. To love him. But was that a possibility? Was he free to want that?

Gordon had been his brother—maybe not by blood but he was by everything else that counted. His mind kept looping back to kissing Suzie in the moonlight. Those thoughts had brought him outside to sit on his porch, letting the calm of the night seep in as he let everything settle in his thoughts.

She wasn't ready for a relationship and he understood that. They had to help Abe first. He understood that and wanted that.

But he also understood what he wanted. And despite the misgivings, he'd fallen for Suzie.

Understood that he loved Suzie and he'd do anything for her. He could only hope that she might return his feelings someday, given time.

Just as had been the plan all along, their priority was Abe. But, from here on out, Suzie was going to know that she was special. That she wasn't alone.

When his phone rang, he glanced at the caller ID fully expecting it to be the dispatcher at the office. He was startled when he realized it was Suzie calling at eleven-thirty. Grabbing the phone up from the table, he punched the button, his heart kicking up a ruckus. "Suzie, everything okay?"

She hesitated. "Tucker." Her voice was quiet. "Can we talk?"

He sat up. "Sure."

"I mean in person."

"Of course. I'll be right there. Meet me on the porch in ten minutes."

"Okay, thank you."

"Anytime."

Her voice had been so soft, so full of the weight of concern, that he knew this was about Abe. But she'd called, and that mattered a great deal to him.

Heading back into the house, he pulled on a T-shirt with his jeans, yanked on his boots and jogged down the steps to his truck, opting for his personal vehicle instead of his official SUV. He was actually not on duty for three days. He was off all weekend unless there was a major catastrophe.

Within the ten minutes he'd allotted himself, he was driving into the yard of the ranch and pulling to a halt in front of the porch. He stepped lightly as he walked up the steps, not sure if Suzie was already outside sitting in the shadows.

"Hey," came her sweet voice from the swing.

"Hey, yourself," he said, continuing to keep his steps quiet, not wanting to disturb anyone inside. "Mind if I sit down?"

She shook her head and he sank into the cushion on the porch swing beside her. Her hair was still damp from her shower and she wore an oversize green T-shirt with a pair of black lounging pants. Her legs were tucked in between them, and her bare feet peeked from beneath the hem of her pants. She looked comfortable and relaxed, but her expression was pinched and her eyes weary.

He laid a comforting hand on her calf, patting gently before laying his arm across the back of the swing. "How are you? What's on your mind?"

She took a deep breath. "A lot. I called the counselor right after you left and she was so accommodating. She had an evening appointment open and urged me to bring Abe in to see her. So I came to the ranch and basically demanded Abe come with me. He wasn't happy, but he got in the car and I took him."

"Sometimes, you have to be firm. I know, if you're worried about the emotional state of your child that makes it all the more difficult." He toyed with a damp strand of her hair. "Not that I have parenting experience—"

"Working with all these boys at the ranch gives you more experience than I have. Don't kid yourself. I value your experience."

He gave her hair a gentle tug. "Thanks. I want to help and I'm glad the doc could see y'all. How was it?"

"Well, I told Abe before we got there that his bad behavior wouldn't be rewarded. That this was our home and that we would not be going back to San Antonio, no matter how much he acted up. After I said that, he didn't talk to me the rest of the hour-long drive to the appointment."

She worried a spot on the swing's arm—rubbing on it and thinking. "When we were in with Dr. Livingston and I brought up the saddle, he just crossed his arms, closing us out, and stared out the window."

"That's tough."

"Yeah, but Dr. Livingston didn't act like it was uncommon." Suzie sighed. "Abe didn't talk for thirty minutes. Just sat there. Dr. Livingston started talking to me, explaining that she'd asked us both in there tonight, but that on the other trips she would see Abe alone. Toward the end of the session she did ask me to step out and she spent a short time alone with him. I think to see if he had anything to say when I wasn't in the room. I'm not certain, but he may have talked a little with her."

"How is he now? Or on the ride home?"

"He was quiet." She looked at him then. "But I think he was resolved. Hopefully he understands that I care, and this is for his own good. I told him that, and maybe some of it is getting through. And hopefully he knows he's going to have to accept that Sunrise Ranch—I mean, Dew Drop is his home."

"Sunrise Ranch is okay, it is his home."

"No, actually, it isn't, Tucker. That's one of the things I wanted to talk to you about. This has been wonderful as a temporary layover. And he will continue to go to school out here, but I need to make a home for him so that he feels like we're a family again. Because the truth is, he isn't exactly like all of these wonderful boys here. He does still have a mother who cares for him. He hasn't been abandoned by both his parents. I hate that so much for the boys, that they have, but Abe hasn't. And this has made me more than realize that we need our own place. I can bring him to school each morning, and he can stay and hang out, work on the ranch whatever needs to be done. But at night he'll go home to his own bed in his own room."

"Okay, I get it. He really may need that separation. So, what can I do to help?"

"Well, I'm going upstairs to the apartment in the morning and I'm going to start cleaning and arranging. It shouldn't take me long at all. We'll start there, and then, that will keep him close. It will give him a place to call home. I hope that doesn't hurt any feelings, but at the moment this is about Abe."

"That's fine. You're absolutely right. In the meantime, I'm wondering if he would enjoy a roundup—an authentic roundup out in the more remote areas of the ranch. It would give him time to see what the ranch is really all about. He's taken to riding with ease and this is more than just riding a fence looking for a hole that donkeys escaped through. The boys love it. And I have a long weekend, and Rowdy mentioned to me that when he got home from his honeymoon, the cattle would have to be driven from the east pastures over to the west pastures. Only problem is it takes two days and requires camping out one night."

She sat straighter as he spoke and smiled, excitement in her eyes. "Oh, Tucker, I think he would love that. It sounds so, so exciting."

He chuckled. "Well, it's a cattle drive. As a cowboy, I love the drive and never miss it if I can help it. There is just something about being on the trail like that that takes you back to the basics. We'd originally put this one off because Rowdy's gone, but we can do it without him. And we could have it set up to start tomorrow if you want."

"I think it's a great plan. Gordon talked about loving the cattle drive, too. I think I remember him saying there was a pass you had to take them through and a cabin with corrals that had been built back in the early days of the ranch."

"That's right. You could come, too. If you think you could take off."

"I'll see what I can do. I might be able to have some-one cover for me for the afternoon, and Camy's already set to work on Saturday."

"Then I'll call Morgan and Dad, and see what I can set up."

She smiled; there was relief and anticipation in that smile. "I'll talk to Abe as soon as he wakes up and fill him in on everything you and I have set up. I'll let you know how it goes."

"We have a plan."

Her eyes melted his heart when she looked at him. "Yes, we do. And that's why I called you, because I knew you would help me think this through and come up with something good. Thank you."

She would never know how much those words meant to him.

Standing, and knowing he needed to put space be-tween them before he messed up and pulled her into his arms, he took her hand and tugged her from the swing. "That means a lot to me. Now, how about you head on inside and get some rest. You're going to need it."

She took a step toward him, as if she were going to come in for a hug—or to rest her head against his thun-dering heart. But she stopped suddenly.

"Thank you. See you tomorrow, Tucker McDermott."

He watched her go. Only after she was inside and the door firmly shut behind her did he leave.

He whistled all the way home.

And didn't sleep a wink for the rest of the night.

Chapter Fifteen

The morning had been a whirlwind. Suzie had actually slept after Tucker left. She'd set her alarm for 5:00 a.m. and by 6:00 a.m. she was dressed in roundup-appropriate attire—just in case Tucker was able to organize everything as discussed. She went into Abe's room, sat on the edge of his bed and gently shook his shoulder to get him to wake up. "Abe, honey, I need to talk to you before I head to the shop."

Groggily he opened his eyes. "Why?"

She needed them to be back on good terms. This was killing her. Leaning down she cupped his face in her hands and laid her cheek against his. "I love you, Abe. I love you so much." When she rose up, she could see a brief glimpse of her son behind the mask of indifference. It was her hope.

"Look, I know last night was hard on you. But I've been doing some thinking." She told him of her plan to move them into town—that he would go to school here and could be friends with the boys, but that they needed their own place. She said she was going to begin preparing the apartment so that the following week they could move in.

"For real?"

"Yes, and since our things are already stored there it shouldn't take too long to get it cleaned and painted. It's nothing fancy but it'll be ours."

He sat up, as if excited at the thought, which thrilled her. Then she told him what Tucker was doing, and asked him if he wanted to help with the roundup, if they had it. She worried briefly that he would say no.

"So, you're coming, too?"

She nodded. "Unless you'd rather I didn't. But when we get home, you can come into town with me and you and I will work on the apartment."

She was relieved to see excitement filter into his eyes. "Okay. Then that sounds good. I'd... Mom, I'd like you to go."

She very nearly started crying. Had that been part of the problem? He'd felt they were at a distance, too? "Then if you don't mind, let Tucker know that we're going if he gets it set up. He'll call me and I'll come straight here. I just need to get to town and line up someone to run the shop while I'm out." She'd been so blessed to have Camy, the teen was so reliable and she really enjoyed the shop. If only she could find someone to keep it open in the day at times like this, when she had to leave.

In the end, she found the most unlikely people to watch the shop and take orders for her—Chili and Drewbaker dropped by when she was about to start calling the handful of applicants.

"We're the perfect candidates for the job this morning," Chili said. "We're here right now, and you've got time to show us what to do before you hit the road to the ranch and hop on a horse."

"That's right. By the time you make a few calls and find one of them there applicants who could start at a minute's notice it could very well be noon, and then you'd have no time to show them anything. It could be a mess."

"A real mess," Chili agreed. "So, you can trust us two to watch the store for you, keep our hands off the flower arrangin' and take money for anything anyone wants to buy off the walls or counters. How does that sound?"

She laughed. "Y'all are really serious?"

"Sure we are," Drewbaker assured her. "You go spend time with your son and Tucker. And the rest of them kids at the ranch. You don't worry about a thing. We'll keep the doors open till Camy gets here and everything will be just fine."

She asked herself if she was just plain crazy. But no, these two sweethearts were competent men who, she was realizing, had hearts of gold.

"Then I accept your offer. I'll pay—"

"You'll do no such thing," Chili got out first, with Drewbaker saying something similar.

"We're doing this because we care and the good Lord saw fit to have us walk in here right when you needed us."

"Thank you, you two are sweethearts." She gave them each a hug then got busy showing them what they needed to know.

She'd run upstairs before opening that morning and had surveyed the apartment more thoroughly than she had the first day. She'd been intent then on staying at the ranch, but today she took in everything. It would work. With elbow grease and dust bunny attacking, she and Abe could be here by the following weekend. Abe could have a home of his own once more.

By noon she was heading back out to the ranch. Tucker had called as she was about to head out the door with a smile and a wave to Drewbaker and Chili.

"We're on," he said, his voice deep and excited against her ear. "We're having a roundup."

Suzie couldn't get to the ranch fast enough. This was about Abe, but in her heart of hearts she knew that something between her and Tucker had shifted. And the anticipation of exploring what and where that could lead had her pressing the gas pedal and driving hard for the ranch.

By midafternoon they were nearing the valley where the large herd waited for them. Tucker had explained that they were driving the small herd of cattle that was ahead of them from the pastures near the ranch house to join a larger herd over the rise. Then they would drive the two herds through the pass and over to fresh grazing lands. Then they would take the cattle in the pastures there and load them in cattle trailers bound for sale.

He explained some of the ins and outs of the cattle business as they rode beside each other, filling time, she knew, but it was interesting. She could tell that he loved the ranch and the ranching aspects of it.

"Can I ask you why, if you love this so much, you are sheriff instead of being more deeply involved in some aspect of the ranch? I know it's personal, and you don't have to tell me, but I'm curious."

"I hadn't planned on being a law enforcement officer. I'd planned on a career in the marines. But I got talked into running by my family. They knew it would help me to feel like I was making a difference. And it has. I needed that after what happened with Gordon."

She'd thought as much. "You're good with the boys, too. And you give back in that way."

He smiled at her, and her insides felt as if she'd just gone airborne over a speed bump.

"Thanks. I know I love this. And I'm glad you've come along."

"Thanks again for getting it together."

They reached the top of the hill. And below them was an enormous valley. Cattle were everywhere.

Tucker reined in his horse, and she did the same, bringing Cupcake to a standstill beside him.

"Wow. Unbelievable."

"Yeah, it's pretty awesome."

"It certainly is."

He pointed across the expanse to where Abe and the other teens were on the far edge of the cattle, riding back and forth, waving their ropes and moving the cattle forward. "Abe's holding his own. Look at him go after that stray that's running the wrong direction."

From this distance they couldn't see the boys' faces; she recognized individuals more from their mannerisms and body size. She had picked Abe out instantly. But so had Tucker. It touched her deeply that he was close enough to her son that he could do that from this distance.

"Oh, Tucker, he is having a blast."

"He's out there learning from some of the best. I'm glad we did this a week early, because it enabled Wes and Joseph to join in before they head back to Huntsville on Sunday. Wes is a cowboy of cowboys. He can't be outridden or out-roped. Abe is hanging close to him.

"You ready to ride down there and get involved?"

"I think so."

"Sure you are," he said with a wink. "I'm going to make a cowgirl out of you yet."

He laughed and nudged his horse into a lope. Cupcake followed—and, ready or not, Suzie rode!

It was amazing as they rode down the hill toward the cattle. She felt free with the wind flowing across her skin. She was very grateful for the day she'd spent riding the fence on Cupcake looking for the donkey escape route. At least she didn't feel as though she was going to topple off the horse and land in the dirt.

Tucker had explained earlier that she was to crowd the cattle so that they would leave the grass they were eating and move along with the others. Once moving, it was fairly easy to keep them going, but every so often one would lag behind or break for freedom. That was when she would have to work with Cupcake to get between the heifer and wherever it was she was trying to escape to.

That was the tricky part.

But for now, she was quite proud of the fact that she was pushing the cattle along almost as if she'd been born to do this. Of course, there was no telling how many roundups ole Cupcake had been involved in. The truth was that Suzie could probably drop the reins, and the horse would have gone on doing exactly what it was doing.

Even so, Suzie felt exhilarated with the ride.

Dust and mooing, mingled with the usual whoops and hoots of the boys, was the music of the day over the range. The sun lifted high and hot in the Texas sky—fitting for such an adventure, Suzie decided, though the beads of perspiration and grime weren't the most endearing aspects of the day.

No, there was no getting around the fact that a roundup was a hot job.

But Suzie found herself smiling most of the way. Smiling so much that her teeth kept drying out and her lips kept getting stuck. Not exactly glamorous, but Suzie could see now there was a reason cowboys were cowboys. There was definitely something about the process that drew a certain type of person.

She was startled to find that she *was* that sort of person. Of course, when her backside started aching it dawned on her that she might not be able to move the next day. Suddenly a cow broke and ran straight toward her, jolting her out of her daydreaming. Cupcake instantly tried to jump in front of the renegade, and Suzie nearly fell out of the saddle. Grabbing the saddle horn, she regained her balance. Then, determined to do her job, she tugged on the reins, wheeled Cupcake around, and they loped after the calf. The old horse knew exactly what she was doing. They rounded in front of the cow and, to Suzie's pride, the animal turned back. "We did it!" she exclaimed, patting Cupcake's neck as they fell back into the lineup.

She caught Tucker smiling at her. She gave him a thumbs-up.

"You're a natural," he called.

"I love it!" Anticipation for the rest of the day filled her. Now Suzie knew exactly why the boys whooped and yelled "Yee-haw!"

The cattle were mooing and plodding along the

streambed that went down the center of the ravine. It made for the perfect containment passage as they moved to the other side of the ranch.

"There's Nana," Suzie said, spying her in the valley.

Tucker grinned. She was cooking on her big barbecue pit, which she always pulled to the area behind her old truck. It was her version of a chuck wagon. "Nana married my grandfather and started driving her truck-wagon out to the roundups to feed the cowboys long before Dad had been born. It's a tradition."

"That's so wonderful. They must have been perfect for each other."

He looked at Suzie, she was so beautiful. "They were."

By the time they arrived, she had the sausage links hot and sizzling on the grill, and the tortillas warm and ready for a feast of sausage wraps followed by peach cobbler. The kids ate as if they hadn't seen food in a week, and even Suzie ate like a cowhand.

"How are you holding up?" he asked, moving to stand beside her.

She was standing real still as she ate, and he figured it might be because it hurt too bad to sit.

"Well, there are parts of my anatomy that I no longer feel, they've gone numb. And then there are other parts that are screaming in pain with every move I make."

He chuckled. "Thought that was why you were standing so stiffly."

"Yup. If I hadn't had such a great morning, I would kick you with my boot—but it would hurt too bad. And I have had the time of my life."

Her eyes were twinkling, and if he'd had a camera he'd have taken her picture.

"I'm sorry about the soreness. Riding does take some getting used to by greenhorns."

"Greenhorns! That's an understatement. And believe me, I have no idea how I'm going to climb back up into that saddle."

"Tucker will help you out," Nana called. "Don't you worry. I've got some great liniment I'll give you tonight that will help. Tucker, do you think the rain is going to hold off?"

He'd been studying the storm clouds and he could see his dad, Morgan and Chet, their top hand, over by the horses studying them, too. He wanted this experience to keep being positive. Rain added a whole different aspect to a roundup.

They especially didn't need the rain on the leg of the trip that was coming up. He could hear the river roaring up ahead as the stream turned and fed into the river that cut through Sunrise Ranch. The cattle would travel a short distance along the flowing river, but then an arm of the ravine would fork and the cattle would walk up an embankment and into the next section of the ranch.

The river flowed pretty good on a wet day, and since they'd had heavy rains upriver two days before, it would be rushing through this narrow, curved section and bottleneck farther downriver into some dangerous rapids.

Suzie was doing a good job riding beside nine-year-old Sammy at the moment. "Y'all stay on the left side of the cattle until we make it to the fork. You know the rules, Sammy," he called, and the kid gave him a nod. Sammy had learned to respect the river's power and Tucker knew he'd follow the rules.

Abe burst from the brush chasing a runaway heifer back into the herd. Then he pulled up beside them.

"That one gave me some trouble but I got it. This is great." He grinned. Tucker hadn't seen a smile from the kid in over a week.

"You're making a top hand, that's for certain," Tucker assured him. "Just stay away from the embankment."

The river was growing louder.

"I'll be back." Tucker rode up ahead through the cattle and toward where his dad, Morgan and Chet were taking the outer positions beside the herd. Each would take the position at the opening as they came to it, waving the cattle off from the water and in the right direction. Then he'd move forward as the next man and his section moved through. Tucker was the last.

Behind him, he heard a shout and saw Abe take off after another runaway. Sammy went to help. Up front, the first of the cattle had reached the river. Everything was going well as the last cattle began feeding through. Tucker took Chet's place on the flat rock that was buffeted by the river as it raced past. Now he could see the water was higher than they'd realized and building small rapids, even this far upstream. He glanced back at Suzie just as she had Cupcake block a calf from making a run for it. The move took her to the very back of the herd, where there were no animals between her and the river.

He was about to yell for her to move up when the heifer Abe and Sammy had followed into the woods came blasting from the trees as if its tail was on fire. Cupcake jumped but held her ground. Suzie, in her excitement to cut the calf off, jabbed the horse too hard with the heels of her boots. Cupcake did what she was asked and bolted after the calf. Everything seemed to happen in slow motion as Suzie came too close to the rock edge. Tucker urged his horse just as the calf twisted around and bolted straight into Cupcake.

Tucker watched, helpless, as the poor horse danced sideways then reared when the frightened calf rammed it.

Eyes wide, Suzie tried to hold on as Cupcake pawed the air. Though the horse found its balance it was too late for Suzie as she pitched backward out of the saddle and into the river below.

Chapter Sixteen

⁓

Tucker yelled to draw everyone's attention as Suzie hit the water and went under, then reappeared flailing in the swift current. The current dragged her under almost instantly. Tucker was already reaching for his rope before she hit the water—his heart stopping but his mind reacting.

Urging his horse forward, he charged down the bank along the uneven edge of the river. Praying for Suzie to reappear again, he knew he was her best shot as she came up fighting downstream. "Yah!" he shouted, urging his horse to increase speed as he started his rope spinning above his head. Suzie was fighting, but he had to get her before she rounded the curve. This throw mattered more than any other he'd ever made, he knew, as he sent the loop after her.

The rope sailed through the air—his prayers flying with it that God would direct its path.

It landed over her and she grasped it. Then he had his horse sit back on its heels and begin backing up, pulling her from the water.

"You got her," Sammy yelled.

When she was almost to shore, Tucker wrapped the rope around the horn and threw himself from the saddle. Letting one hand slip down the length of the line, he raced into the water, pulling her the rest of the way ashore.

His heart pounded as he hauled her from the water and into his arms. Terror gripped him, now that it was done, and he clung to her. She clutched him as he kissed the top of her head.

"You're okay now. You're safe," he said, caressing her hair, trying to soothe her nerves, unable to hold her tight enough.

"Thank you," she gasped. "I'm sorry. I shouldn't have put Cupcake in that position. You told me. I just got excited." She was rambling, looking up at him.

Tucker shook his head. "It's okay, Suzie. It wasn't your fault. You're safe, and that's all that matters."

He'd almost lost her before he'd had the opportunity to tell her he loved her.

"You saved me," she whispered, the sweetest expression on her face.

"I wasn't about to lose you. I love you, Suzie. I couldn't lose you." He kissed her long and hard, not caring who saw—not thinking about who was around. His only thought was he had the woman he loved in his arms and she was safe.

"Mom!" Abe yelled, racing up on his horse, bringing everything around them back into focus. Everyone was rallying around them.

"I'm okay. Tucker pulled me out," she said, though it was obvious what had happened. But Abe didn't seem interested in that. His face contorted in anger.

"You *kissed* him," he accused, his expression twisting with rage.

"Hey, son, hold on," Tucker said, stepping in.

"I'm not your son!" Abe exclaimed. Then he spun his horse and took off riding as fast as he could go.

"Abe," Suzie cried, her hand coming to her mouth.

"I'll get him." Anger, alarm and empathy forged together for the kid. Looking at the ashen expression on Suzie's face, he moved to his horse, swung into the saddle and went after Abe. "Take care of her," he called to his dad as he rode past.

"You need help?"

He shot his dad a look over his shoulder. "No, we'll meet you at the cabin." And he buckled down low and rode like the wind.

Abe needed a showdown. And he wanted it with Tucker.

And Tucker understood it, and was prepared to take whatever the kid needed to throw at him.

But one thing the kid needed to know was that his mother didn't deserve what he'd just thrown at her.

The threatening rain clouds that had hovered over the day had darkened ominously and the wind had picked up. Tucker rode hard, following the path through the trees that Abe had taken.

A storm wouldn't be good for the roundup. They'd planned on camping at the cabin halfway to their destination. But would they make it before the storm hit? He glanced at the sky, then back at the trail. His dad would handle it.

He had to find Abe. He had to get to the root of this…finally.

When he topped the ridge he spotted the boy riding

his horse across the open pasture at a crazy speed. The danger of the horse hitting a hole and breaking its leg, or falling and rolling on Abe, was high.

Yelling wouldn't do any good, since he suspected that even if Abe could hear him, he wouldn't listen.

Tucker prayed again that Abe would make it to the trees and be forced to slow down again. At the speed they were going, it didn't take long to cross the meadow.

Just as Tucker made it to the trees, the skies opened up with torrential rain. God answered prayers sometimes in mysterious ways. Abe would have to slow down now.

Ahead of him a lightning bolt lit the dark sky and thunder instantly shattered the silence with a deafening blast—reminding him of a mortar exploding.

It was too close.

"Abe!" he shouted, just as another bolt of lightning and crack of thunder split the sky open. Texas thunderstorms blew in with unexpected power some days, and this was not weather they'd anticipated when they'd chosen to bring the boys on this cattle drive. He heard a yell up ahead and plunged forward through the brush that tore at him. He pulled up short when he saw Abe, thrown from his horse, lying sprawled on his back. As soon as he saw Tucker, he tried to scramble up but couldn't. Within seconds Tucker was out of the saddle and kneeling beside him.

"Go away," Abe yelled, wiping rain and maybe tears from his face as he glared at Tucker.

Tucker ignored him, too intent on getting him to safety. "Are you hurt? We need to get out of this."

"I can get myself out of this. I don't need you. Stay away from my mother."

Lightning cracked and thunder rolled and the sound of a tree splintering could be heard somewhere not too far away.

"Where does it hurt?" Tucker demanded. His commanding tone, one developed and fine-tuned in war zones, left no room for denial. His unwavering gaze locked on to Abe's.

"My ankle," Abe snapped, giving in.

Tucker wasted no time. Slipping his arm under Abe's, he hauled the teen up. "Here we go, roles reversed from our first meeting."

Abe grunted, and grimaced with pain.

"I'm going to get us out of this weather before we get struck by lightning or hit by a falling tree. You can blast me with whatever you want once you're safe. Hang on."

Abe winced as Tucker hauled him up and over his shoulder. Intent on his mission to get the kid to safety, Tucker moved at a fast pace through the woods.

"Where are you going?" Abe asked, his hands pressing against Tucker's shoulder blades to balance himself.

"There's a cave near here where we can sit out the storm. Rowdy discovered it when we were kids. You were heading right to it and didn't know it." Tucker didn't say it out loud, but he looked at that coincidence as divine intervention. He'd put them not fifty yards from the cave.

In the woods, it was almost as dark as night with the storm clouds blotting out the sun above the canopy of trees. But even still, he knew where the cave was. "Me and my brothers spent many a night in this cave we're going to. Rowdy discovered it after our mother died. It became our shelter when the grief overwhelmed one of us."

Abe didn't say anything, but Tucker felt him tense. The cave came into view, a ledge more than an actual cave, it would provide shelter from the storm.

Ducking low he carried Abe to the farthest corner from the opening and set him down gently so that he could lean back against the rock wall.

Abe wiped water from his face, his gaze dug into Tucker as he pushed the leg of Abe's jeans up and then began to ease off his boot. "Your ankle is swollen, all right. We'll need to elevate it."

"You kissed my mother." The words were accusing.

Tucker had lost his head after pulling Suzie from the water. He shouldn't have kissed her like that in front of Abe and the others. But he'd lost his head…he hadn't been thinking.

"Yeah, I did." The truth was all he could do. "Abe, talk to me," he urged. When Abe said nothing, Tucker moved over to a thick, flat rock that was about a foot wide and he pushed it to the side, exposing a hole where a baggie of matches and lighters were stored.

He held them up for Abe to see. "These have been here for a long time. And the wood, too. We had a rule growing up—anyone could come here when they needed to get away, but they had to leave wood and matches for the next person's first fire." He opened the bag and pulled out the box of matches. "It's a good idea, even all these years later."

Abe had crossed his arms and pressed his back into the rock as if to get as far away from Tucker as he could.

Tucker studied the wood and the matches. "This isn't left over from me fifteen years ago. I think someone else has been visiting here since me and my brothers and your dad were here."

"My dad came here?" he asked gruffly.

"Yeah, he had times when he needed to be alone, too. When your family dies or cuts you loose in the world before your time…it leaves a lot of anger. You aren't the only one who's ever dealt with them, you know. Your dad needed quiet time to think, too. So did I and my brothers. So do most of the boys who come to Sunrise Ranch. And no, you aren't like them. You had two parents who loved you deeply and cared deeply for you. You still have your mom."

Abe looked sullen.

"Being here among these boys doesn't mean you're like them. I know you are having abandonment issues, but there is no reason to, because you haven't been and never were. You need to let that go."

Abe glared at him then looked away, studying the rain pouring over the edge of the entrance like a waterfall blocking out the world. "Yeah, Wes has been talking to me."

Leave it to Wes. The kid might be determined to be a champion bull rider, but his calling was as a counselor.

"That's good. You need to talk to others. Wes is a great one to talk to."

"He told me I need to let it go. I tried. That shrink said the same thing. But…"

"You don't want anyone messing with your mom."

He nodded.

Tucker fought off a sigh that wanted freedom. What could he say? He wasn't about to make promises to the kid he couldn't keep. "I had planned on bringing you here, but things kept getting in the way," he said instead. "I think today God said it was time."

Grabbing a handful of kindling he started working on a fire. Within moments, a small but warm fire glowed between them. Abe had grown more sullen and glared at the fire, lost in his own world of hurt and anger.

After a few quiet moments he rubbed his ankle. "Because of you, my dad is dead."

The words stretched between them like dead weight. "I would have given my life for your dad. But, instead, your dad gave his life for—not just me, but his entire unit. I hate that he died, but, Abe, he would have done it for any one of the guys in the unit. This wasn't about me, at all, but about the kind of man your dad was. I hate it with all my heart that it killed him. But he was a proud marine and his own man. He chose to lay his life down for me and the others."

Abe was so tense that he looked as though he might break in half. His eyes misted. "He left me. Left Mom."

Tucker's heart hurt for Abe. He remembered well the feeling of abandonment he and his brothers felt when their mother died. "He didn't abandon you, Abe. He made the choice he could live with."

Abe glared at him. "But he didn't live."

The truth played across Tucker's thoughts as clear as springwater. "If your father hadn't at least tried to save me—if he hadn't tried to stop the shooter—it wouldn't have been something he could have lived with. Your dad was a man who followed a code of ethics. He would never have walked away from a fellow marine in need without first doing what he needed to do. Even if that meant dying."

Big tears streamed down Abe's face, built-up pain and grief escaping in a river of release. Tucker looked at the small fire and prayed that this could be God's time of healing for this kid. Reaching out, he laid his hand on Abe's shoulder. "You are a strong young man, Abe. You are, after all, your father's child and your mom's."

Abe brushed his damp cheeks with the backs of his hands, and nodded.

Encouraged, Tucker continued, "You are made of tough stuff. The anger you've locked inside is normal. No one wants to lose someone they love. Someone they need. Me and my brothers have walked through this valley, too—and, in many ways, your dad and all of these boys here at Sunrise Ranch. You are not alone."

"I know," he whispered.

"But, Abe, your grief and the pain you feel is uniquely yours, and you have to grieve in your own way. The same goes for your mother."

Abe swallowed hard and stared at him.

"Eventually, you will both have to move forward. To be healthy, it's the only way. Your mother is trying."

Abe remained silent and Tucker prayed his words were sinking in to Abe's heart.

"And that goes for me, too. Your dad's death is similar to Jesus giving His life for all of us so that we could live. It was a gift beyond measure. And I'm unworthy of it but struggling to be a man of honor and strength who Gordon would be proud of. And I'll always be here for you. And for your mother."

Abe studied him.

"Why did you kiss my mother?"

He held Abe's gaze and thought carefully about how best to answer him. "Because I've come to care deeply for your mother. Today, it terrified me when I thought I'd lost her. I kissed her out of relief." It was the truth, part of it anyway. Now was not the time to tell Abe that he loved Suzie.

The flames flickered in the kid's eyes, exposing so much pain. He nodded. "Good. I like you, Tucker, but…"

"It's okay, Abe. You don't have to explain. We'll get through this."

Chapter Seventeen

"They'll be all right," Randolph said, coming to stand beside Suzie at the window of the camp house, where they were escaping the storm. It had been built by Randolph's dad when he'd bought the ranch. "Tucker will find him, and they'll find shelter and sit this storm out."

Chilled to the bone, and not because of the weather, she wrapped her arms around her waist and took a deep breath. "I hope so."

"I know my son and he's resourceful. Plus, he and his brothers have roamed every inch of this ranch and know places to hole up that even I don't know. As soon as this passes over, I'll send all my ranch hands out to search, too, so don't worry. Tucker will know that. As soon as it's safe to travel he'll be on the move."

"If he can. If they're both able," she added.

"Yes. Now, would you want to come help scrounge something up to feed these boys? You don't have to help but it would give you something to do other than stand here and worry."

Morgan and Chet had immediately started a fire when they'd made it inside the cabin, and all the boys were gathered around it to warm themselves after being drenched. Wes was once more entertaining them with stories of his first semester of college and bull-riding escapades.

"Yes, I'll do that. I know they are not going to materialize outside this window in between lightning bolts."

She followed him to the corner where the rustic kitchen area had been set up. There was a gas stove and cabinets where she found large and small containers of canned food. There were several gallon-size cans of chili and they opted for that. There was also a large glass jar with a label on it that said Nana's Cocoa.

"As you can tell, Nana keeps the place stocked up for emergencies, large or small."

Suzie smiled up at Randolph. "I have a feeling she stays on top of any and every situation that could arise."

He smiled the devastating smile that he'd passed down to each of his sons. "My mother is a wonder, that is for certain."

Working as a team they prepared the meal while Chet and Morgan donned slickers from a closet and went out to check on the horses and the livestock.

Time ticked by, and Suzie tried not to think about it. Still, Abe's fury at seeing Tucker kissing her kept flashing through her mind. When she'd been in the river, the undercurrent was so strong, and though she'd been fighting, she'd felt like a rag doll at its mercy. When Tucker had pulled her out of that water and wrapped her in his arms she'd known she never wanted to leave the security and love she felt there.

Love. It had become so clear that she'd fallen for the lawman despite all the reasons not to. Despite the fact that she'd had no desire to fall for anyone, and especially him.

But she had.

Still, Abe's angry outburst had instantly brought her back to the real world. She pushed the turmoil in her mind away and concentrated on boiling water for hot chocolate and stirring the large pot of chili.

When the food was almost ready, Randolph asked her if she could handle it alone, and when she said yes he thanked her, then grabbed a slicker and went out to find Morgan and Chet.

She couldn't help but wonder if he was more concerned than he was letting on.

Randolph had found a stash of paper cups and bowls—bless Nana's heart—and he'd placed them on the rough counter separating the kitchen from the living area where the boys were. Shutting her mind off, she focused on her task.

"Time to eat, boys," she called, and that was all it took to start a stampede.

"Thanks, Ms. Suzie," Sammy said, and more thanks raced from the others as they came through the line and she ladled chili into their bowls.

"You think Tucker and Abe are okay?" B.J. asked.

"Yes, they are," Wes answered from behind the little boy. Wes met her gaze with solid eyes. Eyes that said he believed what he was saying. "Tucker will make sure of it."

He smiled, and Joseph agreed instantly, and through the trepidation that was suffocating her, she smiled back at them. She had fallen in love with all of these boys in the weeks since she and Abe had been here, and in the short time Wes and Joseph had been home she'd done the same with them.

"I believe they are all right," she said, realizing that in her heart of hearts she knew that Tucker would not have stopped until he found Abe. The surety of that wrapped around her reassuringly.

The problem was, had he found Abe yet? After the boys all had their food, she walked to the window and stared out into the storm.

"Please let them be safe, dear Lord. Please," she whispered the words of prayer and worked at forcing herself to believe that God would bring Abe home to her. She couldn't lose someone else…didn't want to think about it.

God hadn't brought Gordon home to them, so she knew there were no guarantees in this life.

The rain was hitting the window sideways, the wind was blowing so hard, and rivers of it ran down the pane making it almost impossible to see anything but a blurry gray evening turning into night.

Lightning sizzled across the sky, and right on its heels another bolt made a jagged stab at the earth so close that she jumped.

Closing her eyes, she prayed harder and fought the helplessness that engulfed her.

Abe had run away because of her. He saw Tucker kissing her, and—if she admitted the truth—he saw her kissing Tucker back.

She'd been trying all evening to deny it, but she couldn't. She had to take the blame and not put it solely on Tucker. She'd known in the water, when she'd believed she could be about to die, that she'd regretted not giving the emotions she felt for Tucker a fighting chance.

And what were these emotions?

She'd fallen in love with the strong, caring cowboy. But what if Abe couldn't accept that?

What then?

The storm had settled in for most of the night, so Tucker and Abe had sat it out inside the dank but dry shelter. He'd worried all night about Suzie and prayed that she knew he had her son safe. Abe had finally fallen to sleep after their conversation. And, somewhere along the way, Tucker had slept for a short while. But the sun wasn't quite up when he shook Abe awake.

"It's cleared up. I think we should get started. Dad and Morgan will have the ranch swarming with folks searching for us if we don't get back soon after sunrise. Plus, your mom is probably sick with worry and no sleep."

He looked ashamed. "I'm sorry for that."

"She'll just be glad you're okay."

"I'm going to try and take care of her."

Tucker gave the boy a nod. "You'll do a fine job of it."

Abe had told him the same thing Suzie had, that they were moving into the apartment. It was probably for the best, and time would make things better. "Where are the horses?"

"They're either near or will have headed back toward the ranch. If they've made it back before us, then that will make everyone worry all the more. So we better get going."

"Okay."

Tucker had already put out the fire. He helped Abe stand, drew Abe's arm over his shoulder, and they started down the hill, moving as fast as they could, given the sprained ankle.

The sun began to peek over the horizon quickly; a good thing, since the ground was slippery.

They worked their way down the hillside they'd ridden up. They didn't talk much, but Abe didn't seem as sullen or angry. When they made it to the bottom of the hill and were on more even land, traveling across an open pasture, Tucker asked how Abe was.

The kid hefted a shoulder. "Fine, I guess. I thought about what you said, and I know my dad would want better of me. For my mom. I'm the man of the house now."

"Yes, that's true. But you don't need to let that pressure you."

Abe gave him a long look as they trudged forward. "I'm going to try and use it like you're doing. I'm going to try and let my dad's death make me a better man. Not that you weren't a good man. I know all about the men you saved and how you are a hero. The guys talk about it all the time. Wes showed me stuff on the internet. Said you didn't put any of your medals out for display. So I'm not saying that. I'm just saying, you know, you're…you're trying to carry my dad's torch along with you."

Emotion clogged Tucker's throat. He nodded.

Abe gave a sad smile. They were halfway across the pasture when Morgan and Chet emerged from the woods leading their horses.

Tucker hadn't ever been so glad to see his brother

and his friend. With their help they'd get back to Suzie sooner.

And she and her son would finally have the fresh start she'd been praying for.

And he would hang in the background and give them room.

The sun was barely up, but everyone was saddled and ready to ride. Tucker's dad hadn't slept all night, either. Neither had Morgan and Chet, who'd headed out as soon as the lightning had eased up and the rain had turned to a drizzle. To ease the wait, they'd told stories of life on the ranch, and as worried as she was, Suzie had found herself laughing at the antics of the kids. With all of the activities that went on, there was never a shortage of stories. But now, she was ready to find Abe. And Tucker.

She was about to climb into the saddle when she heard one of the boys yell.

"They're coming!"

Suzie spun around to see Tucker and Abe riding from the woods with Morgan and Chet.

Relief and love raced through her in a riot of happy emotion.

Rushing forward, she met Abe as he eased from his saddle, hopped on one foot and wrapped his arms around her.

"I'm sorry, Mom," he said, hugging her as tightly as she hugged him. It was the first real hug she'd had from him in months. Her knees almost buckled from the shock and joy of it.

With her heart full to overflowing, she held him

close and met Tucker's eyes. "Thank you," she mouthed silently, and then to her son she said, "Don't worry about any of that, Abe. I love you and am so glad you are okay."

"And you, too, Mom. I didn't even tell you I was glad you were safe after Tucker pulled you from the river."

She assured him she'd known he was, despite what had transpired afterward.

The boys had held back, giving them time for their reunion, but now they rushed forward and encircled them, welcoming Abe and asking what had happened.

She wanted to know as much as they did. It was obvious something had happened to his ankle but he seemed okay. Giving him a last squeeze around the waist, she backed away and let him talk to his friends.

"Tucker caught up to me after the storm hit. It was bad, I sprained my ankle, too. But he knew of a cave and we made it there and spent the night."

"Sweet!" Wes said. "That's *my* cave. It's a good thinkin' place."

"Yeah, that's for sure," Abe agreed. "But me and Tucker mostly talked and watched the fire while the rain and the lightning went crazy. What'd y'all do?"

"We had chili," B.J. exclaimed. "And it was *good, good, gooood!*"

Tucker moved to stand beside her, keeping a distance between them that was obvious.

"Thank you for bringing him back to me." She wanted to reach out and touch him, but she didn't. He was holding himself at a distance, anyway—could she blame him? *No.*

"I think Abe is going to be all right. Talk to him, I believe he may have turned a corner toward healing."

"I'll do that. Are you all right?"

"Don't worry about me." He didn't wait for her to reply. Instead, he went back to his horse and stepped into the stirrup, threw his leg over the saddle and looked down at the boys. "Okay, boys, we started this job and we're going to finish it. We've got cattle to round up."

That was all it took for the boys to head to their horses. Abe was grinning as he limped to his.

"Abe, you need to have that ankle looked at," Tucker warned.

"It's better. Sitting in a saddle's not going to hurt it," he said, using his good foot to saddle up. "Let's roll," he said, looking every bit the born-and-bred cowboy.

Suzie was so proud of him.

They'd talk later.

There were some important issues that had to be discussed.

"Come on, Ms. Suzie, it's roundup time. Ain't you comin'?" B.J. called, riding over to her. She had to smile at the little boy.

"B.J., I wouldn't miss it for the world. Goodness, you look like you grew a foot last night. I was looking down at you and now I'm looking up. What happened?"

He giggled. "I got on my horse."

"Oh, is that what you did? Well, hang on and I'll get on mine, and we can round them up together, how's that?"

He grinned. "Awesome!"

She caught Abe smiling at her from his horse, and

it felt as though the sun had just come out after the terrible storm.

What, she wondered, had gone on between Tucker and Abe out there in the midst of that storm?

Whatever it was, it was an answer to her prayers, and she couldn't wait until there was a private moment where she and Tucker could talk.

About a lot of things.

Chapter Eighteen

Edwina hustled from the Spotted Cow's kitchen, plopped two plates of food in front of a pair of cowboys in the corner, then headed Tucker's way. The sharp-witted waitress took one look at him, poked her pencil behind her ear and grimaced. "Sheriff, you look like roadkill—awful handsome roadkill, but *awful* bein' the key word here. What happened to you?" She held up her hands. "No, wait. You need some strong coffee first, and then you can explain why you have marched in here and completely wrecked my belief that you always look magazine-perfect."

He wasn't going to argue—he needed strong coffee and some of Ms. Jo's coconut pie. And he was proud to see that he didn't even have to ask for it. After loading up the horses in the trailers that the hands had waiting for them at the end of the roundup, Tucker had watched all of the boys and Abe pile into trucks and head back to the ranch.

There had been no time for a private talk with Suzie. He'd just been able to ask if she was all right after her fall in the river. Since there hadn't been much time before he'd gone after Abe, he had simply needed to make sure she was okay. She'd kept her distance. He'd longed to wrap his arms around her, but he didn't want to upset Abe or Suzie. Had she just reacted to his kiss earlier because she'd been terrified?

That question had been eating at him.

Edwina left him at the table and returned with a pot of coffee in one hand and a double portion of pie in the other. "Here," she said, plopping the pie in front of him then carefully filling his cup full of dark coffee. "You need sugar, so eat up. And then tell me what has happened to you."

The coffee burned a trail down his throat and the sweet, creamy pie acted like an IV of glucose as it rushed into his bloodstream. He'd taken a swig of the coffee and downed a forkful of pie before he realized Edwina was still watching him, her arms crossed and the half-full pot of coffee dangling from one hand.

Ms. Jo finished her conversation at a nearby table and came over to stand beside Edwina. Her bright eyes behind her round-rimmed glasses pierced deep as she, too, studied him.

"Somethin's up, Ms. Jo," Edwina drawled, cocking her head toward him. "Tucker's inhalin' your pie like you don't have fifteen more back there he can have if he really wanted them."

"And he looks worn out, to boot. Take care of the customers, Ed. I've got this."

"Sure thing, boss. You just give me the nod on whatever you need. And fill me in later."

Tucker took another bite of pie. Why not? The two of them obviously didn't need him in the conversation they were indulging in at his expense. And he needed the pie, the comfort and the sugar it provided.

Ms. Jo slid into the booth across from him. "That's your mama's recipe, and anytime you're feeling low, you eat that pie like a man dying of thirst."

He swallowed, savoring the pie, remembering how his mother used to make this for him whenever he asked. He took another swig of coffee. "I guess even a grown man needs a little reminder sometimes of the way things used to be."

Ms. Jo laid her hand over his and squeezed. "We all do. What's got you looking so down? I noticed at the wedding the other night that you looked distracted." She dipped her chin, and peeked at him over the rim of her glasses. "I kind of suspected it had a little something to do with Suzie."

Was he that easy to read? He never had been before. As a marine he'd needed to sometimes live behind a shield, but maybe there wasn't any way to hide an emotion as strong as love.

"You see too much, for a little short woman."

One brow hiked. "This little short woman has eyes just like everyone else. Believe me, it wasn't just me who saw you only had eyes for our newest resident. Her business is doing good. Except yesterday she put Drewbaker and Chili in charge of the cash register, so I'm thinking she might have a screw or two loose upstairs." She chuckled. "They had customers backed out the door, it was so full."

He laughed. "Yeah, she was in a bad way and needed to go on the roundup with us. Those two volunteered and she felt spending time with Abe was worth it."

"And with you, maybe?"

He sighed. "Maybe, but it's complicated."

"Love always is."

He dug his fork into the last bite of pie, not willing to admit that to anyone yet. "Ms. Jo, that was wonderful. Can I ask you something?"

"Anything."

"You remember how I was after mom died?"

She looked sad and thoughtful. "Yep. You looked like you carried the weight of the world on your shoulders. It took a long time for you to accept that she was gone and not coming back. You remember that, don't you?"

He toyed with his coffee. "Some of it. A lot of those first months are fuzzy for me."

"Grief does things like that. Why do you ask?"

"Abe, he's better. But I'm not sure he's ever going to completely get over his dad's death."

Ms. Jo shook her head. "Death makes a mark on a soul. But love is patient and kind and perseveres. It never gives up. Do you know what I'm saying? I know whatever is going on between you, Suzie and Abe is complicated. But God can work even complicated out according to His plan. And His plan is always perfect."

If he loved Suzie, he'd have to be patient. And if he loved her, he'd have to be willing to accept what was best for her…even if that meant he wouldn't be in her life.

"Tucker, I know you've had a lot on your plate since returning home. Gordon's death was hard on this entire community. We loved that young man. And for him to give his life for his country—and for you—it just has been hard. But we see that pain that runs through you as you take care of all of our safety, protecting us in our little world. You need to find happiness like your brothers have. And my instincts tell me Suzie means more to you than you want to admit."

Oh, he knew exactly how much she meant to him. It just wasn't that simple. He downed another long draw of coffee and glanced toward the exit, looking for an escape route.

Ms. Jo's knowing smile unfurled. "That's what I thought. Sometimes God's plan for our lives comes from the worst of circumstances. Beauty from ashes, the Bible says."

"And some things are never meant to be."

Her eyes flashed. "You ever see a flower growing out of a tiny crack in the cement or a sliver of dirt in a rock face? It's against all odds that that beauty would rise up out of that hard, unforgiving rock, but it does. It fights the odds and flourishes. If God's in this, then you fight for it. Don't give up on it before it's even had time to root."

He'd come for the pie, but also this. Ms. Jo's encouragement always cut to the quick of the matter. But this time he just wasn't sure if fighting for what he wanted was the right thing to do.

By Wednesday, Suzie and Abe were moved into the apartment over the shop. Everyone at the ranch had acted as if they were moving to Alaska. It was touching, really, and she hoped it made Abe feel good that everyone was sad to see him move from the ranch property. Suzie had been so relieved when Nana and Randolph assured her they understood.

The place still needed painting, but by the time she'd cleaned, thrown out all the stored junk, laid carpets on the floors, placed photos and paintings on the walls, arranged her furniture with help from Tony, Abe and Caleb. And Jake had helped, too. Now the apartment had a homey feel to it and a coziness that helped her feel relaxed. There was nothing like a place of your own to call home. No matter how much she had enjoyed Nana's hospitality, it hadn't been home. No wonder Abe had felt a little displaced. Now they were surrounded by familiar things, *their* things, family items that spoke to their hearts.

They'd also made huge steps toward healing in the past week. And they were building on that.

She'd taken Abe to school then picked him up after work all week and they'd come home together. She'd fixed them supper, and they'd eaten together at the kitchen table that they'd owned since Abe was a baby. There was familiarity in their days. And Abe seemed content.

Everything was almost perfect, as though life was actually going to be good again. Except Suzie realized very quickly that she missed Tucker.

She hadn't seen him since the day he'd returned Abe to her. He hadn't stopped by the shop, and she hadn't been at the ranch as much, so she hadn't seen him there.

She thought a few times about going to his office, but she hadn't.

"Mom," Abe said on Friday evening, as they drove home from seeing Dr. Livingston. "Are you happy?"

"Yes," she said, glancing at him. "Is something wrong? I thought you said everything was better. And you said that you talked to Dr. Livingston and it helped."

His eyes were deeply serious. "I'm doing good, Mom. I asked about you. The doc, she asked me how I thought you were doing, and I told her good. She asked me if you were seeing anyone, if you'd moved forward, and how I would feel about that."

Suzie's pulse jerked and she automatically pressed the brake. They were on the outskirts of town and she slowed as she glanced at him. "What did you tell her?"

He frowned. "I told her you were fine. That you were happy."

"I am." Tucker's smile filled her mind, she missed him so.

"Are you sure?" Glancing at him again, she realized he looked worried.

"What's the matter, Abe?"

"Nothing," he said, and stared out the window.

She wasn't sure what to make of his questions. She knew in her heart that she'd fallen in love with Tucker McDermott. It had happened watching him care for her son's welfare and try so hard to make up for the loss of Gordon. She just didn't know what to do about it.

She didn't know how Abe would feel about it. And suddenly he was asking these questions.

"I'm a young woman, though, Abe. I probably will remarry one day. But I don't want you to worry about that now. I want you to be comfortable with it. My main concern right now is that you grow and adjust to our life as it is now. I don't want you to worry about anything. Okay?"

"Okay, and, Mom, I'm okay. You can stop worrying about me. I promise."

Her heart swelled and thankfulness filled her to the brim. *Thank You, Lord.* She smiled.

Her GED test was in four weeks. She and Jolie had come up with a study plan that worked for her. She was reminded every time she sat down with her books that she might have never thought to do this until Tucker had suggested it to her.

He'd been so encouraging in all aspects of her move here and in her life going forward. And now he'd helped Abe profoundly. The night after they'd stayed in the cave together, Abe told her that Tucker had talked to him about the anger that he'd felt when he lost his mother when he was around Abe's age.

What touched her was that Abe had said he was trying to live a life that would make his dad proud.

There was no better tribute than that. And Tucker was responsible for this turnaround.

Suzie couldn't get him off her mind, and she wondered why he hadn't come by to see them. He'd just seemed to disappear after the roundup.

Of course, she knew he was down the street at the office, but…she knew he knew she'd moved into the apartment in town. If he wanted to see her, wouldn't he come by?

On Saturday morning she woke early. She had decided she needed to talk to Tucker, but first she had to work on flowers for a small wedding. She was unlocking the front of her shop when Tucker passed by in his SUV.

Her heart began pounding at just seeing him. She waved and he pulled into an empty parking space. His elbow rested in the open window. "Morning, ma'am. You're out bright and early."

He was so handsome, she could hardly breathe looking at him. Her fingers itched to cup his rugged jaw, and she realized how much she wanted to feel his arms around her and his lips on hers.

She'd been concentrating on Abe all week, but now…
"I have a wedding today. They need the flowers before lunch, so I wanted to make certain they were done. You're out and about early, too."

"Yeah, I need some bodies to fill up the jail cells so I thought I'd get an early start. Have them full by noon."

She laughed, and his eyes twinkled.

"It sounds like we'll both be finished by lunch," he said.

She took a step toward him, moving to the edge of the sidewalk. "I—I've missed you, Tucker. I was hoping to talk to you."

He looked away, studying some distant point at the end of the street. "I've been busy."

"Oh, sure, I see."

"How's Abe? Jolie told me he's been participating in school all week. And Pepper told me that he's been coming in and cleaning stalls, even though his two weeks of duty ended on Thursday."

"He's doing great, Tucker. And yes, I've had to bring him home from the ranch the last two days with the windows down because he's been cleaning stalls. But he said he was helping the younger boys out with their chores."

Tucker smiled. "He's a good kid, Suzie. He's going to be all right."

She took a deep breath. "Yes, he is. Thanks to you."

Tucker studied her and the distance between them seemed like a chasm. "How are you?"

"I'm good. I—" She ached to touch him. But he hadn't moved, was just sitting there with the closed truck door between them. "I'm good. We're getting settled in and things are more normal now, with our things around us. I'm going to have to paint." She smiled at the thought of the day he'd come by when she was painting. "But no red."

He chuckled. "I won't complain."

"I've started studying for my GED and I've signed up for online classes for the fall semester."

"That's wonderful," he said, pride in his eyes that brought sudden tears to hers. "What's wrong?" he asked, alarmed.

She sniffed, and swiped at her eyes. "Oh, nothing. I— Oh, Tucker, I owe you so much."

He was out of the truck before she could blink. He swiped the tear from her cheek before she could do away with it. "Don't cry, Suzie. I don't want you to cry anymore. You don't owe me anything. You don't."

The intensity of his words startled her. "But I do," she said, meaning it with all of her soul.

"Everyone loved Gordon, and they, we, love you and Abe," he said. "I want you and Abe to be happy and healthy. I want you to move on with your life, not feel like you owe me. No more tears about that."

He stepped closer and the spicy scent of his aftershave, masculine and woodsy, wrapped around her. It was everything she could do not to step close and lay her head on his shoulder.

But he wasn't reaching for her. His arms remained at his sides.

"I do, and I always will," she said, firmly.

His brows dipped over frustrated eyes. "I've got to go to work. What's Abe doing today?" he asked, before he turned to go.

Frustrated by the conversation, she hid her feelings. "I think he said Tony and Jake were going to pick him up and they were going to practice for the rodeo or something. He seemed excited about it."

"Yeah, I think they are holding some sort of exhibition this afternoon. You should come."

"I will."

He tipped his hat. "Good. See you there."

And he was gone. She watched him drive off and felt as if he'd erected an invisible wall between them.

She didn't like it.

They'd come through so much together.

Why, she wondered, did it seem as if he was holding her at arm's length? Why had he not come around to check on them since the roundup?

She'd missed him, but she'd been so busy getting Abe settled that she hadn't let herself dwell on why he was missing from their lives. Instead of going into the shop, Suzie headed back up the stairs. She walked into Abe's room, suddenly knowing that, as wonderful as things had been in the past week, she needed to ask him a question.

Laughter and excitement filled the air inside the arena. Along with dust churned up from the donkeys as the boys ran around trying to herd them into a holding pen. Tucker leaned against the rails with Morgan and Rowdy, waiting to watch the boys rope calves as soon as the donkeys were moved out of the way. The boys huddled up suddenly and then little B.J. broke from the group and came barreling across the arena, his face red with enthusiasm.

"We're gonna ride us some donkeys!" he exclaimed.

"Donkeys?" Tucker asked, glancing at his brothers. They looked as surprised as he was. He'd told the boys that they were going to load them up later and take them back to Chili's, since the fence had been fixed earlier that week. As it turned out, Chili and Drewbaker had saddled up and found the broken fence and fixed it. They hadn't let him hear the end of it, either.

The other boys walked up, expectant looks on their faces. "Y'all planning on riding the donkeys?" he asked.

Tony stepped out of the group. "Well, sir, Chili told us we could. So we were hoping to do it before we take them away. "

"We thought we'd give it a go," Abe added, grinning.

Tucker chuckled, liking the grin on Abe's face.

Morgan crossed his arms and studied them. "You boys think you're up to that?"

Highly insulted expressions instantly swept over the group, and a round of indignant "Yes, sirs" rolled between them.

"Then go for it," Morgan said. It was his call since he and Randolph were in charge of the foster program. "And good luck."

"Yeah, watch those back legs," Tucker warned over the eruption of excited whoops. "They aren't as mild as they look." He should know, remembering the lick his hip had taken.

He glanced toward the house, where Suzie was visiting with Nana, Lucy and Jolie. He'd seen her drive up a few minutes ago and had to fight himself hard to stay away. It had been a fight all week. And that morning, he'd very nearly broken his vow to himself and enveloped her in his arms when she'd gotten emotional thanking him. Talking about owing him.

But that was it. He didn't want her to owe him. He

wanted her to love him. And he wanted Abe to be okay with that. Wanted Abe to love him, in fact.

The shouts and laughter of the boys drew the women's attention and they started toward the arena, probably realizing the roping was about to start.

"Hi," she said, to him and his brothers as she walked up. "The boys seem really excited about the roping."

Rowdy chuckled. "They're excited, all right. But it's not about roping."

"They're about to have a riding exhibition," Morgan said, winking at Jolie. "Y'all need to grab seats in the stands and get ready for a show. And we better get out there to make sure it doesn't get too rank and rowdy."

"What are they going to ride?" Suzie asked, pinning Tucker with curious eyes.

"We're about to have a little exhibition rodeo. The boys are going to *attempt* to ride the donkeys."

All the women's eyes widened in alarm.

"Won't they kick?" Suzie asked first.

"And buck, too?" Lucy added. "I'm just glad I'm not getting roped into this one. You have to watch these fellas, Suzie. The little sneaks will trick you into doing things you wouldn't normally do."

"B-but—" Suzie stammered, glaring at him. "It's too dangerous. Remember how they charged me?"

"Now, Suzie, boys will be boys. We'll be there watching out for them," he said, and knew that he planned to join in the fun…while watching for flying body parts. Anything would be safer today than spending time standing too close to Suzie.

He turned and headed toward the gate. Putting distance between them. It was getting harder and harder to stay away from her.

* * *

"You aren't serious?" Suzie called, startled that Tucker would walk away from her, as if she would be okay with this.

Suzie planted her hands on her hips as her words brought Tucker to a halt in his tracks. He turned—looking shocked that she would ask such a thing.

"Are you seriously about to let these boys ride those…those donkeys? You and I both know that they seem docile but are far from it. Look what that one did to you."

"Now, Suzie, don't get all bent out of shape—"

Her mouth dropped open. "'Bent out of shape,'" she huffed. "I saw firsthand what those measly animals can do. One kicked your legs right out from under you. And then, one charged me—tried to run me over and trample me!"

"Look, yes, there are a few dangers, but these boys know how to watch out for them. I just got a little too close the other day, is all."

"And that is supposed to make me feel better."

"I guess it doesn't, but this is cowboy country. This is what we do for fun. You just need to relax. It's going to be all right. And, despite what you are thinking, it's going to be great for Abe."

He turned and continued on his way as if she'd never said anything. "Going to be fine, indeed," she mumbled, almost going after him.

"Suzie, come sit with me," Nana said, drawing her attention.

"I can't believe this," Suzie said, moving toward Nana.

"This is a ranch," Jolie said, coming up beside her.

"They love doing things like this. It'll be fun. Rowdy and the others will minimize the risk, but honestly, kids get hurt falling off their bicycles. It'll be all right. You can't put kids in a bubble. They have to have some freedom. I think this is especially good for Abe. He needs to know he's tougher than he thinks." This coming from a champion kayaker—daredevil—had Suzie wondering if she was too overprotective.

Feeling as if she would explode with anxiety, Suzie forced a nod. She couldn't always protect Abe from everything. She just couldn't. And the truth was that she trusted Tucker and his family. She did have to let go some. She'd smother Abe if she didn't.

But could she relax enough to watch Abe ride?

The boys were having a blast. The donkeys were giving them the time of their lives and testing their abilities. Tucker wanted to enjoy the event but all he could think about was Suzie.

Abe came bouncing by, laughing even though he was clinging to a wild donkey's neck in his effort not to be thrown to the ground.

Tucker's gaze flew instantly to Suzie. To his surprise she was laughing. Her eyes were alive, just as they'd been in all of Gordon's photos, and Tucker could not look away. Somewhere in the middle of all of this, she'd let go and begun to enjoy the show. Let go and felt the joy in the moment. Had she let go of everything? Had she let go of Gordon?

"Look out," Morgan said, yanking him out of the way of a runaway donkey.

"Distracted just a bit?" Morgan asked, his lip hitching upward.

No sense denying it any longer. "Yeah, I am," Tucker snapped, not at all happy.

Rowdy looked around Morgan at him. "Thought you weren't going to go there."

"Do I look like I planned on it?"

"More like you're having a root canal," Rowdy shot back, eyes serious.

"What are you going to do?" Morgan asked. Both knew the seriousness of what he was facing.

Considering Morgan's question, Tucker watched Abe among the chaos of riders. The kid was doing good, still clinging to the donkey's neck—but one hard buck and he went flying facedown in the dirt. As the donkey ran off, Abe rolled over onto his back.

It took a moment to realize he wasn't getting up.

Tucker bolted toward him the instant he realized it. Running across the arena, he slid to a stop in the dirt, and sank to his knees beside Abe, whose eyes were closed. Suzie came, nearly falling down beside them in her haste to reach her son's side.

"Abe, Abe, speak to me." She grabbed Abe's hand and shook it. When he didn't react she glared at Tucker.

Abe's eyes popped open and a grin spread across his face. "Mom! This has been the best day of my life."

Suzie gasped. "Abe, you scared the dickens out of me."

Tucker stared at the kid, not sure what was going on.

Abe sat up and rubbed his chest. "It's okay, Mom. I just lost my breath for a minute."

"Are you okay now?" Tucker asked, placing a hand on Abe's shoulder. He could feel a crowd gathering behind him.

Abe's grin faded as he studied Tucker and then his

mother. "No. I'm not. I've caused a lot of trouble and I'm sorry. I've been thinking about it all night since I talked with the doc yesterday. And—" He paused, straightened his shoulders and met Tucker's gaze. "I need y'all to know that I'm okay. With everything. Tucker, my mom's young. She's going to remarry one day. She said so herself."

Suzie gasped. "Abe Kent, did you hit your head?"

He laughed. "I'm just saying what you told me. And I've been thinking about it. I saw y'all kissing and, well, I was just wondering…if that means y'all love each other. Because if it does, I'm good with it."

"Abe, honey," Suzie said, "I think we need to get you out of the sun."

Tucker pushed his hat back and studied the kid in shock. He agreed wholeheartedly with everything Abe had said, but it was a startling revelation. Standing up, he reached and grabbed the boy beneath the arms. "Here we go, buddy."

"No, I'm fine." Abe scrambled away to stand beside his friends. The boys were all grinning.

"He ain't hit his head," B.J. said. "He's just got his brains back. He done told us he wants Tucker to be his new daddy."

Suzie stood up and stuffed her hands on her hips. "Abe, this is not the way things are supposed to be handled. And you can't just decide you want something and then think that makes it so."

"I know, Mom, but I was thinking that maybe y'all need to know how I feel. So you— So you can both be happy."

"Th-thank you, Abe, but this is not the time or the place to be telling me this."

Suzie looked at Tucker with big, alarmed eyes.

"Okay," he said, having had enough of being the show. "Abe, thanks for speaking your mind. But now everyone needs to get back to what they were doing. Suzie, could you come with me? I think there are a few things we need to talk about." He ignored the excited looks on every boy's face and refrained from looking at his nana. Morgan and Rowdy were grinning like fools.

"We've got it covered," Morgan assured him.

"Yes," Nana said. "Shoo, boys, get on back to your riding."

Tucker glanced at Suzie, but she was already striding out of the arena. He caught up to her just past the trucks. "Suzie, wait. Abe's right, we do need to talk."

She spun around, anger flashing in her eyes. "I've been waiting for you to come talk to me all week. I've been in town, at the shop or at the apartment and you've stayed away. So shoot, I'm ready to hear what you have to say."

He did like the fire in her eyes. "I was giving you time to get settled. I rushed you both times I kissed you, and so I was just biding my time."

She glared at him, but her voice had softened to butter. "Is that so?"

He stepped close but kept his hands to himself. "Yes, it is. Because every time I get near you, I want to hug you up tight and never let you go. I didn't want to chance running you off or worrying Abe again."

She stepped closer to him, lifting her chin so she met his gaze. "So, about this hugging me. Why do you want to do that?"

He cupped her face in his hands. "Because I've fallen completely in love with you, and I'm hoping you'll fall in love with me. And when you're ready to talk about it… I want to—"

To his surprise, Suzie stood on her toes and kissed him. He'd never before been told to stop talking in such a nice way….

Suzie couldn't help herself and kissed Tucker with all the pent-up love she held for him. He wrapped his arms around her, pulled her close and kissed her deeply. "Tucker," she whispered, drawing away so that she could look at him. "I came to Dew Drop and the Sunrise Ranch as a last resort, because I had no choices. You helped me and Abe come through the fire, and I know he's going to be all right. And much of that was due to you. My life has changed. It was wonderful and it can be wonderful again especially with you in my life."

The most dazzling smile she'd ever seen flashed across Tucker's face. "Then you'll marry me? I love you, Suzie. And I love Abe, and until now I wasn't sure if there was a place for me in y'all's lives."

"I love you so much, Tucker. And Abe is doing great. Whatever happened out in that cave helped free him from the past. He's ready to move forward, and I think he just made it clear that he's ready for you to be a part of our family. And I know without doubt that I am."

"Then, what do you say? Will you make me the happiest man in the world?"

Her heart soared. "Yes."

It was a simple word and it set free the most beautiful promise. Beauty from ashes.

Her life with Gordon had filled her with great joy and happiness, but it wasn't meant to be her future… Life with Tucker was her future.

Wrapping her arms around his neck she kissed him. There were no regrets, no worries, no fears.

Instead there was hope, love and joy.

"I love you, Tucker. I'm so glad you didn't give up on me."

"Never," he assured her, and then kissed her again.

And somewhere in the background she heard clapping—and whoops of glee.

Tucker laughed. "Well, are you ready to go back in there and tell Abe?" Tucker asked, holding her hand gently, his deep blue eyes promising to love her, and cherish her and her son.

"I'm so ready." Holding his hand, she knew she was exactly where she was supposed to be. "I'm so very ready."

As they entered the gate, Abe came jogging their way, a grin plastered across his face and the boys of Sunrise Ranch following him in hot pursuit.

Suzie's heart was so full she had to fight the tears of joy that filled her eyes. "Oh, Tucker, God is so good."

"Yes, darlin', He is."

* * * * *

HER ALASKAN COWBOY

Belle Calhoune

For my nieces—Celina, Kylie and Nina.
May you grow up to follow your hearts
and live out your dreams.

I will praise thee; for I am fearfully
and wonderfully made: marvellous are thy works;
and that my soul knoweth right well.
—*Psalms* 139:14

Chapter One

Honor Prescott sat on her white stallion and stared down from the mountain ridge at the sprawling Diamond R Ranch. From this vantage point, Honor had a bird's-eye view of the property. She could see horses in the paddock and a few ranch hands milling around. Snow from last night's snowfall covered the ground. She let out a sigh of appreciation at the vast acreage. This view had always been spectacular.

A few cars were parked in the driveway by the main house. She spotted Lee Jamison's distinctive yellow-and-tan wagon parked by the house. She felt her lips twitching at the sight of it. That van had to be older than Lee himself. As town attorney and a member of the town council, Lee was a beloved figure in Love, Alaska. Honor had come to the Diamond R Ranch today at Lee's request.

Honor drew her coat tighter around her as the February wind whipped relentlessly against her body. Although the sun was shining, there was a chill in the air. Honor grabbed Lola's reins and cantered toward the property. Riding her horse rather than driving over from the wildlife preserve was a luxury for her. Lately, she'd been so busy with work demands she rarely had the opportunity to spend time with her horse.

A feeling of nostalgia swept over her. It had been years since she had visited the ranch owned by Bud Ransom, the patriarch of the Ransom family. Bud had unexpectedly passed away a few days ago. She would miss him and his warm, solid presence. And she would be forever grateful to him for leaving the ranch to the town in his will.

Bittersweet memories washed over her as she surveyed the property. The two-story log cabin–style home was a generous size. It had been home for generations of Ransoms. Her ex-fiancé, Joshua Ransom, had grown up here with his grandparents, parents and his older brother, Theo. When they were dating, Honor had spent a lot of time at the Diamond R. Too much time, according to her own brothers—Boone, Liam and Cameron. They had been vehemently opposed to her relationship with Joshua, who had been in and out of trouble for the duration of their relationship. Joshua had been the ultimate rebel. Boone, who served as town sheriff, had hauled Joshua into his office on more occasions than she could count for a variety of charges. Drunk and disorderly. Vandalism.

But Honor and Joshua had been head over heels in love and committed to a life together. She had defended him at every turn, much to her family's dismay. In the end, their engagement had imploded after Joshua's involvement in a fire that had gutted a beloved town church and left a man seriously injured. It had been the final straw for her. Honor had given him back his diamond ring and headed off to college in Michigan. They hadn't spoken since.

After Honor had left Love, she'd discovered she was carrying Joshua's child. Weeks later she'd lost the baby. It still crushed her to remember how alone and scared she'd been. Since that time, Honor had turned to her faith and developed a relationship with God. She would never repeat the mistakes of the past.

Joshua had never known about their child. A few months after the miscarriage, she'd discovered that Joshua had gotten married. Joshua's quickie marriage mere months after their breakup had been a terrible blow to Honor's self-esteem. For some reason, it still stung.

Honor let out a sigh. The ranch represented a more innocent time in her life. She had experienced her first kiss in the barn. This ranch was where she'd fallen for Joshua. They had made plans for their future sitting amidst bales of hay. Their love had been genuine. Honor shivered as feelings of loss suddenly crept over her. After all this time, it still wasn't easy to think about losing the only man she'd ever loved. It had broken her young heart to end her engagement. She'd been so naive back then, believing that there might be a happily-ever-after for the two of them.

Joshua. Her first love and former fiancé. She hadn't thought about him in a very long time. Their relationship had ended in such a painful manner for Honor that it was easier now to stuff those memories deep down into a dark hole where they could no longer hurt her.

She had been a mere kid at the time—eighteen years old. What had she really known about love?

As she led Lola toward the stable so she could tether

her to a post while she met with Lee, Honor heard the crunching sound of footsteps walking on the snow. She swung her gaze up and found herself staring into the eyes of the last person she'd expected to see in all of Alaska.

Her heart constricted. Everything came to a standstill around her. The dark head of hair. The cleft in his chin. The sky blue eyes. Joshua Ransom, her high school sweetheart, was back in town. Her first instinct was to hop back onto Lola and ride off as quickly as possible in the opposite direction.

"Honor." The sound of her name tumbling off his lips was startling. It had been six years since she'd last heard it. Truthfully, she had never believed she would ever hear it again.

"Joshua." Somehow she managed to speak past the huge lump in her throat.

"It's been a long time," he said, his mouth quirking. "How are you?"

Her mouth felt as dry as cotton. "I'm doing well. And you?" she asked, marveling at the fact that they were able to exchange pleasantries despite the huge chasm between them.

"I can't complain. What brings you out here?" he asked, his eyebrows knitting together.

"Lee asked me to meet him out here. We understood none of the family was returning since Bud didn't want a service. When did you get back?"

"Yesterday. Theo and I flew in together from Anchorage."

Theo Ransom had moved away from Love years ago and joined the military. To her recollection, neither brother had been back to Love in the ensuing years.

"I'm guessing you didn't hire O'Rourke Charters to fly you here," Honor said. Her voice crackled with sarcasm.

A hint of a frown marred his brow. "No, we didn't."

She shouldn't have brought up the bad blood between him and the O'Rourke brothers—Declan and Finn. It harkened back to when she was dating Joshua and her own brothers had been staunchly against their relationship. There had been a lot of discord. It had all come to a head when she and Joshua had secretly gotten engaged and her family found out about it. Not a single person in town had been happy for them, except Bud. Despite his gruff demeanor, Bud had been a marshmallow at his center.

Joshua ran a hand over his face. "Bud never wanted a proper funeral, but Theo and I figured we should have some sort of memorial service for him. And we need to settle his affairs. Then I'll be heading home to Seattle."

Honor frowned. She hadn't heard a single word about a service for Bud. From what she had understood, Bud hadn't wanted any fanfare. The townsfolk would certainly want to know about the service so they could say a final farewell. Although she wanted to ask Joshua about Bud's desire to leave the Diamond R Ranch to the town of Love, she wasn't sure it was her place to ask Joshua probing questions. It would appear insensitive since his family was in mourning.

"I'm sorry about Bud. He was always kind to me."

Joshua nodded. "Thanks. He thought you were the real deal. I think he hoped you could straighten me up so I'd walk the straight and narrow path." Joshua let out a harsh-sounding laugh, although both he and Honor knew he wasn't joking. Honor couldn't count on two hands the number of times Bud had pulled her aside and asked her to steer his grandson in the right direction. At the time, she had naively believed it was possible. Life had shown her how wrong she'd been to believe it. Being in love with Joshua had given her a pair of rose-colored glasses.

Honor smiled at the memory of Bud. "Well, he always saw the good in people. It was what he did best."

Joshua nodded. "He was a great man. I've always been proud to be his grandson." He grimaced. "I wish I'd been better," he muttered.

He didn't have to say any more. Honor knew exactly what Joshua meant. As a rebellious teenager, Joshua had been in and out of trouble so much it had broken his grandfather's heart and caused his family a world of embarrassment. He had tarnished the Ransom family name.

He jutted his chin toward Lola, then reached out and ran his palm across her side. "It's nice to see you and Lola are still a team."

Honor nuzzled her face against Lola's nose. "She's a part of me. Always will be. I'm glad Boone took care of her for me while I was away at school." Boone had paid for the costs of boarding Lola at a local stable, along with feed costs and her upkeep while Honor attended college and graduate school.

At the mention of her brother, Joshua's body seemed to stiffen. Honor couldn't help but think that after all these years the bad feelings still lingered.

As the small talk between them faltered, tension hung in the air. There were so many things left unsaid between the two of them, words they had never gotten the chance to say to one another. Honor opened her mouth, then shut it. What was the point? It was six years too late for closure.

Both of them had moved on with their lives. End of story.

She shifted from one foot to the other. "Well, I should go see to Lola," she said in a low voice. "Do you know where I can find Lee?"

"I saw him talking to Theo when I was out in the paddock. They were headed inside the house," Joshua said. For a moment he looked at her curiously. She imagined he was still wondering what she was doing here at the ranch. A gut instinct told her Joshua didn't know anything about Bud's bequest. The thought of his being blindsided made her stomach knot. Although she was fairly certain he had no interest in coming back permanently to Love, it still might rankle to learn his family's property had been given to the town he despised.

"Thanks," she said, lightly pulling at Lola's reins as she prepared to lead her toward the stable.

"Mr. Ransom!" a voice called out, interrupting the silence. Honor turned toward the house. Winnie Alden, housekeeper and cook for the Ransom family, was standing a few feet away from them with a crying baby in her arms. "I tried my best to settle her down, but she won't stop crying. I think she wants her daddy."

Winnie held out the child to Joshua. Honor's heart stilled. The little girl wrapped in the pink blanket was Joshua's daughter!

Joshua Ransom reached for Violet and held her against his chest. "Thanks, Winnie. I'll take it from here." He began to make rhythmic circles on Violet's back. Almost immediately, she quieted down.

"The baby whisperer strikes again," he said in a low voice next to his daughter's ear.

He swung his gaze toward Honor. She was staring at him with wide eyes.

"She's yours?" she asked in a shocked tone.

"Yes, she's mine. This is Violet," Joshua said, his voice filled with pride. "Violet Anne Ransom."

Honor's gaze locked onto Violet. She couldn't seem to look away from her. "She's beautiful," she said, darting a glance at his ring finger.

Joshua didn't hold it against her. It happened to him all the time. As a single father raising a little girl, he raised a lot of eyebrows. It was all right. Violet was his whole world.

He nestled her closer against him. "I should get her inside. It's pretty cold out here and her sweater is on the thin side."

"Go ahead. You don't want her to get sick," Honor said, her brow creased with concern.

Joshua sucked in a deep, steadying breath as he turned toward the house. He felt as if he'd been sucker punched. Although he had known it was a possibility to run into her during his stay in Love, he hadn't expected to see her at his family's ranch. And he wasn't quite sure what she was doing here. Her answer had been vague.

She was just as beautiful as she'd always been. Time had only enhanced her good looks. Her hair hung in glossy chestnut waves. Her cheekbones were more pronounced in her heart-shaped face. Now she was more woman than girl, one who exuded a great deal of confidence. It hadn't taken long for one of the locals to mention she was running a new wildlife center here in town. He felt a burst of pride knowing she had managed to achieve her goals.

She was no longer the eighteen-year-old who had dreamed of protecting animals and earning a degree in wildlife biology. Honor had reached out and successfully grabbed the brass ring.

It made him feel a little unsettled to know so much had changed since Honor had been his girl. In truth, it felt like another lifetime.

What did he expect? Time hadn't stood still. In many ways, Joshua felt thankful for the passage of time. It had given him the opportunity to change his life and circumstances. Over the past six years, he'd worked extremely hard to better himself. Redemption had been a huge motivating factor. He was no longer the selfish youth who had been impulsive and reckless. In his younger years, he had stolen a car to go joyriding, destroyed town property and been arrested for underage drinking and disorderly conduct. He had been a fixture at the sheriff's office. It had been easy for the residents of Love to believe he had been responsible for setting fire to the town's church and demolishing it. The townsfolk had already written him off well before the fire.

Joshua had made something of himself through sheer determination and grit. He had adopted Violet, the biological child of his ex-wife who had passed away shortly after Violet's birth. He had an impeccable professional reputation. His parents were extremely proud of the way he had pulled himself up by his bootstraps. And yet, he still yearned for the townsfolk of Love to think well of him. He still wanted their stamp of approval.

It had always bothered him that Honor's brothers had

so thoroughly disapproved of him. He felt heat suffusing his neck as he remembered their vocal opposition to his relationship with Honor. Sheriff Boone Prescott had made it his mission in life to break them up and to catch his every misdeed. Joshua let out a sigh. To be fair, he'd enjoyed being a rebel. Until things had spiraled out of control and his whole life was in shreds.

Being in love with the sheriff's sister and the granddaughter of the town mayor, Jasper Prescott, had complicated matters. Law enforcement had not been on his side. Not that he'd made it easy on them. Joshua had been ornery and wild. He had deliberately pushed as many buttons as he could in his hometown and he'd never backed down from a fight. That had endeared him to very few people, particularly since Honor had been the town's reigning princess.

Despite the opposition to their relationship, Honor had always been his biggest cheerleader. She had believed in him until he'd been arrested for burning down the church. Still, after all this time, it gutted him to have caused her such heartache.

Joshua shrugged off the feelings of guilt and recrimination. He had worked steadfastly over the years to redeem his character. He had painstakingly rebuilt his life, laying the foundation one brick at a time. God was a central part of his world now and he lived life with a purpose.

Coming back to his hometown hadn't been easy, but he owed it to his grandfather to pay him his last respects and to tidy up his affairs. He hadn't realized things with the Diamond R would be so complicated.

Joshua made his way to the room he was using as

Violet's nursery. Once he entered the bedroom, he stood by her crib and gently rocked her from side to side. When he felt her head droop against his chest, he slowly lowered her until she was resting on her back. Her eyelids were closed and she was peacefully asleep. He quietly made his way back downstairs.

For Violet's sake, he felt grateful that he could finally hold his head up high in Love. He had put the shameful events of his past in the rearview mirror. He felt proud of himself, if only because he knew so many people had given up on him. This town had viewed him as irredeemable and broken. They had been dead wrong.

Joshua hadn't expected to feel such a wealth of emotions upon his return to Love. As soon as he had spotted Kachemak Bay from his seat in the seaplane, he'd felt a tightening sensation in his chest. Despite everything, this town still lived and breathed in him, just like Honor Prescott. One look in her blue-gray eyes had shown him that the past was still a powerful force to be reckoned with.

As Joshua walked back toward the homestead and away from her with his baby girl, Honor's shoulders sagged. Her cheeks felt flushed. Joshua had a child!

She'd been composed during their encounter, even though seeing Joshua holding his daughter had shaken her to the core. Her limbs were trembling. Coming face-to-face with her ex-fiancé hadn't been on her agenda for today. And it had been shocking to realize he was a father. She felt as if someone had just thrown an ice-cold bucket of water over her head. Joshua looked even more handsome than she remembered. Age had only enhanced his masculine appeal. At six feet or so, Joshua's frame had filled out, giving him a more rugged appearance. His dark hair set off against his blue eyes made a striking combination. He was the type of man who drew stares when he walked down the street.

Her mind veered toward Violet. It had hurt her to see the child nestled in Joshua's arms. It served as a stark reminder of the child she had miscarried six years ago. Joshua's child. She pushed the painful feelings away. She couldn't allow herself to get consumed by the past. It might drag her under.

As she exited the stable, Honor spotted Lee, who was quickly making his way toward her. With his salt-and-pepper-colored hair and sea green eyes, Lee had a distinguished appearance. There was something so solid about him. He was trusted by the whole town. At the moment he had an intense expression etched on his face. His movements seemed full of urgency.

"Honor, it's nice to see you," Lee said, warmth emanating from his voice.

"Hey, Lee," Honor said. "Good morning."

Lee ran his hand around his shirt collar. His fingers seemed unsteady. "Under the circumstances, I'm sorry to have called you out here. It was a mistake."

She frowned at him. He looked flustered. Normally, he was a calm, unflappable man. It was slightly alarming to see him acting this way.

Was Lee referencing Joshua's unexpected appearance at the ranch? Like most of the townsfolk, he was fully aware of their history.

"There's been a bit of a hiccup regarding the reading of the will and Bud's property," he said, his tone apologetic. His eyes radiated disappointment. "I probably jumped the gun by inviting you here to the Diamond R."

"What's wrong?" she asked. Adrenaline began to race through her veins. Instinctively, she steeled herself for bad news.

Lee let out a ragged sigh. "Bud didn't update his will, Honor. He made no written provisions to donate the property to the land preservation society." Lee threw his hands in the air. "There's not a whole lot more I can say, but I'm very disappointed."

"What?" Honor exploded. "That can't be right. He said it over and over again. Everyone in town knew his wishes."

Lee shook his head. "According to his attorney, Bud had the best of intentions, but he passed away before he could make it official. He never updated his will. Knowing Bud, he probably figured he had plenty of years ahead to make those changes."

Honor felt numb as the ramifications of Lee's disclosure began to settle in. "He verbally stated his intentions on several occasions. We all knew what he wanted to do with regard to the ranch. Isn't that enough?"

Lee stared at her with sadness radiating from his eyes. "I'm afraid not, Honor. Our hands are pretty much tied. We could file suit against the estate, but it would cost a fortune. And to what avail? Alaskan inheritance law is very clear."

Her heart sank. "So what happens now?" she asked. "Who inherits the property?"

"According to Bud's attorney, Theo and Joshua and another relative named Violet are listed as the heirs to the Diamond R and all of its assets and acreage."

Honor let out a deep breath. She felt like a deflated

balloon. The old adage was true: don't count your chickens until they're hatched. In her mind she'd formulated so many plans for the expansion of the wildlife center. Now, in a puff of smoke, those dreams had been dashed.

Lee stroked his chin. "I've heard some rumblings about a developer from Texas who's been circling around trying to buy up property in Love. It seems that Theo has already been in contact with them. They came to the ranch first thing this morning." His chest heaved as he sighed. "There's no easy way to say this, Honor, but I think we have to prepare ourselves for what lies ahead."

Anger flared through her at the idea of Theo making deals to desecrate Bud's ranch. Even as a kid he had never had an appreciation for the ranch. Joshua had been the one who had loved horses, the cowboy lifestyle and riding across the property with Bud. Honor had always thought of Joshua as her hometown cowboy.

"Lee, give it to me straight," Honor demanded. Having grown up with three older brothers, she knew when she was being treated with kid gloves. She had always fought against it. She was way tougher than she might look on the surface.

"Do you remember the town council meeting where we discussed the upsurge in interest from developers in acquiring land here in Love?" Lee asked.

"Yes," she said with a nod. "With the popularity of Operation Love, this town has been in the media spotlight. And now that Lovely Boots has taken off, a lot of developers view this town as a hot commodity."

Operation Love was a matchmaking program created by Honor's grandfather, Jasper Prescott. As town mayor, Jasper had devised a way of fixing the imbalance in the male-female ratio in town by bringing eligible women to town who were seeking Alaskan bachelors. The program had been very successful, with dozens of marriages and engagements. And Jasper's wife, Hazel Tookes Prescott, had created genuine Alaskan boots that the town had mass produced as a way of boosting the local economy. After years of recession, it had been a brilliant way of bringing revenue to a cash-strapped town.

The downside of her grandfather's matchmaking program and Hazel's creativity was the sudden focus on their Alaskan hamlet. Suddenly, developers were viewing Love as a potential moneymaker. The idea of developers swooping down and buying up Alaskan land only to dig it up and build businesses on it made her sick to her stomach.

Lee's features creased with tension. "This one outfit is serious about buying land here in Love and the Diamond R property is on their radar." His mouth tightened. "It seems they have plans to build a five-star Alaskan dude ranch. There's a chain of them all across the country."

Honor's jaw dropped. A dude ranch! Right here in Love?

"Theo and Joshua probably had a big check waved in front of their eyes by these developers." He made a tutting sound. "They might find it hard to turn down such a lucrative offer."

She let out a shocked sound. Joshua was in on it? She was stunned that he would go along with such a materialistic scheme. Was this the real reason the brothers had made their way back to their hometown? To make a quick buck by selling the Diamond R Ranch and the surrounding property?

"He wouldn't," she murmured. "He's always loved this ranch."

Lee narrowed his gaze as he looked at her. "Never say never, Honor. It's been quite some time since you've known what Joshua may or may not do."

"Is there any way to intervene?" she asked, instantly discouraged by the defeated expression stamped on Lee's face.

"There's nothing more for us to do except say a few prayers," Lee said with a shrug. "Maybe the Ransom heirs will do the right thing and fulfill Bud's heartfelt wishes." He shook his head. "It's doubtful though. Theo seemed very cocky about being owner of the ranch. Something tells me he won't budge an inch."

Anger rose up inside her. She felt her cheeks getting heated. How could they even consider such a drastic move? It went against everything Bud had stood for in this world. It would be fine by Honor if the property wasn't handed over to the town, just so long as it wasn't torn up to create a tacky dude ranch. She didn't want the town of Love to become a commercial enterprise. Her hometown was a small fishing village filled with God-fearing people who loved the quaint and charming aspects of their town. If the Ransom brothers decided to sell, it would be a nightmare for the residents of Love.

Her stomach churned with worry. Hadn't Joshua just told her he would be heading home after settling his grandfather's affairs? Clearly he wasn't invested in the ranch or in this town. Honor fumed. Joshua might not care about the fate of the Diamond R or this town, but she cared deeply about its future.

"There may not be anything we can do to change their minds," she said in a fierce tone. "But I'm going to let Joshua Ransom know exactly what I think of him turning his back on a town he used to call home."

Chapter Two

Joshua threw his hands up in defeat as he gave in to temptation and moved toward the side window so he could check up on Honor. Was she still outside? He pushed back the curtain and peered out the window, keeping his eyes peeled on the stables. Honor was standing with Lee and they seemed to be having a very intense discussion. He watched as she threw her hands in the air and kicked her booted foot in the snow. The gesture almost made him chuckle. Some things never changed. Although most of the townsfolk had always regarded her as sweetness and light, Honor Prescott had always possessed a feisty side. He remembered it well. More times than he'd like to admit, he had been the recipient of her ire. He sighed. Joshua knew he hadn't made it easy for Honor to love him.

But she had loved him, hadn't she? *Love never fails.* How many times had Honor said those words to him, quoting the verse from *Corinthians*? In the end, their love hadn't been strong enough to survive adversity. It had withered and died. And he had walked around with a broken heart for years, pining for the one who'd gotten away. That was a long time ago though. He no longer harbored any love for his ex-fiancée. It had taken years, but he'd finally gotten over her.

He probably shouldn't be spying on Honor, but his curiosity had gotten the best of him. What was she doing here in the first place? And what was she discussing with Lee that had become so contentious?

All in all, it had been a strange morning at the ranch. Theo had met not only with Lee and his grandfather's attorney, but with a developer from Texas who had come to discuss the Diamond R Ranch. Joshua hadn't attended the meeting. His hands had been full with wrangling a cranky Violet.

Joshua turned away from the window and gazed at his surroundings. His grandfather was all around him at the ranch, but especially in this very room. The den had been Bud's favorite place in the house. Before she had passed away, his grandmother, Pearl, had always enjoyed teasing her husband about holing up inside his man cave for hours on end. Joshua could hear her voice now. *Bud Ransom, we might as well put a bed and a stove in there with you. Then you'd never come out.*

He missed both his grandparents. They had been two of the most loving, generous people he had ever known. They had doted on him during his childhood and shown him unconditional love. His own parents were living in Singapore, too far away to come back for the memorial service. For all intents and purposes, his family had been reduced to a small circle.

Did a person ever stop yearning for the ones they had loved and lost? Honor's face flashed before his eyes. Beautiful, headstrong Honor. He now knew for certain he wasn't over the events of the past. Not by a long shot. Seeing her in the flesh had proven that point. After all this time he still felt a pull in her direction. Not that it mattered. She had shown him years ago that he was dispensable. Honor had tossed him aside like yesterday's garbage. He imagined the whole town of Love had stood up and cheered her on.

A sudden noise drew his attention. Joshua cocked his ear to the side and listened for any cries. These days it seemed as if he was always bracing for the slightest sounds. It was amazing how a child could alter a person's life. He exhaled as silence reigned. Suddenly, Joshua heard the slam of the front door, followed by heavy footsteps. He was about to give Theo a piece of his mind. How many times had he warned him about making loud, disruptive noises when a baby was in the house?

All of a sudden, Honor was standing in the doorway of the den, her hands strategically placed on her hips. Pure molten fire radiated from her eyes. Little huffing sounds were coming from her mouth. He was fairly certain steam was coming out of her ears.

"Are you seriously considering selling out?" she asked in a raised voice, quickly swallowing up the distance between them.

Honor had come charging up to him like a wild bull reacting to a red flag. If she hadn't looked so angry, he might have laughed at her aggressive stance. Her arms were folded across her chest, and she was breathing heavily as she glared at him. She was tapping one of her feet on the hardwood floor.

Old memories crashed over him in unrelenting waves. How could he have forgotten this defiant side of Honor?

He held up his hands. "Can you lower your voice to a dull roar? Slow down. What are you talking about?"

"Lee said there's a developer who wants to buy the Diamond R. He says they want to build a resort on the property—some bootleg version of a dude ranch for people who want a so-called authentic Alaskan cowboy experience."

Joshua stiffened. Hadn't Theo said to keep things quiet about the offer from the developers? Clearly his brother had been running his mouth about the subject. And he had failed to mention anything about a dude ranch. Typical Theo.

He let out a sigh. "Nothing has been decided yet. I just found out about it myself."

Her face fell. "So you're admitting someone is circling around and making an offer on the ranch?"

"Yes, Honor. It's true. Theo told me there's an outfit from Texas that's very interested in buying the property."

"Bud would never have wanted this place to be sold to a developer. How can you even consider it?" she asked, her voice ringing out in the stillness of the room.

Joshua clenched his teeth at the accusatory tone of her voice. He felt his anger rising.

"Excuse me? I don't reckon you want to pick a fight with me over my family's land." He hadn't meant for his voice to have such a hard edge to it, but so be it. He hadn't come back to Love in order to be pushed around and judged by his ex-fiancée. The days of everyone here in town making him feel less than were over. "It's nobody's business but ours."

Honor let out a shocked gasp. She took a few steps closer to him until he could hear her breathing. He could see the flecks in her blue-gray eyes. She was bristling with rage.

"Do you know what will happen to this land if you sell? This developer will come in and tear up the land and make it some ghastly commercial enterprise."

Joshua frowned. "You're getting way ahead of yourself."

"Am I? These things seem to happen fairly quickly. One minute they're making you an offer and the next thing you know papers are being signed. This is precious land. It shouldn't be transformed into something unrecognizable. And Bud wanted to donate the property so it would be preserved from developers."

"Then why didn't he put it in writing and make it official?" Joshua asked. "Bud was smart. He knew the risks in not following through on his promise."

"I—I don't know, but I do believe it was his intention." She locked eyes with him. "Doesn't that mean anything to you?"

"This isn't just up to me. Theo has some say in this as well. And I'm not convinced Bud wanted to donate the property to land preservation. He was as sharp as a tack. Maybe he changed his mind."

He watched as Honor's eyes widened and her mouth opened. Just as she seemed ready to erupt, a loud wail rang out in the room.

Honor froze at the sound. She turned toward the sound of the cries, which came from a nearby baby monitor.

"Is something wrong with Violet?" she asked. She sounded alarmed.

"I'm sure she's fine. She's been fussy since we arrived here," he answered in a clipped tone. "She must have woken up from her nap."

"She sounds upset." Honor bit her lip and looked in the direction of the baby monitor.

"Sometimes she just needs to settle back down."

She swung her gaze back toward him. "Aren't you going to go get her?"

Joshua frowned. He didn't understand why Honor looked so stricken. Was she suggesting he was neglecting Violet? He opened his mouth to say something, but he shut it. He didn't need to remind Honor that she wasn't a parent. There was already enough acrimony between them.

It really didn't matter what she thought. He was Violet's father. He knew what his own daughter needed better than anyone.

"I need to go see to her," Joshua said in an abrupt tone. He turned on his heel and left the room, his footsteps echoing in his wake. Honor turned toward the baby monitor. She could still hear soft cries emanating from it. It caused a tightening sensation in her chest.

Honor hadn't meant to sound so bossy, but the sound of Violet's cries had been tugging at her heartstrings. There was something so poignant about the sound of a baby crying. Tears sprang to her eyes and she blinked them away. She knew it had everything to do with the baby she had lost. Joshua's child. Although her own pregnancy had been unexpected, Honor had desperately wanted to be a mother. Not being able to hold her child in her arms was something she would never get over. And at moments like this one, the pain of loss came crashing over her in waves.

A few minutes later, the sound of footsteps heralded Joshua's return. Honor's gaze went immediately to Violet. The baby's eyes were slightly red-rimmed and her hair was rumpled. She looked adorable.

Honor's pulse began to quicken at the sight of Joshua and his little girl.

Violet was the perfect name for the blue-eyed stunner squirming in Joshua's arms. With her chubby cheeks and a head of blond curls, Violet was a vision. Unable to stop herself, Honor took two steps toward Joshua, then reached out and grasped one of Violet's fingers.

"How old is she?" Honor asked, filled with curiosity.

"She's ten months old."

Her throat felt as dry as sandpaper. There were other questions she wanted to ask, but she wasn't sure it was really her place. Where was Violet's mother? she wondered. She cast another gaze at his ring finger to make sure she hadn't missed it. He definitely wasn't wearing a wedding band.

"Bud said you'd gotten divorced a long time ago," she blurted out, immediately wishing she could pull back the impulsive words. She didn't want Joshua to think she'd been keeping tabs on him. Bud had hired her to come over to the Diamond R twice a week to check in on his animals. Although he'd never divulged much about Joshua's life, he had slipped one day and confided in her about Joshua's divorce.

"That's right," he said, jutting his chin out. "About five years ago. It lasted all of eleven months. I'm no longer married."

Honor knew the shock was showing on her face. Her entire life people had told her about her inability to hide her feelings. She was certain this moment wasn't any exception. She was reacting to the fact that Joshua hadn't married Violet's mother. It wasn't shocking in itself, but it didn't gel with the Joshua Ransom she had once known.

Joshua Ransom was no longer her business. What difference did it make whether he was single or divorced or had a houseful of babies? It was none of her concern. He was nothing more than a faded memory to her.

"Dada," Violet said in a sing-song voice, looking up at Joshua with a gummy smile.

"Hi there," Honor said in a light voice, smiling at the blue-eyed charmer. "Aren't you the sweetest little thing?"

Violet gifted her with a grin, then reached out and tugged at her hair. Honor let out a squeal as Violet grabbed a few strands and wrapped them around her fingers. The expression on Violet's face was one of triumph.

"Easy there, Vi," Joshua said with a low chuckle. He began disentangling Honor's hair from Violet's grasp. "She loves to latch onto things."

"She's beautiful," Honor said, unable to take her eyes off the little girl. She looked dainty in her pink-and-purple onesie, yet her little body appeared to be sturdy and well nourished. From the looks of it, Joshua was doing a great job in the fatherhood department. There was a funny feeling stirring around in her belly.

"Thank you," Joshua said. "She's changed my life in ways I never could have imagined." Joshua's voice was filled with reverence. "On a cloudy day, this little lady can make the sun peek out past the clouds."

"And her mother? Is she here, too?" she asked, her heart sinking at the idea of coming face-to-face with the woman who had given Joshua a child. It was a petty emotion, but Honor couldn't ignore it. It was an unsettling feeling. After six long years she shouldn't care about Joshua's personal life.

Joshua's expression hardened. His jaw tightened. "She passed away right after Violet was born. I'm raising her on my own."

Guilt clawed at her. Moments ago she'd felt an emotion resembling jealousy. And now she had just discovered that Violet didn't have a mother. The situation was heartbreaking. Joshua was a single father raising a baby daughter. And poor Violet would never know the woman who had given her life.

It was incredibly difficult to reconcile the man standing in front of her cradling Violet with the ex-fiancé who had run wild all over town, leaving mayhem in his wake. He had once stolen a car as a prank and broken into a Jarvis Street shop named Keepsakes on a dare. And in one final act of rebellion, he had gone too far and started a fire that had destroyed the town's beloved church. A local man had sustained burns after trying to put out the blaze. There had been no going back for Joshua after that heinous act. It had earned him a one-way ticket out of Love.

She shook the painful memories off and focused on the present. "I'm sorry to hear that, Joshua. It's terribly sad for both of you," she said in a low voice.

"Yes. It's not fair for Violet. She'll never get to know her mother," Joshua said. He sighed deeply. "Tomorrow is never promised, like Bud always said. Life keeps teaching me that lesson. I thought I'd be able to see my grandfather again. He had plans to fly to Seattle to visit

Violet and me next month." His mouth quirked. "That won't happen now."

There was nothing Honor could say. No words were necessary. They both knew from their own experiences how unfair life could be. At the age of eight, Joshua had lost a baby sister to leukemia while Honor had struggled throughout her life with having parents who were missing in action. But developing a relationship with God during her college years had strengthened her as a person. He had shown her that despite setbacks and disappointments, life was a beautiful journey.

Honor found her gaze straying back toward Violet time and again. She felt a wild impulse to ask Joshua if she could hold his daughter. She wanted to cradle her tightly in her arms and smell her forehead. Babies always smelled like powder and soap and fresh flowers. She knew it wasn't true, but looking at Violet made her believe it.

Seeing Joshua's child created an ache deep within her soul.

"I need to get back to the wildlife center," Honor said, tearing her gaze away from Violet. She needed to get away from Violet and Joshua as quickly as possible. These tender feelings were making her feel all jumbled up inside. A feeling of intense loss swept over her. Thinking about the baby she'd lost was incredibly painful. Joshua's child. Seeing Violet brought back those devastating memories. What she wouldn't have given to have held her own child in her arms just once.

She had only come to the Diamond R Ranch today to meet with Lee about Bud's will. Seeing Joshua had been a complete shock to the system. And finding out that Joshua had a sweet-faced baby girl had been quite the surprise. Her mind was still whirling about the terms of Bud's will. It was all a little much for her to absorb at the moment.

Honor had no intention of allowing herself to get swept up in Joshua's life. When she had ended their engagement, Honor had cut all ties with him. Joshua had torn her world apart and ripped her heart to shreds. Becoming invested in his life was a surefire way to blur the lines she had established between them. She couldn't run the risk of falling for him all over again. The sight of him holding Violet threatened to wear down all her defenses. It made her wonder what kind of a father he would have been to their child.

Joshua eyed her warily. "Are you finished reading me the riot act?"

She locked gazes with him. "For now," she said in a low voice. "I don't want to startle Violet by raising my voice." On impulse, she reached out and swept a finger across the baby's cheek. She was soft and warm. *She is more precious than rubies.* Honor felt a tugging sensation in the region of her heart as she gazed upon the irresistible sight of Joshua's baby girl.

"By the way, no decision has been made regarding the Diamond R," Joshua said in a firm voice. "But make no mistake, Honor. Any decision I make will be in the best interest of Violet and her future. The moment I became her father she became my number one priority in this world. Bar none."

She nodded in his direction as an acknowledgment of the sentiments he had just expressed. Putting his daughter first was noble. She had no idea what that meant for the future of the ranch. If she believed Joshua, its destiny still hung in the balance.

As Honor walked away from Joshua and Violet and out into the brisk February afternoon, a feeling of sadness swept over her. Six years ago she would have given anything to have this version of Joshua Ransom in her life. Steady. Devoted. Strong. Dependable. Instead, she had fallen for a rebellious rabble-rouser who had stolen her heart, then made a fool of her in front of her family and the whole town. Ever since then Honor had been wary of falling in love.

Tears pooled in her eyes as the dreams of her youth came rising back to the surface with a vengeance. She had once dreamed of forever with Joshua. She'd wanted the fairy tale—the white picket fence, the blue-eyed babies who were the spitting image of their father and a happily-ever-after. None of it had come true.

Her brothers had all found their happily-ever-afters. Boone had married the love of his life, Grace, and they now had a baby girl named Eva. Cameron had reunited with Paige and discovered he was a father to baby Emma. Liam had been given the greatest gift of all when he'd discovered that his wife, Ruby, who had been presumed dead in an avalanche, was alive and suffering from amnesia. Their reunion had been incredibly moving. Even Jasper had found everlasting love with Hazel. The list went on and on. Declan. Finn. Sophie. It was as if the whole world was coupling up and finding their happy endings. Everyone but her.

All this time Honor had been telling herself she didn't want love in her life. But it had been a big lie. Being wounded by her failed relationship with Joshua had made her gun-shy. She wanted the same things her siblings had—promises of forever. But having all her dreams go up in flames six years ago had left her with permanent scars. Even though she had a good idea of the life she wanted to live, she had no idea how to reach out and grab it.

Once Honor left the ranch, Joshua brought Violet into the kitchen so he could whip up some lunch for her. Introducing Violet to his ex-fiancée had been a bit surreal. Two worlds colliding. He hadn't bothered to tell Honor that Violet wasn't his biological child. Truthfully, it wasn't anyone's business. In his heart, she was every bit his daughter. When his ex-wife, Lauren, had discovered she had a terminal illness, she had tracked him down and begged him to raise Violet. Although he hadn't seen Lauren in over two years, Joshua had embraced her request. It had been the single best decision he'd ever made in his life.

Joshua let out a low chuckle as he placed his daughter in the wooden high chair he had retrieved from the attic. It looked like something from the Stone Age. He imagined his grandparents had used it for his own father and perhaps him and Theo as well. He had been surprised at its sturdiness. Built to last. He had always thought of the Diamond R Ranch in the same vein. Enduring.

Joshua placed Violet in the high chair, then bent over so he could place a kiss on her temple. "This thing might be old, but it does the job, doesn't it, cutie pie?" Violet looked at him and gurgled. He took that as a yes.

Footsteps announced Theo's arrival in the kitchen. His brother stood in the entryway with a huge grin on his face. With his dark head of hair and azure-colored eyes, Theo could easily pass for his twin. Growing up, they had constantly been confused for one another by teachers and townsfolk.

"Be careful, bro. You're turning into a pile of mush," Theo teased. "That little charmer has you wrapped around her finger."

Joshua felt a slight twinge of embarrassment. He had always prided himself on being rugged and manly. That's the way he and Theo had been raised. Now Theo had caught him in the act of cooing to his baby girl and mashing up peas and carrots and pastini for her lunch.

Why should he worry about what he looked like? He loved his daughter more than anything in this world. He had always cared way too much about his older brother's opinion. Doing so hadn't always been in Joshua's best interest. It had ended up costing him a lot.

"Fatherhood changes a man," he conceded, not even bothering to object to Theo's observation. If being mushy brought him one step closer to being a phenomenal father, Joshua would assume the title as the mushiest guy in all of Alaska.

Theo took off his cowboy hat and rocked back on his heels. "Was that Honor Prescott I just saw beating a fast path away from here on a horse? She was riding like the wind itself was chasing her."

Joshua didn't really want to discuss Honor with his brother, but there was no way of avoiding it. Theo had made it clear on numerous occasions how he felt about his ex-fiancée. *Stuck-up* and *highfalutin* were two words he had regularly used to describe her. It had annoyed Joshua to no end. Theo hadn't known Honor. Not the way Joshua had. She had been sweet and loyal and kind. The best person he'd ever known. And if he hadn't messed things up so royally, she would have become his wife.

"Yes, it was Honor," he admitted. "She came here to

meet up with Lee. And then she blasted me regarding your meeting with the developers. She was really bent out of shape at the idea of us selling the Diamond R." He hated the way Honor had made him feel. The way she had spoken to him had been harsh, as if he was a traitor to his grandfather and the entire town. Even though a part of him rejected her assessment of the situation, he still felt a bit tarnished by her judgment. Old habits died hard. Sadly, it was a familiar feeling in this town.

Theo's expression hardened. "Same small-minded opinions," he scoffed. "Some things never change. These people seem to think they have some say in the matter, when in reality it's Ransom family business."

"Please don't tell me they're really intending to open an Alaskan dude ranch," Joshua said. "That's about the cheesiest thing I've ever heard."

"They mentioned it in passing," Theo said with a shrug. "But, to be honest, it's not my concern. What they do with the property is their business."

Joshua frowned at his brother. "Sounds like you've already made up your mind. We've barely discussed it."

Theo scoffed. "Is there really anything to think about? Let's face it, Joshua. Neither one of us wants to live in this Podunk town. It would be about as exciting as watching paint dry to stay here. I for one could use a big fat check from this Texas corporation. They sound as if they're ready to make a very lucrative offer and draw up contracts."

Joshua's head felt as if it was spinning. He'd barely been back in Love for twenty-four hours and not only had he inherited the Diamond R Ranch, but he might end up a millionaire if he agreed to sell the property.

That type of money would be instrumental in raising Violet and paying for her future education.

Coming face-to-face with Honor had knocked him off balance. She represented all of his young hopes and dreams. There had never been another great love in his life after Honor Prescott. She had imprinted herself on his heart. And even though he shouldn't care about her opinion, he still did. He wanted her to see the new and improved Joshua. It had hurt him to see such condemnation flashing in her eyes.

Everything was happening way too fast for his liking. The idea of selling his family's ranch felt incredibly final. And if Honor was right, it wasn't in accordance with his grandfather's wishes. But Theo wanted to make the deal, collect the money and then head out of Dodge. It was a lot to process.

"Theo, I need some time to wrap my head around all of this. Why don't we focus on the memorial service? After all, it's the main reason we came here, isn't it? To honor Gramps."

Theo nodded. "You're right. Let's give him a fitting send-off." He rubbed his hands together. "How about a rip-roaring barbecue at the ranch?"

"It's February in Alaska. It's far from barbecue weather." Joshua chuckled. "How about a simple church service followed by a nice meal and fellowship with some of his friends?" Joshua suggested.

"A church service?" Theo asked with wide eyes. "Not sure we'd be welcome in church, Joshua. Not after what happened with the fire."

"Our grandfather paid our debts at that church. He donated a hefty sum of money to have it rebuilt. I managed to dodge jail time due to my age, but I still had to attend a program for first-time offenders before I went overseas." Joshua winced. He hated discussing that period of his life. It hadn't been pretty. "Pastor Jack reached out to me and extended an olive branch. He wants us to host the memorial for Bud there. He was beloved in this town. Thankfully, the townsfolk could separate Gramps from the actions of his grandsons." He shook his head, overwhelmed by the pastor's generosity. Not many people would be gracious toward the man who they believed was responsible for burning down the town's church.

"Joshua," Theo said in a low voice. "Maybe it's time for me to set the record straight. It's not fair you've been blamed all this time for something I did."

He waved a hand at his brother. "It's water under the bridge. We made the decision to protect your army career. If I hadn't claimed responsibility, you would have lost your military position."

Theo made a strangled sound. "So instead you lost the woman you loved and were run out of town on a rail. It doesn't seem fair, does it?"

Even after all these years it still hurt to think about the dissolution of his relationship with Honor and being disowned by his hometown. At the time, it had felt like the end of the world. It had forever altered the course of his life.

He shrugged. "I wasn't exactly innocent, Theo. I was right there with you causing trouble. We had no business being in the church at night."

"But I set the fire. You didn't. I was playing around with my lighter and one of the hymnals. When the flame began raging out of control, I had no clue how to put it out. I was frightened."

Joshua nodded. The event was indelibly imprinted on his mind. "So we ran. Probably the worst thing we could have done," Joshua said. "The church might have been salvageable if we'd stuck around and called the authorities." After all this time, he still felt guilty. If only he'd convinced Theo to alert law enforcement. If he was being honest with himself, he knew why he hadn't done so. Sheriff Boone Prescott. He hadn't wanted to give Honor's brother the satisfaction of saying I-told-you-so to his fiancée. They had been caught anyway.

Joshua turned to Violet and spooned a mouthful of food into her mouth. Although he appreciated his brother's desire to make amends, Joshua knew it wouldn't do much good in the present. He had lost Honor because of one foolish decision that had spiraled out of control. The town had been rocked by the torched church and the knowledge that the fire had been started by one of their own.

Joshua raked his hand through his hair. Now he couldn't hold back the groundswell of memories rising up inside him. "Zachariah Cummings spotted us as we fled the scene. He told the authorities I was the one covered in ash and fleeing the church. He mistook you for me. Same hair and eye color. Same build."

"Zachariah tried to put out the fire by himself before the authorities arrived," Theo said, a look of discomfort stamped on his face.

"He suffered serious burns," Joshua said with a shake of his head. "He's lucky to be alive."

Theo groaned. "It was all my fault. And you took the fall because my stint in the army would have been over before it really began."

The brothers locked gazes. So many words had

been left unspoken between them. Joshua had taken the blame to protect his brother's military future. As a result, he had lost everything. "But I'm no longer in the army, and you deserve to be vindicated." Theo's voice rang out with conviction.

"Theo, I've moved on since then. It won't serve a single purpose to rehash the past and dig up old wounds. In a few weeks we'll both be back home in Seattle and Los Angeles living our lives. I can't imagine either one of us having a reason to come back here." Just saying the words out loud caused a tightening sensation smack-dab in the center of his chest. It sounded so final.

For a few moments silence settled over the kitchen. Violet's gibberish was the only sound in the room. She was in her own world and babbling away. Joshua imagined that Theo, much like himself, was consumed by the past, their grandfather's passing and being back in their hometown. Not to mention the dilemma of whether or not to sell the Diamond R.

"We'll have to contact Pastor Jack and get a list together of all his friends here in town," Theo said, breaking the silence.

An invite list. He couldn't help but think about Honor and her big, bustling family. They had always respected and admired his grandfather, but because of the bad feelings between himself and the Prescotts, Joshua wasn't certain if they would attend the memorial service. It made his heart ache a little to think about it. Joshua hoped he hadn't burned all of his bridges in his hometown.

For some reason, being a father had changed his views about Love. It hadn't all been negative. He wanted Violet to know the place where he'd been born and raised. The Diamond R Ranch had been a huge part of his upbringing. He couldn't change the way people felt about his past, but he wanted to show everyone that he had grown and matured.

Even though he had tried to convince himself that he was over the past, it still sat like an anchor on his chest. When he least expected it, memories rose up and threatened to drag him under. Pain. Loss. Heartache. One fateful decision that had altered the course of his young life. He had kicked himself a thousand times for not telling Honor the truth.

Even if he was only in Love for a short duration, Joshua intended to extinguish those painful memories before he headed back to Seattle. Since he'd left town he had worked tirelessly to make something of himself. He now owned a home construction business and he'd been flipping houses to bring in more income. He had stashed away a nice sum of money. In the next few months he intended to purchase a medium-sized starter home for himself and Violet. All in all, life was good.

His life had moved on in the aftermath of the dissolution of his relationship with Honor. When she had broken off their engagement, the very foundation of Joshua's world crumbled. Although he had been forced to adjust to living without her, it had been the most difficult undertaking of his life.

She's too good for you, Ransom.

Those words had been seared into his brain, courtesy of Sheriff Boone Prescott and his brothers. As much as he had hated Boone for being so blunt, Joshua had always known it had been true. Despite having loved her, Joshua knew he hadn't been worthy of the reigning princess of Love, Alaska. Honor had been the shiny brass ring completely out of his reach. Against all odds, he had earned her love, which had made him the happiest man in all of Alaska. But love hadn't been enough.

Joshua winced as bitter memories washed over him. In one reckless moment, Joshua had shown his complete unworthiness and given Honor no choice but to walk away from him. And even though he had moved on, Joshua still wasn't over it. Not by a long shot.

Chapter Three

Honor drove her truck down the snowy streets of downtown Love and hummed to the upbeat tune on the radio. It felt nice to be out and about on a chilly Saturday afternoon. Having brunch with her family provided a well-needed pick-me-up. She had become so isolated working and living out at the wildlife center. As much as she loved her job, it was important to stop every now and again to smell the forget-me-nots.

Her family had been advising her to get out more and start socializing with the townsfolk. Honor knew exactly what it meant. Everyone wanted her to find a nice Alaskan man to settle down and start a family with. It was easier said than done. So far she hadn't been able to let go of the past in order to embrace her future. Her heart had been encased in ice for quite some time. And whenever she thought about opening up to someone, fear of the past repeating itself kept her in the safe zone. It was far better to be single than to be brokenhearted.

As soon as she crossed the threshold of the Moose Café, the tempting smells of freshly brewed coffee and baked bread rose to her nostrils. There was already a bustling crowd scattered about the establishment. Her brother Cameron's café was a very successful eatery here in town. Everyone loved the coffee, the food and the relaxed atmosphere. Honor was proud of her older brother for living out his dreams and pushing past all the self-doubt.

"Honor! It's nice to see you." Sophie Catalano, Honor's dear friend and a waitress-barista at the Moose Café, warmly greeted her. "You barely show your face around here anymore."

"Hey, Sophie," Honor said, wrapping her arms around the beautiful redhead for a warm hug. "It's great to see you. I've been so busy at the wildlife center it's hard to get to town most days."

"I understand," Sophie said with a smile. "You're doing important work over there. Ruby was raving about your workshop on birds of prey. Aidan was mighty impressed," she said, referring to Honor's seven-year-old nephew.

"Wait till he finds out we have some lynx kittens that were orphaned and injured in a fire. He's such a compassionate little boy. I know he'll want to come see them as soon as he can get over there." Just the thought of the lynx kittens made Honor smile. It had been so fortunate that a local firefighter, Hank Jeffries, had managed to rescue them from the fire. They were now out of danger and on their way to a full recovery.

"You're pretty much the bee's knees as far as Aidan is concerned," Sophie said.

Honor grinned so wide her cheeks hurt with the effort. "I think that's probably the best compliment I've ever received." Just the thought of her nephew and nieces filled Honor with joy. Her brothers had made her such a proud auntie. Family meant the world to her and God had blessed her with all of these connections.

"If you're looking for your brothers, they're sitting over there with Jasper," Sophie said, nodding in the direction of a table in the back. Honor followed Sophie's gaze, smiling at the sight of all three of her brothers sitting with her grandfather, along with Declan and Finn O'Rourke, close friends of all the Prescotts. None of her sisters-in-law were present, which made Honor the only female in attendance. She looked around for Hazel. It always felt nice to have some extra estrogen when surrounded by Prescott and O'Rourke men.

Honor walked over to the table and quietly joined her family. She was greeted by a chorus of enthusiastic voices. Warmth settled in her chest. This was home, she thought. A place where you were greeted with joy and open arms. Unconditional love. She settled into a seat beside Boone and Liam. It felt nice to be surrounded by family and good friends. She felt safe and protected from the slings and arrows of life. Honor might disagree with them from time to time, but when times were tough, they all had each other's backs.

Hazel—Jasper's wife and a surrogate mother to Honor and her siblings—strolled over to the table clutching papers against her chest. She looked around the table and flashed a wide smile. "Morning everyone. Glad you could all make it. Isn't it nice to get together and break bread? I can't wait for you to taste my new jalapeño corn fritters."

Jasper looked at Hazel. "You know I don't like spicy food. It gives me heartburn. Can you please just cut to the chase and tell us why you organized this brunch?

You're about as transparent as glass. It's obvious you have something up your sleeve."

Hazel slapped Jasper on the shoulder, causing him to let out a yelp. "Old Jasper here is right. I've made up some flyers and I'm going to be distributing them to our customers today. Then I'm going to hang some up at the church on the announcement board."

"If this is about your over-the-top birthday party," Jasper groused, "we already know you've planned your own shindig. Everyone has already saved the date and placed it on their calendars."

"Once again, you're wrong, Jasper." Hazel swung her gaze around the table. "To be frank, I really don't want to hear any grumbling about this. I just wanted to give you all a heads-up." She placed the papers down on the table with a thump, then eyeballed everyone as if daring them to say something.

Honor picked up one of the flyers. It had the café's logo at the top. She read the words out loud. "Homegoing reception in honor of Bud Ransom."

Liam sputtered as he drank his coffee. "Here? At the Moose Café?" he asked, his eyes bulging.

Cameron held up his hands. "Don't blame me. I had nothing to do with it. I just own the joint," he muttered.

"Was this all your idea, Hazel?" Honor asked with a frown. Never in a million years would she have imagined that the Ransom brothers would be welcome at the Moose Café. It felt like something in the universe had shifted.

Hazel grinned. "Yep. It was all me. I figured after the memorial service we could all come here for some refreshments and fellowship. Joshua and Theo were at the church looking for a place to hold a reception, so I suggested they have it here."

"What in the world did you do that for?" Jasper asked. "Those Ransom boys are nothing but trouble. Always have been. Always will be. And I can't believe either one of 'em had the nerve to step inside a church."

Honor cringed at the harsh tone of her grandfather's voice. By force of habit she opened her mouth to stick up for Joshua, then quickly shut it. It wasn't her job to take up for Joshua anymore. Those days were long over.

"To be fair," Liam said, "that was a long time ago. None of us would want to be judged by our worst moment."

Honor ached at the sincerity in her brother's voice. Of all her siblings, Liam was the one who was the most forgiving. As a physician, he didn't have the luxury to judge others. All who sought medical help from him were treated with equal kindness and dedication.

"Bud was a fine man, but that's where it ends as far as his family is concerned," Boone said, folding his arms across his chest. "Theo and Joshua haven't been part of the fabric of this town for quite some time. They burned those bridges a long time ago, no pun intended. I'm surprised they'd want to host something here."

Declan flashed a pearly grin. "It might be fun to toss them out on their ears for old time's sake," he said with a laugh.

"You should be ashamed of yourselves!" Hazel barked. "Not an ounce of charity to spare, is that it? Those boys just suffered a great loss. Haven't you ever heard that once you're a part of this town you're always welcomed home with open arms? It's practically the town motto."

"Nope," Cameron said with a shake of his head. "Can't say I have." He squinted at Hazel. "Are you sure you didn't just make that up on the spot?"

Hazel glared at him. "I'm not even going to dignify that with an answer. We're going to let those boys host the reception right here at the Moose."

"They're not exactly boys anymore," Finn said with a snort.

"Troublemakers is what they are," Jasper roared. "I can't think of a single good thing either of those two ever contributed to this town. They weren't happy unless they were causing mayhem and madness." He shook his fist in the air. "You mark my words! If they stick around Love, they'll be up to no good in no time." He swung his gaze toward Honor. "You should thank the Lord Almighty that you didn't marry that scoundrel."

Honor gulped. She didn't even want to think about how angry her family would be when they found out Joshua and Theo were courting an offer from a developer to purchase the Diamond R Ranch. She feared Jasper just might have a coronary. He'd already had one heart attack a few years ago. For the moment she was keeping quiet about it. After all, nothing had been decided. And she really didn't want to raise Jasper's blood pressure. The news would surely put everyone on edge.

Hazel planted her hands on her hips. "The last time I checked, I have some say around here. Long story short, I've invited the Ransom brothers to have a reception here after the memorial service. I don't want to hear another word about it."

Everything stilled and hushed for a moment as the news settled in. Even Jasper kept quiet. There was a don't-mess-with-me vibe radiating from Hazel. No one wanted to see her erupt.

"Well, we might as well order some food," Boone mumbled. "I came over here expecting to be fed. And I know better than to fight with you, Hazel."

"I sure wish Jasper would get that memo," Hazel said, letting out a delighted cackle. "I keep telling him he needs to be sweeter to me since my birthday is coming up. He might not make it onto the invite list."

Jasper grumbled and buried his head in the menu, refusing to meet his wife's gaze. Honor knew her grandfather's anger was genuine. He really disliked both Ransom brothers. Honor knew part of the reason was tied up in her history with Joshua, while another reason lay in Jasper's title as town mayor. It was impossible for her grandfather to respect people who he felt weren't law-abiding citizens. Being responsible for the destruction of the town's church had been unforgiveable in Jasper's eyes. Not to mention the fact that Jasper's close friend Zachariah had been hurt in the fire.

Honor let out a sigh. Jasper wasn't the only one. The majority of the townsfolk in Love had vowed to run Joshua out of town on a rail. It hadn't come to that since Joshua had packed up his things and left Love after she'd broken things off with him.

Brunch was a solemn affair. Everyone dug in to their food and tried to focus on anything but the elephant in the room. At the end of the meal, everyone got up and dispersed without lingering for conversation or fellowship. A disgruntled vibe hung in the air. It made Honor feel uncomfortable. She didn't like her family to be at odds. For a long time after her breakup with Joshua, Honor had been angry at Boone. She had irrationally blamed him for her broken engagement and all the troubles with Joshua. It had taken quite a while for Honor to forgive her brother for opposing their relationship.

As she stood up to leave, Liam placed his arm around her and pulled her off to the side. "How do you feel about all of this? It must be strange to have Joshua back in Love after all this time."

"It's fine," she murmured, meeting Liam's skeptical gaze. She shrugged. "I'll admit it is kind of odd. Seeing him for the first time was surreal. And finding out he has a baby kind of threw me for a loop."

"A baby?" Liam asked. "I heard he had one of those quickie marriages a few years back, but if I recall correctly, they split up shortly after the wedding."

Honor wrinkled her nose. "You're right. He isn't married any longer. And he's raising baby Violet on his own because her mother died."

Liam winced. "That's tough. I know what it's like to raise a child by myself. When Ruby was presumed dead, I was both father and mother to Aidan." He scratched his jaw. "It wasn't easy."

"No," Honor said, squeezing her brother's arm. "I know you went through some hard times. Despite what went down between myself and Joshua, I don't want him to suffer the same way you did."

Liam narrowed his gaze as he looked at her. "Honor, I hope you maintain a safe distance from Joshua."

"What do you mean?" she asked.

"You have a heart that's as wide open as the Alaskan tundra. I don't want you to get hurt again." Liam didn't need to say anything else. It was written all over his handsome face. Her brothers had always been her protectors. Years ago they had tried in vain to get between her and Joshua. Like most young women who were head over heels in love, Honor had been stubborn and intractable. She had felt such resentment toward her brothers for trying to sabotage her youthful romance. There had been no convincing her of the unsuitability of Joshua Ransom.

She had been blind to Joshua's flaws until everything exploded in her face.

"He's only come back for the memorial," she said in a clipped tone. "And, believe it or not, I've moved past my relationship with Joshua." She let out a brittle-sounding laugh. "We were kids back then."

Liam nodded. "Kids who were crazy in love," he noted.

Crazy in love. It was an apt description for the way she had felt about Joshua. And the way he had felt about her in return. They had been madly, deeply, happily in love.

All of sudden Hazel appeared at their side, allowing Honor a reprieve from having to come up with a response to Liam's statement. There was no doubt about it. She and Joshua had been so committed to one another that they had dreamed of getting married and spending their lives together. He had proposed to Honor and put a ring on her finger. Their relationship had been so much more intense than youthful infatuation. Even though she had tried to minimize those feelings over the years in order to make herself feel better about the way things had crashed and burned, it had been the real deal.

Hazel cleared her throat. "Liam. Do you mind if I have a word with Honor?"

"Of course not," Liam said. He winked at Hazel. "She's all yours."

Once they were alone, Hazel began shifting from one foot to the other. A sheepish expression crept over her face.

"Honor, I think I might owe you an apology. Jasper, bless his heart, isn't always on target, but he pointed out that I was wrong to offer the Moose Café to Joshua without checking with you first." She bit her lip. "I know how hard it was when things ended between you and Joshua. Never in a million years would I ever want to cause you any pain."

"Please don't worry about me. I'm fine. I think it was very generous of you to offer the Moose Café to Joshua and Theo."

She groaned. "You're just being nice. I'm sorry if I made a mess of things. Sometimes I try too hard to do what I think is right," she muttered. "Maybe I should have just left things alone."

Honor reached out and took her hand. "Hazel. You didn't do anything wrong. Joshua and I are six years older and wiser. We've both moved on with our lives. What kind of woman would I be if I begrudged them the use of the café for Bud's reception?" No matter what had transpired between her and Joshua in the past, Honor couldn't allow it to change who she was as a person. She had cared for Joshua's grandfather. Bud had been her friend.

"That's very mature of you. Can you do me a favor and ask your brothers to kick their vendetta to the curb?" She made a tutting sound. "They need to just let it go already. Joshua was a boy of eighteen when he started that fire. It was a terrible accident and he paid dearly for it."

"Yes, he did," Honor murmured, knowing Hazel was referencing her.

"Call me a softie, but life is too short to harbor bitterness in one's heart."

"Old grudges are silly. I don't want anyone feuding on my account. The way I figure it, if I can be civil to Joshua, no one else has the right to act up." She chewed on her lip. "And I hate to say it, but there could be a legitimate reason for tensions to heighten in the near future."

Hazel frowned. "Do I dare ask what you're talking about?"

Honor bit her lip. "I don't want to gossip, but you'll find out soon enough. Bud didn't sign the ranch over to the town and the preservation society. Joshua and Theo are his heirs. And they're considering selling the Diamond R to a Texas developer."

Hazel's eyes bulged. "No! That can't be right!"

"Unfortunately it is. I heard it straight from Lee's mouth and then Joshua confirmed it." She made a face. "Some outfit from Texas wants to create a posh dude ranch on the property. It seems as if everyone wants a piece of our little fishing village these days."

"I'm afraid for this town if they sell out. Bud was a smart man. I can't believe he didn't make things official in his will," Hazel lamented.

Honor shrugged. "I don't know. Maybe he changed his mind about it. Perhaps he wanted Joshua and his daughter to be comfortable. He's raising her all by himself."

"Joshua has a daughter?" Hazel asked. "Years ago I wouldn't have trusted that boy with a pet rock, but time changes folks. Everyone deserves a shot at getting things right."

"I think so, too," Honor concurred. *Getting things right.* Suddenly, a lightbulb went off in Honor's head. "Maybe Joshua will decide to do the right thing regarding the Diamond R. Perhaps this is his chance to redeem himself," she said.

Hazel eyed her with skepticism. "I wouldn't hold my breath. Joshua and Theo are just passing through Love. Neither one of 'em has any reason to hold on to the ranch. Sad to say, but selling it makes a whole lot of sense." Hazel patted her on the shoulder before walking back toward the kitchen.

Honor shook her head. It wasn't going to happen. Not on her watch! There was no way she was going to sit around on the sidelines as a developer destroyed Bud's ranch and created such a monstrosity in Love. She wasn't certain how she would go about it, but she was determined to make Joshua see how wrong it would be to sell the Diamond R Ranch. Perhaps she could remind him of all the reasons he used to adore his hometown and Bud's ranch.

If there was even a sliver of the old Joshua that still existed, Honor felt certain he would tell the Texas developers to take a hike and find a new town to plunder.

Chapter Four

Joshua looked around the Moose Café with keen interest. The establishment owned by Cameron Prescott had a rustic charm. Copper lights hung from the ceiling, giving the café a warm glow. Forget-me-nots had been placed in small vases on each individual table. He had to admit, the place had a comfortable, cozy vibe. The smell of coffee and baked goods went straight to his empty stomach. It grumbled loudly in appreciation. He could see why this place was successful. It was the perfect spot to sit and eat and enjoy fellowship with good friends.

Not that he would ever hang out here. Too many Prescotts and O'Rourkes lurking around. He imagined they wouldn't welcome him with open arms anytime soon if he happened to stroll in on his own. Clearly Hazel had pulled some strings in order to allow them to host the reception here. At first he had balked at the idea, but in reality, there were few places here in town that would host them.

This wasn't about him or the way the townsfolk felt about him. It was about Bud and giving him a proper send-off. Pastor Jack had given a beautiful eulogy for his grandfather. It had been a nice mix of humor, solemnity and faith. Joshua had been incredibly moved and grateful for the kind words.

The café was packed with townsfolk. Everyone had migrated over after the church service. Folks were milling around and gathering in little groups. He ignored the whispers as best he could. After the scandalous way he'd left town, he deserved them. As far as they knew, he was a fire starter.

He swung his gaze around and locked eyes with Boone. The man's expression was shuttered but his eyes glittered with anger. After all these years, the sheriff of Love still couldn't stand the sight of him. It radiated from his every pore. It made sense, Joshua supposed. He watched as a dark-haired woman with striking features gently tugged at Boone's arm, then placed a baby in his arms. His features softened as he looked down at the child and began to nuzzle his nose against hers. Boone appeared to be the epitome of a family man.

So he does have a heart after all, Joshua thought. He wasn't simply a tyrant with a shiny gold badge.

He stuffed down the spark of jealousy at the sight of the family unit. It was what he'd wanted as long as he could remember. A wife and kids. Years ago he had been convinced he and Honor were destined to live out their days together. Sometimes he still allowed himself to daydream about what might have been if he hadn't claimed responsibility for starting the fire.

Joshua cradled Violet closer against his chest and shook off thoughts of the past. He was blessed to have his daughter. Her presence in his life strengthened his sense of purpose. God had answered his prayers in the form of the blue-eyed little girl.

It felt as if he had just walked into the lion's den. Folks were eyeing him warily. Some were glaring at him with outright hostility while others seemed to feel sympathy toward him. Even though Violet was a baby, he prayed she didn't pick up on any negative vibes swirling around the café.

Hazel appeared at his side holding her arms out. "Why don't you let me take Violet and put her down for a nap? That way you can mingle with the guests. Cameron has a playpen in his office he uses for Emma. I'm guessing she'll settle down just fine."

He looked down at Violet. She was nodding off and heading for sleepy-time. It was way past her nap hour. Joshua handed her over to Hazel, who seemed delighted to be holding a baby in her arms. She began to softly hum as she walked away with Violet. He smiled. At least he had one solid friend here in town. Hazel's kindness humbled him.

He swung his gaze around the café again. Joshua wasn't sure he wanted to socialize with any of the townsfolk. More important, he wasn't certain they had a single word to say to him. The past still stood between him and the town like a rushing river. In their eyes, he was responsible for burning down a beloved church. Although it hurt to be treated like a pariah, Joshua knew it was something most would find hard to forgive.

He looked around the establishment for his brother. Theo was on the other side of the room talking animatedly with some school friends. They were laughing and enjoying themselves. He felt a stab of jealousy. His brother didn't have the same target on his back as he did. In the town's eyes, Theo had been the accomplice the night of the fire. He hadn't been the fire starter. At moments such as this one, Joshua couldn't help but wish the truth had been told all those years ago. Being blamed for the fire had left him with scars he wasn't sure could ever be healed. If he had to do it all over again, he knew he wouldn't take the rap for the fire. It had cost him Honor's love—a price too high to bear.

"Joshua." Honor's honeyed voice flowed over him. He turned toward the sound of her. She was standing next to him looking gorgeous in a royal blue dress that made her blue-gray eyes pop. He hadn't seen her at the church, but it had overflowed with parishioners. It had pleased him to see so many people turn out to honor Bud.

"It was a lovely service. Bud would be proud."

"Thank you," he said. "Pastor Jack is a good man. He really knew my grandfather well." He let out a low chuckle. "Some of the stories he told were highly amusing. Sounded just like Bud."

"He'll be sorely missed. I was proud to call him my friend. He was very supportive of the wildlife center. He backed every single donor drive we held. And every now and again he would surprise me by popping up when I least expected it." A hint of a smile hovered on Honor's lips.

"Sounds like Gramps. Do you know he sent me a twenty-dollar bill in the mail every year for my birthday?"

Honor giggled. It sounded like music to his ears. It had been a long time since he'd heard the lovely sound. "That's really sweet."

Joshua had the sensation of eyes boring into him.

Boone stood across the room, staring at him with an intensity Joshua couldn't ignore. He began to walk over toward where Joshua stood with Honor, his stride sure and steady. Honor eyed her brother warily.

Joshua met Boone's gaze head-on. Something told him Honor's brother hadn't walked over to offer condolences. Boone didn't waste any time. "I hear you've been talking to the Alloy Corporation about the Diamond R."

"That's right," Joshua said, his stare unwavering. A lot had changed in six years. He wasn't afraid of Sheriff Boone Prescott anymore. Back when he had been a teenager, Joshua had been intimidated by Boone's authority and the position he held in law enforcement. Not to mention the fact that he'd been Honor's big brother. Back then he had always been looking for trouble. Now, it was the last thing he wanted.

"Selling to that outfit will hurt this town," Boone said in a clipped tone. His voice was filled with censure.

"That remains to be seen," Joshua said. "It could open up the town to more revenue just like Lovely Boots," he said, referencing the boot company based on Hazel's creation of genuine Alaskan boots. From what his grandfather had told him, the company had helped Love put money back in the town coffers after years of downturn in the local economy.

"To be fair," Honor interjected, "Lovely Boots has provided a lot of jobs for locals. A dude ranch would largely benefit the owner. And it would make Love a tourist trap." Honor shuddered. "That would irrevocably change this town. It wouldn't be a quaint fishing village anymore. It would be unrecognizable."

Joshua bit back an angry retort. He counted to ten in his head before he responded. "A dude ranch would need employees, so it could help the local economy. Surely that's not a bad thing."

Honor didn't respond. Her jaw hardened. She had a mutinous expression stamped on her face.

She didn't need to say anything further. Of course Honor was siding with her brother. He shouldn't be surprised. Nothing had changed in this town. He was still on the outside looking in. But it didn't really matter what the Prescotts or the townsfolk thought. He and Theo had the authority to decide the destiny of the Diamond R Ranch. And there was nothing any of them could do about it. They held all the power. It was a complete reversal of fortune.

He didn't enjoy feeling this way, but for so long he had been powerless against the judgment and the condemnation of this small town. Even before the fire, Joshua had been viewed as a troublemaker and a rabble-rouser. His tarnished reputation had caused a lot of heartache for his mother, who had shed buckets of tears over the situation.

Suddenly, Cameron came over and stood next to Boone. Declan and Finn followed suit. Joshua let out a labored sigh. It was as if the cavalry had just ridden in. So much for a nice reception after Bud's memorial.

"So tell us, Ransom, is selling the ranch to the highest bidder a way of getting back at this town?" Cameron asked, his brows furrowed.

Joshua shook his head. He felt incredulous. Hadn't he established any goodwill in this town? He had lived here for eighteen years. Surely in all that time he'd done at least a few good things.

"For the record, revenge isn't my style," he said, keeping his voice calm and measured. Joshua didn't feel the need to explain that he had developed a relationship with God after leaving Love. He knew the God he served wouldn't want him to harbor hatred in his heart or fight with anyone. He had evolved over the past six years.

Provide things honest in the sight of all men. If it be possible, as much as lieth in you, live peaceably with all men.

Honor's face radiated discomfort. "Can you boys take it down a few notches?" Honor asked. "This isn't the time nor the place. Today is about Bud."

"Bud didn't want his land to be sold to someone who would desecrate it," Declan said. "It isn't what he wanted!"

"I'm getting pretty sick and tired of people telling me what my grandfather wanted!" Joshua gritted his teeth. "Let me just tell all of you at the same time so I won't have to repeat it. Nothing's been decided. Theo and I will take everything into consideration and decide what's best for us."

Finn shook his head. "That's no big surprise. Doing what's best for Love has never really interested you."

Joshua sucked his teeth. It was a low blow. His faith was being tested. *Turn the other cheek.* It was a Bible verse he lived by. But now there were people in his face pushing his buttons. There was only so much he could ignore.

Just then Theo walked up, nudging his way into the circle. "What's going on over here?" he asked. "What did I miss? Are you guys catching up on old times?"

"Something like that," Joshua drawled, making eye contact with his brother.

"We were inquiring about your intention to sell

the Diamond R," Boone explained. "Word has gotten around town. Folks are curious. And concerned about developers trampling all over Bud's land."

"That's mighty neighborly of you to ask," Theo said, grinning at Boone. "We're still weighing our options, but at the moment, selling to the Alloy Corporation is where we're leaning."

Boone scowled at Theo. The tension was so thick one could cut it with a knife.

Joshua could see the concern flickering in Honor's eyes. It was all over her face. She was dead set against the sale of the ranch and still reeling from disappointment about the provisions in Bud's will.

He felt a twisting sensation in his gut. So many years had passed by since they had been in love with one another, yet he still cared about what she thought of him. A part of him had secretly hoped Honor would be impressed by all the changes he'd undergone in the ensuing years. Clearly none of that mattered now. Her focus was on the Diamond R ranch and whether or not it would be turned into a trendy dude ranch.

Truth to be told, they were on opposite sides of the fence.

Despite what he had just said to Boone, Joshua's decision about the ranch had been made early this morning prior to Bud's memorial service. Theo had basically confirmed it just now. Bud's ranch would be sold. Joshua's life was in Seattle. He didn't need to hold on to anything here in Love. Once upon a time he had dreamed of settling down here with Honor, but all of those dreams had gone up in smoke. It was best that he cut all ties with the town that had made him an outcast. His grandfather's passing signified an end of an era.

Theo was right. Selling the ranch to the Alloy Corporation was the best choice they could make. He wasn't going to feel guilty about the decision. The money he would make on the deal would secure Violet's future. And it would permanently sever ties with a town that had never really embraced him.

Heat stained Honor's cheeks as she left the gathering and followed Boone into the kitchen. As soon as they were alone she tugged on her brother's arm and turned him around. "Was that really necessary?" Honor asked. "Why were you being so confrontational? We didn't need a scene at Bud's memorial reception."

Boone frowned at her. "Please don't take up for him. I thought six years would have given you some distance from the situation. I would hope you'd gained some objectivity."

She folded her arms across her chest. "I'm not defending him. Hazel arranged this reception. She went to a lot of trouble to do so. We all promised to respect her wishes. I think part of that meant not picking fights or rehashing old grudges."

Boone let out a snort. "He picked the fight six years ago."

"Don't make it personal," she cautioned. "I understand where you're coming from, but it doesn't serve any purpose."

He clenched his jaw. "He burned down the church our folks got married in. We were all baptized there, all four of us. It doesn't get more personal than that," Boone said in a raised voice.

She let out a sigh. The fire that had gutted the church was still an emotional subject. In many ways, there hadn't been closure to the incident. It was like a scab that had never healed. So much had changed in her life after Joshua burned down the church. In her heart she had always believed it was accidental, but it still had been too much to forgive. There was no defending arson.

She had given Joshua his ring back and headed to college in Michigan at Boone's urging. He had wanted her to get as far away from her ex-fiancé as possible. Although she had initially been angry at her brother for forcing her hand, she'd been grateful to him in the long run.

Tears pooled in her eyes. A tightening sensation spread across her chest. "I know what he did, Boone. Why is it that you always seem to forget what I lost? I was engaged to him. He was my high school sweetheart. I loved him. So I understand you were devastated about the church, but for me it was like a tsunami effect. I lost my entire world!"

Boone reached out and pulled her into his arms. He cradled her against his chest and patted her back in a soothing motion. "I'm sorry, Honor. I let my temper get the best of me. You know I never liked Joshua. I didn't think for a single second he was good enough for you."

Still, after all this time, it hurt to hear Boone talk about Joshua in such a negative way. "But he was good," she insisted. "I realize you never approved of him. I know he caused trouble and he ran wild all over town. You took him into custody more times than I can count. But there were great qualities about him as well. He was kind. Loyal. Sweet. Funny. He treated me well." Her voice began to quiver as thoughts of her ex-fiancé came into sharp focus. "So for me, it's always been hard to judge him by his worst moments when there were so many others along the way."

Boone cupped her chin in his hand. "Honor Prescott, you're a good woman. You believe in people. Sometimes too much. I believe in forgiveness, but when it comes to Joshua I have a hard time with it." He pressed a kiss against her temple. "I'm sorry about earlier. The thought of this town turning into a tourist's haven is weighing heavily on me."

"I know. Me too. It would be a nightmare," she said. "But I'm not giving up on the idea of the Ransom brothers deciding not to sell. It's their birthright after all. Maybe they'll change their minds."

A hint of a smile twitched at Boone's lips. "There you go again with your pie-in-the-sky thinking. It's one of the things I love most about you. You're idealistic." A sigh slipped past his lips. "I hate to break it to you, but Theo and Joshua haven't lived here in quite some time, nor have they been back to visit. What makes you think they harbor warm and fuzzy feelings about Bud's ranch? I think Theo was giving it to us straight. They're selling." His mouth was set in grim lines.

Honor opened her mouth, then shut it. How could she dispute Boone's assessment of the situation? He was right. Theo had pretty much confirmed it. In all likelihood, Joshua would accept a big fat check for the sale of the ranch, then head back to Seattle where he belonged. But she was still going to hold on to a kernel of hope. Joshua had always loved the ranch. It was hard to imagine him selling it.

Her sister-in-law Grace popped her head in the kitchen and regarded them both with a wary expression. "Is everything all right in here?" she asked.

"Everything is fine," Honor said, reaching up and pressing a kiss on her brother's cheek. No matter if they disagreed from time to time, Honor adored her older brother. He, along with her grandfather, had raised her in the absence of their parents. He had always wanted the best for her. She hadn't always been able to see it or appreciate his overprotectiveness, but at this point in her life she knew Boone had led with his heart. No doubt he would do the same with his own daughter.

"Good," Grace said with a grin. "We should probably get going. Eva is fading fast. Jasper's holding her right now and he's telling her stories about her ancestors searching for gold in the Yukon."

Boone shook his head and laughed. "Uh-oh. We better go rescue her."

Honor watched as Boone grabbed a hold of Grace's hand and headed back toward the main area of the café. She felt a little bereft. Watching as other couples happily settled down was getting harder and harder for Honor. She always felt joyful for them, but increasingly she was feeling more and more alone.

What was wrong with her? Why didn't she feel a pressing need to get out there and find love? She was lonely at times and secretly yearning for a perfect match. How amazing would it be if she could find her other half like Liam or Boone, or Jasper and Cameron? Or any other number of couples here in town?

Love one another. Wasn't that God's command?

These emotions always struck her whenever she attended a town event where residents were coupled up. And in a town where Operation Love was in full force, it was hard to avoid romance. It was as if there was this little hole inside her aching to be filled up. Despite what she tried to tell herself—that she wasn't looking for love—Honor knew it was the great big lie of her life. She tended to stuff all of the emotions down so she didn't have to face them. It wasn't working anymore. Those needs were bubbling to the surface.

She shook off the morose thoughts. There was a much more pressing matter at hand. If no one intervened, it was very likely the Diamond R would be sold to a developer. The very idea of it made her sick to her stomach. Feelings of helplessness washed over her. She didn't like being in this frame of mind. Surely something could be done to mediate the situation?

What if she invited Joshua to the wildlife center and showed him what a wonderful haven it was for rescued animals? Perhaps he would see how vital it was to preserve precious Alaskan land. The very land the wildlife center sat on had been given to the town by a resident—Miss Mary Mae Pritchard—in her will. If Mary had sold to a developer, the center wouldn't even exist, nor would the animals have been rescued.

Preserving wildlife and keeping the land intact went hand in hand in Honor's estimation. With the Diamond R bordering the wildlife's property, Honor knew a dude ranch would impact her own way of life. The very thought of it made her feel uncomfortable. Perhaps she could sway Joshua to her way of thinking, or at the very least get him to see a different point of view.

It was a long shot, but Honor truly believed it was possible to change hearts and minds. It was a big part of her faith. Things had gotten out of hand earlier between the Ransom brothers and her own siblings. That wasn't Honor's way. If it was possible, she wanted to try to smooth things over. Like Hazel always said, you could catch more bees with honey than with vinegar. Honor was about to test out that theory with Joshua.

She prayed it wouldn't be too difficult to spend time alone with Joshua Ransom and his adorable baby girl. Hopefully it wouldn't serve as a reminder of everything she'd lost in the past.

Chapter Five

It was a perfect February Alaskan afternoon for a trip to the wildlife center. The sky was as blue as a robin's egg. Although there was snow on the ground and a chill in the air, it was spectacular weather for this time of year. Joshua had bundled Violet up in a snowsuit, hat and mittens. He tended to be overprotective of his daughter. At three months' old she'd contracted bronchitis, which had led to a three-day stay in the hospital. Joshua hadn't left her side for a single moment.

He buckled her into her car seat and tested it to make sure it was secure. Parenthood wasn't for the faint of heart. Violet twisted his heart up like a pretzel. He had never felt like this before in his life. Well, just once, he corrected himself. Honor used to make him feel as if he could soar like an eagle just by looking in his direction. His pulse began to race as he thought about those days. It had been so long ago, yet he remembered every moment as if it were yesterday.

Joshua had been floored by Honor's invitation to visit the wildlife center. If it hadn't been for Violet, he might have declined. Even though she was too young to fully absorb the experience, Joshua still liked to expose his daughter to the world around her. The truth was, Honor still caused his heart to beat a little faster whenever he was in her presence. He wasn't in love with her anymore, but he still felt a tug in her direction. Perhaps it was the abrupt way their relationship had ended. One moment they had been planning to get married and settle down in Love, while in the next Honor was giving back his ring and leaving town to attend college out of state. If he lived to be one hundred, Joshua would never forget the look of hurt and disillusionment in her eyes when she had ended things after finding out about the fire.

He had asked himself the same questions hundreds of times. What if he hadn't taken the blame for the fire? Would he have ridden off into the sunset with Honor? Would they be building a family and working together on their life goals at this very moment?

He shook off the futile questions. One thing he knew for certain. If he hadn't taken a certain path, Violet wouldn't be in his life now. And without his daughter, life didn't really make much sense. She gave him a purpose each and every day. Some might say he had saved her from being an orphan, but in truth, Violet had been the best thing to ever happen to him. She infused his life with colors. Reds. Oranges. Vivid purples. He made sure to thank God each day for making him a father.

As he settled into the driver's seat and began to make his way to the wildlife center, the stunning Alaskan vista came into view. The spectacular view of the mountains always left him in awe. Tall, snow-covered trees dominated the landscape. Hawks flew gracefully up in the sky, dipping down every now and again, then soaring back toward the heavens.

Although many residents of Love preferred to live near town, Joshua had always enjoyed living out in the boondocks. It was serene out here. Nothing but the great outdoors and breathtaking views of Alaska.

As soon as he saw the sign for the wildlife center, Joshua turned down the road and followed the arrows. Before he knew it, he had arrived at a ranch-style house surrounded by several small, flat structures. He could see horses running in a paddock in the distance.

By the time he parked Bud's truck and got Violet out of her car seat, Honor was walking toward them from a nearby building. With her hair pulled away from her face in a high ponytail, she looked like a fresh-faced beauty. She wasn't wearing a hint of makeup, and she was dressed casually in a pair of blue jeans and a navy blue parka. A gray wool hat sat on her head. To this day, Honor was the loveliest woman he'd ever seen.

This invitation to the center had come as a complete surprise, especially after the tension that had flared up between him and her family at Bud's reception.

She waved at them. "Hey, Joshua. Glad you could make it out here."

He nodded at her. "Thanks for the invitation. I thought it would be good for Violet to experience a little bit of my hometown. When she's older I can tell her all about how she visited Love."

Honor smiled at Violet, who turned away and hid her face against his chest. "She's a bit shy at first. It'll take her a few minutes to come around."

"I don't blame her one bit," Honor said in a cheery voice. "After all, I'm basically a stranger to her. And she's here in this new town where she doesn't really know anybody. It's a lot for her to absorb all at once."

He felt grateful for Honor's understanding of the situation. It was hard for Violet to be away from home and trying to acclimate to her new surroundings. The past few nights she had awoken in the wee hours of the morning crying out for him.

"Well, she's at a good age for an introduction to animals. I promise we won't visit any that might frighten her."

"I appreciate it," Joshua said. "She spooks easily, although she loves animals. She's really enjoying the horses at the ranch. Her favorite place back home is the zoo."

Joshua knew he was probably telling Honor way more than she wanted to know, but things still felt a bit awkward between them. They had once had such a familiarity between them, with conversation flowing as effortlessly as a river. But now, with years stretched out between them, he was searching for something to say. He prayed the awkwardness would melt away.

"Zoos are wonderful places to engage children and educate them about animals. I'll never forget my first visit to the Alaska Zoo when I was six years old. It changed my life. From that point forward, I knew what I wanted to do with the rest of my life." Her voice rang out with conviction.

"I've been meaning to say congratulations on all of this," Joshua said. He swung his gaze around the area, amazed by the scope of it. Dragging his eyes away from Honor took effort. She was extremely pleasing to the eye.

"Thanks," she said. "I didn't get here on my own.

Boone and Jasper really helped me with tuition. I received a partial scholarship, but there was still a chunk I had to pay. It wasn't easy, but I held a few part-time jobs to help with the bills. It was a big financial sacrifice for my family, so I wanted to pay for all the incidentals on my own."

It shouldn't matter after all these years, but it still rankled that Boone had orchestrated Honor's moving away to Michigan to attend college. For a long time, he had wondered whether they would have gotten back together if she hadn't left Love so abruptly. Michigan had been so far away and there hadn't been a single way for him to contact her. In the aftermath of their breakup, she had changed her email address and her cell phone number. All avenues had been closed to him since she wasn't active on social media.

It was all water under the bridge now. He had made his peace with all of it a long time ago.

"I wouldn't expect any less from our class valedictorian," he said in a teasing tone. Honor had been the top student in their high school class. She had deserved a scholarship to an excellent university and a pathway to the career of her dreams. It probably wouldn't have worked out if they had both stayed in Love and been married as teens. It would have been yet another mistake.

"You weren't exactly a slouch yourself," she answered. "You were a great student when you weren't goofing off."

They both chuckled, enjoying a moment where they could reflect on the past with frivolity and not bitterness. There had been so many wonderful moments shared between them. Even though he had tried to convince himself otherwise, their love had been real. It just hadn't been built to last.

"Why don't we go take a look at the horses?" Honor suggested. "They're very gentle, and Violet might get a kick out of petting them."

"Let's go," Joshua said, walking beside Honor as she led them toward the paddock. Violet's eyes grew wide as they reached the horses. She couldn't seem to take her eyes off them. She pointed a chubby finger in the direction of a butterscotch-colored Palomino.

"Ba Ba," she said, reaching out to touch the stallion.

"I think she likes him," Joshua said, allowing Violet to pat the horse's side. He knew better than to let her put her hands by the horse's mouth. When Joshua was a kid, Bud had taught him how to stay safe around horses.

"She has good taste," Honor raved. "That's Pecan. She's a real sweetheart. She was my first rescue and rehabilitation. I wasn't certain she would make it at first." Honor visibly shuddered. "She was in really bad shape. Neglected and abused. Ultimately, our goal is for people to adopt the horses, but I've decided to keep Pecan. She holds a special place in my heart. Just like Lola."

Lola had been Honor's horse ever since her thirteenth birthday.

"How many do you have at the moment?" he asked.

"About twenty-five or so. We have some wild mustangs that just came to us. They're magnificent horses but they have some injuries that would make it impossible to be out on their own. So we're rehabilitating them."

Joshua let out a low whistle. "Please tell me you're not doing this all by yourself."

"No way. That would be tough. I have two full-time workers and a few part-timers who come in as needed.

We're all really hands-on since the whole point of the center is to provide a safe, nurturing environment for animals who've been in precarious situations."

"This place is impressive," he said with a nod. "It's nice to see you making a difference in the community. I know it's what you always wanted to do."

She brushed her chestnut locks away from her face. "I consider myself very blessed. Not many people get to work in their dream job."

Violet's shyness faded away after a short amount of time in Honor's presence. She couldn't take her eyes off the animals. Or Honor. Joshua suspected his daughter found Honor fascinating because she herself didn't have a mother. There really weren't too many female figures in her life. Although Joshua had always dreamed of having a wife and kids, he didn't think he was very good at relationships. He'd reconciled himself to the idea of raising Violet as a single dad even though he knew finding a wife would be a dream come true. The thing was, he still couldn't seem to reconcile the word *wife* with anyone but Honor. It was probably one of the reasons his marriage to Lauren had failed.

"Do you still ride?" she asked.

"Not regularly," he admitted. "Riding isn't big in Seattle. It's a large, bustling city."

"I'm surprised to hear that. You loved riding more than anyone I've ever known, including Bud. You were the quintessential Alaskan cowboy."

Honor was right. It had been a huge part of his life. "Those were the days. I miss it," he said, his eyes straying toward the horses in the paddock. "I never felt more like myself than when I was on horseback. I don't know how to put it into words, but sometimes it seemed as if I was one with the horse."

"Spoken like a true horseman. You miss the ranch," she said, a knowing look glinting from her eyes. "I know what it meant to you. You and Bud were an amazing team. Two peas in a pod."

"I never imagined I'd leave," he said in a wistful tone. "In the end I didn't really have a choice, did I?"

"Not really," she said in a soft voice. "Considering everything, it was for the best."

The best? It stung a little hearing Honor felt that way about his exile from Love. It had been the most agonizing period of his life. He was probably being overly sensitive, but he wondered if he'd been wrong after all. Maybe Honor had never really loved him.

"It came out the wrong way," she blurted out. "It sounded harsh, but I didn't mean to sound so cavalier. Bud probably never told you, but things were really tense around here after the fire. People were really up in arms. I remember hearing Boone say if you had stuck around there could have been retaliation against you."

He jammed a hand through his hair. "I'm not surprised. Tensions were running high before I left town," Joshua said. "Bud never said a word about it though. I hated it for him. It makes me angry he had to suffer for our actions."

"Bud was tough. He could handle all the backlash. He was also beloved in this town. The majority of residents had his back."

Warmth settled over him at the idea of his grandfather being supported by the residents. He had deserved no less. Bud Ransom had been a wonderful person.

"So, where did you go when you left Love?" Honor

asked. "I was at school, but I heard a lot of things through the grapevine." She began to giggle, then placed her hand over her mouth. "It's not funny, but rumors were running rampant about your whereabouts. Someone even surmised you'd joined the traveling circus."

Joshua burst out laughing. Never in a million years had he ever thought he'd laugh over the circumstances of his expulsion from town. But, as in the past, Honor had the ability to make him chuckle.

"After completing the first-time offender program, I traveled with my parents. My dad got an assignment overseas. So I was in Singapore for a year. I took some business classes and stretched myself."

Honor's eyes widened. "Wow. Singapore? That's impressive. And here I imagined you were sitting in a dungeon somewhere."

Joshua met her gaze. He sensed her comment was on the passive-aggressive side. Did she think he hadn't suffered? "I didn't get off scot-free in case you were wondering. I had to pay restitution in addition to what Bud paid to repair the church."

"You were fortunate to have Bud in your corner." She avoided looking at him. Instead she reached out and fiddled with Violet's fingers. He heard a slight edge to her tone. Joshua felt a nagging sensation inside him. Honor was still harboring negative feelings from the past. Did she believe he had put his grandfather in a bad position?

Suddenly, he felt guilty all over again. He hated feeling this way. How long would he have to beat himself up over the choices he'd made? Was it a life sentence?

He cleared his throat.

"Honor, you've been gracious to me and Violet. I know most folks here in town wrote me off a long time ago. They've been cordial only because I'm Bud's grandson. You didn't have to invite us over here today, especially considering everything that went down between us in the past."

Her hair swung about her shoulders as she shook her head. "We've both moved on from all that, Joshua. We were kids back then."

Kids. He hated the way she phrased it, as if they hadn't known what they were doing. In reality, they had been very much in love and committed to a life together. Their dedication to each other had been heartwarming, although being intimate with Honor had been a huge mistake. Since that time, Joshua had turned his life over to the Lord. He now knew how wrong their actions had been.

He shook off his irritation with Honor. "It's only fair that I give you a heads-up. The bottom line is that Theo and I have decided to sell the ranch. It's really the only sensible thing for us to do." He pushed the words past his lips before he could chicken out.

A look of shock passed over her face. The lines of her mouth hardened. She raised an eyebrow. "Sensible? That's hardly a word I'd choose to describe what you and Theo are planning to do."

Something about her disappointed expression made Joshua want to reach out and hold her in his arms. It was a reflex from back in the day. He had always strived to soothe Honor's wounds. It was no longer his job to do so, no matter how much he might want to at this moment.

"I know it's not happy news. But, to be honest, we're between a rock and a hard place. Love hasn't been our home for quite some time. We're only passing through town, so to speak. Our lives are elsewhere."

She frowned at him. "Jasper has an expression. You can try as best you can to run away from home, but it's always going to be a part of you."

"I agree with you, Honor. To an extent. And I'm not running away from anything this time. I'm walking toward something. A home for Violet and me. Security. A place where she's always going to know she's loved. We have a great life in Seattle."

Who was he trying to convince? He was making it sound way more idyllic than it really was. But he was being truthful about this town. Love hadn't been home in quite some time.

Honor bowed her head. "And what about the ranch? Can you really just walk away from it, knowing the Diamond R is going to cease to exist as you know it? Can you live with that?" she pressed.

He glanced down at his daughter. Violet was rubbing her eyes and fading fast. In Joshua's opinion, it was the perfect moment to head back to the Diamond R. Honor had been kind and solicitous, but tensions were rising. He didn't want things to completely fall apart. It was best to end things in a civil manner.

"We've made up our minds," he said in a firm voice. "I don't expect everyone to agree with us, but I hope our decision will be respected."

"Well, then," Honor said in a crisp voice. "I guess there's nothing more to be said." Honor's tone spoke volumes. Her voice crackled with anger. There was no mistaking the look of fury on her face.

He shifted Violet to his hip. She had fallen asleep

against his chest. Violet was getting heavier by the day. No doubt she was going through a growth spurt.

Maybe coming here today had been a mistake.

The civil mood between him and Honor had deteriorated. Perhaps both of them had just been going through the motions. The air between them was thick with tension. "We should get going. I need to run into town to get a few things for Violet. Thanks for having us over here, even though I'm beginning to think you had an agenda."

Honor stood with her arms folded across her chest. She appeared slightly shocked and wounded.

"I hoped to talk some sense into you, but clearly I overestimated your ability to see beyond your own needs and wants. I thought you might consider Bud's legacy and the integrity of this town." Her voice quivered with emotion. He could see the pain radiating from her eyes.

He hated himself for hurting her, but there was no point in sugarcoating the situation about the Diamond R. She would have found out sooner or later anyway. Joshua was done living his life for others. He had a responsibility to provide a wonderful life for his daughter. There was no way he could ever do that here in Love where the townsfolk viewed him as a ne'er do well. He didn't owe them anything! Not after the way they had treated him like yesterday's trash.

He turned toward his vehicle and opened up the door. If he looked into her eyes, he just might break in two. Honor stayed silent until he'd buckled Violet into her car seat and settled himself behind the wheel.

"Don't do it. Don't sell! You'll regret it, Joshua," she called out after him. "It's Bud's legacy you would be selling. It's something you can never replace in a million years."

Joshua turned and looked at her from his position in the driver's seat. He hated seeing her so broken up about the ranch, but there was nothing he could do to change things. He didn't bother to respond to her. Joshua revved the engine and drove away from the wildlife center, his soul feeling wearier than it had felt in recent memory. Why, after all this time, did Honor Prescott still have such sway over his emotions? Why did she always make him question the things he thought he knew with a deep certainty?

Honor's words rang in his ears well after he reached the ranch and settled Violet down for a nap.

Don't do it. Don't sell! You'll regret it, Joshua.

Honor couldn't seem to move from the spot she had been standing in when Joshua had roared off in Bud's truck with Violet.

We've made up our minds.

Theo and I have decided to sell the ranch.

Honor couldn't shake her conversation with Joshua. She couldn't believe the words that had tumbled out of his mouth. Her stomach clenched as feelings of betrayal washed over her. Tears of frustration pooled in her eyes. What a fool she had been to believe Joshua would be swayed by her words!

They were selling the ranch! Bud's beloved Diamond R would be transformed into a commercial enterprise. If only Bud had protected his land by making certain his will mirrored his wishes. In her heart Honor hadn't really believed Joshua would be capable of moving forward with the sale. He had always been sentimental about the ranch. Who was this version of the young man she had thought she'd known like the back of her hand?

She felt so hopeless. Her grand plan to convince Joshua to reconsider his position had been a huge flop. He had already made up his mind before he'd stepped foot on the grounds of the nature preserve.

Honor bit her lip. She wasn't a helpless person. She was smart and resourceful. And she believed in this town and the Alaskan environment more than mere words could express.

What if she could figure out a way to prevent the sale of the Diamond R Ranch? What if there was a legal way to stop Joshua and Theo from selling to the Alloy Corporation? Lee had said it wasn't possible to challenge Bud's will. But what if there was a way around it? Something tied in to land preservation. She saw it all the time in the news where people fought against construction in rural areas.

As town mayor, Jasper might be aware of some technicality by which the sale of the land to developers could be challenged. She needed to be certain before she crossed this bridge. Once she headed down this road, there would be no turning back. Joshua would no doubt be angry at her for interfering, but Honor felt strongly about the situation. She would be acting for a higher purpose than the Ransom brothers. Clearly, all they cared about was the almighty dollar.

In this case, the ends justified the means. As an animal rehabilitator and land preservationist, she couldn't bear it if strangers descended on her beloved town and started digging up the land. Having hordes of tourists stomping around Jarvis Street would ruin the town's laid-back vibe. It wasn't just sour grapes about Bud not leaving the land to the town. It was about principles. It was about keeping Love quaint and pristine.

If she had to go head-to-head with the Ransom brothers in order to protect her hometown, that's just what Honor intended to do.

Chapter Six

Joshua stood outside the paddock and gazed at the wide array of horses that had belonged to Bud. Chocolate. Midnight black. Sienna. Bone white. He had always been fascinated by the vast array of colors horses came in. These animals were an integral part of the Diamond R Ranch. A huge lover of horses, Bud Ransom had been proud to call himself a cowboy and a rancher. Gramps had been the one to teach Joshua how to ride when he was five years old. Joshua had fallen in love with horses and with the Diamond R Ranch.

It had been a long time since he had been home, but he was falling in love with it all over again. With each and every day he was falling into old, familiar rhythms and seeing his hometown with fresh eyes.

He had just now ridden across the property on Blaze, his grandfather's favorite horse. He wasn't sure how it had happened over the years, but he had forgotten how wonderful it felt to fly like the wind on a prized stallion's back. It brought back a part of him he had thought was gone forever. The carefree boy who had dreamed of being a cattle rancher and owning his own spread.

There wasn't much riding for him in Seattle due to his hectic work schedule. Getting a business off the ground and raising a child consumed most of his time.

It was a nice change of pace to hang out with the horses.

Pride soared through him as he swung his gaze around the ranch. The property stretched out for miles. Pure Alaskan land. He felt a twinge of regret over his decision to sell the ranch. Theo had worked overtime to convince him of the wisdom of selling rather than holding on to the property for nostalgic reasons. He hadn't told Honor, but he'd been on the fence regarding the decision. Much like the way he'd done in childhood, Theo had pushed him over the edge regarding the sale.

If he closed his eyes he could picture himself as his pint-sized self, following after Bud as he walked around the Diamond R. He'd been his grandfather's shadow, wanting to know everything he could about running a ranch.

He scoffed. What was he being sentimental for? It wasn't possible to keep the Diamond R. It wasn't as if either he or Theo wanted to establish roots here in Love. Been there, done that. Nobody really wanted them to stay anyway. They just wanted his family's land.

He heard the whir of tires crunching on the snow and turned in the direction of the road. It was Theo. He had headed into town earlier in order to meet with Eric Mathers, Bud's attorney. Joshua had been content to stay back at the ranch while Theo sorted through the paperwork regarding their inheritance. Violet was inside the house with Winnie, the Ransom housekeeper. She had cheerfully agreed to watch the baby while he poked around the ranch.

Theo drove right up to the stables, then stopped on a dime. Joshua frowned. His brother had gotten out of the car and was making his way toward him. His stride was full of anger.

So much for his peaceful morning. Instinct told him things were about to take a turn for the worse.

"What's going on? Are you all right? You look like a storm cloud," he called out to Theo as he approached.

"You're not going to believe it!" he announced from a few feet away. His face was twisted up in anger. His eyes flashed warning signs.

"Maybe you need to take a few deep breaths," Joshua said. "You don't look so good."

Theo stopped right in front of Joshua. He was breathing heavily. A vein bulged over his eye.

"We've been stopped in our tracks, Joshua. We can't move forward in selling the ranch. An injunction was filed preventing us from selling to the Alloy Corporation. Eric said that an argument is being made that the property should be blocked from sale to any developers."

"An injunction? On what grounds?" he asked. His mind raced with the impact of the news. This had Boone written all over it. In his eyes, Joshua would always be the villain. He had probably jumped at the opportunity to make trouble for him. No doubt he wouldn't be content until he left Love forever.

"An argument was made that since the land borders the wildlife preserve, it's federally protected land. Since some of those animals are endangered, construction could hamper their ability to thrive."

Joshua's jaw dropped. It was a slick move, designed to put a wrench in their plans. He wasn't sure if the argument had merit, but it would surely grind things to a halt. "Sounds like they threw whatever they thought might stick against the wall."

Theo jammed his hands into his back pockets. "Yes. I think you're right. Now a judge has to decide on the matter. It really messes things up for us. The Alloy Corporation might not want all this hassle and legal wrangling. And it's going to cost us a small fortune if it's litigated."

Litigation! This could seriously affect both of them financially. He didn't have money to defend lawsuits!

"I can't believe Boone would go to those lengths," Joshua muttered. He was well aware of the sheriff's ill will toward him, but he'd never imagined Boone would resort to filing legal papers to impede them. This situation had truly spiraled out of control.

"It wasn't Boone. Matter of fact it wasn't any of the Prescott men. Or the O'Rourkes." Theo chewed on the inside of his lip. "It was none other than your ex-fiancée, Honor Prescott."

Honor? Theo must have gotten his information wrong. There was no way Honor would go the route of filing an injunction against them.

"No. That doesn't sound right," Joshua said, shaking his head in disbelief. Sweet, kind Honor. "She wouldn't do such a thing."

Theo twisted his mouth. "Yes, actually she would. And she did! That's exactly what Eric told me. She filed legal paperwork to impede our sale of the ranch. She's citing imminent harm to the animals at the wildlife preserve."

A fierce anger raced through Joshua's veins. She had used the information he had given her the other day regarding selling the ranch to try to undermine them. Who did Honor think she was to tie their hands in such a manner? This was a spiteful act. Honor had never been a vindictive person. Was this payback for the past? Bitterness over the will? Or just a way to let him know he had no business here in town. If so, he wasn't just going to roll over and play dead.

"Can you let Winnie know I need her to watch Violet for another hour or so?" Joshua asked.

Theo frowned at him. "Where are you going?"

"To the wildlife center. It's about time I got a few things straight with Honor."

Theo called out after him, imploring him to come back. Joshua didn't heed his brother's pleas. He strode off toward the direction of Bud's truck, feeling grateful the keys were in the ignition. He didn't want to have to go back inside the house and allow Violet to see him like this.

His youthful years had been full of swagger and rage. As a grown man he had made a conscious effort to be even-tempered and calm. In many ways, his past troubles had been a result of his inability to control his temper.

Let every man be swift to hear, slow to speak, slow to wrath. In his estimation, it was one of the most powerful Bible verses. It had always resonated with him.

At this very moment, Joshua knew his anger was beyond anything he'd experienced in adulthood. A part of him felt like the wild, reckless boy of his youth. The feelings surprised him. He'd been of the belief that he had gotten rid of that boy a long time ago. But Honor had pressed every last one of his buttons by embroiling him and Theo in a legal battle. He felt like a volcano that was about to blow sky-high.

Honor held a baby lynx in her arms and firmly placed the bottle in her mouth. She grinned as Glory greedily guzzled the milk. The baby lynx was finally showing signs of thriving. She had rejected food for days, raising alarm bells with Honor. Seeing Glory eating caused a feeling of triumph to surge up inside her. For all intents and purposes, Honor was serving the role of mother. Honor wrinkled her nose. Some might find it silly, but she loved her ability to mother and nurture the animals. It filled up an emotional void in her life.

It filled, she realized, her own yearning for motherhood. Ever since laying eyes on Violet, her own loss had been pressing on her heart. She still mourned the loss of her child. Sometimes, in the still hours between darkness and dawn, she thought about what might have been.

The quiet of the center settled around her like a warm, cozy blanket. It was such an idyllic setting. It was a great place to listen to her own thoughts as they rambled around her brain. It was important, especially in the past few days.

As someone who had grown up in a big, bustling family like her own, it was a wonder she didn't mind the isolation of the wildlife center. There was something calm and peaceful about being out here with all of the animals. She loved what she did for a living. It had been worth all the years of being in Michigan away from her loved ones. Running the wildlife center was a dream come true. She still wasn't sure what she had done in this lifetime to receive such a blessing.

Heavy footsteps sounded in the distance. Perhaps it

was Clay Mathers, one of the workers. He didn't usually stomp around the place though. She turned toward the door, watching as it swung open with a loud crashing sound.

Joshua stood there, all six feet of him, bristling with a ferocious anger. It radiated from him in waves. His blue eyes glittered with animosity. Honor shuddered. She had never in her life seen Joshua look at her with such condemnation in his eyes. Even at his worst, he had always gazed at her with love radiating from his eyes. It was a bit unsettling to see this version of Joshua.

"What do you think you're doing?" Joshua demanded.

"You need to lower your voice. I'm trying to get her to sleep," Honor said, placing her finger to her lips in a shushing motion.

Joshua's face hardened. "I need to talk to you. Now!"

"I know why you're here," she said in a loud whisper. "And I'm very sorry if you're upset with me, but I had to take action before you sold the ranch."

"No, you didn't," he said in a low voice. "You could have just let things be instead of meddling. This doesn't concern you."

She glared at him. "Meddling? I'm doing my civic duty for this town."

"It's not your business!" he spit out. "It's Ransom land."

She sat up straight. "It is my business. I'm from this town. Love flows in my veins. I could no sooner turn my back on the fate of this town than I could forsake my own family. And Bud wouldn't want this. Someone needs to speak for him! It's his legacy you're keen on destroying."

Joshua scoffed. "So now that you're a wildlife biologist you're suddenly saving the world from developers? Riding to the rescue? Is that it?"

"I have principles that guide me," she said. "I always have."

He threw his hands in the air. "You're affecting my future by what you're doing. And Violet's. How could you do that?"

"It's not about you, Joshua. It's about this town. The people. We deserve better than to have developers come in and twist Love into something it isn't and can never be. Doesn't that bother you?" she asked in a voice choked with emotion. "Don't you feel sad about the idea of Bud's beautiful ranch being turned into something ridiculous and frivolous? A dude ranch," she sneered. "It's utter nonsense."

"When did you become so judgmental?" he asked. "When did you appoint yourself as judge, jury and executioner?"

She jutted out her chin. "Probably around the same time you became so money hungry. Let's face it, there's only one reason you're considering this offer from the Alloy Corporation. And it has to do with you and Theo fattening up your bank balances. You're selling out for cold, hard cash."

"Do you know what I think?" Joshua asked, taking a step closer to her. "I think you've been spending too much time around your brothers and Jasper. They've rubbed off on you. You never used to be cynical. Or coldhearted."

"I wonder why?" She asked. "You made me more jaded than all my family members combined."

He frowned at her. "So is that what this is about? Settling old scores? Getting even with me?"

"Clearly you think I have no integrity. I'm not doing this for personal reasons."

Joshua narrowed his gaze as he studied her. "So it has nothing to do with any lingering feelings you might have for me?"

Honor sucked in a shocked breath. She couldn't believe what Joshua was insinuating. What had she done to make him believe she was harboring residual feelings for him? She met his gaze head-on. "Everything I ever felt for you died the moment you lit the church on fire."

She could see the hurt in his eyes. He tried to shake it off, but she had seen the glint of pain before it disappeared and he shuttered his expression.

"We're going to fight you on this, Honor. And we'll win. You don't have a leg to stand on. If you really love this town, you might want to think about it before you drag it through a very expensive legal case." Joshua's words hung in the air like a thinly veiled threat.

He turned on his booted heels and left the building. Moments later she heard the engine of a vehicle revving up. She let out a shudder. Going head-to-head with Joshua had been painful. But she had no one to blame but herself. She had served the first volley by going to Jasper and working with him and Lee to get papers filed against the sale of the Diamond R.

She felt bad about the animosity between them, but she wasn't going to crumble into dust. Years ago she had been defenseless against Joshua. She'd been so naive and trusting. His actions had made a fool of her after all the lengths she'd gone to in order to defend him to her family and the townsfolk. He had shattered her belief in him with one horrific act. All of her dreams of marrying him and building a life together had evaporated. She had been left with nothing but pain and regret. Discovering she had been pregnant with their child and then losing the baby had been devastating.

Being vulnerable to Joshua had never served her well. She had vowed to herself a long time ago to never allow herself such weakness again. Dealing with her ex-fiancé meant hardening her heart against him. Joshua Ransom knew how to worm his way into her good graces like no one else.

She couldn't afford to let that happen. Loving and losing Joshua had already torn her world apart once before. Honor was going to focus on making sure the Diamond R wasn't turned into a tacky dude ranch. She couldn't afford to consider Joshua's feelings or picture Violet's angelic little face. If she did, Honor knew she would be in a world of trouble.

Chapter Seven

Joshua sat back in the leather love seat in the living room and sighed in contentment. His hands were resting behind his head while his feet were perched on the matching ottoman. The only sounds were coming from Violet, who was happily playing with her toys. He had set out a large blanket and scattered her favorite playthings around so she could explore them to her heart's content. He got a kick out of watching her scoot around.

They had the house all to themselves this evening. Theo was reconnecting with an old friend here in town while Winnie was spending the evening with her own family. Joshua enjoyed the silence. Quiet moments with his daughter meant the world to him. He had never imagined fatherhood would be his most sacred role. Violet had given his life a true purpose. He was no longer searching for meaning. God had been good to him.

And it hardly ever crossed his mind that his blood didn't flow in Violet's veins. It simply didn't matter. The love he felt for her came straight from the deepest parts of his soul.

The lights began to flicker for the third time this

evening. Joshua frowned. He needed to locate the lanterns and flashlights in case they lost power. Although he had looked around earlier, he'd been unsuccessful in finding anything. He had a vague memory of Bud going down to the basement after a power outage and coming back with an armful of supplies. He unfolded himself from his comfy chair and stretched.

"I'll be right back, Vi. I need to make sure we have some flashlights and supplies in case the lights go out." His daughter just looked at him and gurgled, then went back to playing with her doll. Joshua quickly moved toward the hallway and yanked open the basement door. He flipped the light switch, bathing the darkened basement in light. He walked down the steps and began poking around in bins and drawers. Bingo! A whole drawer full of flashlights! The lanterns had to be around here somewhere.

Suddenly, the silence in the basement was broken. He heard a succession of loud thumps as if something had fallen. For a moment, he completely froze. Fear grabbed him by the throat. When he heard the loud cries, he pivoted toward the steps. Violet was lying at the bottom, her features contorted in pain. Her loud wails pierced his heart. He raced to her side, murmuring words of comfort.

Joshua gently scooped his daughter up in his arms and brought her back upstairs. With his free hand he reached for his car keys, wallet and cell phone. There was no question in his mind that she needed immediate medical attention. All could he do at the moment was pray that Violet wasn't too seriously injured.

As far as Saturday nights in Love, Alaska, went, hot chocolate and s'mores before a roaring fire at the Moose

Café was a rip-roaring good time. Honor sighed. She truly loved her hometown, but every now and again she yearned to kick up her heels. For the most part, Honor worked at the wildlife center and watched as everyone else in town settled down to domestic bliss. With each couple that paired off, it became harder and harder to tell herself she was fine being single and unattached.

Dear Lord, one of these days, I would like to find someone who'll sweep me off my feet. I haven't been ready to plunge into the dating world, but with every day that passes by, I think I'm getting closer. Could you please make him tall and handsome and a good dancer? And this time around, could you let my brothers approve of him and not give him a hard time?

Was she ready for God to point someone in her direction? She believed so. It had been so long since she'd had romantic feelings for someone or even gone out on a romantic date. Being burned in the past by love wasn't a strong enough reason anymore to stay single. And after seeing how thoroughly Joshua had moved on with his own life, she was determined to follow suit.

Thanks to Jasper, her brothers, as well as Declan and Finn, had been apprised of the injunction she had filed against the Ransom brothers. They had invited her to a little celebration at the Moose Café. Although she felt a little bit guilty about celebrating Joshua's misfortune, Honor was now being hailed as a conquering hero. The niggling sensation in the pit of her stomach sure didn't feel like victory.

"Let's raise a mug of hot chocolate to Honor!" Cameron said in a triumphant voice as he raised his drink high in the air.

Everyone joined in, shouting her name and offering her congratulations. She looked around the table. Her nephew, Aidan—Liam and Ruby's son—had a whipped cream mustache that made her grin. He was sitting next to his best friend, Oliver, Finn's stepson from his marriage to Maggie Richards. Finn had recently adopted Oliver, so he was now Oliver O'Rourke. Grace was giving baby Eva a bottle as Boone sat beside her, while Liam was sitting back in his chair as Ruby rested her head against his shoulder. Even Jasper and Hazel looked peaceful and content. As much as they fussed and feuded with one another, Honor knew their love story was epic. Cameron's wife, Paige, was gently blowing on her daughter Emma's hot cocoa, making sure it wasn't too hot for the toddler.

Honor felt a sense of pride as she gazed upon the members of her family. Finn and Declan O'Rourke and their wives, Maggie and Annie, were honorary members of the Prescott brood. And Sophie was also, along with her husband, Noah Catalano. *This should be enough*, she realized. A fantastic family and great friends who showered her with love and affection. She was an auntie several times over. If she never met the man of her dreams, she would still be loved. Always.

Liam began to loudly clink his mug with a spoon. "Attention! Attention!" he called out. "Since we're all gathered here celebrating Honor's brilliant move to protect this town, Ruby and I wanted to make an announcement." There was a feeling of expectation hovering in the air. Everything stilled and hushed.

Ruby smiled at her husband, then swung her gaze around the table. "We're expecting a baby!" she announced.

A deafening roar erupted at the table. Everyone

began hooting and hollering. Jasper was yelling louder than anyone. Grace made a point to cover baby Eva's ears.

Honor got up from her seat and made her way to her brother's side. She threw her arms around his neck. "Oh, Liam, I'm so happy for all of you. You must be over the moon about it."

Liam grinned, making him look even more handsome. "I'm thrilled. We've been blessed with such abundance. I didn't dare to hope for more." He shrugged. "But the good Lord saw fit to add to our family."

"He sure did," Honor said. "No two people deserve it more than you and Ruby. You're wonderful parents." After everything the couple had endured when Ruby was presumed dead in an avalanche, Honor couldn't be more overjoyed for their incredible news. It had taken them years to find their way back to one another, but their love had endured adversity.

"I can't wait till it happens for you," Liam said, squeezing her hand. "You're so supportive of everyone else's happy news."

"From your lips to God's ears," she said in a teasing voice. "I think I'm ready to move forward in that area."

"Good," Liam said. "It's about time."

Boone stood up and raised his mug. "Now, let's make a toast to Ruby and Liam. And big brother-to-be, Aidan. May your new addition be healthy and happy." Aidan was grinning from ear-to-ear.

The café was filled with joy and euphoria. It had turned into the perfect family night. A cell phone rang out amidst the chaos.

"Sorry, I'm on call at the clinic," Liam said, holding up his phone and walking away from the table.

"I can't believe I'm going to be a great-grandfather again," Jasper said, rubbing his grizzled jaw. "It seems like just yesterday I was sledding with Boone, Liam and Cameron on Cupid's Hill when they were little tykes."

"I want to go sledding!" Aidan cried out. "Can you take me, Jasper?"

Hazel shook her head. "Aidan. Jasper might break a hip if he takes you sledding." She leaned in toward him and said in a loud whisper, "He's not as young as he thinks he is."

Jasper shook a finger at Hazel. "I heard that. A person is only as old as they feel."

"So you're one hundred and five," Hazel cracked, throwing her head back in laughter. Jasper frowned at his wife, but his lips twitched with amusement.

Liam rushed back to the table, his expression tense and full of concern.

"Guys, I've got to head over to the clinic." His gaze swung toward Honor. "It seems Joshua Ransom's daughter took a bad fall. He's on his way into town with the child right now."

Honor jumped up from her seat and walked over toward Liam. Her pulse was skittering. She couldn't imagine how frantic Joshua would be under these circumstances. Violet was his entire world.

"Is it bad?" she asked.

Liam's expression was grim. "I'm not sure. I need to head over right now. I want to be at the clinic when he arrives."

"I'm coming with you, Liam," she said.

He frowned down at her. "Are you sure that's a good idea?"

She bit her lip. "Not really, but if I was in his shoes,

I'd want some company. I have no idea if I'll be welcome, but I think considering what we meant to each other in the past it feels like the right thing to do."

"Okay," he nodded. "Let's go."

She went back to her seat and grabbed her purse and coat, then quickly trailed after Liam.

"Honor!" Boone called after her. She turned around and eyed him warily. He had caught up to her. His expression radiated concern.

"Boone. I've got to go. It's an emergency."

"Why don't you just stay here with us? It's not wise to get wrapped up in Joshua's personal life," he warned. "You don't need to get pulled back in."

Why was Boone continuing to treat her like a child? It was beyond irritating. "The last time I checked I'm an adult. I'm gainfully employed and I live on my own. I'm no longer the naive teenager who had stars in her eyes. Please stop questioning my decisions!"

Boone opened his mouth to reply, but she turned on her heel and raced to catch up with Liam, who had left the café. When she walked outside, Honor spotted her brother revving up his car across the street. She raced over, then hustled into the passenger seat.

Please, Lord, she prayed. *Let Violet be all right. It will destroy Joshua if his baby girl is seriously injured. We might not be in the best place right now, but I still care about what happens to Joshua. I don't want him to be in pain.*

And therein lay her truths. She still cared. Their love story had ended a long time ago, but it didn't mean she had ever stopped loving him as a human being. It was different from being *in* love with him, but it was still powerful. The ties binding them together meant she couldn't turn her back on him when he was in need. And beautiful, sweet Violet had touched something inside of Honor that had been dormant for a long time. It had frightened her to feel such intense emotions for Joshua's daughter, but she knew exactly where they stemmed from—the loss of the baby she and Joshua had created.

It wasn't easy dealing with all the feelings she had stuffed down for so many years, but Honor knew she needed to offer support to Joshua and Violet. She prayed Joshua wouldn't be upset by her presence at the clinic, because there was no force on earth that could stop her from being there.

Joshua couldn't remember a time in his life when he had been so terrified. He had broken every speed record in Love, Alaska, in order to get Violet to Dr. Liam Prescott's clinic. Violet screamed the entire way. His heart had broken listening to her cries. All he'd wanted to do was hold her in his arms and make her feel better. Joshua had uttered more prayers than he'd ever imagined possible.

Because neither Theo nor Winnie had been at the house this evening when Violet had fallen, he was all alone in a very scary situation.

As he pulled up in front of the clinic, he immediately noticed it was ablaze with lights. He vaulted out of the truck and raced to unbuckle Violet. Her face was blotchy and red. She was whimpering and her eyes were pink from crying. Joshua cradled her as gently as he possibly could in his arms. The last thing he wanted to do was inflict more pain on her.

As soon as he walked up to the front door, it swung

open. Liam stood in the entranceway, ushering him inside.

"Come on into the examining room," Liam said, leading him down the hall.

Honor was standing there with wide eyes, wringing her hands. There was a look of strain on her face. "I thought you might need a friend," she said.

Although he was still furious with her regarding the injunction, Joshua couldn't ignore the sense of relief he felt upon seeing her. Even though they were at odds over the Diamond R, Honor knew him on a level most people didn't. They had history. Somehow it made him feel better to have her here. Now he didn't feel so alone.

He nodded at her, tacitly giving her permission to come with them into the examining room. Once they were inside the room, Liam began to pepper him with questions.

"Can you tell me what happened, Joshua?" Liam asked.

Joshua had to talk over the sound of Violet's wails. Every now and again she would stop crying, only to start up again. "She fell down the basement stairs." He let out an agonized sound. "I ran down there to get something. I left her playing in the living room. I can't believe she toddled all the way over to the basement door." He scratched his jaw. "I should have realized she could scoot over there in the blink of an eye."

"These things happen. You can't dwell on that part," Liam said in a gentle voice. "I'm going to lay her down on her back so I can examine her. Just stand right next to me so she stays as calm as possible."

Joshua laid Violet down on the examining table. She held out her arms so he would pick her up. Joshua was in agony. His daughter was too little to understand what was going on. As Liam examined her, Joshua spoke to her in a calm, soothing voice. He began playing peek-aboo with her and trying to distract her. After a few minutes, Liam sat Violet up.

"I'm going to do some X-rays on her left arm. Judging by the way she's holding it and her reaction to my touching it, it could be broken. And I'd like to check on her leg as well. She could have broken several bones in the fall. We just have to make certain. She's not showing any signs of a concussion, but we should watch out for them. Loss of balance. Headache. And I also want to rule out any internal injuries."

Joshua ran a hand over his face. He felt incredibly guilty. "I can't believe this," he muttered. "She's just a baby."

"It's going to be all right, Joshua. Violet is in great hands. Liam will figure out what's going on," Honor said in a comforting tone.

"Why don't we just take her down the hall to get the X-rays and then I'll be able to see what's going on with her," Liam explained. "I'll give you a vest to wear, Joshua, so you can hold Violet and not have to worry about exposure to any radiation."

Joshua nodded, handing Violet over to Honor. She didn't fuss or make a peep. Violet's big blue eyes were focused on Honor. Clearly, she'd won her over with her sweet, honeyed voice and warm smiles. Honor projected a caring, sensitive vibe. It was one of the many reasons Joshua had fallen for her.

Honor swayed back and forth with Violet as Liam took Joshua into the X-ray room and helped him into his vest.

"We'll be done shortly," Liam said to Honor, taking Violet from her arms and bringing her into the room with Joshua. Honor gave him an encouraging thumbs-up sign before the door was closed.

Taking the X-rays wasn't as simple as Joshua had hoped. Violet wriggled around like a fish on a hook. He let out a huge sigh of relief when Liam told him he'd managed to get a great picture of Violet's extremities.

As soon as they returned to the examination room, he began to pace back and forth. It killed him that his daughter was in so much pain. Violet had begun to softly cry again. He'd been negligent. He didn't think he could ever forgive himself for hurting Violet. Honor didn't overstep. She stood by as a support system without being overbearing.

"This is all my fault!" he said in an agonized voice as he gently held Violet in his arms. He worried about hurting her by moving her body or brushing against her.

He felt a soothing touch on his shoulder. "Don't blame yourself, Joshua. It was an accident," Honor said. "The way you feel about Violet speaks volumes. You would never hurt her intentionally."

"I should have watched her more closely. In the past few days she's been extra curious about her surroundings. I know how fast she can move when she's motivated."

"Blaming yourself is wasting a lot of energy. Why don't you focus on next steps? What can you do to make Violet feel better? Does she have a favorite treat, like Popsicles or chocolate milk? What about a blanket that makes her feel better or a favorite doll?"

"That's a great idea, Honor. Thanks." He shook his head. "I just hope she's going to be all right."

Honor sent him an encouraging smile. "I think she will be. She's not crying as much as when you first arrived. I know she's in pain, but I think she's probably scared, too. Taking a tumble is frightening."

"You're right about that." Perhaps her injuries weren't as terrible as he'd imagined on the drive to the clinic.

Dear Lord. Please grant Violet favor. She's just a baby. She doesn't even understand what's happening. Please give her comfort and healing.

"I appreciate you being here, Honor. A few hours ago I never would have imagined feeling this way, but despite what's going on with the ranch, when I saw you standing by the exam room door, I was grateful."

"It must have been terrifying for you." She made a tutting noise. "And for Violet."

"It all happened so fast. I'm still wondering how it all happened so quickly."

Suddenly, Liam reappeared in the room. "I've studied the images. The arm is fractured. But the good news is, no other broken bones. Due to her age, she'll heal quickly. There aren't signs of a concussion or anything more ominous. Please keep me in the loop if she exhibits any additional symptoms, although I'm confident she'll be on the mend soon."

"Praise the Lord," Honor cried out, clapping her hands together.

Joshua let out a ragged sigh. He pressed a kiss on Violet's cheek, overcome with relief and joy. He carefully maneuvered so as not to give her any additional pain or aggravate the injury. She nuzzled her face against his chest and stuck her thumb firmly in her mouth. He looked down at her, knowing full well he was wearing his heart on his sleeve. "What a blessing! I'm grateful for your dedication, Liam."

"That's what I'm here for, Joshua. To make things better. Now I need to put a cast on her arm." He made a face. "At her age, it isn't easy to sit still, especially when you're in pain."

Joshua looked down at Violet. She was so small and vulnerable. He couldn't wait until this night was nothing more than a memory.

"Why don't you hold her in your lap and I'll get it done as fast as I possibly can?" Liam suggested in a gentle voice. Joshua was thoroughly impressed with Dr. Liam Prescott. Six years ago he'd intensely disliked Honor's brother. He was convinced the feeling had been mutual. It was amazing how people could grow and change for the better.

Joshua sat down and held Violet in his lap. He held her free hand as Liam placed the cast on her arm. Considering everything she'd been through this evening, Violet barely fussed. Part of his heart ached at the weary expression imprinted on his daughter's face. She'd been put through the wringer. Her little body was near exhaustion.

"Why don't you take this little lady home? My work here is done. Violet looks like she's ready to crash." Liam tousled Violet's blond curls. "I can't say I blame her. She's had quite an eventful night."

"She's been a trouper," Honor said, reaching out and brushing Violet's hair out of her eyes.

Joshua stuck out his hand to Liam, who didn't hesitate to shake it. "Thank you for responding so quickly to my call. And for everything you did for my daughter. I won't ever forget it. You can send the bill to the ranch."

"I'll do that. You're very welcome." Liam nodded. "Goodnight. I'm going to lock up the place."

Honor held the door open for Liam as he walked outside. Snow was gently falling from the inky sky. Violet turned her face upward and giggled as snowflakes landed on her face. Joshua glanced over at Honor. They met each other's gaze and smiled. Seeing Violet so full of joy was an amazing blessing.

"She's something else, isn't she?" Joshua asked.

"She sure is," Honor murmured. An emotion he couldn't pinpoint flickered in her blue-gray eyes.

He busied himself settling Violet into her car seat. Within seconds her eyes were firmly shut and she was fast asleep.

"Poor little thing," Honor said. "She needs a good night's rest."

"I won't disagree with you on that. 'Night, Honor."

"Good night, Joshua." She began to fiddle with her fingers. "I know my being here tonight doesn't change anything regarding the injunction and the Diamond R Ranch, but I'm really happy it all worked out this evening."

He felt something inside him toughen up at the mention of the injunction and Bud's ranch. When Honor had invited him and Violet to the wildlife center, he had viewed it as an olive branch being extended. A beautiful act of grace. But then she had stabbed him in the back by filing an injunction against him and Theo. When she had shown up at the clinic, it had felt so comforting and amazing. But, he had to admit, now that his fear for Violet had diminished, he was beginning to see things more clearly. It wasn't all roses and moonlight between him and Honor.

Now he had to wonder if she had a hidden agenda. Why was she bringing up the issue right now? Couldn't she let it go for one evening?

"I appreciate the fact that you came here tonight, but you're right. It doesn't change a thing. We're still on opposite sides of a very tense situation."

"I wasn't trying to make you angry," she said.

"I guess I'm beyond anger." He shook his head. "I've been racking my brain trying to reconcile the woman I used to know with the person who filed legal paperwork against me. It seemed almost spiteful." He let out a frustrated sigh. All he wanted to do was go back to the ranch and tuck Violet into bed. But he couldn't leave without getting a few things off his chest.

Honor met his gaze head-on. "It couldn't be helped. I felt you and Theo left me no choice but to explore other avenues to shut down this sale of the ranch. And I know you've had a rough night, but I'm not sorry about what I did." Sparks were practically flying from her. She seemed defiant.

"You're just prolonging the inevitable, Honor. We're Bud's heirs. Myself, Theo and Violet. I know you thought the property was being willed to the town, but that ship has sailed. Ultimately, my brother and I are going to be in control of the ranch and property. We'll decide what happens to it. Not you. And not the townsfolk!"

"I don't agree with you. An injunction is in place. That didn't happen on a lark. I think we set forth some excellent reasons why the land shouldn't be sold to a developer. We might win this."

Joshua let out a strangled sound. "We're not just going to lie down and let you run all over us. Theo flew to Anchorage the other day to meet with legal counsel." He furrowed his brow. "That injunction isn't worth the paper it's written on. I don't want to see you crushed, Honor, but you're not going to win this. You might as well resign yourself to the idea that the ranch is going to be sold."

A wounded expression passed over her face. "Tonight wasn't about legal wrangling or injunctions or Texas developers descending on this town. I actually came here this evening as a friend." She tilted her chin up. "I'm sorry that I actually thought that might be possible. Good night, Joshua."

Honor turned around and walked back toward the clinic. He opened his mouth to call out to her and apologize for his harsh words, but he reined the words back in. Joshua shouldn't feel guilty. He and Honor weren't friends. Not in the truest sense of the word.

Friends kept in touch. He hadn't seen Honor in six years. They hadn't been a part of each other's world in a very long time. She had been the great love of his life. And he didn't want or need a friend here in Love because he wasn't staying. This town had brought him nothing but pain and rejection. As soon as the lawyers were able to have the injunction withdrawn, Joshua intended to move forward with the sale of the ranch.

He was tired of allowing people to stomp all over him simply because he'd made some mistakes in the past. Who among them was perfect? When he had first arrived back in Love, Joshua had hoped the townsfolk would see he'd made something of himself. He had only been fooling himself to think they would even care. With the exception of Hazel, all the residents seemed to care about was whether or not the Ransom brothers were selling the Diamond R.

From this point forward, Joshua wasn't going to feel an ounce of guilt about selling the ranch to the Alloy Corporation. In the past few days the ranch had gotten under his skin. He had been awash in memories of a childhood and adolescence spent at the ranch. But the ranch didn't represent his future. And as he had done for the past six years, Joshua would simply stuff down the past.

He would always treasure the memories of life at the Diamond R Ranch with his family, but he had already made his peace with letting go of the property Bud had loved so much. Now if he could only relinquish his feelings for Honor.

As he drove away from the clinic he cast a glance in his rearview mirror at the back seat. He couldn't see Violet's face due to the rear-facing car seat, but he suspected she remained fast asleep. His heart swelled with love for her. Every step he took in this lifetime mattered due to his little girl. She was the reason he drew breath each and every morning. Feeling a tug in Honor's direction after all of these years was merely a distraction. He had come back to Love only for a short period of time, to properly say goodbye to his grandfather and to help Theo settle the estate.

It was far too dangerous to get invested in this town or in Honor Prescott.

Honor couldn't remember the last time she'd been so incensed. Actually, she could. Six years ago when she had discovered from Boone that Joshua had burned the church down, Honor had been consumed with unbridled rage. It had seemed incomprehensible to her. How could he have done something so horrendous? In doing so, it had dealt their relationship a final devastating blow. All their plans for the future had been extinguished by his dangerous actions.

And now he had treated her with such cruelty and condescension. She didn't care what he thought! Her presence here tonight at the clinic hadn't been motivated by anything other than concern. The moment Liam had told her about Violet's fall, Honor had wanted to be by his side to help him deal with the situation. She had acted on pure instinct.

As she sat down in the passenger seat of Liam's car, she slammed the door behind her.

"Hey! Easy on the door. What's wrong?" Liam asked as he revved his engine. "Did something go down between you and Joshua while I was locking up?"

Honor clenched her teeth. She felt like exploding. "I don't want to talk about it," she muttered.

"Uh-oh," Liam said. "That doesn't sound good. Whenever Ruby utters that phrase, I head for the hills."

Honor threw her hands in the air. "Joshua had the nerve to question my motives. He brought up the injunction and we got into it. I came here tonight with the best of intentions. He should be—"

"Grateful?" Liam asked, shooting her a pointed look before turning his eyes back toward the road.

"Yes, he should. Don't you think so?"

A small sigh slipped past his lips. "Honor, I think you should give Joshua a break."

She sucked in a shocked breath. "What do you mean? You can't stand Joshua. Why are you taking his side?"

"Simmer down, cowgirl. First of all, I don't dislike

him. I hated what he did to the church and this town."
His voice softened. "And to you. As your big brother,
it gutted me to see you with a broken heart. But I let go
of all those feelings a long time ago. My faith tells me
to turn the other cheek. So that's what I did."

A groundswell of love for her brother rose up within
her. He had always been the most tenderhearted of all
her siblings.

"Can you really expect Joshua to be focused on gratitude when you filed the injunction against him?"

Tears welled in Honor's eyes. "It wasn't personal."

Liam pulled up in front of the Moose Café and put
his car in Park. He turned toward her, wiping away a
stray tear on her cheek with his thumb. "I'm not criti-
cizing you. I think it was a brilliant move designed to
protect this town. I admire you more than mere words
can express. You showed pluck and grit and ingenuity."

Honor's lips quivered. "Why can't Joshua see it that
way? He made it seem as if I'm being malicious."

"Sis, you don't have a mean bone in your body. If
Joshua blew up at you tonight, I would say he's simply
hurting and frustrated. He looked scared tonight. Really petrified. He's under a lot of strain on the heels of
Bud's passing. And he was terrified for Violet."

Suddenly, she felt ashamed of herself. Liam was
right. Joshua was in mourning for his grandfather.
Maybe it had been wrong of her to file the injunction
when he was at a low moment. She bit her lip. "I know.
I can't imagine how terrifying it must have been for
both of them."

"I know what it feels like to be a single father," he
said. "It can be really lonely and you question whether
or not you're doing a decent job as a parent. I empathize

with him. That being said, why do you care so much? Isn't he leaving soon to go back home?"

Honor knit her brows together. Liam's question threw her for a loop. "What? I—I don't really care all that much. It's just that I'm trying to be cordial with him. Isn't that turning the other cheek? I've tried to move beyond what happened between us in the past. As painful as it was for me to go through all of it with him, I realize he's grown and changed. He's been married. He's a father now to a beautiful little girl. I've moved on."

She met Liam's gaze. "Have you, Honor? Really and truly? Because from where I'm sitting, it doesn't seem like it. The look on your face when I told you about Violet's accident was very telling."

Honor rolled her eyes. "I'm not in love with him anymore if that's what you're insinuating. Those feelings died a long time ago."

"I'm not saying you're still in love with him. But what I am saying is that if you're not careful, you're going to fall in love all over again with your ex-fiancé."

Chapter Eight

Joshua stood in the stables saddling up Blaze for a ride across the property. He felt excitement bubbling up inside him at the prospect of being at one with the Alaskan landscape. Since he'd been back home, riding had become one of his favorite pastimes. There was really nothing like it. It filled something inside his soul like nothing else could.

There had been a small snow squall late last night, but it had barely added to the accumulation already on the ground. Love, Alaska, was a wintry wonderland. He couldn't deny how much he enjoyed being back at the ranch. It brought back to life a part of him he thought he'd buried a long time ago. It was hard to imagine not ever being able to ride across this landscape again.

Theo was on Violet duty while Joshua was taking this opportunity to venture out on the property. His brother had felt awful about not being around when the accident took place. As a treat, Uncle Theo had brought a huge teddy bear for Violet from a local gift shop called Keepsakes. Violet had embraced the stuffed animal with open arms, smothering it with hugs and endless kisses. She had gifted Theo with a million-dollar smile in return for his kindness. He shook his head at the irony in Theo purchasing the toy at the same store that he'd broken into on a dare back in his rebellious years.

Joshua couldn't wait to have some alone time out on the range. He needed to clear his head regarding last night. Had he been too harsh on Honor? Or had he been right on point? He had no way of knowing since, when it came to Honor, he always seemed to lose his objectivity.

Last night when he had returned to the ranch, he'd gotten down on his knees and prayed about the situation. He was now a man who didn't like volatile situations or drama. It reminded him all too much of things he would rather forget.

"Mr. Ransom. Can I have a few minutes?"

Joshua swung his gaze up. Cal Abilene, the ranch foreman, was standing in front of him with a look of concern carved on his face. He had his cowboy hat in his hand and his eyes swirled with strong emotions.

"Sure thing, Cal. What's up?" he asked. From everything he had heard from Bud, as well as what he had seen with his own eyes, Cal was a great ranch foreman. Hardworking and honest, Cal had been at the Diamond R for almost twenty years. The ranch's success was directly related to Cal's strong work ethic.

Cal raked a hand through his shoulder-length dark hair.

"Would you mind telling me if you're going to be selling the place? If so, I need to start looking for a new position here in town or head to the Kenai Peninsula where there are more opportunities to work on a ranch."

Joshua felt his heart sink. How could he and Theo have been so thoughtless? The Diamond R had employees who counted on their paychecks to stay afloat. Selling the ranch would have a trickle-down effect.

"Honestly, Cal, things are up in the air at the moment. I'm sure you heard about the injunction filed against us?"

Cal nodded. "I sure did. Honor has a lot more pluck than I ever gave her credit for," Cal said with a light chuckle.

"I'll be straight with you. As soon as the injunction is lifted, Theo and I plan to accept an offer for the ranch. To be honest, I'm not sure if the outfit buying the Diamond R will keep you and the others on. That hasn't been discussed."

Cal's face fell. "I'd like you to know the people who work on this ranch have been here for years. We work hard. We've always been invested in this place." He twisted his mouth. "It's hard to imagine this ranch changing hands. Bud poured his heart and soul into the Diamond R."

Joshua felt a prickle of guilt. "I know he did. And if it's okay by you, I'll make sure to inquire as to whether the Alloy Corporation will be in need of a foreman and ranch hands."

Cal scoffed. "For the dude ranch? No, thanks, Mr. Ransom. That doesn't interest me. But I appreciate your giving it to me straight about selling the ranch. Now at least I know what I need to do." With a nod of his head, Cal strode away from the stables.

Joshua stood by Blaze and watched as Cal quickly disappeared from sight. He felt awful. He had been so consumed by his own agenda and concern for Violet's future that he hadn't considered the people whose lives would be drastically altered if the Diamond R was sold.

Cal had driven the point home. Many lives were going to be affected by the sale of the ranch. Not just the townsfolk of Love, but the dedicated employees who had worked at the Diamond R for years. They would all have to seek employment elsewhere, or even leave Love in order to make a living. It wasn't fair to them, but there was nothing he could do to change things. He had already agreed to sell. His future was in Seattle.

As he mounted Blaze and headed out across the property, Joshua let go of all the things that were burdening him. He took a deep breath of the fresh Alaskan air and began to gallop away from the ranch. Craggy mountains stretched out before him in the distance. There was nothing but wide-open spaces in front of him. He turned his face up toward the sky and allowed the sun's rays to wash over him. He flew like the wind on Blaze's back, feeling unfettered for the first time in ages.

From a distance, he spotted a person on horseback galloping toward him. As soon as the rider drew closer, Joshua recognized Honor seated on Lola. He had forgotten how close he was to the property line for the wildlife center.

"Honor," he said, tipping his cowboy hat in her direction by way of greeting.

She reined in her horse, bringing Lola to a stop not far from him. "Hi, Joshua. I was just heading toward the Diamond R so I could check on the newborn calves."

The calves. He had almost forgotten all about them. "It's nice of you to take time out from the wildlife center to check on them."

"Bud trusted me to do it a few times a week. He and I stayed close over the years. I wouldn't feel right about stopping until a decision is made about the ranch."

"I'm headed in that direction. We can ride together." He frowned. "Unless you'd rather not."

"I think the great outdoors is big enough for both of us," she cracked, making a none-too-subtle reference to their war of words the other night.

"You're right about that. It's beautiful out here. Majestic. Seattle is a nice place to live, but it's not this," he said, scanning the area around them. This Alaskan vista was one of the most spectacular sights he had ever seen.

"How's Violet this morning? If I may ask?"

"Of course you can. She's doing well. Theo is probably spoiling her as we speak."

"It's all right to do so now and again. After all, she went through the wringer due to her accident. And she wasn't the only one. I saw the alarm on your face. The love you feel for Violet is palpable."

"Once you become a mother you'll see how it is," he said. "You always worry."

Honor visibly winced. "I can imagine," she murmured.

"I remember riding out here with you a lot," Joshua said, meeting Honor's gaze. Were the memories as indelible for her as they were for him? He could picture in his mind's eye her long chestnut-colored hair whipping in the breeze and the look of joy on her face.

A slight smile twitched at her lips. "I remember the time we were looking for a herd of wild mustangs."

Joshua laughed. "Bud told me if I caught one of 'em, I could keep him."

Honor made a face. "Little did we know it was easier said than done."

His grandfather had been a mischievous person. It had tickled him to no end to play jokes on him and

Theo. On this occasion Bud had convinced Joshua to go out looking for wild mustangs. He'd fallen for it hook, line and sinker, not realizing that catching one was a near impossible task. In the end, he had come up empty-handed.

"I miss him," he said, blurting out the sentiment that had been sitting on his heart ever since he'd learned of his grandfather's death.

"Me too. He was truly one-of-a-kind. Sort of like Jasper."

Joshua wrinkled his nose. "I'm not sure anyone on earth is quite like Jasper."

They both laughed. God had broken the mold when He had created Mayor Jasper Prescott and everybody knew it.

"I will say he's done something amazing with Operation Love. At the end of the day, people want to find love and a soft place to fall," Honor said. "That's happening here in town now thanks to my grandfather."

A soft place to fall. That's exactly what he'd wanted to give Honor all those years ago. And he knew she would have given it back in return. He wasn't sure he would ever fully get over it. But he hoped life would bring him a loving partner and a mother for Violet. Everyone needed someone to lean on, to pray with, to grow old beside them. Perhaps one of these days God would hear his most fervent prayer.

"What about you?" he asked, blurting out the question he'd been dying to ask. "Are you signed up for the program?"

Honor looked at him, startled. "No, I'm not, but I appreciate what Jasper is doing for this town. Lately I've begun to realize that we all need that special someone in our lives. Who doesn't want the fairy tale?" Her voice sounded soft and vulnerable. It made him want to sweep her into his arms and hold on to her for as long as she would allow.

"It sounds like you're right where you need to be. There are lots of Alaskan bachelors in this town." Joshua tried to stifle a sudden spurt of jealousy. He wanted Honor to be happy, but the thought of her settling down with another man bothered him. He couldn't shake the feeling off or stop the images racing through his mind of Honor walking down the aisle and cradling a newborn in her arms.

Still, after all of this time, Joshua felt cheated out of the life he had envisioned leading with Honor.

Silence descended upon them as they neared the Diamond R. For a moment something hung in the air between them. Neither one mentioned the tension of the other night, but it hung between them like a live grenade. He didn't know whether to broach the subject or simply leave it alone.

"Well, I should go see to the calves," Honor said. "I'm glad Violet is feeling better. You must be relieved."

"Thanks. I'm a happy man," he said, his apology getting swallowed up by his pride. He stood by everything he'd said to her, but his timing and delivery was questionable. Joshua should never have barked at her when she'd showed up at the clinic simply to offer support. It had been less than gracious.

And be kind to one another, tenderhearted, forgiving one another even as God for Christ's sake hath forgiven you. The Bible verse from *Ephesians* ran through his mind, serving as an admonishment for the harsh way he had treated Honor. Despite the fact that she had filed the injunction, Joshua needed to forgive her. Hadn't he wanted the townsfolk to offer him the same grace?

Joshua watched Honor dismount from Lola and head toward the barn. He felt a knot in his stomach as his gaze trailed after her. Why did it always seem as if Honor was leaving him? Pretty soon he would be leaving Love, never to return. The ramifications of it sat heavily on his chest. The thought of never seeing Honor again made him ache inside. Despite the anger he felt toward her for filing the injunction, Joshua couldn't forget what they'd meant to each other in the past.

Joshua led Blaze toward the stables and placed him in his stall. The horse was working his mouth, letting Joshua know he'd enjoyed their ride across the property. After cleaning his tack and picking out his hooves, he treated the horse to an apple. As Joshua headed toward the house, he felt as if he was coming home. *Home.* He had never quite felt that way about Seattle. He'd always believed it was because he hadn't yet bought a house to live in, but he now realized it wasn't true. Home was a feeling. It settled inside you like a warm, comfy blanket.

Seattle didn't have this stunning vista. He couldn't ride to his heart's delight at a moment's notice. He didn't have history there. Seattle was a blank slate. He had always considered that a good thing, but now that he was back in his hometown, he was beginning to think it might not be.

Joshua could honestly picture himself settling down here with Violet. Living at the ranch would be a dream come true. The thought served as a jolt to the system. Where had it come from? He wasn't sticking around Love any longer than was absolutely necessary. It was silly of him to imagine a life that could never be possible. He needed to be realistic and focus on moving forward with his life, not only for his sake, but for Violet's as well.

While she checked on Bud's calves at the ranch, Honor tried to keep her thoughts from straying toward Joshua. Seeing him enjoying a ride on Blaze had been a little surprising. It really shouldn't have been, considering how much he had always loved horses, but she'd convinced herself that Joshua had changed over the years from the young man she'd known.

She had been wrong. The adult version of Joshua clearly still enjoyed riding. A warm feeling settled over her at the realization that he was still the same person she had loved so dearly. Seeing him seated on Blaze took her back to all of the adventures they had enjoyed on Bud's property. The Diamond R Ranch had been their stomping grounds. Those carefree moments were permanently seared on Honor's heartstrings.

"You like all this undivided attention, don't you?" Honor asked as she gently patted one of the calves. She wasn't sure if it was her imagination, but the calf seemed to be smiling at her. There were five calves in all who had been born in the last few weeks. Two had been born early, but all five of them were in good condition.

"Can you blame him?" The rich tone of Joshua's voice startled her. She swung her gaze up to meet his. He was standing a few feet away with his arms folded across his chest. He was leaning against a wooden beam. She had no idea how long he'd been standing there.

"I don't mean to interrupt. I was sitting up at the

main house and feeling curious about the calves. Violet is napping, so I figured I'd pop my head in. Winnie is keeping an eye on her."

"It's fine. They're your calves, after all," she said. "I'm pleased to report they're all in fine condition."

Joshua nodded. "That's in large part due to you, Honor."

Honor grinned. Bud had called her over to the ranch when each of the calves had been born. The memory was a sweet one. "Bud had me wrapped around his little finger. This ranch was his whole world. He cared about every aspect of it."

For a moment they locked gazes. Her words hung in the air, serving as a reminder of the huge divide between them regarding the Diamond R.

Her cell phone began buzzing insistently, shattering the silence. She took her phone out and glanced at the caller ID. It was a call from the wildlife center. "Sorry. I have to take this call."

"No problem," he murmured. "Take your time."

The voice of Priscilla Walters, one of her employees, rang in her ear as soon as she said hello.

"Honor! I've been looking everywhere for you."

"Hey, Priscilla. I'm at the Diamond R checking on Bud's calves. I let Clay know before I headed over here so there would be coverage at the center." There was an urgency to Priscilla's voice that was unsettling.

"Clay is out checking the fences," Priscilla quickly explained. "He forgot to mention you'd headed over to the ranch."

There had recently been an issue when one of the animals had managed to slip through a gap in the fence. She had spent the better part of a day out in the van trying to locate the heifer. They were now regularly making the rounds to ensure no more animals got loose.

"What's going on?" Honor asked. "Is something wrong?"

"We just got a call from Gunther. He spotted a small arctic fox over by Nottingham Woods not too far from the entrance. Gunther said it's been there since yesterday and it may be hurt or abandoned since it hasn't moved. He's not sure how old it is."

Honor made a clucking sound. "Gunther probably thought the mama fox was nearby at first, but if it's still by itself something may have happened to the mother. She may not be alive or she's rejected the baby fox for some reason."

"Can you ride out there?" Priscilla asked. "There's a few preschool kids who are coming for a tour today so I'd like to stay put. And I can't reach Clay. There's probably no service where he is."

"Sure thing," Honor said, not wanting to leave the children in the lurch.

Although she hated to miss the visit by the small group of children, locating the arctic fox and making sure it was safe and sound was important. A young fox who was on its own and possibly injured was a pressing matter.

"I'll head right over there and check it out," Honor said.

When she hung up, Joshua shot her a questioning look.

"There's an arctic fox out in the wild. It might be hurt or abandoned. We're not sure how old it is. I need to head out to Nottingham Woods to check on it," she explained.

Joshua's eyes widened. "How are you going to do that without a vehicle?"

Honor sighed. She had completely forgotten that she'd ridden Lola over to the Diamond R. It would take her forever to ride all the way to the Nottingham Woods on her horse. And if the arctic fox needed medical attention, Honor wouldn't be able to transport it to the wildlife center.

"I'd be happy to drive you over there," Joshua offered. "It's been a while since I've been to Nottingham Woods."

Honor shook her head. "I couldn't ask you to do that."

"You're not asking me. I'm offering," he said in a firm voice. "I can also have one of the ranch hands bring Lola back to the wildlife center for you."

"Thank you, Joshua," Honor said. "I accept. Do you mind if we leave right now?" she asked, anxious to find the fox.

Joshua laughed. "No problem. I just need to let Winnie know I'm going to be out for a while so she can watch Violet. I'll be right back," he said, beating a fast path out of the barn and heading toward the main house.

After grabbing her belongings, Honor walked toward Bud's truck. She only had to wait a few moments before Joshua came back outside and met her by the vehicle. He opened the door for her and she stepped up into the truck. Joshua got behind the wheel and headed off toward Nottingham Woods. It was roughly a fifteen-minute drive from the ranch. As Joshua drove, they passed moose crossing signs and a desolate patch of road with nothing more than snow-covered trees decorating the landscape. The view of the mountains became even more magnificent the closer they drove toward the woods.

As they approached Nottingham Woods, Honor made a mental note to come back up here soon to do some hiking. As a kid, Jasper had taken her and her brothers spelunking in one of the nearby caves. As a teenager, Honor had brought Joshua to the caves. In a wildly romantic gesture, Joshua had carved their initials in the stone wall. *J.R. loves H.P. forever.* To this day, no man had ever made Honor feel the way Joshua had in that moment. Adored. Treasured. Well loved.

Once they arrived, a large cedar sign welcomed them to Nottingham Woods. Joshua turned the truck into the entrance and put it in Park. Honor opened her door and stepped down. She immediately began scouring the area. She knew from experience that arctic foxes could easily blend into the scenery due to their white coats. Honor began walking toward the trail and searching the area for any trace of the animal. Joshua walked a few feet behind her. It was nice to have another set of eyes and ears.

Frustration and worry set in after a half hour. Trying to look on the bright side, Honor reckoned the fox could have been reunited with its mother or found its way back to the den.

All of a sudden, a slight sound caused her to stop in her tracks. "Did you hear that?" she asked Joshua. He nodded instead of speaking. Clearly, he was trying not to spook any animals.

She turned her head to a patch of trees twenty feet away from the trail. As she moved closer, the sounds became more distinct. Honor picked up her pace. She gasped as she came face-to-face with a pure white arctic fox. It was curled up and emitting whimpering sounds. Although it wasn't a baby, it appeared to be under a year old.

Honor saw its weakened condition and the signs that the fox hadn't been eating. It was clear to her that the fox had been injured, which explained why it appeared malnourished. It hadn't been able to forage for food. It meant Honor needed to transport it back to the center. Getting the arctic fox proper nourishment and shelter was crucial for its long-term survival.

She reached out and touched the fox. It was shaking like a leaf. "I'm not going to hurt you, sweet pea." Honor tried to make her voice reassuring and tender. With the utmost gentleness, she lifted it up on its legs. Joshua knelt beside her, allowing her to take the lead but staying close for support. Almost immediately, the fox collapsed. Honor could see there was something going on with its legs.

"She can't walk on her own," she said to Joshua. "I'm going to take her to the center for rehabilitation."

"Why don't you head to the truck and open up the back for me? I'll carry her," Joshua said.

She watched as Joshua reached out and scooped the small fox up into his arms. Honor took off at a fast clip and began walking toward the vehicle. She flung open the back door of the truck, not wanting to waste a moment in getting the animal inside.

After the harsh words they had exchanged, Joshua would have been the last person she would ever want to help her out. At this moment, she wouldn't want to be with anyone else but him.

Chapter Nine

Honor stood by the truck and watched as Joshua gingerly held the arctic fox in his arms. She couldn't help but admire Joshua as he strode toward her, his steps full of power and purpose. A sigh slipped past her lips. He was dressed in a nice-fitting pair of blue jeans and a hunter green parka. A cowboy hat sat perched on his head. There was no debating he was much better-looking than all of the single men in this town put together. A true Alaskan hottie! Her cheeks felt heated at the admission.

He placed the arctic fox in the back of the truck on top of one of her blankets, then firmly closed the door. Honor quickly situated herself in the passenger seat. Joshua sat in the driver's seat and cast a glance behind him at the fox. He reached to turn on the radio, his arm brushing against hers in the process, causing an electric pulse to run through her. Being so close to Joshua was doing a number on her. There was an awareness that always flared between them whenever they were in close proximity. At the same time, Honor felt comfortable in his strong, steady presence. Their shared history bonded them for life.

He revved the engine and began to drive away from Nottingham Woods.

"Thanks for bringing me out here, Joshua. You've been a big help," Honor said, gratitude welling up inside her.

"Hanging out with you twice in one day is pretty suspicious. I'm beginning to think you're following me," he said in a teasing voice.

Honor rolled her eyes. She snapped her fingers. "You figured me out. And here I was trying to be subtle."

"Isn't that how we started dating? You used to trail after me all the time until I noticed you."

"You wish, Ransom," she said, shaking her head.

His low chuckle sounded like it radiated from deep inside him. They both knew the true story. Joshua had been the one to chase Honor. He had worn down her initial defenses with his tenderness and boyish charm. She had been defenseless to resist him.

"So what's your theory on the fox? Was she abandoned?" Joshua asked.

Honor nodded. "No, I don't think so. She's not a baby. I would say she's about nine months old or so. Arctic foxes are on their own from a fairly young age and are forced to fend for themselves. Judging by her weakened state, she's malnourished. She really needs some TLC."

"Sounds like she's in good hands," Joshua said.

"The wildlife center is the perfect place for her. I'm feeling very blessed that we were able to find her in the woods."

Joshua winked at her. "Haven't you heard? There are no accidents in life. Everything happens for a reason."

No accidents in life? Honor agreed with the sentiment. Everything had a divine purpose. She had been scratching her head trying to figure out why God had placed Joshua back in Love. Surely it wasn't so he could sell Bud's ranch to the Alloy Corporation? There had to be some other reason, she reckoned. Her faith told her so.

"Well, I'm glad there's a happy ending for Bashful." The helpless look on the arctic fox's face tugged at Honor's heart.

"Bashful?" he asked with a raised eyebrow. "Like one of the seven dwarfs?"

Honor nodded. "It's the perfect name for her." She chuckled at the skeptical expression on Joshua's face. "I'm serious. She has that shy look on her face and those big ears."

"Now that you mention it, she does look a little on the bashful side," Joshua noted.

"See! I told you!" Honor said, her tone laced with triumph.

He turned toward her. "So what will happen to her?"

"First, we'll get her up to speed nutrition-wise. Then we'll rehabilitate her. She can't stand on her legs. She's been injured in some way. I'll call the vet out so he can come on over and check on her. Then we'll go from there." She found herself smiling. Although she hated the sad circumstances that led animals to the wildlife center, Honor enjoyed being the one who helped bring them to a place of healing. It was truly her calling in life.

"You really love what you do, don't you?" he asked.

"I really do. I'm so blessed. From the moment I start

work in the morning until I clock out, I'm filled with such joy. Being an advocate for these animals is a huge responsibility, but it's one I completely embrace."

Joshua quirked his mouth. She could tell he was thinking about something. He was listening to every word she was saying with such rapt attention.

"What about you?" she asked, curious about his business. Bud had told her a little bit about Joshua's company. His grandfather had been extremely proud of his grandson's success, although he had always seemed wary to share information with her. Perhaps Bud had believed it would reopen old wounds. He certainly had never breathed a word to her about Violet.

"I like working in home construction and flipping houses, but I can't say I'm passionate about it. To be honest, I never really thought about it before." He frowned. "You're one of the rare ones, Honor. Most people work jobs. You have a vocation. You're living the dream."

Joshua's words made Honor's chest swell with pride. Following her passion hadn't always been easy, but she had forged through and completed her education. With her family and the Lord by her side, Honor had persevered. Boone had always advised her to keep her eyes on the prize. And she hadn't lost sight of the big dream—creating a wildlife center in Love.

As Joshua turned into the entrance to the wildlife center, Honor took a moment to survey the property. It wasn't as big as the Diamond R Ranch by any means, but it was spectacular in her opinion. She didn't want to dwell on the fact that Bud had mentioned merging the properties. It was all water under the bridge. There wasn't a single thing she could do to change it. Filing the injunction had only been about preventing the Ransom brothers from selling to a developer. If the wildlife center never gained another acre, Honor would still be content.

"Seems like you've got company," Joshua said as he pulled up to the house.

A car sat parked outside the main building. Its motor was still running.

Honor would recognize the distinctive vehicle anywhere.

"It's Lee," Honor said. Her heart sank. The timing of the attorney's visit couldn't have been worse. Joshua knew full well that Lee had helped her pursue the injunction against him and Theo.

The mood in the truck immediately became tense. She and Joshua had been getting along so well, with little or no discord. She'd thought they had turned a corner. The appearance of Lee served as a reminder that sides had been taken in the matter of Joshua's inheritance. It was as if there was a huge neon blinking sign up ahead reminding Joshua of the injunction.

Honor couldn't help but notice the change in Joshua's demeanor. His jaw was tightly clenched. He was gripping the steering wheel so hard she could see his veins threatening to burst through the skin.

Perhaps there was still some way of salvaging their goodwill toward one another.

"Would you like to stay for a bit and see how Bashful gets acclimated?" Honor asked.

"No, thanks," he said tersely. He nodded in Lee's direction. "It looks like Lee wants your time and attention."

"Joshua, I don't want—"

His expression softened. "You don't need to say anything. We're just on opposite sides of things. That's just the way it is." He shrugged. "Maybe it's always been this way."

"What do you mean?" she asked.

"Think about it. When we first fell in love, your family tried to put up roadblocks at every turn. Then I created a bunch of them myself. Theo always had a problem with you. There was always one thing or another separating us. We never had a shot, did we?"

"That's not true!" she said. "I can't believe you've become so cynical."

"Do you blame me?" he asked in an anger-filled voice.

"Yes, I do," she said. "I guess you've forgotten what we shared, Joshua. Because it was real. It mattered. And you can try to reduce it to something trivial if you want, but it wasn't. It was pretty epic."

Their gazes locked. Honor reached out and swept her palm across Joshua's cheek. "I'm sorry if my filing the injunction hurt you. Or if you feel I've tied your hands. I truly am. But it's separate and apart from what we once meant to each other. Our love was real. And after everything I went through, I'm not going to let you say otherwise." Honor wrenched open the door and hopped out of the truck. She might have slammed the door behind her if Bashful wasn't resting peacefully. She moved toward the back of the truck and tugged the blanket toward her, bringing Bashful along with it. Next thing she knew, Joshua was beside her, lifting up the arctic fox.

"Where do you want her?" Joshua asked, looking around him.

"I can take her," Honor said, reaching out her arms for the animal. Joshua tenderly placed Bashful in her arms, then nodded at her, murmuring a quick goodbye. Lee raised his hand in greeting as soon as he spotted her. He knit his brows together as his gaze veered toward Joshua. Honor saw the questions lurking in her friend's eyes, but she had no intention of addressing them. At the moment, she was all talked out.

As Joshua roared away from the wildlife center, Honor found herself wondering how things had ever gotten so complicated between them. It seemed that they were destined to be at odds over every little thing in this world.

It had been several days since Joshua had assisted Honor with locating the wounded arctic fox at Nottingham Woods. He and Theo were making great progress on tidying up Bud's estate, with the glaring exception of the ranch. According to their lawyers, they had immediately filed all the necessary paperwork to dispute the injunction. They appeared to be very optimistic about the injunction being lifted based on similar, precedent-setting cases. The judge could render a decision any day now.

Violet seemed to be as happy as a clam despite her broken arm. Joshua was blown away by her resilience. He loved taking her out to the paddock every day so she could greet the horses with her natural brand of enthusiasm. He had even taken her to church for Sunday service. His elementary school teacher, Mrs. Henrie, had made a beeline to him after the service. It had been a nice interaction, with Joshua introducing her to Violet and Mrs. Henrie telling him how proud she was about his turning his life around. It had left Joshua feeling a tad emotional. There were still some folks in this town who thought he was worth something after all.

"I'm going a little stir-crazy," Theo announced with a loud moan as he walked into the great room and flopped onto the love seat. Violet, who was playing in her playpen while Joshua worked on the computer, stood up and held on to the sides with her hands. She gurgled at Theo. He covered his face with hands and said, "Peekaboo," causing Violet to cackle with glee. It amazed Joshua how easy it was to entertain kids. All they needed were simple things to keep them laughing and joyful.

"What does that mean? Do you want to fly the coop?" Joshua asked. He should have known Theo was bored. It had always been difficult to keep him focused.

"Yes. Don't you? This place has gotten old really quickly."

Joshua shrugged. "Not really. I like being here at the ranch. It's peaceful. And I get to ride whenever I want. Despite her broken arm, Violet seems really content. To be honest, I can't wait to teach Violet to ride when she gets old enough."

Theo snorted. "You always did love this place more than I did. That's one of the reasons I joined the army at such a young age. I wanted to spread my wings. You're like Bud. He lived and breathed this place."

"I would have been completely happy to stay and grow old here," Joshua said in a voice clogged with emotion. Since he'd been back, Joshua had been opening himself up to the things he had buried inside him a long time ago. His hopes and dreams. His emotions. The love he'd felt for Honor. Even though he hadn't let her know it, her words had chipped away at him. She had made him feel ashamed of doubting their past relationship. Even though it hadn't resulted in a happily-ever-after, it had been the real deal.

Theo furrowed his brow. He was staring at Joshua with an intensity Joshua couldn't ignore. "Grow old? With who? Honor?"

He nodded. "That's what I wanted more than anything. We all know that didn't exactly go according to plan," Joshua said in a curt voice. What was the point in discussing Honor with Theo? He'd never been a big believer in their love story. Bringing it up would only dredge up painful memories Joshua might not be able to handle. As it was, he felt as if he was dealing with a groundswell of memories crashing over him in unrelenting waves.

"There's no reason we should have to hole up here at the ranch. We haven't done anything wrong."

Joshua made a face at his brother, then raised his eyebrows. "That's debatable."

"Well, beside the fire, but that was six years ago."

"I can think of a few things I did back when I was a teenager."

"Surely there's a statute of limitations on youthful indiscretions?" Theo asked. "God forgave me a long time ago. No one has the right to judge us. 'Judge not, lest ye be judged.'"

Joshua had to chuckle. Theo hadn't seen the inside of a church in many years, with the exception of Bud's service. As far as Joshua could tell, his relationship with God was shaky at best. And now he was quoting from the Bible.

"Theo, I know something in the universe has shifted when you're quoting the Bible."

"You're not the only one who can change, Joshua." For once Theo wasn't making a joke. A serious expression was carved on his face.

"That's good to hear," he said with a nod. "Throughout all of the dark times in my life, I always knew the Lord was with me. That's my prayer for you as well."

Joshua reached out and clasped his brother's hand. He and Theo had always shared a tight relationship, although time and geographical distance had chipped away at it a little bit. Joshua knew he was no doubt harboring some pent-up feelings regarding the fire and taking responsibility for it. Ultimately, he'd made the decision to do so all on his own. Theo hadn't forced his hand. But he wished Theo had acted like a big brother and shielded him from the fallout.

"What do you say we head into town for Hazel's birthday celebration? It's supposed to be a big town event according to a few of my friends."

Joshua shook his head. "No, thanks. I'm not in the mood to deal with the Prescotts."

"Come on, Joshua. Hazel invited us. She wants us to be there," Theo said. He stood up and went over to the side table, then rummaged through some mail. He held up a brightly colored envelope. "Here it is. Hazel's Ageless Birthday Party. Don't you remember I mentioned it the other day?"

Joshua chuckled at the ageless theme. Leave it to Hazel to put a novel twist on celebrating a milestone year.

"Sorry. I forgot all about it. Where is it being held?" Joshua asked.

"At the Moose Café," Theo said.

He let out a groan. "Are you serious?"

"Of course I am. Hazel has been good to us. I for one want to go to the party and wish her a happy birthday. What are you afraid of? Running into the townsfolk?"

Theo's question prickled his pride. He didn't want it to seem as if he was running from the residents of Love. He wasn't a coward by any means.

"I'm not afraid of anything or anyone in this town. They've already done the worst they can do to me. And frankly, I'm a little bit over it." He inhaled deeply. "Why shouldn't we go? An invite from the birthday girl herself means something."

"That's great. I picked up a little present and a birthday card for Hazel just in case we were going to attend."

Joshua scooped up Violet from the playpen and said a little prayer about attending the celebration. If he ever wanted folks in this town to treat him with an ounce of respect, perhaps he needed to show them who he was rather than hiding away at the ranch like a hermit. Time had changed him for the better. He was a father and a businessman now. Surely they could see he had worked hard to earn redemption.

Maybe, just maybe, they would decide to show him a measure of grace.

Chapter Ten

Honor placed her gift for Hazel on the oval table laden with gaily wrapped presents. Hazel had told everyone not to buy her any gifts, but clearly, no one had listened. Knowing Hazel, Honor wouldn't be surprised one bit if she donated her gifts to a charitable organization.

"Sorry if this sounds gossipy, but isn't that your ex-fiancé who just walked in?" Her sister-in-law's blue eyes were twinkling with interest. As a journalist, Grace was always interested in people, places and things. More times than not, she couldn't keep her curiosity in check.

Honor turned her head toward the entrance. Joshua had just walked in with Theo. He was holding Violet in a baby carrier. She dragged her gaze away from the sight of him.

"That's him," she said in a cool voice to Grace.

"I saw him at the memorial for Bud. Quite a memorable face," Grace said, her lips tilted upward into a smile.

"He was always handsome," Ruby added. "It used to get him out of a lot of scrapes when he was younger."

"Not enough though," Honor said, remembering all of Joshua's brushes with the law.

"He has a kind vibe," Grace noted. "And that baby is adorable."

"I'm surprised they showed up here, although Hazel has made it quite clear she's crazy about those Ransom brothers," Ruby added.

"Let's not stare at him," Honor said, feeling a bit flushed. "He'll think we're talking about him."

"But we are," Ruby teased, her brown eyes full of mischief.

Honor watched with interest as the Ransom brothers navigated their way around the party. Honor would have guessed that Joshua would rather eat glass than show up at a birthday celebration at her brother's establishment. Perhaps Hazel herself had been the inducement. There wasn't a single soul in town who didn't adore Hazel. And she had helped Theo and Joshua host Bud's reception. Clearly, she was a fan.

She caught his eye from across the café. He waved in her direction. She nodded back. In his dark shirt and a nice-fitting pair of faded jeans, he made an eye-catching figure. Her palms began to moisten. Honor reminded herself to breathe deeply in and out. Inhale. Exhale. Why did the sight of Joshua rattle her so badly?

"I—I should go check on the cake," she muttered before turning on her heel and heading toward the kitchen. She let out a deep breath as soon as she was away from the main area of the café.

It was fairly pathetic that she was hiding out in the kitchen rather than socializing with everyone. Leave it to Hazel to have invited the Ransom brothers to her birthday party. Her kindness was legendary, and she'd always harbored a soft spot for Joshua. Back in the day it had been sort of sweet. Now it was an annoyance.

"Everything okay in here?" Hazel barked as she entered the kitchen.

Honor turned her back to Hazel as she pretended to wash her hands. Without turning around, she answered, "I'm fine. Just washing up."

"I was worried about you. You disappeared as soon as Joshua arrived. I can't help but think you're running away from something. Old feelings, perhaps?"

Honor turned around and faced Hazel. "It's just a coincidence, Hazel. You're being a bit fanciful, don't you think?"

"Believe it or not, I know a little something about love," Hazel said. "After all, I pined after Jasper for years when he barely knew I was alive."

"That's your story, not mine. I'm not pining for Joshua," she protested. "He's an ex. We're trying to be civil with one another considering we're at odds regarding the Diamond R. There's nothing more going on between us."

"Maybe not, but ever since Joshua's come back, there's been something different about you. It's as if you're lit up from the inside. You radiate a certain type of energy now that wasn't there before." She squinted at Honor. "Reminds me of how you looked when you first fell in love with Joshua. Your cheeks were always pink and you had stars in your eyes." Hazel leaned in and peered into her eyes. She nodded and let out a sound of satisfaction.

"Yep. I knew it," she said, clapping her hands together.

Honor shook her head, words of denial dancing on her tongue. What was Hazel talking about? She was being absolutely ridiculous.

"Hazel!" she said in a sharp voice. "Just because it's your birthday doesn't mean you can just spout such nonsense."

Hazel looked at her knowingly. "You don't need to say another word. Some things are as plain as the nose on your face."

There was no point in arguing with Hazel. She always liked to get the last word on any given subject. And her middle name was *matchmaker*. According to Hazel, she had paired up more people in town than Operation Love.

"I'm going back to the party," Honor said. "You should, too. After all, it isn't every day you turn... thirty-five."

Hazel burst out laughing. "Bless you, Honor. A girl after my own heart. I'll catch up to you later on."

As soon as Honor walked back in the room, she spotted Joshua standing with Grace and Paige, who were each holding her nieces in their arms. It seemed as if they were introducing Violet to their girls. Even from this distance, Honor could see it was achingly sweet. She felt a little hitch in her heart. If her own child had lived, he or she might be standing alongside his or her cousins. Her chest tightened as she watched from a distance.

She stood there for a moment, unsure of whether to join the group or walk off to another area. Hazel's comments were still ringing in her ear. Paige saved her from having to make that decision for herself.

"Honor! Come see. Isn't this the cutest thing?" Paige called out, waving her over.

Honor walked over and watched as Emma and Violet gave each other kisses and tightly held hands. They had made fast friends. It was a bittersweet moment for Honor. Although it made her feel happy to see Violet making friends with Emma, thoughts of her own child raced through her head. She couldn't help but think of what might have been.

"They're adorable together," Honor said, her eyes straying toward Joshua. Standing so close to him was a bit of an assault on her senses. The spicy smell of his aftershave rose to her nostrils. He was looking at her with an intensity that made her want to look away from his gaze. The energy between them was palpable.

"I think it's time we changed some diapers," Grace said, tugging Paige by the arm and quickly leading her away. After Grace and Paige made a fast exit, she and Joshua were standing there together, just the two of them.

"This is some birthday party," Joshua said, letting out a low whistle.

Jasper had transformed the eatery into a replica of a tropical island. There were palm trees, flower necklaces, grass skirts, tiki torches and pineapple centerpieces. Honor really had the feeling she had been transported to another world.

"Jasper really outdid himself," Honor said. She was proud of her grandfather for stepping up to do something spectacular for Hazel. Ever since Honor could remember, Hazel had been there as a steady, guiding presence for the Prescott family. She deserved to be the center of attention tonight.

"It's more like a Fourth of July celebration. Someone said there are actually fireworks later on." Joshua's eyes went wide.

Honor giggled. "Hazel is the grand dame of Love.

Everything revolves around her," Honor said with a shake of her head. "She deserves it though. I've never met a more gentle, supportive person in my life."

"She's gone out of her way for Theo and me ever since we came back to town. I'm still in awe over the fact that she allowed us to host the reception here. I know she must have called in a lot of favors for that one."

"She always did favor you. It used to drive me crazy in Bible class. She let you get away with everything and anything!" Joshua had been a really cute little kid. He had managed to wrap Hazel completely around his finger.

Joshua threw back his head and laughed. "Spoken by the princess of Love. Everyone in this town always adored you. They all thought butter wouldn't melt in your mouth."

She scoffed at the notion. "There was always too much tomboy in me to be a princess."

"That's what made me fall in love with you," he said in a low voice. "You knew how to ride Lola bareback in the morning and go for a manicure in the afternoon."

Violet reached out and grabbed Honor's necklace. Joshua gently admonished Violet and extricated her chubby little fingers from the gold chain.

"Sorry about that," he apologized. "She loves shiny, sparkly things."

"Joshua. Can I hold her?" she asked, wanting desperately to hold the precious little bundle in her arms.

A huge grin broke out on his face. "Of course you can." He transferred Violet into Honor's arms. "You look like you know what you're doing, that's for sure."

"I have two nieces and a nephew, with another one

on the way. I've got skills," she said, gently swaying from side to side. Violet was studying Honor's face, her big blue eyes taking it all in. She raised her hands and place them on either side of Honor's face. She leaned in and placed a kiss on Honor's cheek.

Joshua chuckled. "She really likes you. She's fairly stingy with her kisses."

Honor thought her heart might crack into a million little pieces.

Violet was Joshua's child. In many ways, it was the closest thing to the child she had lost. A baby she had never been able to hold, or rock to sleep, or soothe at bedtime. Tears pricked her eyes. She blinked them away. It was embarrassing for Joshua to witness her being so emotional about his daughter.

"Are you all right?" Joshua asked. His voice sounded tender, which made her want to sob.

"I'm fine," she said, sniffing away tears. There was no way she could tell him the truth about their child. There was too much water under the bridge for her to resurrect it. "I just feel honored to be holding your daughter." Surprise flashed in Joshua's eyes.

All of a sudden a loud clinking noise rang out in the café. Jasper stood up on a bench and looked out over the crowd.

"Attention, everyone. Attention. I have a few words to say about the birthday girl." The guests gathered around Jasper. Hazel made her way through the crowd until she was standing near her husband.

"I want to wish my lovely wife, Hazel, a happy and blessed birthday. Before Hazel came into my life, I was getting by just fine. I was content. But then something wonderful happened. I looked at her one day and realized that she held my heart in the palm of her hand. I wanted to be her guy. Forever. And thankfully, she let me put a ring on her finger."

Everyone began to cheer loudly.

"Wishing you many more birthdays, Hazel," Jasper said, dipping his head down to place a kiss on his wife's lips.

As Hazel and Jasper kissed, the guests thunderously clapped. Honor wiped away a stray tear. This was what she wanted. Real, enduring love. Life wasn't an easy road to navigate. Her grandfather and Hazel were a testament to true, abiding love. They were far from perfect, but they were perfectly made for each other. Their love story was unique.

When Jasper came up for air, he shouted out, "Everyone head outside for the fireworks in celebration of my sweetheart's birthday."

"I love fireworks," Honor gushed.

"I'm not sure Violet will enjoy it," Joshua said. "She doesn't like loud noises. It might startle her."

Honor felt a stab of disappointment. It was nice to spend time with Joshua in a relaxed setting where they weren't fussing about injunctions and the sale of Bud's ranch. She'd forgotten how good it felt just to talk to him. For once her brothers weren't glaring at Joshua and creating an uncomfortable vibe. Something told her she had Paige and Grace to thank for reining her brothers in.

"That's a good point. I always forget how kids and dogs react to fireworks," Honor said, trying to hide her disappointment.

"Go ahead and join the festivities, Honor. Don't worry about us. We'll be fine staying behind," Joshua said.

Grace, who was standing beside them, turned in their direction.

"Joshua. Why don't you let Violet stay with me back here at the café? Eva is way too young for fireworks and I'm watching Emma as well so Paige and Cameron can enjoy the fireworks."

"Are you sure it wouldn't be too much for you?" Joshua asked. "Three little ones can be a handful."

"Of course I'm sure," Grace said with a dismissive wave of her hand. "I've got eyes in the back of my head."

"That's nice of you, Grace," Joshua said, grinning at her. "I'll take you up on the offer."

"Sure thing," Grace said, reaching out for Violet, who easily went into the crook of her arm. With a girl on each hip, Grace said, "Go on and enjoy the fireworks. I'll set the kids up in the back room. Cameron keeps a playpen and toys and blankets in there. It'll be a party for the baby and toddler set."

After grabbing their coats, Joshua and Honor walked outside to Jarvis Street and followed the other guests as they walked over to the town green. Honor and Joshua walked side by side down the street. A few of the towns-folk openly stared at them. Honor was past the point of caring. She wanted to be on civil terms with Joshua. It felt good to know that they'd managed to push past the drama and the conflict, if only for this moment in time.

The sound of fireworks exploding in the sky above them rent the air. Honor let out a gasp as a myriad of colors lit up the onyx sky. Greens and reds. Purples and whites. Threads of silver and gold. She gazed up at the sky, marveling at the fiery beauty of the explosion of colors.

"It's spectacular, isn't it?" Honor asked, turning toward Joshua. He wasn't looking up at the fireworks. He was staring at her, his eyes full of an intensity that made her shiver.

"I can't argue with you on that," he drawled. "You are spectacular, Honor Prescott. You always have been."

Honor let the compliment wash over her. It felt nice to hear it from Joshua's lips. Back in the day he had used his silver tongue to court her, and she'd quickly fallen for his smooth delivery and boyish charm. She felt butterflies tumbling around in her belly. She should be guarding her heart against the threat Joshua represented, but all she wanted to do in this moment was revel in his company and bask in his sweet compliment. No other man had the ability to make her feel the way Joshua did.

As fireworks continued to burst in the sky up above, they stood side by side with their arms touching, watching the brilliant pyrotechnic display. As it died down, folks began to meander away from the town green.

"Let's take the long way back," Joshua suggested. "It'll give me an opportunity to take a walk down memory lane and check out the new additions to this area. I really haven't had an opportunity to explore."

"Okay," Honor agreed, stuffing her mittened hands in her jacket pockets as they headed toward Jarvis Street. The temperature had dipped down, making it much colder than it had been this afternoon. "There are a few changes here in town you might not have seen yet."

"Looking forward to it," Joshua said. "Bud used to talk my ear off about Hazel's boot company and the cannery that never opened. He really loved this town."

"And we loved him back. I used to enjoy it when he would come sit with me for a cup of coffee at the Moose Café. He would just saunter over and sit with me at my table." She let out a ragged sigh. "I miss his sly sense of humor and his knock-knock jokes. They were terrible, but I pretended to love each and every one of them."

"That was awfully sweet of you. Theo and I used to tell him not to give up his day job because he was never going to make it as a comedian."

They both laughed as the memories of Bud Ransom washed over them like a cool spring rain.

"That was a pretty great speech Jasper made about Hazel. I have to admit, I didn't think he had it in him. He always struck me as the curmudgeon type."

Honor smirked. "Jasper is full of surprises. And marriage to Hazel has truly enriched his life. It's really been gratifying to watch their love story unfold."

"It reminds me of my grandparents. Bud lost a huge chunk of himself when my grandmother died. They were soul mates."

"Speaking of marriage, you never wanted to remarry and give Violet a mother?" she asked. She must be a glutton for punishment for even inquiring. It hurt to imagine Joshua with a wife and family.

"Not really. Of course I've thought about it, but I want something that's built to last," he answered with a shrug. "Lauren and I didn't make it very long. Our marriage was a train wreck. I would love for Violet to have a mother, but I certainly don't want a second marriage to fail."

"I'm sorry. It must have been painful to go through that," she said, her mind whirling with questions. Their marriage had been short-lived, yet they had clearly reunited years later and conceived Violet. Although she yearned to ask Joshua that very thing, Honor didn't feel she had the right to probe.

"You're probably wondering about Violet, huh?" he asked.

She let out a sigh of relief. "To be honest, I am. Bud said you got married not that long after you left Love. There are some gaps in the story I can't quite figure out. The timing doesn't add up."

"You're right. I met Lauren in Singapore about four months after I left town. She was over there with her parents who were missionaries. We got married after a whirlwind courtship, then set up house as soon as we landed stateside." He clenched his teeth. "It was foolish on both our parts. She was getting over someone who'd been killed in the army." He locked gazes with Honor. "And I was still very much in love with you."

Her stomach tensed. Joshua was basically telling her he had married his ex-wife on the rebound. It made her heart ache to hear it. At the very same time, Honor had been struggling to get over him and mourning the loss of their child.

Her throat felt dry. "Did you ever love her?"

He shook his head. "I cared about Lauren and I thought I was in love with her, but I don't think either of us truly loved each other. Not in the truest sense of the word. If we did, I think we would have fought harder to stay together. It didn't even come close to the way I felt about you."

Something flickered between them. An electric pulse hummed and crackled in the air. Honor could almost feel her heart swelling inside her chest.

Honor frowned. "But clearly you must have reunited with Lauren when Violet was conceived?"

"There's something I didn't tell you about Violet," Joshua said, a hint of strain in his voice. He hesitated for a moment. "It will probably answer all your questions. She's not my biological child."

Honor gasped. He could see the surprise on her lovely face. Her blue-gray eyes widened. Her lips parted. Joshua could see the questions emanating from her eyes.

"Lauren and I stayed in touch after the divorce. Every now and again she would drive from Tacoma to see me and we would go to church together or eat at a nice Italian restaurant. She even introduced me to her boyfriend once. I got the impression she was looking for my approval. I didn't hesitate to give it to her, Honor. He seemed like a good enough guy and I wanted her to be happy. She wanted the same for me.

"About a year ago, I got a call from her begging me to travel to Tacoma to see her. When I got there, I noticed two things. She was heavily pregnant and she looked really ill. She had dark shadows under her eyes and she was rail-thin despite her pregnancy. It was alarming."

Honor frowned. "What was wrong with her?"

"She had breast cancer. And she suspended all treatment while she was carrying Violet. More than anything in the world, she wanted a healthy baby. The cancer was very aggressive though. Lauren knew she wasn't going to make it. She was just holding on long enough to deliver her baby girl." He swallowed past the huge lump sitting in his throat. "It turns out her boyfriend dumped her and bailed when he found out she was sick. He refused to step up as a father, so I agreed to assume that role. It gave her the peace she needed before she passed. I've never regretted it for a single second."

She raised a hand to her throat. "Oh, Joshua," Honor said, wiping away stray tears. Sniffling noises emanated from her. "Of course you don't regret it. How could you ever?"

"Honor, she's mine in every way that matters. It's thicker than blood. I chose to be her father. I've been on my own with Violet since she was a few weeks old. I had no clue how to care for a baby or even change a diaper. But I knew I was her father. I loved her from the day she came into this world."

Watching Honor's emotional reaction caused a fierce response inside him. It felt as if his heart was being squeezed inside his chest. He hated to see her cry. He reached out and wiped away a tear as it slid past her lower lid.

Her lips trembled. "Joshua. What an unselfish act! You didn't have any legal ties to Lauren, but you stepped in to raise her child. If you hadn't done so, she might have ended up in foster care. She's one fortunate little girl."

"To be honest, I think I'm the blessed one. Being Violet's father is the most important role I've ever played. It gave me a shot at redemption for all the rotten things I did here in town. It made me a grown-up."

"I get it. God was watching out for Violet. And you as well. He put the two of you together and now you're a family."

Joshua grinned. "Yes, indeed. Now we're a family. She's my entire world."

"I appreciate you sharing all of it with me. I know it's quite personal."

"So, now that I've told you my story, I have a question for you. Why are you still single?"

Honor bit her lip. "Hmm. That's rather tricky to explain. After I refused to be a part of the Operation Love program, I think the local men gave up on me." She twisted her mouth. "A lot of them are afraid of my brothers. Some folks think they're intimidating." She arched an eyebrow in his direction.

"Hey! I wasn't afraid of them!" Joshua protested, holding up his hands.

Honor giggled and shook her head. "Whatever you say."

"Well, maybe I was a little bit afraid of Boone," he conceded. "He was mean. And he walked around with that gold sheriff's badge on his jacket pocket. From the first time he saw me, your brother didn't like me."

"I don't think that's true, Joshua. To be fair, he only started to dislike you when we began dating."

The Prescott brothers had always been protective of their little sister. She had been the jewel in their crown. As the oldest, Boone had taken it upon himself to act as Honor's guardian. It had driven her crazy to be treated like a child, which had led to many fights between Honor and Boone.

Being a father provided Joshua with insight. He knew without a shadow of a doubt he would protect Violet's heart the same way Boone had tried to safeguard Honor. And Lord help the young man if he acted as wild and foolish as he once had.

"I sure gave him plenty of reasons to dislike me," Joshua said, reflecting on his teenage antics. "It must have been hard to see your boyfriend go head-to-head with your brother so often. Sadly, I never really stopped to consider how my actions affected other people. I wonder sometimes how things might have been different if I had acted accordingly."

"It's impossible to go back and change the past." There was tension laced in Honor's voice. He wondered if she was thinking about what might have been if the circumstances had been different.

He reached for her chin and lifted it up so their gazes locked.

"I'm sorry for every ounce of pain I inflicted on you," he said in a tender voice. "And I hate that we're on opposite sides regarding Bud's estate."

Honor shrugged. "It can't be helped, can it? It's just the way it is."

"I suppose not," he said, gently stroking the line of her jaw with his finger. "Honor Prescott, you're still the most beautiful woman I've ever seen. For the record, any man would be fortunate to have you." His own words served as a reminder of how blessed he'd once felt to have been loved by Honor. "And I know it's been a long time since we've done this, but I'd like to kiss you."

Chapter Eleven

I'd like to kiss you.

It had been a long time since Honor had kissed a man. The last time she had kissed Joshua he'd been more boy than man. If she was being honest with herself, this kiss had been in the back of her mind since she'd first seen him at the ranch a few weeks ago. But with so much standing between them, a kiss had seemed impossible.

Her mouth felt dry. All she could do was nod. He dipped his head down and placed his mouth over hers in a tender, romantic meeting of their lips. He tasted sweet like cinnamon. As his lips moved over hers, Honor wished it could go on forever and ever.

Kissing Joshua felt like coming home. It was familiar and achingly gentle. It took her back to a more innocent time when she had believed in fairy-tale endings and enduring love. Her nostrils were filled with the rich, woodsy scent of him. She raised her hands up and trailed her fingers along the nape of his neck. Her fingers brushed against his hair.

When the kiss ended, Joshua swept his lips against

her temple. His touch was feather light. He threaded his hands through her hair and pulled her back toward him for another kiss. When they finally broke apart, Honor felt breathless.

This is what had been missing from her life for all this time. Sparks. Not a single man had ever made her feel the way Joshua did. This feeling of being one with another person. A connection that withstood separation and pain and disappointment.

Joshua ran his palm against the side of her face. "Honor. You're making me feel like I'm sixteen all over again."

She looked up into his eyes. "I haven't felt like this in a long time. Not since we were together," she whispered.

"I feel the same way," he said, letting out a deep breath.

Fear rose up inside her. Joshua felt something, too. It made it all the more real and frightening. She had been down this road before and gotten terribly hurt in the process. It was like playing with fire. This pull she felt toward Joshua could cause her heartbreak down the road. Sharing a kiss didn't change a thing. There were still huge chasms between them.

For so long Honor had stuffed her emotions down, fearful of cracking into little pieces. She had mourned the loss of Joshua so fiercely that her heart hadn't been able to open itself up to anyone else ever since.

Was she just getting carried away by the moment? She was a very sentimental person. Perhaps that's all this was. Nostalgia over the past and her first love. An inability to close the door on something that had ended a long time ago.

"I can tell your brain is racing with a hundred different thoughts." He reached out and smoothed a spot on her forehead with his fingers. "And this little frown needs to go away. Stop worrying so much."

Honor couldn't think of a single thing to say. She had been worried ever since Joshua stepped foot back in town. It always felt as if raging rivers stood between them. On some level they both knew that this brief interlude would quickly fade away in the harsh light of day. When they each woke up tomorrow morning, nothing will have changed. If the injunction held out, there would be resentment simmering between them. And if the sale of the ranch was approved, Joshua would be leaving Love and returning to the life he'd built in Seattle.

It was best to focus on lighter things. If only for tonight. When Joshua had told her about embracing Violet as his own despite the fact that she wasn't his biological child, Honor had felt a strong urge to tell him about the child they'd lost. But what good would it have done? Much like the rest of their relationship, it was water under the bridge.

"You said that you wanted to see any new additions to town. I have something to show you," Honor said, tugging Joshua by the arm and leading him a few feet down the street.

She stopped in her tracks and pointed at the building. "Look! It's the Free Library of Love. Isn't it magnificent?"

"Wow. It's fantastic," Joshua said as he admired the building. "Love is patient. Love is kind. *Corinthians*." He read the words imprinted on the front of the library.

"Love never fails," Honor said, wishing in her heart it was true. Love had failed both of them in the past.

And here she stood with Joshua in the moonlight having just shared a fantastic embrace with him. She must be all kinds of crazy to have ventured down that road with him again.

"A brand-new library is a great addition to Love," Joshua said, admiring the structure. "I'm not sure if I would have spent a lot of time here as a teenager," he said with a chuckle, "but it's great for the town."

"A lot has changed in six years," she noted. The town of Love had gone through a recession, lost beloved members of their town, created a lucrative company, Lovely Boots, and created the innovative program, Operation Love. They had gone through some difficult times, but the town was still standing. The town of Love had endured. Yet, Joshua had missed all of it. The tragedies and the triumphs. The townsfolk coming together to rebound from financial ruin. And he hadn't been aware of Bud's determination to bequeath the Diamond R to his beloved hometown.

Both she and Joshua had changed. They were no longer the high school sweethearts who had been head over heels in love with one another. They were two strong-willed people who might be headed for a legal showdown in court over Bud's property. They didn't believe in the same things. She sighed. No matter how fantastic their kiss had been, it couldn't alter reality.

"It really has," he agreed with a nod. He locked gazes with her, his eyes filled with intensity.

Honor bowed her head. She was beginning to think kissing Joshua hadn't been such a good idea. Looking into Joshua's eyes complicated matters. They were pulling her in. "We should be getting back. Violet will be looking for you," she said in a brisk tone.

He nodded his agreement. They began to walk down Jarvis Street toward the Moose Café. Joshua's mood seemed contemplative. Perhaps he, too, was coming to the realization that the kiss between them had only served to complicate an already messy situation.

Silence reigned as they walked back toward the café. From this point forward, Honor was determined to avoid being alone with Joshua. She didn't need any more trips down memory lane with him or tender kisses in the moonlight. Joshua had the ability to make her forget all of the reasons why they shouldn't be kissing in the first place.

Honor needed to focus instead of getting distracted by Joshua. She wasn't going to allow a tender kiss to deter her from the main objective—preventing the Ransom brothers from selling the Diamond R to the Alloy Corporation. If Joshua Ransom thought he had softened her up tonight with his boyish charms, he had another think coming.

On the ride home to the ranch after Hazel's party, Joshua had plenty of time to reflect on his impulsive decision to kiss Honor. Kissing her had been an act of sheer nerve on his part. And, although it had felt good in the moment, he was having deep regrets. Honor wasn't the type of woman a man should casually kiss. Everything about her screamed home, hearth and forever. But he couldn't give her any of those things. Their one shot at a happy ending had fallen apart six years ago. He clenched his jaw and let out a ragged sigh. It had been foolish to give in to nostalgia. There wasn't a single thing tying them together in the present.

Theo kept giving him curious sideways glances. He

knew his brother wanted to ask him about his mood, but so far Theo hadn't peppered him with any questions.

He began tapping his fingers on the steering wheel. Suddenly, he was a bundle of nervous energy. Irritation bubbled up inside him. If he had been alone in the truck, Joshua knew he might roar with frustration. Life wasn't fair.

Theo grumbled. "All right, already. What's up with you tonight?"

Joshua feigned ignorance. He didn't need Theo coming down on him about the foolishness of kissing Honor. His brother had made it clear years ago he didn't care for her. Theo had always believed Honor hadn't loved him as much as he'd loved her. And he had been of the belief that they had been way too young to commit to a future together.

"I'm just tired. It's been a long day."

Theo scoffed. "Gimme a break, Joshua. I've known you all your life. It's not simply fatigue. Fess up."

Joshua sighed. "Honor and I shared a special moment." He was trying to be discreet, while at the same time letting his brother know they'd connected in a meaningful way. Joshua needed someone he could trust to confide in.

"A special moment?" Theo asked. "What does that mean?"

"I kissed her," he blurted out. "And she kissed me back."

Theo began to mutter in an angry tone. "What in the world did you do that for? Are you a glutton for punishment or what?"

"Whoa! Take it easy. Haven't you ever acted on impulse?"

Theo shook his head and muttered angrily. "Why are you doing this to yourself? She demolished your heart six years ago. What do you think is going to happen this time around? Roses and moonlight?"

Joshua looked away from the road for a quick moment, shooting Theo a deadly glare. "I made a mistake by kissing her. I'm already kicking myself for doing it. If you can't say anything supportive, don't say a word. Okay?"

Silence stretched out between them. The radio was the only sound in the car. Violet was peacefully sleeping in the back seat.

"I'm sorry, Joshua. You know how I am. I shoot from the hip. I'm sorry if it sounded harsh." He quirked his mouth. "I'm only watching out for your best interests. I'm worried about you. And you know I always have your back."

Joshua knew how difficult it was for his brother to apologize. It always had been, ever since they were kids. "It's all right. I know you're trying to protect me, but I've got this under control."

"Do you?" Theo pressed. "Because it seems to me that despite all reason, Honor still has a hold on you. It makes no sense to me! Her main goal is to prevent us from selling the ranch. What happens if the injunction holds and we can't sell the Diamond R?"

Joshua swallowed past the huge lump sitting in his throat. "We'd have to accept it. I would try to see the bigger picture and find meaning in the judge's decision."

"How do you think this town will react if we get the green light to move forward with the sale of the ranch? It won't be pretty."

He felt his jaw tighten. Why was his brother so intent

on hammering his point home? It wasn't as if Joshua was dreaming of a happily-ever-after with Honor. Their opposing views on the future of Bud's property represented the huge chasm between them. And he wasn't putting down roots here in Love, no matter what the judge decided.

"They'll rebound from it," he said, answering Theo's question. "This is a town with a lot of faith and fortitude. Love has endured much worse than this. I'm guessing it might not be an ideal outcome, but everyone would learn to live with it, including Honor."

The thought of it caused a tightening sensation to spread across his chest. Honor's face flashed before his eyes and he pushed the thought of her away. He didn't want to think about her being hurt or disappointed. Joshua needed to focus on his own wants and Violet's needs.

"Honestly, we probably won't even have to deal with the fallout. We're not sticking around Love any longer than necessary," Theo said. "If I were you, I would avoid any more tender moments with Honor. It only serves to muddy the waters."

"You're right," he said with a nod. "Things don't need to get any more complicated than they already are."

Try as he might, Joshua couldn't completely snuff out the memory of the kiss he'd shared with Honor. It was probably the last one he would ever share with his ex-fiancée. Soon enough he and Violet would be back in Seattle, settled into their normal routine. Honor would be nothing more than a bittersweet memory from his past.

As they approached the gates to the Diamond R

Ranch, Joshua cast his gaze across the property. Illuminated by the moonlight, it was the most stunning vista he had ever laid his eyes upon. It would always be near and dear to his heart. The memories would have to be enough to sustain him.

Joshua had come back to Love, Alaska, for the sole purpose of tying up his grandfather's estate. Honor Prescott wasn't part of his future. He needed to work harder to put her firmly in the past.

After the guests from Hazel's party dispersed from the Moose Café, Honor stuck around to help with the cleanup. Her staying to pick up the mess allowed Hazel and Jasper to head home without having to worry about the nitty-gritty details. Boone decided to send Grace home with baby Eva so he could stay and help Honor tidy up the place. The Moose Café would be open for breakfast first thing tomorrow morning and they wanted to make sure everything was in pristine condition.

After forty-five minutes or so, they were done. Boone grabbed two sodas from the fridge and sank down onto a seat at one of the tables.

He patted the chair beside him. "Come sit with me. I need to talk to you."

A feeling of panic immediately seized her by the throat. Having a talk with her older brother rarely boded well. More times than not, Boone subjected her to a lecture of epic proportions. She wasn't in the mood tonight.

Boone began to chuckle. "You look like a deer caught in the headlights. I want to talk, not torture you. Have a little faith, sis."

Honor moved toward the table hesitantly. Boone

stood up and pulled a chair out for her. She sat down and folded her hands in front of her on the table.

"You look like a little kid sitting like that."

She squirmed in her seat. "I feel like one. I have an idea what this is about."

Boone arched an eyebrow. He sat back in his chair, arms folded across his chest. "Really?"

"It's about Joshua. Am I right?"

"Yes. You are." He stroked his jaw. "There are a few things I'd like to say about you and Joshua."

She slammed her hands down on the table. "Boone, there really isn't anything between Joshua and me other than an uneasy truce. So you can save your speech. I really don't want to hear a lecture from you about how unsuitable we are for each other and how rotten Joshua is. I know you think he's a terrible, irresponsible person. You thought our engagement was the worst thing possible. And I know you must think I'm the biggest fool in the world for ever falling for him all those years ago."

Boone's jaw dropped. "Is that really how I sound?"

"Honestly, yes," Honor admitted in a soft voice.

He reached out and took her hands in his. "I'm so sorry, Honor. It seems I've overplayed my position as eldest brother of the Prescott clan. I only ever wanted to protect my baby sister. I never for a single second ever wanted to clip your wings or make you feel less than for your choices.

"When I met Gracie we were opposites in many ways. Despite everything we fell for each other. Things fell apart when I found out she was lying to me and this town. In the end, I realized that Gracie made a mistake. I forgave her." Boone looked down for a moment. His expression was full of emotion. "We've had it a bit rough, haven't we? Two parents who bailed on us. We've all had to raise each other and rely on ourselves, haven't we?"

The look of pain on her brother's face was enough to bring her to her knees. Boone was a tough guy, one who had never shown a whole lot of emotion, especially about their upbringing. "We did," she said through a haze of tears. "We got through it though. Prescotts are made of strong stuff." She wiped tears away with the back of her hand.

"Here's the thing. Loving Gracie taught me something important. You can't help who you fall in love with. You just can't. When you and Joshua fell in love as teenagers, all I could see was the negative. I was so scared for my little sister I never stopped to appreciate your love story. And when the church burned down, it gave me a legitimate reason to hate him."

Honor's eyes widened. "That's all in the past, Boone."

Boone sighed. "Not really. It's crept into the present. I don't like harboring negative feelings toward people. As a man of faith, it's been a failing of mine. So I decided that I can't do that anymore. I can't hate Joshua for a mistake he made when he was barely of age. I don't want to carry that burden around anymore. It's too heavy."

"Oh, Boone. That's wonderful. Forgiveness is such a powerful gift. Not only for Joshua, but for yourself as well." She reached out and squeezed his hand.

"I was watching you tonight with Joshua while the fireworks were going off. It made me wonder if you still had feelings for him."

Honor bowed her head. "I'll always have the memories of what we shared, but that's all in the past. As it stands now, we're on opposite sides of this issue regarding the Diamond R. Joshua can't wait to head back to Seattle and put this town in his rearview mirror. There's no way things could ever work out between us. Even if the injunction holds, it's still a messy situation."

"I just wanted to let you know that I'll support you, no matter what. I didn't have your back six years ago, and I know it caused you a lot of pain."

"That means a lot to me," she said, fighting back tears.

"Now, if he decides not to sell the ranch to the Alloy Corporation, that might change things between you. Am I right?"

Honor frowned. "I don't think he will, Boone. He's made no secret of his plans."

"I'm really sorry to hear that. It would be a blessing if he changed his mind," Boone said. "For all our sakes."

She jutted her chin up. "It would be wonderful, but I learned a long time ago not to hope for the impossible." She felt exhaustion sweep through her. The entire situation was taking a heavy toll on her.

"Oh, Honor," Boone said in a voice clogged with emotion. "I'm so sorry."

Something about Boone's tone caused her to crack wide open. Honor got up from her seat and threw herself against Boone's chest. She began to cry—tears of frustration and loss. She had no idea what might happen to the Diamond R, but Honor knew that she and Joshua were hopelessly at odds over it. Filing the injunction had been a long shot, and even though no decision had yet been made, she could almost sense that it wouldn't hold up.

Joshua and Theo would sell Bud's beloved ranch to developers. The Diamond R would cease to exist as they had always known it. And Joshua and Violet would head back to their lives in Seattle. The very thought of it made her heart ache way more than she wanted to acknowledge.

Chapter Twelve

Joshua gazed out the window of Bud's study. The ranch was blanketed in white, with a recent snowfall leaving the ground packed with snow. Everything was white, for as far as the eye could see. A few of the ranch hands were leading horses into the paddock. Maybe he would bring Violet outside later on to play in the snow. He was in an antsy mood. Last night he had tossed and turned for hours, torn apart by the moral dilemma over the Diamond R. Selling the ranch and returning to Seattle was the only thing that made sense. But every time he thought about going through with the sale he felt sick to his stomach.

Theo walked into the study, his face lit up with a huge grin. "I just got the call. The judge has lifted the injunction," he announced in a voice full of triumph. He raised his fist in the air and shook it.

Joshua knew he should be feeling on top of the world at the moment. Hadn't this been what he'd been waiting to hear? Why wasn't he rejoicing? All he felt was emptiness.

"Did you hear me? It's over. We can sell Bud's property to whomever we choose." Theo was practically jumping up and down with joy at the news.

"I heard you," he said. "It's a lot to take in."

Theo narrowed his gaze as he looked at him. "It's a victory, Joshua. We're one step closer to leaving this town behind us." Theo shook his head at Joshua. "I'm beginning to think you were hoping we would lose." Theo glared at him, then stormed out of the room.

Joshua sighed raggedly. The legal victory had hit him like a ton of bricks. He hadn't been expecting to hear anything definitive today. Instead of rejoicing, his head was filled with Honor. He had no idea whether or not she'd received word about the injunction. The news couldn't have come at a worse time. She was scheduled to come to the ranch this morning to check up on the calves, as well as some other livestock. One of the calves seemed to have taken a turn for the worse. Joshua had called Honor to let her know about the situation.

He had no intention of telling her about the injunction being lifted. It would only cause more strain between them.

While Winnie tended to Violet, Joshua found himself listening for any signs of Honor's arrival at the ranch. He was pacing back and forth in the den when he heard the crunch of tires from outside. One glance out of the window confirmed Honor's arrival. He quickly put on his parka and headed outside to greet her.

She was just getting out of her car when he reached her side. Dressed in a pair of nice-fitting jeans and a snug winter parka, Honor looked casual yet lovely. The gray knit hat perched on her head gave her a wholesome look. Joshua stuffed down a wild impulse to kiss her. But he knew it wasn't his place to do so. It would only serve to make things messier than they already were, he reckoned.

"Honor. Thanks for coming over."

"Of course. I came as soon as I could. What's going on with the calf?"

"It hasn't been eating or moving all that much. It doesn't seem to be thriving."

Honor nodded. There were crease lines around her mouth and eyes. He knew she took her job seriously. The welfare of animals was of the utmost importance to her. Part of her profession involved wildlife rehabilitation.

They took off toward the barn with Honor leading the way. She made a quick beeline to the area where the calves were situated. He didn't need to tell Honor which calf was doing poorly. It was evident by the way she sat off to the side, not interacting with the other calves.

Joshua stood and watched as Honor gently examined the calf. After a few minutes, her shoulders slumped. She turned toward him. "You were right. She's not doing well. It could be dehydration or a virus, although I would think if it was viral the others would be doing poorly as well. I'm not a vet, so you might want another opinion, but it's not looking good." She shrugged. "She needs special care. There's not a whole lot we can do if she continues to struggle." She bowed her head.

"Honor. Don't feel bad. Sometimes it's just nature's way. You've been incredible. You've got such a nurturing instinct with animals and with people. You'll make a great mother one day."

Honor looked up at him with tears swimming in her eyes. She held up her hand. "Please don't say that," she said, her voice quivering.

Goose bumps raised up on the back of his neck. There was something going on with Honor that surpassed her worry about the calf. Clearly, his comment about motherhood had struck a nerve. He needed to know what was going on with her. Had he done something?

"What is it?" he asked. "What did I say to upset you like this?" A sudden tension hummed and pulsed in the air between them.

"I was a mother, Joshua," she said, swiping away tears with her fingers. "For a brief moment in time I was pregnant with a child. Our child!"

"I suffered a miscarriage." Finally, after all these years it felt good to say the words out loud. She had been carrying this secret for such a long time.

Joshua's jaw went slack. He let out an agonized sound. "Honor. When did it happen? You never said a word."

"It was shortly after I arrived at college. I was under a lot of stress and I hadn't told anyone about the pregnancy. By that time, I had no idea where you were or what you were doing. When I lost the baby, I figured it no longer mattered."

Tears pooled in his eyes. "I'm so sorry. I wish I'd known. I'm so sorry you had to go through that type of pain. It guts me to know you had to go through all of it alone."

She winced as painful memories swept over her. Honor hadn't told a single person about the pregnancy or subsequent miscarriage. "And I was all alone to deal with it. I didn't have a single person to confide in or to cry on their shoulder."

"I wish I could've helped you through it," Joshua said. She could hear the agony laced in his voice. "We could have mourned the loss together."

Why hadn't she confided in Paige or Ruby or Hazel about her pregnancy? She had felt such shame. As an unmarried woman, Honor had felt ashamed about conceiving a child. She and Joshua had both been struggling a bit with their faith at the time of conception. Neither had lived up to the values of their faith by having sex without the benefit of marriage. Although it had been a mistake to do so, Honor had dearly loved her baby. She had been committed to raising the child with love and faith. It had all been ripped away from her in the most devastating way.

"Honor, please. Let me hold you," Joshua begged. "I don't want you to carry the weight of this on your shoulders. I can carry the burden from now on." Tears were streaming down his face. She could see how much pain he was in. It mirrored her own emotions.

Joshua reached for her and pulled her into his arms. She felt almost weightless. For so long she had been holding this secret close to the vest. Finally, she was able to share it with the person who should have known from the beginning. Her baby's father. Joshua's strong arms held her tightly. She relaxed against him, giving in to the need to be comforted.

All of a sudden, Theo was standing at the stall entrance, his expression somber as he looked back and forth between them. She pulled away from Joshua.

"Oh, I'm sorry. I didn't know you were here, Honor," Theo said, his eyes widening as he looked back and forth between them. With her tearstained face, Honor knew she must look like a mess.

She ducked her head down, feeling embarrassed that Theo had seen her in such an emotional state.

"I'm sorry you're upset, Honor. I guess you heard the news?" Theo asked, looking at Honor with sympathy radiating from his eyes.

"Theo!" Joshua said in a sharp voice. "It's really not a good time."

"What news?" Honor swung her gaze back and forth between the brothers.

Theo's eyes widened. "She doesn't know?"

"I'll tell her in my own time!" Joshua said, furious that Theo had barged in and practically blurted out the information about the injunction.

"I'm sorry. I never meant to butt in," Theo said, quickly retreating and leaving the room.

As soon as he left the room, Honor took a step away from Joshua. She looked at him with suspicion radiating from the depths of her eyes. "What's going on? Theo isn't very subtle. What was he getting at?"

There was no point in hiding it any longer. Honor would find out before the day was done. "The judge rescinded the injunction. As of this afternoon, we're free to sell the Diamond R to whomever we choose."

A shell-shocked expression crept over her face. "I—I can't believe it," she said, stammering. "I was so sure we were on the right side of things."

"I'm sorry," Joshua said. "I know how disappointed you must be."

Her expression was one of utter disbelief. Joshua felt a pang in his heart. She was clearly crushed. It killed him to see her like this. This felt like anything but a victory.

Dear Lord. Please help me find the right words to buoy her spirits. I never wanted her to feel deflated or to feel defeated. It hurts to see her so incredibly wounded. Honor is tough, but at this moment she looks as if she's ready to shatter. Please let me be the one to help her pick up the pieces.

She bowed her head and didn't meet his gaze. Honor raised her hand to her temple. "I really need to go home. I'll write up some instructions for the calf and send them over. I'm not feeling so great." She turned away from him and reached for her bag.

"Honor, please don't leave. Let's talk this out."

Honor turned and faced him. Her cheeks were red and her eyes were rimmed with moisture. She looked away from him.

"Let's face it. There's nothing really to discuss. You won. You can now sell Bud's ranch and head back to Seattle with the proceeds. You should be rejoicing. Isn't this what you wanted?"

His mouth felt dry. The truth was he had wanted the injunction to be lifted, but not at the expense of Honor. Not if it meant he would be moving back to Seattle, never to lay eyes on Honor again. Not if it signified the end of them. At the moment, he wasn't certain what he wanted.

"I never wanted us to be at odds with each other. Surely you know that."

She shook her head. "I don't know anything anymore. Everything has turned upside down. I really don't believe this is what your grandfather wanted. And that breaks my heart."

"This is a terrible situation. It doesn't feel right to be on opposing sides."

She frowned. "What does it matter? You're going to leave, aren't you? Please don't think I'm foolish enough to think you're going to stick around Love, especially since you have a buyer lined up to purchase the property." Her voice had now gone up a few pitches. She clenched her jaw. Storm clouds were brewing in her eyes.

"Honor, my life is in Seattle. It's the only home Violet has ever known. I don't have much of a choice."

She bit her lip. "I understand. But, considering everything, I think it's best you find someone else to check up on the animals from now on. I can't bear to come back here knowing what's going to happen to the Diamond R."

"Please don't say that." It felt like Honor was slipping out his life yet again. He couldn't explain why, but it left him feeling completely bereft.

"Why not? It's the truth!" she snapped.

She zipped up her coat, then jammed her hat back on her head.

Joshua reached out and gently grasped her by the arm. She shook him off and backed away from him.

Her mouth was a hard, thin line. "I'm sorry, Joshua. There's really nothing left to be said."

Joshua felt numb as he watched Honor run toward her car as if her feet were on fire. She couldn't get away from him fast enough. And given what she had just found out about the injunction being lifted, he couldn't say he blamed her.

He was still reeling about Honor's miscarriage. She had been forced to deal with the pregnancy and the monumental loss of their child all by herself. So many things were weighing heavily on him at the moment. Anger and frustration rose up inside him.

He stormed into the house, eager to confront his brother. Theo had somehow managed to make a bad situation worse. And he couldn't help but wonder if his brother had done it on purpose to put an even deeper wedge between him and Honor. Theo was sitting in the study at Bud's desk, riffling through a stack of papers.

"Thanks for making a mess of things," Joshua said in a raised voice.

Theo twisted his mouth. "It wasn't on purpose, Joshua. Take it easy. She was going to find out sooner or later."

"Why did you come barging in like that?" Joshua asked. "Did you honestly not know she was here? Her car was parked right outside the house. Surely you saw it."

"I can't believe you're angry at me. We should be celebrating our legal victory and all you can think of is the precious Prescott princess."

Joshua stepped toward his brother. They were standing eye to eye. He was bristling with rage. "Watch yourself, Theo. Don't say a word against Honor. She's innocent in all of this."

Theo sneered. "Are you kidding me? Honor set this whole thing in motion by filing that injunction." He let out a harsh sounding laugh. "What makes you think she's the victim?"

"She didn't do it to be malicious. Honor has principles she lives by, Theo. Her whole professional life revolves around wildlife and land preservation. It actually tears her apart to think about the desecration of Bud's property. Is that something you've even thought about once?"

Theo wrinkled his nose. "What's wrong with you? Are you changing your mind about selling the ranch?" he asked.

Joshua knit his brows together. "No. Yes. I don't know," he moaned. "Ever since we came back here, my head has been spinning. Half the time I don't know if I'm coming or going."

Theo's expression softened. "Is this about Honor? Why is it that all roads lead back to her? You were kids when you got engaged. It was a lifetime ago. You need to let go of it already. Put it in your rearview mirror."

"Don't you think I've tried? I've spent six years trying to move past all the painful things that happened in this town. It wasn't easy rebuilding my life, but I did it. For some reason, I still can't move past Honor. And I know it's crazy and pointless, because she can't deal with the fact that we're selling the ranch. She'll hate me for it." He bowed his head down. "I wish I'd come clean with her all those years ago about the fire. Things might be very different today if I had."

Theo gazed at him with sad eyes. "I'm so sorry you're in pain, Joshua. You deserve happiness more than anyone I've ever known."

Joshua shrugged. Hadn't he been a happy man before his return to Love? Maybe he should have just stayed put in Seattle and skipped all of the drama.

All of a sudden he felt defeated. Crushed. His conscience was eating at him. Honor's words kept replaying in his mind, over and over again. They nagged at him relentlessly.

For what shall it profit a man if he shall gain the whole world and lose his own soul? If he moved forward and sold the Diamond R Ranch, Joshua feared he would regret it for the rest of his life.

Chapter Thirteen

Honor wasn't sure how she made it back to the wild-life center in one piece. She had sobbed the entire drive from the Diamond R Ranch. It broke her heart to know that the Diamond R was going to be desecrated. The more she cried, the more she realized that she wasn't simply upset over the injunction being lifted. Joshua was leaving Love. In all likelihood, she would never see him again. The sale of the Diamond R would permanently sever all of his ties to Love. And, by extension, to her.

It was now hitting her all at once. She hadn't just been fighting the sale of the Diamond R. Honor had been unwilling to let go of Joshua. She had been fighting it tooth and nail.

What a fool she'd been to actually believe he might change his mind about the Diamond R. Her feelings for him had made an idiot of her once again. Joshua was going to sell the ranch for a large sum, then leave town so he could continue his life in Seattle. Just like the last time, Honor would be left behind to lick her wounds.

She shook her head, trying to make sense of the

events of the past few weeks. Her prayers regarding the Diamond R Ranch had been all for naught. Everything was slipping through her fingers. She had failed Bud. Joshua would be leaving town again. And it hurt even more than the first time.

Lord, please help me. Give me the strength to deal with the pain of losing Joshua all over again. Grant me the grace to let go of him, once and for all.

The sound of someone knocking heavily on her door brought her out of her thoughts. She hoped Joshua hadn't followed her back to the wildlife center. There really wasn't anything else left to say. Everything was pretty cut-and-dried. As a result, she felt incredibly empty.

Honor moved toward her front door and wrenched it open. For a moment she thought it was Joshua standing at her doorstep. She quickly realized it was Theo. Although the resemblance between the brothers was startling, Honor had always seen a lot more kindness on Joshua's face.

Seeing Theo standing on her doorstep was surprising. He had never been a member of the Honor Prescott fan club. Most of the time he'd looked straight through her like glass.

"I just need a few minutes if you can spare it," Theo said, his expression intense.

"This isn't a good time," she told him.

What could Theo possibly have to say to her? Hadn't he already crowed about the injunction being lifted? Had he come over to rub her nose in it?

"I really need to speak to you, Honor. This is very important."

Honor sighed, exasperated. "All right, Theo, but

please make it quick." She ushered him inside toward the living room.

"Take a seat," she said, waving him toward the sofa.

"I'd rather stand if it's all right with you. I won't be staying long," Theo said. He took a deep breath. "My brother is a good man. One of his best qualities is his loyalty. If he makes a vow to do something he'll uphold it, even when doing so causes him to lose everything."

She shrugged. "Why are you telling me this?"

He clenched his jaw. "It was all my fault."

Honor frowned. "What are you talking about?"

"The church fire. I started it by playing around with a lighter and a hymnal. I was young and selfish. I was heading back to the army and I knew my service would be negatively impacted if word got out that I started a fire that demolished a church."

She let out a strangled sound. "So Joshua was innocent?"

Theo nodded. His expression was somber. "Joshua was with me, but he had nothing to do with the blaze that burned out of control. It all happened so quickly I was powerless to stop it. I was immature and reckless. Joshua stepped up and volunteered to take the blame once he was identified as the culprit. He could have pointed the finger at me, but he claimed responsibility for the fire. I know it sounds crazy, but he came up with the idea on his own." Theo ran a hand over his face. "As the older brother I should have protected him by telling him it was out of the question. It was my job to watch out for him. But I felt desperate."

"So you let him take the blame?" Honor asked. Although she still felt a little bit dazed by the news, it was slowly starting to sink in. Joshua had been innocent of the charges! And Theo had benefited immensely from Joshua's sacrifice.

Theo bowed his head. "I did. Because of the close resemblance between us, Zachariah Cummings mistook me for Joshua. It wasn't unusual for people to get us confused. So when Zachariah initially reported it to law enforcement, it was Joshua's name he put out there. Everything just spiraled out of control after that. Even though I wanted to take responsibility… I didn't. I left town to return to the army." Theo winced. "Joshua was left holding the bag."

She felt an all-encompassing rage take hold of her. "How could you? You were the older brother. You should have protected him."

"I know, Honor. And even though it's six years too late, that's why I'm here. It's what I'm trying to do now. I reckon your future with Joshua was a casualty of that lie. Joshua would never rat me out by telling you what really happened, but I needed to right that wrong."

"I respect your telling me the truth, but the past is behind us. I'm through with allowing it to have such a strong hold over me. What we had was a youthful romance."

"Are you saying you don't have any feelings for Joshua?" Theo pressed.

Honor raised a hand to massage her forehead. She had a raging headache. Everything was weighing heavily on her. "Does it matter? Too many things are standing between us. Not just the past, but the present as well."

Theo rocked back on his booted feet. "But don't you see, Honor? If he hadn't taken the blame for my actions, the two of you might still be together."

Honor could hear the agony in Theo's voice. He must have been carrying this guilt around with him for years. Although she and Theo had never been on the same page about anything, Honor's heart went out to him. It was impossible for Theo to go back in time and change the decisions he'd made in the past. Now he just had to find a way to live with it.

"I appreciate your coming here, Theo, but it doesn't change anything. You're still selling the ranch. Joshua still plans to head back to Seattle with Violet. There's nothing I can do to change those things." She wouldn't even know how to go about doing so.

Theo threw his hands up in the air. "Joshua is a great man and an even better brother. He stepped up and claimed Violet as his daughter even though they don't share a single strand of DNA. He's grown into the type of man people look up to and admire. You fought us over the future of the Diamond R. Why are you so willing to roll over and play dead when it comes to fighting for my brother?"

Honor's jaw dropped. Theo was being mighty presumptuous to assume she held romantic feelings for Joshua. Her heart was beating fast. Her palms were sweaty.

She yearned to give him a piece of her mind, but she was done fighting. Honor was all worn-out. At this point in her life she wanted to move forward. She wanted tranquility. Being with Joshua wouldn't give her that. They would always be fighting over Bud's property or the actions of the developers. She would always wonder about the child they'd lost. Some wounds couldn't heal. It was too messy.

"I think it's time I left," Theo said. "Just some food for thought."

Theo nodded at her and strode toward the door. He hesitated a moment at the threshold, then turned to face her. "Pride is a powerful thing, but so is love."

Before she knew it, Theo had made his way toward his vehicle. She sucked in a deep breath. His parting words left her reeling. Was she being prideful? In her opinion it was a matter of being realistic. A person could only surmount so many obstacles. She could only withstand so much pain.

Honor now knew without a shadow of a doubt that she was in love with Joshua. Always had been. Always would be. Finding out the truth about the fire had driven home the point she had always known. Joshua was a good man.

Despite the way he had always been regarded here in town, Joshua had evolved into a wonderful man. He had raised Violet as his own and protected Theo by taking responsibility for the terrible mistake his brother had made. And she would have to love him from a distance, because Joshua would soon be nothing more than a memory.

All she knew at this moment was the ache of her heart shattering into tiny little pieces.

Joshua's thoughts were full of Honor. Every time he'd looked at Violet this afternoon he couldn't help but think of the child Honor had lost. Their child. She had been forced to deal with the heartbreaking situation on her own, with no one to turn to for comfort. The very thought of it made him sick to his stomach. He should have been there to help the woman he loved through the loss of their baby. His mind kept whirling with thoughts of what might have been. What if he hadn't taken the fall for Theo? Would they have stayed together? Or would it all have fallen apart anyway?

It was all so crushing. He should have been there to help Honor shoulder her grief. Joshua should have held her in his arms and mourned alongside her. His faith told him God was in control, but for some reason, that knowledge didn't soothe him. It didn't make it any less agonizing.

He had come out to the stables to spend some time with the horses and to clear his head. He'd almost considered riding Blaze, but his heart wasn't in it at the moment. As he stood in Blaze's stall brushing her coat, Joshua prayed for closure. How could he go back to his life in Seattle with so many issues pressing on his heart?

Lord, I'm really hurting right now. And so is Honor. I never imagined coming back to Love would be such an emotional experience. I thought I could come back to Love, handle my grandfather's affairs and go back to Seattle without skipping a beat. But there are so many things weighing on me right now. If I'm doing the right thing by selling the Diamond R, why do I feel so bad about it?

"I've been looking for you everywhere." He hadn't even heard Theo's footsteps, but here his brother stood a few feet away from him. Theo's brow was furrowed with concern as he gazed at Joshua. "You look like you're in agony."

Joshua looked at Theo through a haze of pain. He didn't even bother to deny it. "That's a good word for it." He let out a tremendous shudder. His shoulders heaved with the effort. "When we arrived here in town everything seemed so crystal clear. But, in a matter of weeks, it's clouded over. I don't know what's right anymore. And I'm afraid if we sell the Diamond R, I won't know who I am any longer."

"You don't want to sell the ranch, do you?" Theo asked. "You didn't give me a straight answer earlier."

Joshua had spent a lifetime trying not to disappoint his older brother. He had always been the classic younger brother looking for Theo's approval. After all these years, he was still yearning for it. He bowed his head. "I don't, Theo. Honestly, I've struggled with the notion ever since the offer was made to us. I can honestly say I don't think it's the right thing to do. It's not in keeping with our grandfather's ideals."

Theo didn't say anything for a few moments. Joshua looked up and met his brother's gaze. As usual, they could easily communicate without a word being spoken. Theo let out a sigh. "All right then, we won't sell. I can't see myself living back here in Love and running the ranch, but from the looks of it, this lifestyle fits you like a glove."

Joshua couldn't believe his ears. "Theo! Are you serious? You were so determined to sell the ranch. What's changed?"

"Seeing you so torn up about everything has forced me to take a good look at myself. The Diamond R is Bud's legacy. It wouldn't work for me to stay here and run it, but I could easily picture you doing it. After all the sacrifices you've made for me, Joshua, it's the least I could do for you and Violet. Money isn't everything."

Joshua ran a shaky hand across his face. Never in a million years would he have imagined things turning on a dime like this. All he could think about was Honor.

How would she react to the news? Joshua leaned in and placed his arms around his brother in a warm hug. His gratitude was overflowing.

"What about you and Honor?" Theo asked. "Will this change things?"

Joshua shrugged. "It doesn't change anything. We've never really managed to bridge the gap between us."

Theo reached out and forcibly shook his shoulders. "Joshua! Wake up. You're in love with her. Are you really going to let this opportunity to make things right between the two of you slip through your fingers? Tomorrow isn't promised. We've got to make the most of today. Isn't that what Bud always told us?"

Bud's image flashed before his eyes. Their grandfather had done so much for both of them throughout their lives. He knew without a doubt Bud would want him to fight for his happiness.

"You're right, Theo. I love Honor. I always have. There's nothing I'd like more than to go to her and tell her how I feel, but I have no idea if she feels the same way."

"Really? Because I can see it whenever the two of you are within a ten-mile radius. You love each other."

Joshua felt buoyed up by Theo's words. He was openly saying what Joshua felt in his own heart. It's what he had always known deep down. The love between him and Honor had never been extinguished. Joshua did love her, with every fiber of his being. He had adored her for as long as he could remember. And he knew now he always would.

He smiled at his brother. For the first time in a long time he had reason to hope. "There's love there. I felt it, but I pushed it down because of everything that happened between us in the past. I didn't put my feelings out there due to false pride or fear of getting hurt again. I can't let it go unspoken, especially now that we're keeping the ranch. There's not a single reason we can't be together."

Theo flashed him a grin. "Sounds like you're going to get that happy ending after all." He slapped Joshua on the back.

"I need to go to her, Theo. I haven't told her how I feel. She doesn't know that I'm still in love with her."

"I heard that the town council is holding a meeting. I can't imagine she would miss it." He glanced at his watch. "It starts in about fifteen minutes."

Joshua reached for Blaze's saddle and placed it on his back. He picked up the reins and busied himself placing the bit in the horse's mouth. Then, with one fluid motion, he mounted Blaze.

"Joshua! You're not riding all the way into town on Blaze are you?" Theo asked. "Bud's truck would be a lot faster."

Joshua grinned at him. "Honor fell in love with an Alaskan cowboy. I want to remind her of the fact that I'm still that hometown boy. I've changed in many ways, but I'm still a cowboy, born and bred."

Theo threw back his head and chuckled. "Go get the woman of your dreams, Joshua. Don't worry about Violet. Between me and Winnie, she's in good hands."

Joshua tipped his cowboy hat at his brother and prodded Blaze to get moving. As he galloped across the property and away from the Diamond R Ranch, Joshua felt as if he was soaring. For so long he had told himself he wasn't worthy of a happily-ever-after with

Honor. Now he was riding toward a dream he hoped and prayed would come true.

It hadn't taken long for word to spread around Love about the Ransom brothers' legal victory. The residents were very upset at Bud and his grandsons. Jasper practically had a conniption fit. Honor was grateful for Hazel, who'd managed to calm him down and remind him of his responsibility as town mayor.

"You've got to be calm, cool and collected in the face of adversity," Hazel had reminded him.

"Who says I'm not?" Jasper had roared.

"Experience," Hazel had muttered.

Jasper had decided to call a meeting of the town council in order to address the controversial issue with the entire town. Her brother Boone, as well as Hazel, Paige and Jasper, were members of the town council. Honor knew the event would be heavily attended by the townsfolk. Everyone seemed to have an opinion about the possibility of a dude ranch replacing the Diamond R Ranch. Most were vehemently opposed to it, while a few said it might be good for the town.

Honor arrived early for the town council meeting. She was hoping to meet with Jasper beforehand so she could implore him not to rile up the townsfolk. Bad things happened when people became agitated over things they couldn't control. Honor didn't want Joshua or Theo to be a target of any negativity. She made her way through the throng of people gathered at the town hall. It was standing room only from the looks of it. Thankfully she had asked Ruby to hold a seat for her. She was blessed to have three sisters-in-law who had her back at all times.

When she entered the meeting room, Ruby was standing up toward the front of the room, wildly waving in her direction. Honor rushed toward her so they could sit together.

"This room is really packed," Honor said as she and Ruby hugged by way of greeting each other.

Ruby made a face. "It's insane. Liam stayed home with Aidan tonight. He would hate this crush of people."

"Thanks for saving me a seat, Ruby," Honor said, craning her neck to get a glimpse of the crowd in the back of the room. "I'm fortunate to have even made it inside the room."

"You're welcome," Ruby said. "I'm anxious to hear what everyone has to say."

"Me too," Honor murmured, placing her hand over her belly in order to quiet down the nervous rumbles.

At 5:30 p.m. sharp, Jasper pounded a gavel and called the meeting to order.

"Good evening, friends. We're here tonight to discuss the legal decision rendered regarding the Diamond R Ranch. I'm sure by now you've all heard the news. But for those of you who've been living under a rock, a so-called judge decided that Bud's kin can do what they like with his beloved ranch." Jasper ran a hand over his face. Honor couldn't help but think he looked extremely weary. This issue had taken a toll on him, which was alarming.

"It's an outrage as far as I'm concerned. Poor Bud is probably rolling around in his grave at this development. That man loved this town and he adored his ranch. It meant the world to him. Rumor has it that the ranch will be sold to an outfit of vipers who want to suck the life out of this town." He let out a ragged breath. "All I know is that I've been in constant prayer about it. And I'm not done praying yet. Maybe Theo and Joshua will have a change of heart. I pray they do."

As Jasper sat down, Boone leaned toward him and clapped him on the back. Honor watched as her brother whispered something in her grandfather's ear that made him grin. It lightened Honor's mood to see it. Jasper wasn't as tough as he seemed to be from the outside looking in. He'd been through a lot in his life.

Pastor Jack stepped up to the microphone. "Jasper asked me to be here tonight so I could share some thoughts with you. Bud—bless his heart—didn't leave the town his property. Perhaps there's some meaning there," Pastor Jack said.

"What kind of meaning could there be?" Jasper asked in a raised voice. "The last thing this town needs is a stinkin' dude ranch."

Pastor Jack smiled serenely. "Grace can be found in all types of situations, Jasper. We, as a town, just need to tap into it. This town has been through the best of times and the worst of times. Some of our ancestors searched for gold in the Yukon in the hopes of making it rich and providing for their families. Instead of finding riches, they met with tragedy. Somehow, their families endured. Not too long ago this town was rocked by a financial downturn. Friends became enemies, lovers became estranged. At our worst moment, this town banded together to save ourselves. We endured."

The crowd began to clap thunderously.

Pastor Jack grinned. "If the worst happens and Bud's ranch is transformed into the worst dude ranch in creation, this town won't crumble. We'll endure. As we've always done."

Pastor Jack was right, Honor realized. It wasn't the end of the world. Dealing with this situation with grace and conviction would go a long way in healing the wounds. She needed to play a role in soothing ruffled feathers rather than riling them up against the legal decision. Love had always endured. It would continue to do so. After all, a town was the sum total of its residents. And the townsfolk here in Love were the best people she had ever known.

As the meeting came to a close and everyone filed outside, Honor felt a feeling of calm wash over her. Snow was gently falling all around them. The air was crisp and biting. The wind was whipping her hair all about her face.

"Honor! Honor Prescott!"

Honor turned toward the sound of the voice calling out her name. She gasped. Was she seeing things?

Joshua was riding Blaze at a full gallop down Jarvis Street and he was heading straight toward her.

Chapter Fourteen

Joshua pulled gently on the reins as he spotted Honor standing next to Ruby outside town hall. There was no mistaking the heart-shaped face and the waves of chestnut hair cascading over her shoulders. She had a pretty pink hat perched on her head.

"Whoa, Blaze." A ripple went through the crowd as they spotted him. People began to whisper Joshua's name and point in his direction. He let out a sigh. Once again, he was the talk of the town. Everyone was gawking at him. Even Hazel was giving him a strange look.

He dismounted from Blaze, then turned toward Honor, who was gazing at him with a shocked expression on her face.

"Joshua! What are you doing here?" Honor asked.

A sudden case of nerves struck him. Did he have the strength to follow through with this? What if she just laughed in his face? What if he was wrong about her returning his tender feelings?

Go big or go home. He had come too far to turn back now. It was time to lay it all on the line.

All of a sudden, Jasper appeared at Honor's side.

"What's with all the dramatics, Ransom?" Jasper barked. "Did you show up here to rub our noses in your victory? We get it. You won. You're about to turn Bud's legacy into a dude ranch. Congratulations."

Joshua swung his gaze toward Honor. "I'm only here for one reason, Mayor Prescott. I need to say something to your granddaughter and it's important. If it's all the same to you, I'd like to speak my piece without being interrupted."

"Oh, brother," Jasper muttered. "Here we go again."

"Hopefully it won't take long," Joshua said with a plucky grin. He turned back around to face Honor. She had been watching and listening intently.

"I came back to Love in order to honor my grandfather. But along the way, something remarkable happened. I fell back in love with you, Honor. Matter of fact, I'm not sure I ever stopped loving you."

Jasper stomped his foot in the snow. "Do we have to listen to this nonsense?"

"Pipe down, Jasper," Boone said in a voice that meant business.

Jasper, muttering under his breath, took a few steps back. He glared at Boone.

"Keep talking, Joshua," Hazel implored him. "Just ignore Jasper's claptrap. We're all ears."

Joshua sent her a smile of gratitude. "Six years ago, I knew without a shadow of a doubt I wanted you to be my wife. There was no question in my mind we were meant to be. I would have joyfully walked down the aisle with you. I was ready to pledge forever to you. But life intruded on our plans."

"Is that a genteel way of saying you set fire to the church?" Jasper barked.

"If you don't hush I'm going to stick you in a snow-bank," Hazel said, jabbing Jasper in the side. He let out a howl.

"I've spent the past six years spinning my wheels and trying to rebuild my life. I've never managed to find anyone who makes me feel even a fraction of what you do. What I should have told you a long time ago is that we got it right the first time around. We knew we were destined to be together. Even at that tender age we knew our hearts." He moved closer to Honor and pulled her toward him.

"In case you didn't hear me earlier, I love you, Honor. I'm head over heels, crazily, helplessly in love with you."

"Oh, Joshua," Honor said, tears flowing down her cheeks.

"Please don't cry," Joshua begged, reaching out and swiping her tears away with his fingers.

"I—I'm just so happy. Hearing you say those words is a healing balm to my soul."

"God led me back home. He led me straight to you. And Bud… I think he knew that by leaving the ranch to me it would cause me to remember all the things I loved about living here. That's what he wanted, Honor. I'm certain of it."

"But you're selling Bud's property to a developer," Dwight Lewis, town treasurer, said in a scandalized voice. "Do you expect Honor to be okay with that? She'll never turn her back on her hometown."

Joshua turned toward Dwight. "Actually I'm not sell-ing to the Alloy Corporation, Dwight. I'm keeping the ranch. Those developers are going to have to find another town to target. They're not getting Ransom land. Not on my watch!"

"Are you serious?" Honor asked, looking up at Joshua with tears pooling in her eyes. "When did this happen? I thought it was a done deal."

Joshua reached out and cupped Honor's chin in his hand. "In my heart it was never a done deal. With each and every day I began to fall in love all over again, not just with you, but with this town and the Diamond R. I can't imagine a better place to raise Violet. She'll be happy here. And hopefully, so will we."

Honor threw her arms around Joshua. "I love you, too, Joshua. I always have."

He leaned down and pressed a kiss against her lips. For a moment it seemed as if they weren't standing in front of a crowd in the middle of Jarvis Street with snow falling all around them. To Joshua, it felt as if it was only the two of them.

"That's enough smooching," Jasper barked.

Hazel raised a tissue to her nose and blew loudly. "I haven't seen anything this romantic since our wedding," she said, sniffing back tears.

"What about Theo?" Honor asked him. "I know how much he wanted to sell to the Alloy Corporation."

"Theo knows how much Joshua sacrificed for him in the past." Theo had made his way toward them. He was standing a few feet away from them with Violet in his arms. "I pretty much owe him everything. Joshua took the blame for the church fire when I was the one responsible. I wish I'd been more courageous at the time." He turned toward the townsfolk. "I want to briefly explain what happened. I set the fire by accident. It was stupid and irresponsible, but not deliberate. Running away from the scene was cowardly." He shook his head. "Joshua was with me at the time, but he didn't have anything to do with starting the fire. Because I was in the army, he wanted to make sure my future was intact, even though his own was compromised because of it. He showed me such grace."

"Such an incredible act of brotherly love," Honor said, squeezing Joshua's hand.

Joshua clapped Theo on the back. "Theo wanted to give me something to show his unconditional love for me. He's giving me the Diamond R."

Theo nodded at him. "Unconditional love. That's what you gave me when you shielded me from responsibility for the fire. It was the most unselfish act I'd ever known. So it's my turn to be altruistic."

"You're giving him controlling interest in the ranch?" Boone asked.

Theo grinned. "Bud's will didn't just name myself and Joshua. It mentioned Violet as well. So, to my way of thinking, Bud wanted Violet to have a say in things. Now she can grow up on the ranch and enjoy the sort of childhood we experienced. I know Joshua would have sold if I pressed it, but it wasn't the right thing to do. Bud just wanted us to sort it out on our own. He had faith in us that we would make the right decision."

"The bottom line is, the Diamond R Ranch is staying in the Ransom family," Joshua announced. "No one's going to be opening a tacky dude ranch on Ransom land."

"Or anywhere else in Love!" Jasper shouted. He raised his fist in the air in a triumphant gesture.

A thunderous clapping rang out. No one was cheering louder than Honor. Joshua loved the transformation on her face. She was radiating joy like a beacon. Jasper stepped forward, quickly followed by Boone and Hazel. Jasper strode over to Joshua and stuck out his hand.

"You've done a good thing, son. I'm proud to shake your hand," Jasper said, grinning at Joshua as if they were best buddies.

"Thank you, Mayor," Joshua said, feeling overjoyed at the notion that Jasper was thawing toward him.

"What's with the mayor nonsense? Call me Jasper." He wiggled his eyebrows. "After all, it sounds like you might be getting hitched to my precious grandbaby."

Honor cried out and covered her face.

"Don't embarrass her!" Hazel scolded, rolling her eyes toward the heavens. "You're about as subtle as a sledgehammer."

Boone stepped forward. He looked Joshua up and down. "It seems I may have been wrong about you. Back in the day, you were a real troublemaker."

Joshua looked Boone straight in the eye. "You're right. I caused a lot of mayhem in this town."

"I appreciate a man who can admit his mistakes and change for the better. What you did for Theo was selfless. I probably would have done the same thing myself," Boone acknowledged.

Relief flooded him. He couldn't believe how this night was turning out. Boone—who had once been his harshest critic—was offering him an olive branch. And he would happily accept it. It brought him one step closer to being with Honor for the long haul.

"Thanks, Boone. Your goodwill means the world to me."

Boone reached out and shook Joshua's hand. Honor stood beside them, awash in tears. Ruby stood next to her wiping at her eyes. Everyone seemed to be giving in to sentimentality.

Hazel blinked away tears. She cleared her throat. "Let's all head over to the Moose for a celebratory round of espressos and hot chocolates. I'm liable to turn into a pile of mush if I stick around here any longer."

"That's the best idea I've heard all day," Cameron said, placing his arm around Hazel's waist.

Ruby held up her cell phone. "Let me call Liam. He and Aidan can meet us over there since it's not a school night."

"I'll take Violet home so the two of you can celebrate," Theo said. "By the way, I'm really happy for you." He winked at Honor. "I told you he was a good man."

"Thanks, Theo. For everything," Honor gushed. Her eyes were shining brightly and she couldn't seem to stop smiling. "I'm not sure any of this would have happened without you."

"I don't deserve any credit. Just be happy," Theo said.

Honor leaned up and pressed a kiss on Theo's cheek.

As soon as Theo and Violet walked off toward Bud's truck, Honor turned toward Joshua. She had a sheepish expression on her face. "Sorry about Jasper. He shoots from the hip whenever he opens his mouth."

"He's growing on me by leaps and bounds," Joshua said in a teasing tone.

"Jasper does have that effect on people," Honor said with a giggle.

Joshua reached out and pulled Honor toward him. His hands were on either side of her waist. He was looking deeply into her eyes. All he could see in their depths was love and contentment. It was amazing how quickly things could turn around. With love, hope and faith anything was possible.

He traced her lips with his fingertip. "I want to put down roots right here in Love. With you, Honor. And Violet. I think that's what Bud wanted. He was a pretty romantic guy. One who believed in true love conquering all."

"I have the feeling he's looking down on us and grinning like crazy. I'm proud of you, Joshua. Selling the ranch would have given you and Theo a big payday."

"As long as I have your love, I'll be rich in all the ways that matter most."

She reached up and placed her arms around his neck. They were gazing into each other's eyes. "I can't wait to see what the future holds for us."

"Nothing but blue skies, from this point forward," Joshua said, his words ringing out as a promise for the future.

Honor galloped on Lola across the wide expanse of Ransom land as the wind whipped across her face and hair. March had come in like a lion with a big snowstorm that had wreaked havoc on the small town of Love. After days of being snowbound, the townsfolk were all coming out of hibernation. Honor and Joshua were celebrating their freedom by riding across the Diamond R property.

Joshua was right behind her on Blaze. Honor pulled on Lola's reins and brought the horse to a stop near a stream. She dismounted Lola and led her over toward the partially thawed water. Soon, Joshua joined her. He patted Blaze, murmuring words of praise as he led her to drink.

"Look at all of this beautiful land," Honor said, spreading her arms wide as she whirled around with her face upturned to the sky.

"It stretches out for as far as the eye can see," Joshua said in a voice filled with awe. "Bud created a lasting legacy for his family."

"He was one in a million. A true pioneer." Honor smiled at Joshua. "Thank you for coming back home."

"It's where I belong. God led me straight back to you. And to this amazing town."

"You're a real-life hero. I think the residents are going to put up a statue in your honor since you decided not to sell the Diamond R. You earned everyone's undying devotion. And respect." Honor could hear the pride ringing out in her voice. The man she loved was an amazing human being.

Joshua chuckled. "Let's just say I'm most relieved to find myself in Jasper's good graces. Being on his bad side wasn't pleasant." He scrunched up his face, which made Honor chuckle.

"And my brothers have given us their blessing," she said, blinking away tears. It had always been important to her to know that Liam, Boone and Cameron approved of the man she intended to spend the rest of her days with. They had all rallied around Joshua in the aftermath of the town council meeting where he'd announced his plans to keep the Diamond R Ranch in the family.

He let out a low whistle. "I almost can't believe it. They've been very gracious to me."

"As they should be," Honor teased. "You're all kinds of wonderful."

"You're not so bad yourself," Joshua said.

She shook her head. Sometimes she couldn't believe how beautifully everything had worked out. Right before the town council meeting Honor had been at her lowest point. It had been nearly impossible to hold on to hope.

"Our path has been anything but smooth," she said.

"True. But the beauty of our situation is that our love never died. Not really. I never stopped loving you, Honor."

She looked up at him, her heart brimming with joy. "It feels as if I've always loved you."

He ran a hand across her face. "I hope you always will."

"After everything we've been through, I can't imagine not loving you." She grinned at him. "Joshua. I have something important to ask you."

"You can ask me anything."

Give me courage, Lord, she prayed. *I want a future with Joshua and Violet more than anything else in this world. I want to spend the rest of my life loving and being loved by them.*

"A little more than six years ago you proposed to me. You said that despite our age and the lack of support from my family, we could withstand anything and everything life threw in our direction. Unfortunately, we couldn't live up to that promise we made to one another." She reached for Joshua's hands and squeezed hard. "I want to ask you, Joshua Ransom, to marry me. We're six years older and wiser now. And we have the full and unwavering support of our families. I want to be your wife. Through good times and bad. And I want to be Violet's mother. I'll be there for her come what may. Through the terrible twos, potty training, the teen years and her first romance. I can't offer you perfection, but I won't ever forsake either one of you, Joshua. Not ever." Tears were streaming down her face and Honor didn't bother wiping them away. She wasn't hiding her feelings anymore. This man was who she wanted to grow old with and shelter from the storms of life. It would be her privilege to be his wife.

"Honor, marrying you would be the supreme honor of my life. I wanted you to be my wife six years ago. That hasn't changed in all this time. I still want you. It would make me the happiest man in all of Alaska to be your husband."

He dug in his pocket and pulled out a shiny diamond solitaire ring. Honor gasped. She covered her mouth with her hands.

"I guess you recognize it. So many times over the years I was tempted to throw it into the river." He shook his head. "I couldn't even think about us because it hurt too badly to go down that road. But something made me hold on to this ring. I couldn't let go of what it represented. When I bought it, I didn't have a whole lot of money to spend on it. But when I gave it to you, it was as if I'd given you the sun, moon and the stars. You didn't care that it wasn't the biggest or the brightest. Because you loved me." He held it out to her. "This ring signifies the most wondrous love I've ever known. Or ever will know."

"Oh, Joshua. It's still the most beautiful ring I've ever seen," she exclaimed.

"Honor, will you wear my ring? Again? And this time promise never to take it off. Will you marry me?" Joshua asked.

Honor began laughing through her tears. "Hey! No fair. I asked you first. You never gave me an answer."

Joshua reached for her hand and slid the ring onto her finger. "This is my answer. Yes, Honor. I'll marry you. Anytime. Anyplace. Anywhere."

Honor threw herself against Joshua's chest and wrapped her arms around his neck. He placed his hands on either side of her waist and whirled her around. Honor let out a squeal of delight and hung on for dear life. Finally, after all these years, they were getting married. And she would be a mother to Violet. All of her dreams were coming to fruition. She was incredibly blessed.

She had never imagined Joshua's return to Love would result in their falling in love all over again. Their reunion had been given a push in the right direction by the good Lord above. She just knew it!

All things were possible with love, truth and faith. She truly believed it now. She and Joshua had been through the fire and come through the ashes to form something stronger than they had ever imagined. And there was no force on earth that they would ever allow to separate them again.

Like their beloved hometown, their love would endure.

Epilogue

Joshua stood at the front of the church dressed in a dark suit and tie. His wedding day had arrived. Hazel had placed a red carnation in his lapel to match the brides-maids' flowers. The way he saw it, he was a simple man who finally was getting his heart's desire—mar-rying the woman of his dreams. After all this time, they were making it official. Mr. and Mrs. Joshua Ransom.

He shifted from one foot to the other as nerves began to grab ahold of him. His palms began to moisten.

"Are you okay?" Theo asked, nudging him in the side. "You're fidgeting quite a bit."

"I think so. I mean, yes, of course I am. It's just that I forgot something important." Joshua fumbled with his words. He turned toward his brother. "I need to go talk to Honor."

Theo's eyes bulged. "Now? Are you serious?"

"Don't worry. I'll be right back," Joshua said, walk-ing quickly toward the back of the church, past all the guests who were seated in the pews and staring at him with wide eyes. People began whispering and pointing.

As he headed toward the changing room where the bridal party was gathered, Hazel cut him off at the pass.

"Joshua! What are you doing back here?" Hazel asked. "The wedding is about to start." She frowned at him. "You're not having second thoughts, are you?"

He leaned down and kissed Hazel on the cheek. "Of course I'm not. Marrying Honor is all I've ever wanted. I just need to say something to her before we exchange our vows."

Hazel began fanning herself with her hand. "Praise the Lord. You just scared the life out of me. An image flashed in my head of all the Prescott men running you out of town on a rail."

Joshua grinned. He could actually laugh at the idea of it, now that things had been smoothed over between him and Honor's family. They had finally shown him grace and acceptance. Hopefully, they would forge a good relationship in the years to come.

"There won't be any drama today, Hazel. I'm marrying the woman of my dreams. I just need for Honor to stand on the other side of the door. If you open it a crack I can talk to her from the other side without seeing her."

Hazel looked at him skeptically. "Okay. I'll pass it on to her." A few minutes later Hazel waved him toward the partially opened door. "She's standing right behind the door. Make it quick, partner. There's a whole church full of people waiting with bated breath for this wedding to start." She winked at him. "After all, it's been six years in the making." Hazel patted him on the shoulder as she walked past him down the hall.

Joshua walked toward the door and faced away from it. He reached out his arm through the opening and said,

"Honor. Are you there? I'd like us to pray before Pastor Jack marries us."

"I'm here, my love." He felt Honor's hand join with his own. She squeezed his hand and he heard her from the other side of the door. "Of course I'll pray with you, Joshua."

Joshua smiled. He closed his eyes and began to pray out loud. "Lord. Thank You for giving us this day and for bringing us back together. You have brought us forgiveness, healing and restoration. Without You I don't think we would have found our way back to each other. Your love humbles us. Please bless our marriage with kindness and faith and devotion. If we make mistakes, give us the grace to forgive one another. And if we ever face any health challenges, may the stronger one hold the other one up. If You see fit, please allow us to grow our family, so that Violet can be a loving big sister and we can cherish more children. And can You please watch over the child we lost until we are all reunited one day. Amen."

"Amen." Honor's voice resonated from the other side.

He squeezed her hand. "Thank you for praying with me."

"Thank you, Joshua. For being the type of man who wanted to pray with me before you greet me at the altar."

Joshua let go of her hand. "I'll see you in a few minutes."

Ten minutes later the wedding march was playing and Ruby, Grace, Paige and Sophie were walking down the aisle scattering rose petals. Aidan followed closely behind them carrying a pillow as the ring bearer. Suddenly, Honor was walking down the aisle toward him.

His heart caught in his throat. He could barely catch a breath. She was radiantly beautiful.

Honor was walking down the aisle, with Jasper by her side. She was dressed in a long-sleeved ivory gown with a sweetheart neckline and a veil trailing past her shoulders. There were shiny rhinestones on the bodice of her dress. She came toward him with a big smile on her face. Her expression radiated love.

"I'm handing over to you our Prescott princess," Jasper said, sniffing back tears. "She's the very best of us, Joshua. Protect her. Love her. Give her a pair of strong arms to hold her when the world gets tough."

Joshua looked Jasper straight in the eye, then shook his hand. "I will always love and honor her, Jasper. I promise."

Jasper was beaming. "You're part of our family now, Joshua. An honorary Prescott."

"I never thought I'd hear you say that," Joshua teased, gaining a chorus of laughter from the guests. "I'm grateful we can be a family."

Jasper leaned over and kissed Honor on the cheek. He pulled a handkerchief out of his jacket pocket and began wiping his eyes with it. He walked over to the front pew and sat down with Hazel and Violet.

Violet reached out and yanked on Jasper's beard. He let out a slight yelp. The sound of Hazel's laughter rang out.

Pastor Jack began to speak. "Of all the couples I've married, I think the two of you make me feel the most hopeful. Your love endured a lot of trials. You faced a lot of obstacles. You climbed mountains in order to be together. Your love won't be shaken. It's a mighty thing indeed."

"You may now recite your vows," Pastor Jack intoned.

Joshua cleared his throat. "You were my first love, Honor. And now you're my forever love."

She reached for his hand. "You've been imprinted on my soul since I was a teenager. That hasn't changed one iota. I'll be by your side, come what may. That's my solemn promise to you."

After Pastor Jack declared them as husband and wife, Joshua leaned down and placed a tender kiss on Honor's lips. The guests began to clap enthusiastically.

Hazel handed Violet over to Joshua, who held her tightly against his chest with one hand and gripped Honor's hand with the other.

As they walked out of the church, a shower of flower petals rained down on them. The sky was shining beautifully. The blue skies above were the color of a robin's egg and cloudless.

Honor looked around her. Joy hummed and pulsed in the air. Operation Love had surely blessed this town. Love was all around her. Boone, Grace and baby Eva. Cameron, Paige and Emma. Liam, Ruby and Aidan. Jasper stood hand in hand with Hazel, who was looking up at him with adoration. Declan had his arms around a heavily pregnant Annie. Finn, Maggie and Oliver were smiling and laughing. Sophie and Noah still were acting like newlyweds and seemed head over heels for each other.

Honor had always believed in happy endings. She had hers now. There wasn't a single doubt in her mind that she, Joshua and Violet would live happily-ever-after. She would continue her work at the wildlife center and Joshua would be running the Diamond R Ranch—their new home. Bud's legacy would live on and thrive.

This was it. She had found her happy place and all the things she had never thought were quite possible. Joshua squeezed her hand then brought it up to his lips and placed a kiss on it. "Are you ready, my love?" he asked, resting Violet on his hip. Dressed in a lilac dress with a big bow in front, she looked adorable.

"Yes, Joshua. I've been waiting for this moment all of my life." She reached out and began to pat Violet's back in a soothing manner. "God has blessed us both in abundance."

"He has," Joshua said. "He gave me redemption and an opportunity to win back the love of my life."

Honor reached up and pressed a kiss on her husband's lips. "He sent you back to me. That was the best gift of all. God is good!"

"All the time," Joshua said in a voice filled with conviction.

This time around Honor and Joshua weren't going to falter when hard times came knocking. They were going to fight for their marriage and bask in their love story. There was a quiet strength in knowing their love was an enduring one. Their union was strong enough to conquer any storms. With an abundance of love, anything was possible.

* * * * *

"Isaac, we have a visitor. This is Leah Porte. She's an *Englischer* friend of ours, staying with us a few months. Leah, this is Isaac Sommer."

For a moment Isaac was struck dumb by the newcomer. With her dark hair tamed back under a *kapp*, and her chocolate eyes, he barely noticed the ugly red scar bisecting her right cheek.

Leah stepped forward. "How do you do?"

"Fine, *danke*. Where do you come from?"

"California."

"Please, sit. Both of you." Edith Byler gestured toward the table.

Isaac found himself opposite Leah and gazed at her as the family gathered around the table. When all heads bowed in silence, he found himself praying he could get to know the visitor better.

At once, chatter broke out as the family reached for food.

"We hope you'll have a pleasant stay with us." Ivan Byler scooped corn onto his plate .

"I…I'm not familiar with your day-to-day life." The woman toyed with her fork. "I don't want to be seen as a freeloader."

"What is it you did before you came here?" Ivan asked.

"I was a television journalist," she replied. Isaac saw her touch her wounded cheek and glance toward him. "But after my…my car accident, I couldn't do my job anymore."

LIEXP0820

Journalist! What kind of God-sent coincidence was that? He smiled. "Maybe I should have you write some articles for my magazine."

"Magazine?"

Edith explained, "Isaac started a magazine for Plain people. He uses a computer to create it. The bishop gave him permission."

"An Amish man using a computer?"

"Many *Englischers* have misconceptions of how much technology the *Leit* allows," Ivan intervened. "You won't find computers in our homes, or cell phones. But while we try to live not *of* the world, we still live *in* the world, and sometimes technology is needed to keep our businesses running. So, some bishops have decided a little technology is allowed."

"What's the magazine about?" Leah asked.

"Whatever appeals to Plain people. Farming. Businesses. Land management."

"And you want *me* to write for it?" she asked. "I don't know anything about those topics."

"But that's what a journalist does, ain't so? Learn about new topics," Isaac replied. Her opposition made him more determined. "Besides, you're about to get a crash course while you stay here. Maybe you'll learn something."

"I already said I had no intention of being a freeloader."

He nodded. "*Gut.* Then prove it. You can write me an article about what you learn."

"Sure," she snapped. "How hard could it be?"

He grinned. "You'll find out soon enough."

Don't miss
The Amish Newcomer *by Patrice Lewis,*
available September 2020 wherever
Love Inspired books and ebooks are sold.

LoveInspired.com

IF YOU ENJOYED THIS BOOK
WE THINK YOU WILL ALSO LOVE

⊞ HARLEQUIN
SPECIAL
EDITION

Believe in love. Overcome obstacles. Find happiness.

Relate to finding comfort and strength in the
support of loved ones and enjoy the journey
no matter what life throws your way.

6 NEW BOOKS AVAILABLE EVERY MONTH!

SPECIAL EXCERPT FROM

H HARLEQUIN

SPECIAL EDITION

*An explosion ended Jake Kelly's military career.
Now his days are spent alone on his ranch, and his
nights are spent keeping his PTSD at bay. But the
ex-marine's efforts to keep the beautiful Skylar Gilmore
at a distance are thwarted by his canine companion.
Every time he turns around, Molly is racing off to the
Circle G looking for Sky. Maybe the dog knows that two
hearts are better than one?*

Read on for a sneak peek at
The Marine's Road Home,
the latest book in Brenda Harlen's
Match Made in Haven miniseries!

"Actually, I think I'll try a pint of Wild Horse tonight."

She moved the mug to the appropriate tap and tilted it under the spout. "Eleven whole words," she remarked. "I think that's a new record, John."

He lifted his gaze to hers, saw the teasing light in her eye and felt that uncomfortable tug again. "My name's not John."

"But as you haven't told me what it is, I can only guess," she said.

"So you decided on John...as in John Doe?" he surmised.

She nodded. "And because it rolls off the tongue more easily than the-sullen-stranger-who-drinks-Sam-Adams, or, after tonight, the-sullen-stranger-who-usually-drinks-Sam-Adams-but-one-time-ordered-a-Wild-Horse." She set the mug on a paper coaster in front of him. "And I think that's a smile tugging at the lips of the sullen stranger."

"I was just thinking that next time I'll order a Ruby Mountain Angel Creek Amber Ale," he said.

"Careful," she cautioned with a playful wink. "This exchange of words is starting to resemble an actual conversation."

He lifted the mug to his mouth, and Sky moved down the bar to serve a couple of newcomers, leaving Jake alone with his beer.

Which was what he wanted, and yet, when she came back again, he heard himself say, "My name's Jake."

The sweet curve of her lips warmed something deep inside him.

Don't miss
The Marine's Road Home *by Brenda Harlen,*
available August 2020 wherever
Harlequin Special Edition books and ebooks are sold.

Harlequin.com